T0311238

WORLDS APART

WORLDS APART

Narratology of Science Fiction

CARL D. MALMGREN

INDIANA UNIVERSITY PRESS

Bloomington and Indianapolis

The paper used in this publication meets the minimum requirements of American
National Standard for Information Sciences—Permanence of Paper for Printed
Library Materials, ANSI Z39.48-1984.
⊗™

Manufactured in the United States of America

Library of Congress Cataloging-in-Publication Data

Malmgren, Carl Darryl, date.
    Worlds apart : narratology of science fiction / Carl D. Malmgren.
       p. cm.
    Includes bibliographical references (p.   ) and index.
    ISBN 0-253-33645-7 (cloth)
    1. Science fiction—History and criticism—Theory, etc.
    2. Narration (Rhetoric)   I. Title.
    PN3433.5.M35   1991
    801'.953—dc20   90-25045

1 2 3 4 5 95 94 93 92 91

He, who through vast immensity can pierce,
See worlds on worlds compose one universe,
Observe how system into system runs,
What other planets circle other suns,
What varied being peoples every star,
May tell why Heaven has made us as we are.

—Alexander Pope, "Essay on Man"

To romance of the future may seem to
be indulgence in ungoverned speculation
for the sake of the marvellous. Yet controlled imagination in this sphere can be a
very valuable exercise for minds bewil-
dered about the present and its potentiali-
ties. Today we should welcome, and even
study, every serious attempt to envisage
the future of our race; not merely to grasp
the very diverse and often tragic possibilities that confront us, but also that we may
familiarize ourselves with the certainty that
many of our most cherished ideals would
seem puerile to more developed minds. To
romance of the far future, then, is to attempt to see the human race in its cosmic
setting, and to mould our hearts to entertain new values.

—Olaf Stapledon, Preface to English
Edition, *Last and First Men*

CONTENTS

ACKNOWLEDGMENTS

In preparing this manuscript I have benefited from the insights, assistance, and support of many people. I would first like to thank Rick Barton, John Cooke, John Gery, and John Hazlett—colleagues at the University of New Orleans who read portions of the manuscript and made helpful suggestions and revisions. I would also like to thank the students in ENGL 4391: Science Fiction and Fantasy (Fall 1986), whose collective enthusiasm and insight clarified my ideas about science fantasy. I am also deeply indebted to the good people at the Americanistics Institute at the University of Innsbruck—in particular, Arno Heller, Sonja Bahn, and Renate Guggenberger—who supplied both "a room of one's own" and various forms of encouragement during the initial phases of this project. The UNO Graduate Council provided a Summer Scholar Grant in 1986 that enabled me to get started on the project.

A revised form of part of chapter 1 appeared in *Utopian Thought in American Literature*, ed. Arno Heller, Walter Hölbling, and Waldemar Zacharasiewicz (Tübingen: Gunter Narr Verlag, 1988). Part of chapter 4 appeared in *Science-Fiction Studies* 15 (November 1989). I would like to thank the editors of those volumes for permission to reprint those materials.

Finally I would like to borrow from Olaf Stapledon part of his original dedication to *Last and First Men*: "To my wife's devastating sanity I owe far more than she supposes." I dedicate this book to my wife, Gertraud.

WORLDS APART

I

WORLDS APART
A THEORY OF SCIENCE FICTION

The important thing in a scientific work is not the nature of the facts with which it is concerned, but the rigor, the exactness of the method which is prior to the establishment of these facts, and the research for a synthesis as large as possible.

—Freud, quoted in Todorov, "The Structural Study of Narrative"

The aim of theoretical thinking . . . is primarily to deliver the contents of sensory or intuitive experience from the isolation in which they originally occur. It causes these contents to transcend their narrow limits, combines them with others, compares them and concatenates them in a definite order, in an all-inclusive context. It proceeds "discursively," in that it treats the immediate content only as a point of departure, from which it can run the whole gamut of impressions in various directions, until these impressions are fitted together into one unified conception, one closed system. In this system there are no more isolated points; all its members are reciprocally related, refer to one another, illuminate and explain each other.

—Ernst Cassirer, *Language and Myth*

All fiction, in that it is necessarily mediated (someone stands between the reader and the narrated events), presents its audience with two main systems of signification—the sign-vehicles making up the *histoire*, or the world of the narrated events, and the sign-vehicles making up the *discours*, the speech act of the mediating narrator. One can use either of these systems in classifying or characterizing fictional forms. When it comes to the question of genre theory, however, one must focus on the *histoire*, on the fictional universe and its events. Any study attempting to establish generic distinctions between fictional forms necessarily relies on comparisons between the fictional world and the "real world"; this has been the case for narrative theory ever since Clara Reeve used these criteria in *The Progress of Romance* (1785) to distinguish between Novel and Romance.[1] It follows, then, that the genre of science fiction must be defined by its unique fictional

1

world or worlds, a truth that many readers of SF come to intuitively: SF can be defined by its peculiarly "science-fictional" worlds. In order to pursue this line of inquiry, we must analyze fictional worlds in general, determine what their components are, and then describe the transformations that SF works on those components. Before doing this, however, we must turn back to the question of *discours*. The discourse of SF does not define the genre (it shares the same discursive formations with other narrative forms, such as historiography and naturalistic fiction), but it rests on a number of fundamental assumptions that must be elucidated and examined.

1.1 The Discourse of SF

> Science fiction is defined in many ways, but as long as we retain the name it seems logical to insist on some relation to science: that is, to man's ways of coming to know himself and his environment through observation, hypothesis, and experiment.
>
> —Brian Attebury, "Science Fantasy"

> "Ah," Sam said . . . , "but the episteme was *always* the secondary hero of the s-f novel—in exactly the same way that the landscape was always the primary one."
>
> —Samuel R. Delany, *Triton*

Most critics agree that SF was "born" in the nineteenth century, singling out the appearance of Mary Shelley's *Frankenstein* in 1818 as the birth date of the new genre.[2] Scholes and Rabkin point out that "from the time of Galileo onward, prototypes of modern science fiction appeared," but that Shelley's novel was the "first work of fiction that has all of the characteristics of the science fiction genre."[3] Scholes and Rabkin do not, however, go on to spell out exactly what those characteristics are. Another critic has noted that the "intrusion of the scientific imagination on the general field of literature in the 16th, 17th, and 18th centuries seems, by modern standards, rather anemic."[4] The reason for this is that SF as a genre is predicated upon certain assumptions about the way the world works, assumptions that first surfaced during the Enlightenment but were not fully in place until the nineteenth century. The nineteenth century witnessed the consolidation of these assumptions and the concomitant creation of a new narrative genre. In order to identify the discursive features of that genre, we need to define briefly the culturological matrix from which it sprang.

As Horkheimer and Adorno have shown in *Dialectic of Enlightenment*, one of the distinguishing characteristics of Enlightenment thought is the whole-sale alienation of humanity from Nature, the reformulation of Nature as something threatening "out there" that needs to be analyzed rationally and systematically and thereby mastered. The whole idea of "natural law" represents one way to domesticate or harness Nature. The Industrial Revolution, itself in part a product of the Enlightenment, represents a more tangible means of harnessing Nature, of putting Nature to work. The steam engine, created by James Watt in the 1760s, made possible forms of loco-motion which did not rely on Nature. It also powered the new industries and factories which came into being after 1760 and which transformed landscapes in the West. The Industrial Revolution remade the everyday world in the nineteenth century, which witnessed the impact of steam on transportation systems, increasing urbanization, and a plethora of tech-nological appliances, including the electrical lamp, the telegraph and tele-phone, new explosives and weapons, the photograph and the phonograph, and the internal combustion engine. The ever-more-apparent evidence of social and technological change necessarily registered on humanity at large, which saw in these developments an ever-increasing command over Nature and natural forces. This new view of the relation between humanity and Nature is one of the preconditions for SF. As one critic concludes, "Not until the facts of change created by man through his growing control over nature and the possibility of controlling change became apparent to per-ceptive men and then to most men . . . did science fiction become possible: that is, somewhat after the Industrial Revolution, generally dated around 1750."[5]

Mary Shelley was in some ways "ahead of her time," because the vision informing SF also rests on certain "breakthrough" discoveries and devel-opments in the natural sciences which redefined the notion of time, many of which came in the middle of the nineteenth century.[6] Charles Lyell's *Principles of Geology* (1831–1833) began this redefinition by putting to rest the biblical time scheme and replacing it with geologic time. His theory of uniformitarianism—of slow changes across vast periods of time caused by natural processes such as erosion and sedimentation—reimagined the world as something very much created in time, over time. The discovery of Neanderthal man in 1856 at one and the same time confirmed Lyell's sense of time and extended its domain to include the biological world, an extension which Darwin's *On the Origin of Species*, published three years later, verified and theorized. The new sciences destroyed notions of time as cyclic or static, undercut the possibility of an origin or teleology for time, and obliterated the dimensions of time in both directions. All the new sciences were dominated by temporal methodologies, by a basis in time. Even physics, in the latter part of the century, acquired a time direction, in the form of thermodynamics and the concept of entropy. The dominant paradigm in scientific thought, which in the eighteenth century had taken the form of a self-regulating mechanism, became in the nineteenth century the concept of evolution, of gradual, irreversible, inevitable change in time.

The application of this paradigm was not limited to the physical sciences; in the nineteenth century, one critic argues, "all the sciences of man— biology, anthropology, psychology, even economics and politics—became 'historical' sciences in that they recognized and employed a historical, ge- netic, or evolutionary method."[7] Informing this paradigm was what Darko Suvin refers to as the "master code" of nineteenth-century ideologies: "the convention of development in linear historical time," whereby "in all cases, history was thought of as a strictly causal sequence going upward or down- ward."[8] Historiography itself became a "scientific" inductive discipline, "an empirical study devoted to the amassing of facts without preconceived theory or metaphysical assumption,"[9] and at the same time the model for the other social sciences. By 1874 John Morley could single out "the growth of the Historic Method" as the most salient feature of the moral and in- tellectual climate of his time, a development he deplored because of its inherent potential for moral relativism.[10] Frank McConnell has generalized about the overall import of the "nineteenth-century discovery of history- writing as science" as follows:

> Besides its far-reaching effects on Western man's whole sense of time, the growth of scientific historiography had an immediate and decisive effect upon social analysis and revolutionary theory. If the future could be extra- polated from the structures of the past, it could also be planned, and planned in accordance with the "true," "natural," or "ideal" shape of a human society as discerned beneath the failed experiments of previous cultures.[11]

The possibility that the present had evolved from the past and that the future could be extrapolated from the present opened up both of these domains to the narrative imagination; it is thus not surprising that historical fiction and science fiction made their appearance in the same century. The latter narrative genre, SF, is predicated upon a world-view which takes for granted that the future will be different from the present, that there exists a spectrum of possible futures all with their germs in the present, and that articulation of one of those possibilities can be of real value. SF, by defi- nition, "sees the norms of any age, including emphatically its own, as unique, changeable, and therefore subject to a *cognitive* view."[12] Because this world-view was not firmly in place until the nineteenth century, SF is a relatively "modern" phenomenon.

It remains for us to articulate the narrative assumptions and discursive features entailed by a world-view predicated upon scientific rationalism, linear time, and the ineluctability of historical change. In general, we can say that SF rests upon a scientific epistemology, one which assumes, first and foremost, that the external world is both real and phenomenal. That is, it consists in discrete, physical events that are available to us through our senses and that can be recorded as facts. This world is also axiologically neutral: it is not informed by a superordinated or metaphysical system of value; value is seen as something superimposed on phenomena. At the same time, that world is subject to a system of discoverable and codifiable order, in the form of a set of interlocking "natural laws." These laws are understood to be universal—they obtain not merely for local observed phenomena but throughout the universe and for all time.[13]

Classical scientific thought rests on the conviction, first, that at some level the universe is simple, if only because it is governed by fundamental laws, and second, that these laws may be discovered by the systematic application of the scientific method, such method being, as T. H. Huxley argued, "the same for all orders of facts and phenomena whatsoever."[14] Among the more important features of that method are an acceptance of logical causality and before-and-after chronology, belief in the possibility of formulating coherent models of the external world and of making such models more and more inclusive, and an acceptance of certain method-ological procedures or givens, such as the notions that experimental results be reproducible, that results be independent of the identity of the inves-tigator, that the investigator work inductively from specific observations toward general laws, that laws so generated have predictive power, and so on. It is not that all SF unilaterally appropriates each and every assumption listed above, but that the genre as a whole accepts the validity of the scientific epistemology and the applicability of the scientific method to the study of the external world. The epithet *science* in science fiction is totally appropriate just because of "the basic premise of science and science fic-tion—that is, the assumption that there is an inherent order in the universe and that this order can be discovered through the scientific method and expressed as natural law."[15]

SF was also born in the century which reconceived time and thereby "discovered" history, which made the "Historic Method" the scientific paradigm for all the other social sciences. In so doing, the nineteenth cen-tury "redefined reality as the historical process of becoming."[16] The world was seen as radically contingent, as a realm in which change is the only constant rule. Science, of course, and consequently SF, necessarily shared this view of reality. According to Stanislaw Lem, the world of SF must be a "real world," by which he intends "one in which no one is privileged from the start, in which no fate is predetermined, whether in favor of good or evil."[17] This radically contingent world lacks an overarching teleology or an informing axiology. In such a world, thinking about the future, whether in the form of historical planning, scientific forecast, or futuristic fiction, "is a kind of protest against being time-bound in the present, and it expresses humanity's determination to control its environment and direct its own destiny."[18]

Rosemary Jackson has observed that the modern fantastic emerged in the nineteenth century when faith in a supernatural order or presence was being undermined and when forms of otherness had to be displaced toward the natural and/or the subjective.[19] Modern SF, I would argue, represents one form that that displacement took, one kind of attempt to create "natural" otherness. Given its grounding in a scientific episteme, however, the genre was constrained to provide plausible scientific rationales for its factors of estrangement. In his "Preface to *The Scientific Romances*," Wells articulated one of the basic rules of the genre: "For the writer of fantastic stories to help the reader play the game properly, he must help him in every possible unobtrusive way to *domesticate* the impossible hypothesis."[20] While I would take issue with the word *impossible* (see 1.4), I would argue that Wells has touched upon a distinctive feature of the discourse of SF, one built into its episteme, the need to base its factors of estrangement in scientific possibility and to provide for them a convincing scientific motivation or rationale. SF rigorously and systematically "naturalizes" or "domesticates" its displacements or discontinuities. This scientific grounding is not, as some critics maintain,[21] merely a literary device, a requirement of the form or a mark of the SF style. It is built into the narrative ontology of the genre; without it, we shall see (see chapter 4), SF metamorphoses into adjacent narrative forms.[22] But before investigating adjacent narrative forms, we need to define SF itself, and to do that we must examine the distinctiveness of the fictional worlds that make up the genre.

1.2 The Worlds of SF

Science fiction . . . gives some of us hope. We have come to suspect anything that speaks of the Truth. We suspect that we are being lulled to sleep by these marvellous "truths," always inapplicable to ourselves. An instinct tells us that the truth is likely to be stumbled on in unlikely places. And what more unlikely the place than in science fiction, which claims many things but does not claim to be literally true?

—Robert Sheckley, "The Search for the Marvellous"

The first step in defining the worlds of SF is to determine the components of a fictional universe in general. Working inductively, we can say that a fictional universe invariably consists of two major components or systems, roughly equivalent to the lexicon and syntax of a language—a *world* and a *story*. The former includes the total repertoire of possible fictional entities, that is, the characters, settings, and objects (in SF these would include gadgets, inventions, discoveries, and so forth) that occupy the imaginal space of the fiction. The story connects and combines the various entities that make up the world; at an abstract level it consists of a systematic set of rules, a *combinatoire*, governing the order and arrangement of those entities and concatenating their interactions.

A marked tendency in the critical analysis of SF has been to define it on criteria essentially based on story. One notes this tendency in the names for various story types which are employed to discuss SF or to organize SF anthologies—the *voyage extraordinaire*, the time-travel story, the post-holocaust story, the alien encounter story, the space opera, the gadget story. It is not that these categories are totally irrelevant to the definition of the genre but rather that they tend to derive from *what happens* in the fiction, from its story. But the generic distinctiveness of SF lies not in its story but in its world. The various plots of SF, once divested of their alien, other-worldly, or futuristic appurtenances, tend to coincide with the plots of realistic fiction. Thomas Clareson gives the following example of what can happen when one locates the uniqueness of SF at the level of plot: "The protagonist, an alien creature, invades and struggles to survive amid a hostile society which dominates the planet—as in *The Invisible Man* [*sic*] by Ralph Ellison." As Clareson points out, "the same old story can be told in a number of ways."[23]

A similar confusion occurs when one tries to generalize about the essential narrative kernel of SF, as when Gary Wolfe argues that "the transformation of Chaos into Cosmos, of the unknown into the known, is the central action of a great many works of science fiction."[24] One might point out that it is also the "central action" (itself a word connected with plot) of *all* mystery stories and of many initiation stories. It follows, then, that in order to understand the nature of SF and its cognitive possibilities, we must examine the unique configuration of its worlds.[25] Darko Suvin, the foremost theoretician of SF, gives precedence to its worlds, defining the genre as "determined by the hegemonic device of *locus* and/or *dramatis personae* that are . . . *significantly different from the empirical times, places, and characters* of 'mimetic' or 'naturalistic' fiction."[26] When discussing the fictional worlds of SF, to avoid the implicit assumption that the characters are human and the settings terran, I shall use the term *actants* and *topoi*. By the latter term I intend not only the settings through which the actants move, and the social order that structures their interactions, but also the implicit time frame (historical, futurological, etc.) of the action and the operative laws that govern the topological domain. To summarize, then, a world consists of a number of actants who populate, occupy, or exist in certain implicit or particularized topoi.

The second step in our definition involves establishing a standard with which to compare the object of inquiry. In this respect, Lubomir Dolezel offers the following suggestion: "The study of possible narrative worlds will be facilitated, if we can define a *basic* narrative world to which all others will be related as its alternatives. It seems natural to propose for this role the narrative world which corresponds to our actual, empirical world."[27] We need, however, to make a minor revision of this formulation in order to accommodate SF worlds. Following Suvin, we must specify that the basic narrative world corresponds to "the 'zero world' of empirically verifiable properties *around the author*"[28] (emphasis added). It happens in SF that narrative motifs or entities which, at the time of their inscription, represent a departure from the author's empirical environment become actualized in a later empirical environment (e.g., submarines, space flight, atomic energy). In this respect, it is also useful to borrow from Eric Rabkin the term *grapholect* to designate a writing practice whose discourse is diacritically marked by the imprint of a specific historical, sociological, and cultural matrix. "Grapholects," according to Rabkin, "mark the writing 'voice' as coming from a particular time, place, and social group. The date of publication may or may not be active in one's mind during the reading of any given text, but the grapholect of that text, and the associated set of perspectives it vivifies, is always present."[29] Verne's *Twenty Thousand Leagues under the Sea*, for example, could perhaps be read today as a possible, if implausible, sea adventure story if its grapholect did not identify for all competent readers as nineteenth-century SF.

Armed with these postulates, we can begin to make some discriminations about the nature of the worlds of SF. Samuel Delany, in a seminal article entitled "About Five Thousand One Hundred and Seventy-five Words," notes that all fiction exists at a certain level of subjunctivity. Realistic or naturalistic fiction, he says, exists at a level of subjunctivity defined by the phrase *could have happened*. Other forms of fiction exist at other levels of subjunctivity; the mood for fantasy fiction, for example, is *could not have happened*. Delany identifies the mood of science fiction as *has not happened* and goes on to enumerate the possibilities that inhere in this particular narrative ontology.[30] His general point is well taken. The distinctiveness of SF rests in its generic license to create worlds *other* than the basic narrative world. This license identifies SF as a narrative species belonging to what is traditionally known as romance (it is no accident that Wells referred to his fictions as "scientific romances").[31]

When we pick up an SF text, we automatically make certain assumptions about that text, among them that it will not re-present (represent) reality, that it will rather constitute an addition to reality. It is as if written in bold letters across the cover of the text were the words *as if* or *what if*, signaling the peculiar essence of the fictional world. Several writers have made note of this particular quality of SF: Ursula LeGuin, in a preface to *The Left Hand of Darkness*, refers to the disjunction between SF and basic narrative worlds as the product of a "thought experiment"; Darko Suvin, in his theoretical study of the genre, argues that "SF is distinguished by the narrative dominance or hegemony of a fictional 'novum' (novelty, innovation)"; and Robert Scholes asserts that SF creates its worlds by means of a "representational discontinuity."[32] For our immediate purposes Scholes's formulation is most pertinent in that it specifies that the fundamental discontinuity is representational, which suggests that the informing transformation involves the fictional world.

An SF world, then, contains at least one factor of disjunction from the basic narrative world created by an actantial or topological transformation. One of the advantages that accrue to this type of narrative ontology has to do with the imaginative latitude granted the author. The author who inscribes an SF world is cut loose from some of the exigencies of mimesis; he or she is free to speculate, to fabulate, to invent. But the discourse of the genre does not grant total license to the fictionist. Once the author has posited the representational discontinuity (and there may be more than one such factor), the discursive rules dictate that the author adhere thereafter to the laws of nature and the assumptions of the scientific method (such as validity of cause and effect, the irreversibility of time, and the concepts of verifiability and repeatability). Brian Aldiss, noted SF author and critic, has charged that "most science fiction is about as firmly based in science as eggs are filled with bacon."[33] This simile is misleading in that it asserts that science and SF have little if anything to do with one another. Aldiss thus passes over the telling fact that the genre is firmly grounded in a discourse that assumes the validity of a scientific epistemology (see 1.1). Moreover, the SF writer must provide a scientific rationale for the discontinuities that he or she introduces into the fictional world.[34]

In terms of practice, some SF writers, most notably Heinlein, have tried to distinguish between discontinuities that violate scientific *fact* and those that contravene scientific *theory*. As Gregory Benford notes, "a commonly held standard is that an SF author should not employ elements which contradict known scientific *facts* though he may deal as he likes with currently accepted scientific *theory*."[35] Heinlein uses this somewhat invidious distinction to justify using faster-than-light (FTL) travel, time travel, even ghosts in SF just because these elements are not explicitly "contrary to scientific fact," but only to "present orthodox theory."[36] Stanislaw Lem, on the other hand, states that in his "serious SF," "I have avoided like the plague the problematic of 'time travel,' 'travel with infinite speed,' ESP, psychokinesis, *et cetera*, for the very simple reason that I don't believe they can come about."[37] Lem's comment is perhaps ingenuous, because it passes over the times he implicitly or explicitly relies on FTL travel, as a conventionalized enabling device, to transport his actants to an SF world elsewhere (in *Solaris* and *The Invincible*, for example). Heinlein's position, on the other hand, all too facilely separates fact from theory, fails to recognize their interdependence. As modern science well knows, theories help to determine what facts are significant. The point is that Heinlein's SF does uniformly adopt certain epistemic principles that are part of the discourse of SF, as can be proved by the fact that it carefully grounds any revisionist theory it might propose in a naturalizing scientific discourse. The general rule for SF is, as another SF author puts it, "You cannot contravene a known and accepted principle of science unless you have a logical explanation based on other known and accepted principles."[38] The science in SF is not merely a matter of embellishment; it informs the epistemology of the narrative, subtends the rhetoric of the fiction, and constrains the aesthetic configuration of the tale.[39]

An SF world is thus to a certain extent heterotopic; it incorporates supernatural, estranged, or nonempirical elements but grounds those elements in a naturalizing discourse which takes for granted the explicability of the universe. According to John Huntington, SF possesses a "deep structure that unites in some way scientific necessity and imaginative freedom."[40] The genre is thus characterized by a fictional world whose system of actants and topoi contains at least one factor of estrangement from the basic narrative world of the author, and by a discourse which naturalizes that factor by rooting it in a scientific episteme. The factor of estrangement, or *novum*,[41] at once defines the genre and determines the range of aesthetic and cognitive functions that it is able to serve.

As Horace, among others, has observed, the primary functions of art of any kind are to entertain and to instruct. The unique narrative ontology of SF particularly enables it to answer these functions. The simple fact of SF's otherness (predicated upon the informing novum) ensures to some degree that the fiction exerts a certain fascination—whether sympathetic, xenophobic, or disinterestedly intellectual. The strangeness of SF worlds guarantees to some extent that they will satisfy some sublimative or affective needs.

But it is not enough that fiction speak to our unspoken dreams, fears, and desires; we also insist that it in some way help us to know ourselves or teach us something about the way we live now. In even the best of times we ask that fiction give us "an adequate notion of what it is to be alive today, why we are the way we are, and what might be done to remedy our bad situation."[42] A fiction that takes as its domain the basic narrative world can presume that the lessons learned by its actants obtain in the "extratextual" world (which is, after all, contiguous and coterminous with the textual world). The epiphanies of the characters are valid insights into the "nature of reality" both within and without the text. Jonathan Culler has argued that making sense of fictonal texts consists in discovering and applying the correct culturally sanctioned models of *vraisemblance* (an untranslatable word connoting the systematic nature of correspondence between literary texts and the text of the real). The first two such models he discusses derive directly from experiential reality; they involve an awareness either of what is "real" or of what is general human knowledge.[43]

Clearly these models of vraisemblance are not available to the reader of SF who is confronted by a world that in a crucial respect proclaims its difference from the basic narrative world. The reader must discover or invent other models in order to recuperate or "naturalize" an SF world. And it is just this process of recuperation which constitutes the genre's cognitive value. The fact that the text adheres to the logic of the scientific method and constraints of natural law in part assures the reader that retrieval is possible, that relations of correspondence do exist. The world of the fiction has all of the predicates that we associate with the basic narrative world—logical consistency, predictability, regularity, comprehensibility— and standards of comparison between the two worlds can therefore be established. But at the same time that world is structured by its novum, a distancing element which forces the reader to look at the basic narrative world from the estranged perspective of a new optic. Ernst Bloch has said that the "real function of estrangement is—and must be—the provision of a shocking and distancing mirror above the all too familiar reality."[44] So it is with the novum of SF, which distances the reader from the empirical world, generating a cognitive space which the reader must negotiate. An SF world is thus less a reflection *of* than a reflection *on* empirical reality. Indeed, part of the attraction of the genre rests in the fact that systems of correspondence between real and fictonal worlds are generated primarily by the labor of the reader. The reader knows that he or she must work to achieve cognitive satisfactions. The challenge of all serious SF lies in the working out of its vraisemblance. Mark Rose has said that "the familiar in relation to the unfamiliar, the ordinary in relation to the extraordinary, is always, at least at one level of generalization, the subject of SF."[45] I would add that this relation, since it must be articulated by the reader, warrants for the genre the lofty title that Suvin has given it, the "literature of cognitive estrangement."[46]

1.3 Extrapolation and Speculation

It is the policy of *Science Wonder Stories* to publish only such stories that have their basis in scientific laws as we know them, or in the logical deduction of new laws from what we know.

—Hugo Gernsback, Editorial, June 1929

I make use of physics. He [H. G. Wells] invents.

—Jules Verne, in a letter

An SF world by definition contains at least one novum, or factor of deviation from the basic narrative world, a factor which informs that world and its unfolding events. We must now examine the creation of this novum as a mental process and make a further discrimination. The degree of "newness" or alternity of the novum is, as some critics have suggested,[47] dependent upon the kind of mental operation the author employs in generating it. The author may, for example, proceed by extrapolation, creating a fictional novum by logical projection or extension from existing actualities. What might happen, John Brunner asks in *Stand on Zanzibar*, if the world population keeps increasing at near-geometric rates? Or the author may rely on what I term *speculation*[48] in the generation of a novum. A speculative discontinuity involves a kind of quantum leap of the imagination, itself the product of poetic vision or paralogic, toward an entirely *other* state of affairs. In *Solaris*, for example, Stanislaw Lem depicts the mystery and grandeur of an almost completely nonhuman sentient planet.

Extrapolation, as is implicit in the word's etymology, is basically a logical and linear process. The author accepts the current state of scientific knowledge, projects from it either in time or in space, and tries to imagine and articulate the resultant situation or conditions. In "pure" extrapolation one must adhere strictly to the current state of scientific theory and fact. Writers firmly committed to extrapolative SF occasionally find themselves in an embarrassing position when subsequent scientific discoveries invalidate the facts which they had presumed to be true while writing the story. Thus Poul Anderson feels compelled to make the following admission in his "Author's Note" to the reprinted story "Life Cycle":

> A science fiction writer may, of course, speculate about things that science has not yet discovered. But whenever he deals with what is already known, he should get his facts straight.
>
> That's what I tried to do in this story. The planet Mercury was depicted as accurately as possible by me, according to the best available data and theories, as of 1957.
>
> The trouble is, scientific "facts" won't stay put. In the spring of 1965, radar and radio observations indicated that Mercury does *not* eternally turn the same face toward the sun and that the dark side—even in the course of a very long night—does not get especially cold.
>
> So perhaps this story should not be reprinted, or perhaps it should at least have been rewritten.[49]

Extrapolative SF has sometimes been labeled the "if this goes on" variety, while speculative SF is contrasted as more of the "what if" variety. Unfortunately, the two phrases, though catchy, are not really helpful. True, some extrapolative SF does derive from the "if this goes on" formula (stories of population problems, fuel or food shortages, increasing technologization, even Cold War confrontations), but much of it does not. Heinlein's *The Moon Is a Harsh Mistress* is basically extrapolative SF based on a "what if" premise—what if the moon is used in the relatively near future as a penal colony? Part of the attraction of that novel lies in the rigor and detail given to its extrapolated world, including its language, customs, and economic and social arrangements.

Speculation is, as has been suggested, a more "creative" or "freer" mental operation, in that the writer who chooses to speculate is cut loose from the current state of affairs (but not from the convention which dictates that any novum must be grounded in scientific necessity). An ethnologist, Henri Frankfort, has defined speculation as follows:

> Speculation—as the etymology of the word shows—is an intuitive, an almost visionary, mode of apprehension. This does not mean, of course, that it is mere irresponsible meandering of the mind, which ignores reality or seeks to escape from its problems. Speculative thought transcends experience, but only because it attempts to explain, to unify, to order experience.[50]

The emphasis here upon the intuitive nature of speculation and upon its desire to transcend experience, to discover as it were a deep structure of reality, pertains, I think, to the creation of speculative SF worlds. Working metaphorically rather than metonymically, the speculative writer tries to inscribe a world whose relation to the basic narrative world is less logical than analogical or even anagogical; there are systems of correspondence between the two worlds, but they are not linear or one-to-one, and they are consequently more problematic, more difficult to establish with certainty.

A speculative writer can assume new scientific principles or make innovative hypotheses (such as the existence of parallel universes, alternate time tracks, or hyperspace) as long as they do not contravene existing scientific principles or laws and are inscribed within a naturalizing discourse. The limit case or "pure" speculation, admittedly an ideality, would present the reader with an articulated novum essentially free of vestiges of anthropomorphism and anthropocentrism. This, of course, is impossible; as Patrick Parrinder points out, "any meaningful act of defamiliarization can only be relative, since it is not possible for man to imagine what is *utterly* alien to him; the utterly alien would also be meaningless. To give meaning to something is also, inescapably, to 'humanize' it or to bring it within the bounds of our anthropomorphic world view."[51] So speculation is necessarily a relative phenomenon, since the absence of any correlation or resemblance between a speculative SF world and the basic narrative world would render the fiction incomprehensible; one needs a background in order to distinguish the salient features of the foreground.

The above analysis perhaps suggests that the distinction between extrapolation and speculation is clear-cut and stable; such is not the case. It sometimes happens that a particular novum, at the time of its inscription within a particular grapholect, can be characterized as speculative, but that with subsequent usage in other SF texts, it becomes part of the repertoire of SF conventions, thus losing its speculative "force." Examples might be FTL travel, time machines, and the like. In these cases it should be noted that these devices have generally become just that—devices—and that they serve as a means to an end, namely, the introduction of the dominant or foregrounded novum in the fiction. In other words, the conventionalized novum has in fact lost its status as a novum and now serves as simply a device subtending the introduction of the "real" novum, as when FTL travel is used to transport the reader to an alien world (which may be predicated upon either an extrapolative or a speculative discontinuity).[52] The distinction between extrapolative and speculative discontinuities is also obscured by borderline cases, such as ESP. There does seem to be some evidence that parapsychological phenomena exist, but that evidence is suspect, in large part because it is nonrepeatable.[53] So how should fictions which employ as their dominant novum telepathy or other "psi" powers, fictions such as Van Vogt's *Slan* or Sturgeon's *More Than Human*, be characterized, as extrapolative or speculative? I would argue that in some cases the discourses in which these discontinuities or novums are embedded help to determine their status—are these powers treated as logical extensions of human faculties or are they seen as a radical departure from existing actualities?—and that even these problematic examples do not subvert the heuristic value of the distinction between the two mental operations.

There remains only to relate extrapolation and speculation to some of the other binary oppositions that have been used to characterize SF. One temptation is to equate this distinction with that between "hard" and "soft" SF. But if we understand the epithets *hard* and *soft* to refer to the sciences in which the fictional novum is grounded,[54] then this equation does not work. That is, if we understand by "hard SF" that species rooted in the "hard" sciences—those dealing with "objective" data, whose results or findings are predictable, repeatable, and verifiable, such as physics, chemistry, or biology—and if we understand by "soft SF" those fictions based on the "soft" sciences—those whose findings are more "subjective," probabilistic, less subject to predication and verification, such as anthropology, sociology, and psychology—then we cannot set up the homology Hard : Soft :: Extrapolative : Speculative. For it is possible to find examples of extrapolative SF based on the soft sciences (Asimov's *Foundation*, for example) or, for that matter, of speculative SF grounded in the hard sciences (Gregory Benford's *In The Ocean of Night* or Stanislaw Lem's *The Invincible*). It is certainly true that hard SF frequently focuses on the changes wrought by the physical sciences or technology and that it therefore relies on the extrapolative mode. Hard SF, after all, tends to endorse wholeheartedly the basic premise of the physical sciences, "that the universe could be understood by an organized application of observation and thought."[55] Such a view lends itself to objectivity, logical prediction, and extrapolation. It is also true that soft SF tends to deal with problems of human consciousness and identity and that it not infrequently locates itself in alternate worlds and dimensions and therefore relies more on visionary or speculative modes of world building. But despite these affinities, we should not confuse the mental operation employed with the sciences in which the novum is grounded.

Turning from synchronic analysis to an examination of the history of SF, we can say that the distinction between extrapolation and speculation supplies for us a critical tool of some value. For example, it is clear that Gernsbackian "scientifiction" of the early pulp era was, by design, meant to be extrapolative. In his *Amazing Stories* journal, Gernsback featured a spectrum of "scientific romances," from the fictions of Poe, Verne, and Wells to those of his contemporaries, but he seemed to prefer "gadget" or "hardware" stories, in which an extrapolative invention of some sort brought about marvelous changes in the human condition. But soon after Gernsback began promoting "scientifiction" there appeared the "superscience" story (dating, according to some, from the publication of E. E. "Doc" Smith's *The Skylark of Space* in 1928), in which the constraints of time and space, scientific possibility and narrative plausibility were exploded; the result was the galactic "space opera" story, decked out in "unstoppable forces and immovable objects, in hyper-spatial tubes and super-weapons and planets full of stupefying life armed with terrible mental capabilities."[56] Superscience stories were, I would argue, a juvenile form of speculative SF, created in part as a "freer" alternative to the more plausible, rationalistic scientifiction. One SF writer has compared the two as follows: "Superscience is not simply scientifiction made more of, although it was arrived at by commercial pressure to find something that would sell bigger. Scientifiction is a cool, intellectual form; superscience is hot, and despite all naivete, fundamentally artistic"[57] (by which I assume he means "imaginative").

One might pursue the line of argument by suggesting that the main difference between Verne and Wells, within the grapholect of their time, can be subsumed under the extrapolation/speculation polarity, or that one might distinguish between the Golden Age and the New Age according to their respective propensities to favor extrapolative or speculative modes of world building. As a matter of fact, one can construct a valid history of SF around the genre's oscillations between those two poles. This in itself argues for the heuristic value of the extrapolation/speculation distinction. But this distinction also has typological value, as will be shown in the next section.

1.4 The Model

Physical theories provide patterns within which data appear intelligible. They constitute a "conceptual gestalt." A theory is not pieced together from observed phenomena; it is rather what makes it possible to observe phenomena as being of a certain sort, and as related to other phenomena. Theories put phenomena into systems.

—N. R. Hanson, in Mooij, "The Nature and
Function of Literary Theories"

A heuristic model is a theoretical structure based on analogy, which does not claim to be transcendentally or illusionistically "real" in the sense of mystically representing a palpable material entity, but whose use is scientifically and scholarly permissible, desirable, and necessary because of its practical results.

—Darko Suvin, *Metamorphoses of Science Fiction*

Drawing on the postulates and distinctions made in the previous sections, we can construct a tentative model of SF worlds. We have argued that a fictional world consists of a set of actants who exist continuously in an implicit or particularized topos. The latter includes both the topography through which the actants move and the social system which structures their interactions and informs their behavior. In addition, both the configuration of those topoi and the morphology of the actants presuppose an operative system of natural laws. A world, then, is composed of four interlocking and interanimating sets of systems, as shown in the following diagram:

It should be clear that in any well-constructed and consistent world these systems are interdependent and self-regulating and that the analysis above is to a certain extent *ex post facto*.

SF is characterized by the introduction of a novum into one of these four systems, a factor of estrangement which transforms the basic narrative world into an SF world. This factor may be introduced into any of the four systems. For that matter there might be more than one such factor; a particular fiction might be characterized by actantial, societal, *and* topological transformations. LeGuin's *Left Hand of Darkness*, for example, features ambisexual aliens, two contrastive nation-states, and a world caught in the grip of an ice age. It can be argued, however, that in any particular fiction one set of transformations serves as the narrative "dominant," thus establishing the typological identity of the text. The dominant, as defined by Roman Jakobson, "rules, determines, and transforms the remaining components" of a given literary system.[58] Within an SF world one set of transformations, by virtue of its precedence, instrumentality, or centrality, takes priority over the others. In the aforementioned novel, for example, the actantial system is the dominant one, and LeGuin's central drama involves the encounter between terran self and alien other. It follows, then, that any particular SF world can be classified according to the type of novum which generates it, serves as its dominant, and establishes its typological identity. Using the novum as the distinguishing feature, we can construct the following typology of SF (see chart, p. 18).

To the model elaborated above, we have, in the chart, added the distinction between extrapolative and speculative discontinuities; we have also supplied representative examples and tendered some tentative remarks about the thematic thrust of the various SF types. For it can be argued that the nature of the novum determines to some degree the cognitive concerns of each SF type. In this respect it is useful to examine each type in turn.

The transformation of the system of actants involves the introduction of an alien entity into a system that is totally human in realistic fiction. One or more of the actants are nonhuman or superhuman or subhuman. The alien novum can take the form of a sentient computer (Harlan Ellison's "I Have No Mouth, and I Must Scream"), a monster (Mary Shelley's *Frankenstein*), or an extraterrestrial (Don Stuart's "Who Goes There?" or, for that matter, *E.T.*). The story paradigm for fiction using this transformation would be encounter with an alien. The reader recuperates this type of fiction by comparing human and nonhuman entities. In general, the fiction tends to broach the question, "What is it to be human?" and the cognitive thrust involves a better understanding of Self and Other. Given her abiding concern with this issue,[59] it is not surprising that many of LeGuin's fictions are of this type. This theme also tends to figure largely in Arthur C. Clarke's work; in *Childhood's End*, for example, he stages for the reader the successive encounters between humanity and an extrapolative Other (the Overlords) and humanity and a speculative Other (the Overmind).

SF presents the reader with a societal novum when it locates its story within an estranged or alternative social order. The story paradigm here typically entails the excursion to a utopic or dystopic elsewhere, a "brave new world" or a "new map of hell," and the reader is invited and encouraged to make comparisons between the fictional society and the originary one and to establish normative frameworks. The basic thrust of this SF type is toward better understanding of the dialectic between Self and Society. To this type belong many of what are considered SF "classics"— Huxley's *Brave New World*, Orwell's *1984*, Zamiatin's *We*, Brunner's *Stand on Zanzibar*, Pohl and Kornbluth's *The Space Merchants*, and Bradbury's *Fahrenheit 451*—in part because the estranged feature (the social order) figures so heavily in any criterion of relevance and significance, in part because the estranged element invites the kind of particularization that gives a fiction weight or density. It is also true that the majority of these fictions are extrapolative in nature, perhaps because it is difficult to imagine a social order that is quintessentially Other. Nevertheless, I would argue that Sta-

Typology of Science Fiction

World Component	Novum	SF Type	Representative Examples		Themes
			Extrapolative	Speculative	
ACTANT	Alien/Monster	Alien Encounter	Shelley, *Frankenstein*	Lem, *Solaris*	Self/Other
SOCIAL ORDER	Utopia/Dystopia	Alternate Society	Zamiatin, *We*	Delany, *Dhalgren*	Self/Society
TOPOS:					
OBJECT	Invention/Discovery	Gadget SF	Asimov, *I, Robot*	Strugatskys, *Roadside Picnic*	Self/Technology
PLANET	Catastrophe/Alien Landscape	Alternate World	Niven, *Ringworld*	Dick, *Ubik*	Self/Environment
NATURAL LAW:					
SCIENCE	Magic/Occultism		Leiber, *Conjure Wife*		
THEORY	Time Looping		Heinlein, "All You Zombies"		
SCIENTIFIC FACT	Reversal/Denial	Science Fantasy	Bradbury, *Martian Chronicles*		Epistemology and Ontology
HISTORICAL FACT	Reversal/Denial		Dick, *Man in High Castle*		
NATURAL ACTANT	Counternatural Actant		Sturgeon, *More Than Human*		

pledon (*Last and First Men*), Delany (especially in *Triton, Dhalgren*, and *Stars in My Pocket Like Grains of Sand*), and other writers have undertaken radical, speculative re-visions of possible social orders.

The third type of transformation involves the insertion of a novum into the topological domain of fiction. Here we must distinguish between possible levels of transformation. If we understand the topos of a fiction to include both the physical settings and the objects (in the broadest sense), then a topological estrangement can be effected at either level. At the local level, the estrangement occurs when a new and revolutionary object (gadget, invention, discovery) is postulated. The simplest form that this type could take would be the "gadget story," in which the invention of a single piece of hardware creates new possibilities or causes narrative complications. A good example of such a story is Lewis Padgett's "The Proud Robot," in which a brilliant but erratic inventor devises a robot in a drunken stupor but loses control over it because he cannot remember what he programmed it to do. Once he remembers its programming, he is able to reassert control over it. The story seems to say, as Gary Wolfe notes, that "if we lose sight of the simple purposes of our machines, . . . the machines will turn in on themselves and rebel against human control."[60] A simple and perhaps obvious message, but an instructive one as far as gadget SF is concerned, for in general gadget SF takes as its basic subject the possibilities and dangers of the products of technology. By its very nature, it explores the relation between man and machine, between Self and Technology. Asimov's *I, Robot*, for example, can be seen as an extended series of gadget stories, meant individually to puzzle and entertain but collectively to mediate the general problem of the correct relation between humanity and its technologies.

For the purposes of our typology, we must distinguish between a simple gadget story and what might at first be mistaken for a gadget story, namely, one which introduces an invention or process which in turn catalyzes a metamorphosis in society or in the human condition. Kate Wilhelm's *Where Late the Sweet Birds Sang*, for example, employs as its originary novum the process of cloning in a world stricken by catastrophe and sterility. But the novel focuses not on the process itself but on its products and its repercussions, on the conflicts that develop between clones and humans in subsequent generations. Here the process of cloning serves only as an enabling device within a fiction whose narrative dominant is the encounter between human outsider and clone society, between Self and Society. Not infrequently, an SF writer relies on a gadget or invention in order to create a world whose typological identity is not that of gadget SF.

There is, however, another level of possible topological estrangement which corresponds to that of gadget SF, the global level of an imaginary landscape, a new planet, or an alien topography. Here the writer posits, not an innovative object within a familiar world but an entire world itself. The world may be our own Earth, transformed by catastrophe or cataclysm into a strange or foreboding environment, as in J. G. Ballard's *The Drowned World*. Or it may be a totally natural, if highly unusual, imaginary world, like the disk-shaped planet Mesklin in Hal Clement's *Mission of Gravity*. It may even be an artificial construct, the product of "terraforming" or planetary engineering, a kind of global gadget, as in Larry Niven's *Ringworld*. In all *alternate world* SF, the author is more concerned with working out the nature, properties, and idiosyncrasies of the imagined world than with examining the actants who populate it or the social order that governs those actants. In general, alternate world fiction addresses questions dealing with the relation of humanity to its physical environment, such as how the environment shapes and conditions all forms of life, how humanity might adapt itself in order to accommodate new environments, or how humanity might remake or modify alien environments in order to make them amenable to human existence. Alternate world SF thus surveys actantial struggles to survive in the diverse topographies of an indifferent universe.

Actants, social system, and topography all presuppose a system of natural laws which in general remain consistent and universal in all SF proper (this, of course, is implicit in that part of our definition which specifies that the discourse of SF is grounded in a scientific epistemology). The final world-transformation, involving as it does the universal natural laws which subtend the genre and inform its discourse, results in an "impure" SF form called *science fantasy*.[61] Science fantasy is created when a novum is inserted into the system of natural laws or into the scientific epistemology. It is thus an unstable hybrid form combining features of SF and fantasy. Like fantasy, science fantasy contains at least one contravention of natural law or empirical fact, but, like SF, it grounds its discourse in the scientific method and scientific necessity. It assumes "an orderly universe with regular and discernible laws"[62] but allows at least one violation of the laws derived from the current state of science. Because a science fantasy world has all of the predicates that we associate with SF worlds, an organized or "scientific" explanation can be formulated for whatever happens, even if that explanation draws on questionable analogies, imaginary science, or counterfactual postulates.

Because science fantasy is a hybridized form, it can take many shapes, but I think that some sort of classification is necessary, even if it is not exhaustive. A science fantasy world is predicated on the violation or contravention of five different kinds of "scientific givens": the epistemology of science itself, an accepted scientific theory, an accepted scientific fact, a given historical fact, or "natural" actantial possibility. A science fantasy violates the epistemology of science when it presumes that magic is the operative discipline in humanity's relation with the external world; it violates scientific theory when it explicitly ignores basic scientific principles (such as the unidirectionality and irreversibility of time); it reverses a given scientific fact when it assumes, for example, the viability of sentient or humanoid life on Mars, and a historical fact when it posits the existence of alternate time tracks based on such reversals; finally, it violates actantial possibility by introducing a counternatural actant into the system of actants, an entity whose morphology, powers, or existence itself contravenes scientific possibility. The above impossibilities, it should be remembered, appear in a world otherwise compatible with scientific necessity and inscribed in a scientific discourse.

Turning back to the chart on p. 18, we notice first that science fantasy cannot be modally either extrapolative or speculative. This is because its defining feature, a reversal of natural law or empirical fact, obviates this kind of distinction; a reversal is by definition 180 degrees and does not admit of gradation. It should be noted, however, that the reversals of science fantasy share affinities with the imaginative strategies of speculative SF and that cognitively the two forms work in similar fashion. Because their respective transformations involve an imaginary quantum leap or occur at a level of the deep structure, the re-visions entailed by those transformations are wholesale. As a result both forms resist neat and clear-cut formulations of their thematic fields. C. S. Lewis has suggested that science fantasy worlds are created mainly to serve sublimative ends, that readers visit these "strange regions in search of such beauty, awe, or terror as the actual world does not supply."[63] This is certainly true, but it passes over the very real, if problematic, cognitive functions that science fantasy serves. The situation is complicated, and not simply because science fantasy can take some diverse forms and pose a wide range of questions. Perhaps it is because any reversal of natural law seems so arbitrary, so unmotivated, so unscientific. Nevertheless, I would submit that science fantasy does have a somewhat circumscribed area of thematic concern. In taking on the laws and principles which we take for granted, it tends to ask ultimate philosophical questions having to do with the nature of reality itself, and about the discourses in which we inscribe reality. It approaches these thematic fields obliquely, and generally in a more exploratory than definitive way, so that its meanings are generally multiple and problematic. But science fantasy ultimately does speak to both our hearts and minds.

In closing, I should like to make some remarks about the advantages and strengths of the model articulated above. First of all, it can accommodate the seemingly inexhaustible and admittedly multifarious forms that SF takes, because it is rooted in an elaboration of fictional worlds. Indeed, it enables us to identify certain problematic cases, such as the *voyage extraordinaire*, which, given its historical pedigree, is sometimes lumped in with utopic fictions or, more frequently, identified as proto–science fiction. Texts such as Poe's *The Narrative of Arthur Gordon Pym* and Verne's *Journey to the Center of the Earth* should rather be seen as science fantasies (within the contexts of their respective cultural grapholects) and can profitably be studied as such. The model also enables us to specify differences that were perhaps indistinct, such as the difference between the "what if" extrapolation Heinlein uses in *The Moon Is a Harsh Mistress* and the "what if" extrapolation Clement uses in *Mission of Gravity*. The difference lies in the dominant extrapolated novum: the former novel focuses on the extrapolated society, examining the relation between Self and Society; the latter novel focuses on the extrapolated world itself, its topography and idiosyncrasies, foregrounding the interplay between Self and Environment. The distinction thus helps us to read these novels.

More important than the discriminations and identifications that the model makes possible are the "deep structural" affinities between apparently disparate fictions that it makes manifest. The model lumps together SF motifs which are elsewhere treated as separate storylines or "icons."[64] In the model, for example, stories featuring sentient computers, robots, aliens, nonhuman monsters, mutants, or clones are revealed to have as a common denominator a structure involving the encounter between Self and Other. It follows that these stories can be read in a similar fashion, using a limited number of models of vraisemblance (e.g., Other-as-Enemy, Other-as-Object, Other-as-Other). This kind of grouping obtains not only for stories which share an obvious structural feature (such as the encounter) but also for stories whose ground situations are apparently completely different. At first glance Heinlein's "Universe" has very little in common with Harlan Ellison's "A Boy and His Dog." The former is set in a colonizing spaceship which has undertaken a multigenerational journey to another star system; the latter recounts the adventures of a self-sufficient adolescent in a postholocaust world. But when we realize that both stories revolve about a basic conflict between an alienated free-spirited individual and a comparatively closed society, then we can identify the stories as having the same typologic identity—that of the extrapolative dystopia—because they share a common dominant novum (an estranged social order). Consequently, these apparently dissimilar fictions are meant to be recuperated in a similar way, as examinations of the relation between Self and Society. The model reveals that apparently different SF worlds can actually share the same dominant novum and thus belong to the same SF type.

In chapter 3 we will look at a spectrum of fictions whose dominant novums establish them as representative SF types and try to circumscribe their respective thematic fields. But first we need to examine in more detail the reader's role in the recuperation and naturalization of SF worlds.

II

SF AND THE READER

In an account of the semiotics of literature someone like the reader is needed to serve as the center. The reader becomes the name of the place where the various codes can be located: a virtual site. Semiotics attempts to make explicit the implicit knowledge which enables signs to have meaning, so it needs the reader not as a person but as a function: the repository of the codes which account for the intelligibility of the text.

—Jonathan Culler, *The Pursuit of Signs*

Much of literary competence is based on our ability to connect the worlds of fiction and experience. And much of our literature quite rightly insists upon that very connection.

—Robert Scholes, *Semiotics and Interpretation*

2.1 Reading SF

Every narrative addresses itself to a hypothetical audience; a story is narrated by someone, for someone. In regard to prose fiction, the audience of which I speak is not the auditors who sometimes appear in narratives employing a tale-within-a-tale, nor is it the flesh-and-blood reader who sits in an easy chair with the text before her or him. The reader I refer to is a "metonymic characterization of the text,"[1] consisting of a set of textually conditioned and culturally sanctioned mental operations which are performed upon the text. These operations are predicated upon a reader's prior exposure to and familiarity with a narrative tradition, upon previous literary experiences which determine the competence of the "native reader." In terms of SF, the most important operations which the reader performs upon the text are *concretization* and *interpretation*.

2.1.1 Concretization: Constructing the Absent Paradigm

In science fiction, the world of the story is not given, but rather a construct that changes from story to story. To read a science fiction text, we have to indulge a much more fluid and speculative kind of survey. With each sentence we have to ask what in the world of the tale would have to be different from our world in order for such a sentence to be uttered—and thus, as the sentences build up, we build up a world in specific dialogue with our present conception of the real.

—Samuel R. Delany, "Generic Protocols: Science Fiction and Mundane"

The first and most elementary operation which readers perform upon a prose narrative can be referred to as concretization. Before "doing" anything with the fictional world that they encounter, readers must endow the fictional entities and motifs with imaginal substance. They must realize or "concretize" the fiction by investing its sign-vehicles with dimensionality and presence, bringing them into imaginal actuality. Reading a Faulkner novel, a reader must bring Yoknapatawpha County into "existence"; beginning an Austen novel, a reader must gradually create from imaginative resources the image of a spoiled, immature, and willful Emma Woodhouse; poring over a Hemingway text, a reader reconstructs, *ex nihilo*, the image of an old man, a turbulent sea, and a monster fish. In the concretization process, the reader verifies the motifs that have been decoded by comparing them with a preacquired encyclopedia of knowledge encompassing the models and laws of physical phenomena, the norms of verisimilar behavior, and a compendium of "real world" information brought to the text.

All narrative invokes and provokes this primary act of concretization. But SF, in that its worlds depart or deviate from the basic narrative world, complicates this process. SF is defined by the novelty of its world, by the novum or novums which inform that world; unlike the worlds of realistic fiction, which are to some extent given, the worlds of SF must be constructed, or, better, reconstructed, the reader responding to the "clues" which the author has encoded in the text. As Marc Angenot has noted, SF elicits or requires a "conjectural reading,"[2] a trial-and-error process of hypothesis, confirmation, and/or disconfirmation, a process that has its roots in the scientific method.

This reconstruction, this concretization of the estranged world apart, is not simply a matter of happenstance guesswork. The discursive conventions of SF (see 1.1), rooted as they are in the scientific episteme, assure the reader that the SF world shares many essential features with the reader's empirical world—namely, materiality, regularity, predictability, and, most important, intelligibility. The worlds of SF are not only possible, they are consistent and coherent:

> Science fiction's hypothetical situations are based on the concept of the "model," a tight self-consistent construction that makes logical sense, worked out from a set of predetermined postulates or hypotheses. On a very small number of speculative postulates a world is built that adheres

closely and logically to the selected parameters, forming a self-consistent and closed system.[3]

The reader, decoding the SF sign-vehicles in the text, works backward to reconstruct that closed system, filling in the "absent paradigm,"[4] the model or structure which is implicit in each recognizably science-fictional sign or syntagm. Let us consider, for example, the following statement, which LeGuin has said served as the narrative germ for *The Left Hand of Darkness*: "The king was pregnant." In a realistic text, such a statement could only be metaphorical. But an SF reader has no problem processing the statement literally, immediately postulating a world in which males could somehow be impregnated. Other sequences in the text enable the reader to determine that the actants of Gethen are perfectly ambisexual, becoming either male or female during regular but intermittent periods of sexuality; thus gradually does the reader build up a more comprehensive paradigm for the estranged world. As Marc Angenot has succinctly summarized, "While reading SF, one slowly drifts from the narrative sequence as such (syntagm) to these illusory general systems (paradigms)."[5] Indeed, it can be argued that this filling in of the paradigmatic "phantasm"—this re-creation of an absent but consistent and coherent possible world—constitutes one of the real pleasures of reading an SF text. Concretizing the worlds of SF requires a certain amount of inferential labor on the reader's part, the successful completion of which entails its own satisfactions.

2.1.2 Interpretation: The Novum, Estrangement, and Cognition

The sf writer is able to dissolve the normal control that the objects (our actual environment, our daily routine) have; he cuts us loose enough to put us in a third space, neither the concrete nor the abstract, but something new, something connected to both. We are cut loose, but with ties so as never to forget that we do live in one specific society at one specific time.

—Philip K. Dick, "Who Is an SF Writer?"

If we must acknowledge that reality inevitably eludes our human languages, we must admit as well that these languages can never conduct the human imagination to a point beyond this reality. If we cannot reach it, neither can we escape it. And for the same reason: because we are in it. All fiction contributes to cognition, then, by providing us with models that reveal the nature of reality by their very failure to coincide with it.

—Robert Scholes, *Structural Fabulation*

A paradigmatic moment occurs in an SF text when the hero-actant, the one who has been off visiting some brave new world, returns to his/her own place and time and people and confronts them. Invariably he or she sees them in a new light, from an alienated or estranged perspective. Ransom, the hero of C. S. Lewis's *Out of the Silent Planet*, experiences such an encounter. He has spent a period of time with the "enchanted" Malacandrans, and then one day a hunting party brings back some strange specimens to the village:

> After [the leaders] came a number of others armed with harpoons and apparently guarding two creatures which he did not recognize. The light was behind them as they entered between the two farthest monoliths. They were much shorter than any animals he had yet seen on Malacandra, and he gathered that they were bipeds, though the lower limbs were so thick and sausage-like that he hesitated to call them legs. The bodies were a little narrower at the top than at the bottom so as to be very slightly pear-shaped, and the heads were neither round like those of the *hrossa* nor long like those of the *sorns*, but almost square. They stumped along on narrow, heavy-looking feet which they seemed to press into the ground with unnecessary violence. And now their faces were becoming visible as masses of lumped and puckered flesh of variegated colour fringed in some bristly, dark substance. . . . Suddenly, with an indescribable change of feeling, he realized that he was looking at men. The two prisoners were Weston and Devine and he, for one privileged moment, had seen the human form with almost Malacandrian eyes.[6]

Ransom undergoes, in an almost pure form, what for the Russian Formalists was the quintessential literary experience, *defamiliarization*, the "making strange" of the familiar. For the Russian Formalists, defamiliarization is an artistic technique which removes an object from habitualization or the automatism of perception by presenting it in a deformed or estranged manner; it is, in other words a *local* device. For SF, however, defamiliarization is at once a *global* principle and a *terminus ad quem*. The estranged worlds of SF are systematically and rigorously unfamiliar. Prolonged exposure to such worlds bestows upon the reader an estranged perspective, a new set of eyes, as it were. The reader necessarily brings that new perspective back to his or her everyday world, which consequently has been "defamiliarized."

It may be helpful here to elaborate a little on the difference between defamiliarization as a literary device and estrangement as a structural principle. Defamiliarization is a local formal device, the making strange of an object or motif in such a way as to make that object unfamiliar and to cause us to look at it with renewed attention. Defamiliarization of an object is valuable because it prolongs the time of perception devoted to the object: "The technique of art is to make objects 'unfamiliar,' to make forms difficult, to increase the difficulty and length of perception because the process of perception is an aesthetic end in itself and must be prolonged. *Art is a way of experiencing the artfulness of an object; the object is not important.*"[7] Defamiliarization is thus a product of verbal devices that "lay bare" the artwork or artifice that has gone into making that object unfamiliar or strange, that foreground the artfulness of the art object.

The estrangement of SF, on the other hand, is a structural principle, more conceptual than verbal or formal. In SF, as Scholes says, "it is the new idea that shocks us into perception, rather than the language of the poetic text."[8] The heterocosmic worlds of SF thrust upon the reader a new and different optic or perspective; prolonged exposure forces the reader to inhabit this perspective and necessarily to bring it back to his or her normal, everyday world. The systematic estrangement brought about by SF worlds serves not only perceptual but also cognitive ends. SF presents the reader with not simply an estranged object but an estranged world, the nature of which necessarily comments upon the basic narrative world. The estrangement which a reader experiences while concretizing and assimilating an SF world compels him or her to bring that world into relation with the basic narrative world, establishing models of correspondence between the two worlds. As will be shown later, the nature of those models is to some degree dependent upon the nature of the novum. By constructing such models (which the reader must do, since in most cases they are underdetermined by the text), the reader interprets the text; interpretation in SF (and in much estranged fiction in general) is thus a function of its world. In making an interpretation, in establishing systems of correspondence, the reader comes to know or understand his or her own world better; his or her interpretive labor can reap cognitive rewards. I say *can* because the degree or amount of cognition is to some extent contingent upon the nature, validity, and function of the novum informing the estranged fictional world.

2.1.3 Noncognitive Novums

> SF can act as a mirror or as a window depending on how it is maneuvered by the author. It is like a pane of glass that can behave in two ways. If held so that the light shines directly through it onto the author's creations, the reader is sometimes fooled into thinking that the glass is not there, that he is seeing genuine aliens, genuine futures, genuine other worlds that have nothing to do with him, the wonders of other places and times, of pure escape. But if held in a slightly different way, a pane of glass also reflects, and the onlooker might catch a glimpse of himself, might see his own image even stronger than that of a new scene.

—A. Wendland, *Science, Myth, and the Fictional Creation of Alien Worlds*

Trying to describe the possibilities available to the writer of "fiction about the future," H. G. Wells engages in the following "thought experiment." Suppose, he says, that biological discoveries made it possible to create female children only, without the intercession or offices of fathers at all. One can extrapolate from that hypothesis a totally female society—a "manless world." One way for the author to treat that world would be comically, stereotypically; the author need merely treat the resultant society as not unlike his or her own and then play upon all the stereotypes that adhere to women today, "jokes about throwing stones, not keeping secrets, lipstick and vanity bags," and so on. The result, Wells concludes, would be "the Futurist Story at the lowest level."[9]

It would also be an SF story with little or no cognitive import, a story whose world does not use its novum in such a way as to estrange the basic narrative world and thus to reveal the latter's inner workings or assumptions. In one way or another, this type of SF "plays" with its narrative *données*; its novum, the originary source of possible cognition, is backgrounded or trivialized or compromised, and the fiction tends to serve functions of entertainment or escape. This sort of science fiction insists that the more things—manners, mores, even man himself—change, the more they stay the same. Given such a world-view, the possibilities for cognition remain limited.

Suvin, in his exhaustive survey of Victorian SF, has identified four forms that noncognitive SF takes—the banal, the dogmatic, the incoherent, and the invalidated. By banal SF, he intends that kind of fiction whose novum takes a back seat to its stereotypic plot and is "drowned in the non-S-F details and/or plot gimmicks of a *banal* mundane tale."[10] Examples might be much space opera and adventure SF. Dogmatic SF is that which overcodes or overdetermines relations between the estranged SF world and the basic narrative world. The text incorporates treatises and/or lectures about the differences between the two worlds; because "the reader is referred directly to the relationships in his empirical environment,"[11] his or her imaginative freedom is circumscribed, and prospects for real cognition are reduced. An example might be Wells's *In the Days of the Comet*, an alternate society SF with limited cognitive value because much of the novel deals not with the postcomet world but with the evils of the precomet days; the discourse of the novel is weighed down with normative pronouncements indicting the evils of contemporary society.

Suvin's definitions of incoherent and invalidated SF are less precise and less clear. The former, he says, contains narrative details about the novum which are "too disparate"; the latter, narrative details which are "qualitatively unsatisfactory" because they "oscillate between a cognitive and a noncognitive or anticognitive validation—genologically speaking, between SF and fantasy, fairy tale, or kindred metaphysical genres."[12] His argument seems to be that these fictions contain novums that are inconsistent or which violate natural law or the scientific method. A novum which is not informed by a consistent narrative logic would indeed be noncognitive (one thinks here of the gadgets and devices of space opera), but I would argue that there exists a hybridized narrative form, science fantasy, which mixes elements drawn from SF and from fantasy *and* which can serve important cognitive functions (see chapter 4).

Suvin argues elsewhere that any SF novum "has to be differentiated not only according to its degree of magnitude and of cognitive validation . . . but also according to its *degree of relevance.* . . . Not all possible novelties will be equally relevant, or of equally lasting relevance, from the point of view of, first, human development, and second, a positive human development."[13] While it may be true that some novums are inherently more telling or potentially more fruitful than others, I would argue that almost any novum, successfully deployed and elaborated, can be turned to cognitive advantage. By the same token, even the most "relevant" novum can be trivialized or "wasted" when it is somehow backgrounded to other narrative functions. It happens that some SF (especially of the short-story variety, where the matter of length can obviate the full working out of the novum's potential) uses its novum only to elaborate a puzzle or create an effect.[14] An example might be the much-anthologized Golden Age short story "Time Locker," by Lewis Padgett, in which the titular novum enables an evil actant to reach into the middle of next week to kill himself. Even this story has limited cognitive value; at a minimalist level, it suggests, as do other gadget stories (see 3.3), that by misusing our technologies we can destroy ourselves. But stories such as these, which subordinate the cognitive potential of their novums to narrative design or effect, are generally intended to speak to sublimative satisfactions; they hope to achieve what Tolkien has argued is "the primal desire at the heart of Faerie: the realization . . . of imagined wonder."[15]

2.1.4 Cognitive Novums

[SF's] specific modality of existence is a feedback oscillation that moves now from the author's and implied reader's norm of reality to the narratively actuated novum in order to understand plot-events, and now back from those novelties to the author's reality, in order to see it afresh from the new perspective gained.

—Darko Suvin, *Metamorphoses of Science Fiction*

In science fiction the relation between the "secondary universe" of fiction and the actual universe is both implicit and intermittently more or less perceivable. It consists not of what is on the page but in the relation between that and the reader's knowledge of actuality.

—Joanna Russ, "The Subjunctivity of Science Fiction"

As a genre, SF necessarily presents the reader with "worlds in collision," with a contrast between the norms of the SF world and those of the basic narrative world. The confrontation between the two worlds, which may be explicitly encoded in the text or left to be inferred by the reader, "foregrounds their respective structures and the disparities between them."[16] The cognitive value of the contrast depends, in large part, upon the nature and treatment of the fiction's dominant novum. The best (in the sense of most intellectually rewarding) SF offers its readers a novum which is at once scientifically possible, consistently worked out, and axiologically relevant. The relevance of a novum is a function less of formal properties than of axiological assumptions; to some extent, then, it is a function of subjectivity. But any novum which is consistently worked out presupposes an axiological bias, and the best SF tends to foreground that bias, in order to affirm it, subvert it, or more generally interrogate it. In the best cases, the shuttling back and forth between estranged SF world and basic narrative world tends "to feed back into the reader's own presuppositions and cultural invariants, questioning them and giving him/her a possibility of critical examination."[17]

The best SF, then, foregrounds or puts in relief certain assumptions or presuppositions that a reader brings from his/her world to the estranged SF world. Can we formulate a systematic set of possible relations between the broad range of SF worlds and the basic narrative world?[18] Are there a limited number of possible logical relations between the contrastive norms of the two worlds—such as inversion, subversion, affirmation, extenuation, etc.? It may perhaps be so, but at this point I would argue that we must proceed by looking separately at each SF type (alien encounter, alternate society, etc.), working from there to define possible sets of relations between the worlds (see chapter 3). I would suggest, however, that we can identify the governing or dominant cognitive thrust of SF as pertaining to science itself (understood in the broadest sense). In part because its discourse is rooted in a scientific epistemology, in part because its novums are drawn from or tied to developments in science, the most significant SF necessarily investigates the dominant scientific paradigms of the day; it draws upon these models regardless of the way in which it treats them. The best SF, as Suvin has noted, foregrounds "the political, psychological, and anthropological *use and effect of knowledge, of philosophy of science.*"[19] In a sense the genre simultaneously affirms and interrogates science, resting as it does on faith in reason and the scientific method while at the same time probing the assumptions, limits, and blind spots of each.

This can best be shown by looking at some representative SF types. But first it might be helpful to look at a couple of classic fictions—one extrapolative, the other speculative—which foreground the reading process in order to examine in more detail how we read SF and, in so doing, to articulate some basic reading strategies used to decode the two modes.

SF can present its estranged worlds to the reader either "raw" or "cooked," unprocessed or processed, with a "zero degree" of interpretation or with one degree. In the former case readers are from the first page immersed in the fiction's estranged world, without intervention or mediation; they are There without any transit from Here:

> The "zero degree" of the interplanetary motif involves projecting a different planet without any provision for intrusion in either direction, by its inhabitants into our world or by earthlings into their world: worlds in collision without the collision. A classic example is Frank Herbert's *Dune* (1965), which constructs an integral self-contained planetary world, nowhere explicitly related to our Earth. Here the confrontation between the projected world and our empirical world is implicit, experienced by no representative character but *reconstructed* by the reader.[20]

In the zero degree case, then, the reader must, single-handedly as it were, concretize the text by constructing the absent paradigm and interpret it by establishing models of correspondence or vraisemblance between the two worlds.

The obverse situation involves an encoded, explicit confrontation between (representatives of) the two worlds. Either a terran actant voyages to the estranged world (as in LeGuin's *The Left Hand of Darkness*), or our terran topos is invaded by some alien novum (as in Leiber's *The Wanderer*). In either case there is a direct collision between the two worlds, and the main terran actant acts as the reader's ambassador or representative, in many cases supplying his or her reactions to the novum and thus giving the text "one degree of interpretation." In this way the actant manages to circumscribe thematic concerns and lay out possible areas of cognition. As Suvin notes, this type of SF often "uses the plot structure of the 'education novel,' with its initially naive protagonist who by degrees arrives at some understanding of the novum for her/himself and for the readers."[21] In some exemplary SF, this first degree of interpretation highlights the process of reading SF in general; these examples of worlds with one degree of interpretation become meta-SF, meditations upon, and models for, how to read SF. Wells's *The Time Machine* and Lem's *Solaris* are two cases in point.

2.2 Reading Extrapolative SF: Wells's *The Time Machine*

> It was still possible in *The Time Machine* to imagine humanity on the verge of extinction and differentiated into two decadent species, the Elois and the Morlocks, without the slightest reflection upon everyday life. Quite a lot of people thought that the idea was very clever in its sphere, very clever indeed, and no one minded in the least. It seemed to have no sort of relation whatever to normal existence.
>
> —H. G. Wells, *The Fate of Man*

When the Time Traveller finds that mankind will have become separated
into two races, the gentle ineffectual Eloi and the savage Morlocks, the idea
that these are descended respectively from our own leisured classes and the
manual workers comes as a mere explanation, a solution to the puzzle; it
is not transformed, as it inevitably would be in a modern writer, into a
warning about some current trend in society.

—Kingsley Amis, *New Maps of Hell*

In his latter years, H. G. Wells tended to derogate both the quality and
the value of the works created during his prolific "scientific romance"
period. Indeed, he held all "fiction about the future" in low esteem, re-
ferring to it as "ephemeral but amusing."[1] In a preface to the collected
edition of his romances, he labeled these works "fantasies." "They do not
aim," he deprecatingly explained, "to project a serious possibility; they
aim indeed only at the same amount of conviction as one gets from a good
gripping dream."[2] Unlike Jules Verne, who dealt with actual possibilities,
with inventions that might come into being and futures that might be actualized, with the practical, "hands-on," everyday world, Wells saw himself
as merely exercising his imagination; his stories did "not pretend to deal
with possible things."[3] Wells wrote these assessments of his early work
during the years immediately preceding World War II. Within such a
gloomy and foreboding context, he could see these works only as "escapist"
entertainments. These *fin de siècle* romances were composed during a comparatively happier time, when it was still possible to indulge in inconsequential or fanciful "fantasies."

Curiously enough, certain contemporary critics have, for far different
reasons, expressed opinions similar to Wells's—namely, that these fictions
should be absolved of any overt moralizing or didactic purpose, should be
seen as somehow divorced from the social context or cultural matrix. Re-
acting in part to allegations that Wells's work is generally stigmatized by
overt didacticism, these critics are at pains to emphasize the degree to which
the scientific romances at least are pure inventions and artful constructions.
Jean-Pierre Vernier, for example, has said of *The Time Machine* that in it "the
divorce between the real world and the imaginative universe is total: *The
Time Machine* is above all a work of art, and it is typical of its age only to
the extent that all art is a re-creation of the world of the moment within
the artist's own vision." Within the world of the Elois and the Morlocks,
he insists, "we are in the realm of fantasy, and there is no conscious urge
to instruct us or warn us."[4] Kingsley Amis generalizes this idea to cover
all the brilliantly original novums of Wells's romance period; the time machine, the invisibility serum, the invasion from Mars—all, he argues, "are
used to arouse wonder, terror, and excitement rather than for any allegorical

or satirical end."[5] In one sweeping statement, then, Amis categorizes Wellsian SF as sublimative in nature, with entertainment as its primary function.

Amis links the affective thrust of the scientific romances with the kind of mental operation that brought them into being. Wells, according to Amis, liberated SF from its "dependence on extrapolation." By dispensing with the Vernian preoccupation with the realm of the physically possible, Wells is able to indulge a "simple delight in invention," in so doing expanding the repertoire of SF motifs.[6] His viewpoint echoes that of Wells's rival, Verne, who, in an oft-quoted and deprecatory passage from a letter, made the following contrast:

> [Wells's] books were sent to me and I have read them. It is very curious, and, I will add, very English. But I do not see the possibility of comparison between his work and mine. We do not proceed in the same manner. It occurs to me that his stories do not repose on very scientific bases. No, there is no *rapport* between his work and mine. I make use of physics. He invents.[7]

Invention should be understood here as unwarranted narrative license, as groundless speculation. He who invents breaks faith with scientific givens and the laws of physics, violates norms of possibility, or indulges in mere fantasy. In conclusion, then, although they operate on different principles and apply different criteria, Verne, certain contemporary critics, and even Wells himself tend to emphasize the fanciful, wonder-ful, "invented" quality of the scientific romances and, correspondingly, to undercut or downplay their cognitive possibilities or dimensions.

This line of argument, I think, totally misrepresents Wells's narrative assumptions, his method of operation, and his thematic intent. Wells's various novums, for example—though frequently predicated upon a "what if" (and therefore more speculative) hypothesis—are firmly grounded in extrapolative logic within their respective discourses. In comparison to Verne, Wells did rely more on speculative leaps; in positing his novums, he allowed himself more imaginative latitude, from a historical perspective. But within any synchronic study of SF, Wells's work must be located within the extrapolative domain. His novums are more daringly conceived than Verne's, but within the fictional world their justifications and repercussions are rigorously worked out with extrapolative logic. Wells himself described the genesis of *The Sleeper Awakes* as follows: " 'Suppose these forces go on,' that is the fundamental hypothesis of the story."[8] In fact, "if this goes on" logic tends to inform the discourses of all the scientific romances; as will be seen, this is particularly true for *The Time Machine*. Despite what Verne says, Wells's SF is firmly grounded in the before-and-after, cause-and-effect, classical kind of scientific epistemology that lends itself to extrapolation.

By definition extrapolation assumes that there is a direct and discernible relation between here and now and there and then, and Wells's romances are firmly predicated on that assumption. In the same preface in which he speaks disparagingly of his romances, Wells admits to an admiration for Swift that reveals itself in "a predisposition to make the stories reflect upon contemporary political and social discussions."[9] The admission suggests that Wells, despite his disclaimers, is aware of the way in which the romances do reflect upon or call into question contemporaneous practices and beliefs. It should be noted that the interrogation of society that Wells undertakes in the romances is not sporadic or local; it does not consist in "palpable hits" here and there. Using his novums as estrangement devices, Wells ultimately holds up to examination the fundamental assumptions, hopes, and beliefs of late Victorian society. Above all, he systematically interrogates the ruling deity of his time—science itself. The romances can best be seen, says one critic, as parables about what it is like to be "living in a world in which science is all there is."[10]

The Time Machine is a case in point. It is, in many respects, an exemplary extrapolative science fiction. The world in which the Time Traveller finds himself, some 800,000 years in the future, is extremely estranged. There are no recognizable landmarks, no shared mores, no common language; even the human species has evolved into forms that are drastically different. Gradually, however, we come to realize that this alien world is somehow connected to the world which we know. Step by step, the world of the Elois and Morlocks is domesticated, recuperated, brought into relation. Moreover, that process of recuperation is explicitly encoded in the text, in the form of the Time Traveller's successive conjectures. In this regard, the Time Traveller is the key figure in the text; he acts as the reader's ambassador to the alien world, someone who shares the reader's epistemological disadvantages. As he notes, he is not supplied with a "convenient cicerone" who could explain to him the manners and mores of that world, or its relation to his own world.[11] The ways in which the Time Traveller comes to terms with the world of A.D. 802,701 foreground the *how, what*, and *why* of making connections with estranged worlds, of establishing models of vraisemblance. Gary Wolfe has said of SF in general that "more than any other modern genre, [it] provides a narrative realization of the new dogma of reason-for-reason's sake. One of its essential structures is a codification of the scientific method itself, a kind of systematized speculation."[12] In the Time Traveller's successive speculations, *The Time Machine* renders the systematic recuperation of an extrapolative SF world; in this way, it becomes at once the enactment of, and a model for, how and why one goes about reading extrapolative SF.

As the reader's ambassador to the future world, the Time Traveller embodies a number of salient characteristics. He is, first and foremost, a scientist. This is figured not only in his vocation and avocations but also, more pertinently, in his attitudes and modus operandi. He seems interested only in the future, at no time betraying a desire to travel backward in time. Once he has encountered an entirely new set of circumstances in the future, he sticks rigorously to the scientific method. He first surveys the scene dispassionately, acquiring data. After a while he renders a tentative hypothesis and tries to square it with the facts. He then attempts to explain how this state of affairs might have come about, using extrapolative logic to connect that future with his Victorian present. The discovery of new, anomalous data forces him to discard his theory entirely or to adapt it to accommodate those data. Whenever he is stymied or frustrated, he emphasizes the need for scientific detachment, for patience, for disinterested observation. When his time machine is stolen, for example, he first indulges in a paroxysm of despair. Later, however, when his emotions are spent, he convinces himself that his problems can be overcome only if he adopts a scientific posture:

> "Patience," said I to myself. "If you want your machine again, you must leave that Sphinx alone. If they mean to take your machine away, it's little good your wrecking their bronze panels, and if they don't, you will get it back as soon as you can ask for it. To sit among all these unknown things before a puzzle like that is hopeless. That way lies monomania. Face this world. Learn its ways, watch it, be careful of too hasty guesses at its meaning. In the end you will find clues to it all. (Pp. 50–51)

He firmly believes that mastery of this new and strange world is contingent simply upon gathering enough evidence and constructing an adequate (scientific) model.[13]

His attitudes and procedures, it should be clear, are exactly those that should be adopted by a reader of extrapolative SF. As one critic says, "The Time Traveller and the reader are engaged in the same activity: they try to understand the nature of the temporal contrast presented and then to discover connections. Like evolutionary biologists, they must first understand what distinguishes two species and then they must reconstruct the evolutionary sequence that links them."[14] A closer analysis of one set of the Time Traveller's interpretations should help to clarify the parallel and to illuminate the reading process.

After spending some time in the world of A.D. 802,701, the Time Traveller has determined that he has happened upon "humanity on the wane," during the sunset of a Golden Age brought about by the complete "subjugation of Nature" (pp. 42, 43). The end result has been the effete, indolent Elois, who wander through a garden world free of pests, disease, toil, and struggle. This model—a communistic, paradisiacal world in decline and decay because of the "perfect conquest of Nature" (p. 44)—seems to comprehend the available evidence. But there remain certain facts that cannot be assimilated under this paradigm. First and foremost, there is the inexplicable disappearance of the Time Machine, the removal of which gives the Time Traveller "the sense of some hitherto unsuspected power, through whose intervention [his] invention had vanished" (p. 47). There are the curious covered wells, which, he supposes, constitute part of a system of underground ventilation, a supposition which, though entirely reasonable, is "absolutely wrong" (p. 52). Other puzzling facts include the absence of elderly or infirm, of cemeteries or sepultures, of the machinery necessary to supply the Elois' minimal needs. Finally, there is the Elois' curious fear of the dark. Given such anomalies and incongruities, the Time Traveller admits that "his first theories of an automatic civilization and a decadent humanity did not long endure" (p. 53). At this point he has discovered that the paradigm he has constructed—the world he has inferentially built up from a smattering of clues—is inadequate and must be discarded for another, more inclusive paradigm.

His eventual encounter with the nocturnal, horrific, but human Morlocks forces him to come up with a better "reading." He realizes that man has differentiated into two distinct species, the "graceful children of the Up-perworld" and the "bleached, obscene, nocturnal Thing[s]" (p. 59) that dwell beneath the surface. The existence of this second species solves the "economic problem that had puzzled" the Time Traveller. He infers, quite logically, that this subterranean species sees to the needs and wants of the Upperworlders.

Having constructed a new model which accounts for more of the available data, the Time Traveller then tries to bring the future world in relation with his own world. He poses to himself a crucial question: How did humanity get from his world to a world of two subhuman forms? Implicit in this question is the possibility of some sort of critical relation between the two worlds. And whenever he asks himself this question, he is able to answer it by drawing on extrapolative logic. In this particular instance, the phrases he uses to connect the two worlds are as follows: "At first, proceeding from the problems of our own age, it seemed clear as daylight to me . . . " (p. 60); "and yet even now there are existing circumstances to point that way" (p. 61); "Evidently, I thought, this tendency had increased till . . . " (p. 61). Whatever his interpretation or model, the Time Traveller thinks that it can be accounted for by direct extrapolation from circumstances existing during his own era.[15] He thereby insists that this strange new world necessarily reveals, in a logical and readily decipherable fashion, something about his own world—some inner truth or tendency. In this particular case, he concludes that the two species descend from Disraeli's "two worlds," from the Capitalists and Laborers of his time: "So, in the end, above ground you must have the Haves, pursuing pleasure and com-fort and comfort and beauty, and below ground, the Have-nots, the Workers getting continually adapted to the conditions of their labour" (p. 61).

Once the Time Traveller has adequately explained the what and where-fore of the world of the future, he takes the next logical readerly step—he passes judgment on that world, dispassionately but firmly. For him the world of the future necessarily makes some sort of normative statement about the world of the present; in this instance, a monitory statement about industrial capitalism and the scientific ethos: "It had been no such triumph of moral education and general cooperation as I had imagined. Instead, I saw a real aristocracy, armed with a perfected science and working to a logical conclusion the industrial system of today. Its triumph had not been simply a triumph over Nature, but a triumph over Nature and the fellow-man" (p. 62). Always the methodical and scrupulous scientist, the Time Traveller notes immediately that there are some data not accounted for by this reading, namely, the Elois' fear of the dark and their inability to return the Time Machine. He also reminds his auditors, as he has carefully done with each of his theories, that what he has given them is simply one interpretation, a reading which may completely miss the mark: "This, I must warn you, was my theory at the time. My explanation may be absolutely wrong" (p. 62). In a similar way he undercuts and problematizes even his final reading: "So I say I saw it in my last view of the world of Eight Hundred and Two Thousand Seven Hundred and One. It may be as wrong an explanation as mortal wit could invent. It is how the thing shaped itself to me, and as that I give it to you" (p. 90). With disclaimers such as these, the Time Traveller in effect declares that the reading process—constructing the absent paradigm—must remain open, able to accommodate new data into more inclusive paradigms.

This process, then—gathering data, inferring a model, rendering an explanation, and passing judgment—recapitulates the reader's activity in the recuperation of an SF world. It is an ongoing process, one which must be continually repeated as more evidence accumulates. In the case of *The Time Machine*, the Time Traveller proposes a fourfold series of cognitive appropriations of the alien world, each validated by extrapolative logic. The four successive readings may be paired as follows:[16]

A1: Communist paradise, based on the perfect subjugation of Nature (p. 41)
A2: Degeneration of that paradise, given the absence of struggle (pp. 42–44)
B1: Capitalism *in extremis*, based on the total differentiation of Capitalist and Laborer (pp. 59–62)
B2: Capitalism *in extremis* inverted, with the Morlocks in ascendancy, preying on the Elois (pp. 74–76)

The above pairings reveal some interesting features informing the Time Traveller's process of appropriation. Each set of pairs has as its basis a fundamental opposition or conflict. The first set, A1 and A2, is predicated upon the struggle between Man and Nature; the second set, B1 and B2, puts in an adversarial relation Man and Man, Capitalist and Worker. The first member of each set postulates the triumph of one of the adversaries:

in set A, "one triumph of a united humanity over Nature had followed another" (p. 43); in set B, the "real aristocracy" (the Elois) had prevailed "over Nature and the fellow-man" (p. 62). It should be noted, then, that Wells is dealing here with *power relations* of the broadest sort, and that therefore his critique, however indirect, is political at heart. Wells is delineating and calling into question here fundamental assumptions about seemingly "natural" relations between Man and Nature and class and class.

This is made even clearer in the second member of of each pair, which represents an inversion of the previously asserted relationship. In A2, Nature has again asserted herself, as man gradually adapts to conditions of peace, prosperity, and security, and lapses into "languor and decay" (p. 45). B2 presumes that the exploited class, the Morlocks, has turned on its exploiters, reversing the power relationship and turning the Elois into human cattle. The double inversion subverts totally the complacent assumptions of Wells's fellow Victorians about science, progress, and class relations. A similar sort of subversion is effectuated by the logical movement from set A to set B. That movement presupposes, as John Huntington correctly notes, "the transformation of an economic social division into a biological one, of an ethical issue into an evolutionary one. Clearly, Wells's moral point here is to impress on an audience which tends to accept the economic divisions of civilization as 'natural' the horror of what it would mean if that division were truly natural."[17] By linking set A to set B, Wells is able to blur hard and fast distinctions between Nature and Society, between biology and economy, while at the same time problematizing assumptions about the relation between evolution and ethics and the nature of the "natural."

It has been noted that, in proposing these sets of relations and validating them, the Time Traveller consistently relies on extrapolative logic. The pairings above also suggest the degree to which his extrapolations are built upon the two preeminent "scientific" thought systems of his time, Social Darwinism and Marxist economic theory. Social Darwinism, the application of principles of natural selection and evolution to human society and history, is not necessarily an optimistic doctrine, as Leo Henkin points out: "Evolution itself, it must be remembered, does not necessarily mean, applied to society, the movement of man to a desirable goal. It is a neutral scientific conception compatible either with optimism or with pessimism. According to different estimates it may appear to be a guarantee of steady amelioration or a cruel sentence."[18]

The Time Machine was written during a period of general optimism and complacency. Many popular writers, intellectuals, and even scientists took it for granted that scientific advancement, progress, and moral improvement were inevitably handmaidens. They believed, as Henkin puts it, that they "were living in an era which, in itself vastly superior to any of the past, need be burdened by no fear of decline or catastrophe, but, trusting in the boundless resources of science, might securely defy fate."[19] *The Time*

Machine stands that complacent assumption on its head, quite literally; it gives us, as Wells says, a "glimpse of the future that [runs] counter to the placid assumption of the time that Evolution was a pro-human force making things better and better for mankind."[20] The novel demonstrates vividly that evolution is a value-neutral force which can easily convert progress into something very like its opposite, and that scientific advancement can be self-defeating. This inversion, this counterfate, adheres rigorously to the dictates of the same "biological science" (p. 44) that Wells's contemporaries were advertising as mankind's vindication and savior. In *The Time Machine*, Wells is the scientist who turns the Darwinian coin over and looks at the dark underside.

The Time Traveller's last set of theories performs a similar inversion upon the Marxist theory of class history. The mere existence of the subterranean Morlocks refutes the notion of a gradually evolving classless society; the Morlocks, after all, represent an ultimate form of the exploited and de-humanized working class. But Wells takes the repudiation of Marx one step farther in the Time Traveller's final realization that power relations have reversed themselves and in the revelation that the Morlocks exploit the Elois in the most basic way, as fodder. This final inversion goes far beyond the mere invalidation of Marxist historiography; it reinserts into the human economy not only exploitation but also aggression, predation, bestiality; it makes into a kind of social law the idea that "cruelty is an inevitable product of a cruel system."[21] Although the Time Traveller is not really capable of viewing the Morlocks' cannibalism "in a scientific spirit" (p. 75), he does realize that the Morlocks cannot be held responsible for this final state of affairs, that cannibalism is somehow the natural end product of the value-neutral working of the system: "Man had been content to live in ease and delight upon the labours of his fellow-man, had taken Necessity as his watchword and excuse, and in the fullness of time Necessity had come home to him" (p. 75). The Morlocks are not so much evil, cruel, pitiless, inhuman as they are the inevitable product of pitiless and inhuman sets of relations. The very relations which Marxist proponents would see as tending toward a more favorable outcome, classless society, are shown to carry in them the seeds, not of their own destruction but of the complete inversion of the Marxist dream. *The Time Machine* thus stands both Dar-winism and Marxism on their heads, in so doing calling into question the assumptions behind them and problematizing any unexamined faith in either of these forms of "science." Wells has thus succeeded in doing what he set out to, namely, "to comment on the false securities and fatuous self-satisfaction of everyday life."[22]

What does *The Time Machine* reveal about extrapolative SF in general and about its readerly recuperation? First, the modus operandi of the Time Trav-eller suggests that extrapolative SF is a relatively "cool" form, the paradigms for which are to be constructed in a regular, step-by-step manner; like the Time Traveller, the reader confronted with an extrapolated world must proceed patiently, drawing on logic, system, and method, and maintaining always the proper scientific detachment and objectivity. The scientific method will eventually discover systems of relations or vraisemblance between the extrapolated world and the basic narrative world simply because extrapolative SF rests on the originary assumption that one avenue to the There and Then follows a straight line from the Here and Now; even "what if" novums are tied tightly to the basic narrative world with tethers of extrapolative logic. Also, in part because of its inherent metonymic relation to the basic narrative world, an extrapolated SF world tends to broach thematic areas that are functional and pragmatic in nature. Extrapolative SF, in other words, concerns itself more with praxis than with theory, examining what we are doing and what we can do about it.

It should also be noted that readerly recuperation of extrapolative worlds inevitably draws on culturally sanctioned models, especially those which lend themselves to extrapolation (such as Social Darwinism and Marxist historiography). The extrapolated world may adhere rigorously to the common acceptance of such models, it may invert them (as happens in *The Time Machine*), or it may embody a more problematic mean involving affirmation, inversion, interrogation, etc. But in any case the model itself occupies a prominent place within the logic of the fiction. In a case such as *The Time Machine*, where the models are inverted, the assumptions informing these models are called into question. And when those same models in some sense underpin and define the basic relations between humanity and the external world, they are "scientific" in the broadest sense—they govern the ways in which humanity apprehends, comprehends, and appropriates that world. Thus Wells can properly be seen as the grand inquisitor of science, someone whose stories "embody moral judgments and dark, anxious feelings about the nature of science and about the human consequences of the scientific vision of reality."[23] *The Time Machine*'s basic novum, the machine itself, acts as the central metaphor in Wells's critique of science. Mark Rose admirably summarizes the thrust of the novel as follows:

> The presence of the machine, the symbol of science and rationality, points to the fable's central concern with power: through science man may be able to dominate time. But what the novel finally reveals is that any such hope is false: not man but time is the master of the universe. Indeed, in the course of the story the very title develops an ironic second meaning as we come to see mankind imprisoned in the relentless turning of history, trapped in a diabolical mechanism whose workings lead to death.[24]

It should be emphasized, however, that even when extrapolative SF critiques the models, projects, or rationales of science, its relation to science and the scientific method remains fundamentally ambiguous. The logic informing extrapolative SF rests on an *a priori* acceptance of the virtues of the scientific method even when the objects and projects to which that method is applied are being interrogated. Decoding extrapolative worlds entails the very same process upon which science as a cumulative discipline relies. This fundamental ambiguity helps to explain the delicate balance between optimism and pessimism that some extrapolative SF strikes. In terms of *The Time Machine*, for example, we are told that the Time Traveller himself "thought but cheerlessly of the Advancement of Mankind, and saw in the growing pile of civilization only a foolish heaping that must inevitably fall back upon and destroy its makers in the end" (pp. 103–104), a view that his story of the future confirms. But, as the narrator reminds us, "it remains for us to live as though it were not so" (p. 104). In this case the source of our hopefulness can only be the powers of comprehension, of foresight, of cognition, which inhere in the scientific method itself, a way of approaching and knowing the world which extrapolative SF finally vindicates. As Frank McConnell says, "in the imagination of disaster, Wells manages to give a name and a shape to forces and tendencies that threaten his—and our—age. And by naming them he helps to render them visible and controllable."[25]

2.3 Reading Speculative SF: Lem's *Solaris*

> Many people in the world of science, however, especially among the young, had unconsciously come to regard the "affair" as a touchstone of individual values. All things considered, they claimed, it was not simply a question of penetrating Solarist civilization, it was essentially a test of ourselves, of the limitations of human knowledge.
>
> —Stanislaw Lem, *Solaris*

> He simply felt an urge to participate in this murky mystery, whose significance, he was quite sure, would forever remain beyond his understanding.
>
> —Stanislaw Lem, *The Invincible*

In much of Stanislaw Lem's SF, the storyline adheres to the following partial "grammar." The protagonist, a scientist or detective who is distinguished by his ordinariness, his susceptibility, is thrown into an alien environment or mysterious circumstances, either here, as in *The Investigation* and *Chain of Chance*, or on some other planet, as in *Solaris* and *The Invincible*. The mystery the protagonist confronts can be rather commonplace (a series of corpse snatchings) or quite uncanny (a sentient ocean). The protagonist, naturally enough, tries to "solve" the mystery, and in the course of the novel various theories are proposed to account for it, some of which are disconfirmed, the others providing only a limited or partial explanation. Eventually the protagonist, by either design or circumstance, finds himself in the heart of the mystery, in direct confrontation with Otherness. He *experiences* the mystery without really solving it, and he returns from the experience a chastened, but somehow wiser, human being. It should be clear from the above summary that the protagonist's experience directly parallels that of the reader of the novel, who also travels from Here to There, a There whose relation to Here remains provisional or problematic. In this respect Lem's novels can be seen as models for encountering and deciphering strangeness or Otherness of a radical or extreme nature.

Certainly, one of the strangest novums that Lem has created and "investigated" has to be the sentient ocean/planet Solaris. Given what happens in the novel of that name, there should be no real debate that the being which occupies Solaris is, in some way, sentient.[1] That is, the "ocean" demonstrates an awareness of the existence of others and an ability to act purposefully (if mysteriously) upon that awareness. This means that the encounter between the ocean and its investigators can be identified as of the Self/Other type, in this case an encounter with speculative Otherness that somehow manages to reveal things about the human Self.

In the living planet Solaris, Lem presents the reader with Otherness on a grand scale, "some seven hundred billion tons."[2] It is not only size which makes the ocean so unfathomable but also its epiphenomenal activities (the surface phenomena) and its mysterious actions (especially the creation of the Phi-creatures). It is the ocean's invariably strange "behavior" which makes the novel, as Mark Rose says, "the most radical, and . . . the most interesting, late treatment of the alien-contact theme," the ocean proving to be "as problematic a sign of the nonhuman as possible."[3] In terms of our typology, we can say that *Solaris* supplies an extreme example of speculative Otherness in the form of its ocean, a being that Lem has rendered so "unyieldingly problematic" as to shift "narrative emphasis from the object to the process of inquiry."[4] As Marc Angenot says, the "object of the story is not so much the mysterious planet Solaris as 'Solaristics' itself, the science dealing with it."[5] Lem stages an alien encounter of the most extreme form in order to explore the limits of our ability to *know* the truly Alien, the limits of scientific cognition, in so doing providing us with a model for reading speculative SF in general.

In many ways, Lem has chosen a particularly apt form to give his alien— that of the ocean. In the first place, to refer to the being on Solaris as an "ocean" (as both protagonists and critics are forced to do) is in some ways to misrepresent that being, to geomorphize it. It is a vast fluid body that covers its globe "with a colloidal envelope several miles thick in places" (p. 24), but there is nothing aquatic about it; it is more a chemical soup than a body of water. And yet "ocean," given its terran significations, is an appropriate and suggestive name. The ocean has frequently served as a symbol of Nature in the "raw," Nature in its most chaotic, mysterious, and inhuman form. To stand at the edge of the ocean is to mark off, like a lighthouse, the end of man's domain and the beginning of Nature's. The vast expanse of an ocean represents that which is both other and unknown. In a similar way, "the enigmatic Solaris ocean can be understood as a version of the infinite void, a metaphor for the vast and unknown universe."[6] Finally, in literature the ocean has been something which, despite its otherness, is forever personified, anthropomorphized. The ocean may well be an entity that stands in no personal relation with its observers or investigators, but poets and writers have insisted that that relation—perhaps hostile, perhaps friendly—exists. The ocean, as represented in literature, is a perfect example of the human need to anthropomorphize, and thus the perfect choice for an alien in *Solaris*.

Stephen Potts has identified the "tragedy of Solaristics, and the theme of the novel" as the fact that "though everyone loves a mystery human nature cannot bear one that insists on remaining a mystery."[7] Certainly, there are mysteries galore in the novel, most of which remain unsolved, but I would argue that its real focus (and the crux of critical debate) is the question of the possibility or impossibility of knowledge, the extent to which humans can come to know the truly alien and how they come to obtain that knowledge. In other words, *Solaris* is a novel whose thematic dominant is epistemology *in extremis*.

The overall critical consensus concerning the ocean is that it defies or confounds human understanding, if only because all human understanding is colored by an anthropomorphic bias or slant.[8] One critic summarizes the process of "knowing" the planet as follows: "We get the concept of the alien world, then many different perceptions of that world, and then in turn different *conceptions* of the planet, interpretations resulting more from subjective observers than the impartial object itself."[9] As has been suggested above, even first-level perceptions of the phenomenon, attempts to describe it in neutral, "scientific" terms, are tainted by the geomorphism implicit in calling it an ocean in the first place. Stuck with this conceptual frame of reference, new arrival Kelvin automatically "sees" the ocean as characterized by "slate-covered ripples" and "waves like crests of glittering quicksilver" (p. 10), by "thick foam, the color of blood" (p. 14). Even the attempt by the "scholarly classifier" Giese to formulate a precise scientific nomenclature with which to describe the polymorphic formations of Solaris—the "tree-mountains," "extensors," "fungoids," "mimoids," and so on—can be seen as inherently anthropomorphic in nature. The problem of taxonomy and classification tends to confirm Snow's claim in the novel that "we simply want to extend the boundaries of Earth to the frontiers of the cosmos. For us, such and such a planet is as arid as the Sahara, another as frozen as the the North Pole, yet another as lush as the Amazon basin" (p. 81). Wherever we go, we see only extensions of the Earth.

In addition, the study of Solaris reveals that the process of description cannot be separated from the act of theorization; the former presupposes or entails the latter:

> The fact is that in spite of his cautious nature the scrupulous Giese more than once jumped to premature conclusions. Even when on their guard, human beings inevitably theorize. Giese, who thought himself immune to temptation, decided that the "extensors" came into the category of basic forms. He compared them to accumulations of gigantic waves, similar to the tidal movements of our terran oceans. In the first edition of his work, we find them originally named as "tides." This geocentrism might be considered amusing if it did not underline the dilemma in which he found himself. (P. 120)

"Human beings inevitably theorize." Even the most neutral description is predicated upon the assumption that there is some similarity, some basis for comparison, between terran and Solarian phenomena. Theoretical attempts to define the ocean in general, whether drawn from the natural sciences—"homeostatic ocean" (p. 24) and "protoplasmic ocean-brain" (p. 24)—or from the human sciences—"ocean yogi" and "autistic ocean" (p. 30)—are shown to be hopelessly geocentric and/or anthropomorphic. The question becomes, then, to what degree they are shown to be invalid or inadequate.

When Kelvin arrives on the planet, it has been under study for more than one hundred years. During that period of time the scientists' attitude toward their object of study has gone through three pretty distinct phases. At first the planet had drawn all the best minds to its study, and Solaristics blossomed. During this period of "open assurance and irresistibly romantic optimism" (p. 174), scientists were convinced that the ocean was indeed a sentient being with which they would eventually establish Contact. Failure to do so led to the second phase of the investigation, a time of consolidation, a "holding" period, during which the data were compiled, sifted through, classified, and put into archives. Gradually, though, given the incredible amount of data accumulated, the fact that much of it was contradictory or anomalous, and the fact that Contact eluded them, scientists began to adopt a more cynical attitude toward the planet. Theories about the ocean were inevitably colored by this cynicism; they were

> unanimous in their concentration on the theme of the ocean's degeneration, regression, and introversion. Now and then a bolder, more interesting concept might emerge, but it always amounted to a kind of indictment of the ocean, viewed as the end product of a development which long ago, thousands of years before, had gone through a phase of superior organization, and now had nothing more than a physical unity. The argument went that its many useless, absurd creations were its death-throes—impressive enough, nonetheless—which had been going on for centuries. (P. 175)

In other words, scientists were reduced to hurling "insults" at the planet, behaving like "a rabble of leaderless suitors when they realized that the object of their most pressing attentions was indifferent to the point of obstinately ignoring all their advances" (p. 176). The history of Solaristics demonstrates the extent to which supposedly "scientific" fields of study are necessarily tainted by matters of subjectivity. As one critic summarizes, "the *attitudes* of the people involved were determining the 'scientific' theories; the adventurous period led to a respect for the ocean, while the despairing era, in frustration and disguised vengeance, produced ideas that were little more than slander."[10]

The radical Otherness of Solaris, then, generates in its observers theories which are at once inevitably anthropomorphic and ineluctably colored by subjective attitudes and emotions, all of which tends to call into question the ultimate "know-ability" of the planet. The question is complicated by the fact that the ocean behaves in such a way as to frustrate the scientific method itself. Since the ocean rarely responds to the same stimuli in the same way, it violates the principles of repeatability and verifiability. Also, its various activities can be theorized in very different, even contradictory, ways, as when a proto-mimoid formation is thought to be a "stillbirth" by one observer, a "necrosis" by another (pp. 122–23). The result is, at the time of Kelvin's arrival, that there is not a "single indisputable conclusion" about the planet (p. 29).

The situation on Solaris has been complicated by the appearance, just before Kelvin's arrival, of the Phi-creatures, created apparently from a "read-out" by the ocean of the investigators' subconscious or unconscious minds. In some respect these creatures embody perfectly the "problem" of Solaris, literalizing as they do the idea that scientists necessarily project a human face upon the unknown. In the negotiation between human and alien, the Phi-creatures occupy a middle ground; at once clearly human and yet utterly alien, they constitute a "third term on the boundary between the two categories."[11] As "deputies" of the ocean, they do indeed represent some sort of acknowledgment, if not exactly a form of Contact. The problem they present is figured nicely in the number of names given to them; they are variously referred to as "ghosts," "Polytherian forms," "simulacra," "visitors," "phantoms," and "Phi-creatures." Even more mysterious than the question of what they are is *why* they were created. Any number of theories are propounded to account for their appearance. Kelvin suggests sarcastically that they might be a form of torture devised by a "huge devil, who satisfies the demands of his satanic humors by sending succubi to haunt the members of a scientific expedition" (p. 82). Later Satorius proposes that they are the products of a "bungling" experimenter (pp. 112–13). Toward the end of the novel, Snow suggests that the creatures might best be seen as a sort of gift, "presents" sent by an ocean that is taking "account of desires locked into secret recesses of [the scientists'] brains" (p. 200). Speaking with his own Phi-creature Rheya, Kelvin summarizes the problem of motivation as follows: "You may have been sent to torment me, or to make my life happier, or as an instrument ignorant of its function, used like a microscope with me on the slide. Possibly you are here as a token of friendship, or a subtle punishment, or even as a joke. It could be all those things at once, or—which is more probable—something else completely" (p. 153). That "something else completely" remains a distinct possibility throughout the novel.

What should be emphasized is that the creatures are linked with the deepest and most strongly felt *emotions* of the scientists. In this way they foreground the extent to which science is an emotional enterprise, one necessarily caught up in the affective faculties of its supposedly objective investigators. The Phi-creatures are literal manifestations of that fact. In this respect, it is entirely appropriate that those who study Solaris are called Solarists, a designation which confuses them with the occupant or inhabitant of the planet.[12] The object of their study is, to some degree, themselves, a circumstance which the Phi-creatures highlight. Given, then, the fact that science is an emotional enterprise in which the object of study is frequently confused with the subject of the study, given the inevitable anthropomorphism of any and all scientific theories, the conclusion would seem to be that any progress in understanding the truly alien is impossible, that, as Stephen Potts puts it, "there remains little question that the endeavor is doomed, hopeless."[13]

Another critic goes so far as to argue that the Solarists (and readers of *Solaris*, for that matter) are "compelled to entertain an idea that necessarily casts grave doubts on the basis of their lives as scientists: that there is no clear line between reason and unreason, reality and illusion."[14] Such a view, I think, misreads an important episode in the novel and betrays the novel's ending. After his second encounter with the dead Gibarian's "visitor," a huge black woman, Kelvin panics and begins to question his own sanity. He wonders if everything he has experienced to this point has been part of an elaborate hallucination induced by toxic fumes from the ocean. For a while he is stymied; he can think of no way to confirm or disconfirm the possibility of madness. As he says, "It was not possible to think except with one's brain, no one could stand outside himself in order to check the functioning of his inner processes" (p. 57). This confusion of observer and observed, of course, is identical to the problem posed by Solaris and by the Phi-creatures. But in time Kelvin *is* able to devise an experiment confirming the reality of his experiences, an experiment using the mathematics of orbital mechanics. In other words, he is able to make use of physical observations and the laws of physics to confirm that the external world does exist, apart from himself. As he says, "I was not mad. The last ray of hope was extinguished" (p. 59).[15]

The point proved by this episode is that, despite what Kelvin might think at the moment, the "last ray of hope" has just been kindled, that proving that the Other exists apart from the Self is the first step in coming to terms with Otherness. By the end of the novel, Kelvin has not, as Potts maintains, "renounced mankind's foolish endeavor to comprehend rationally the non-human with human models,"[16] even if he has learned quite painfully about the limitations and liabilities of such models. Both Snow and he agree, for example, that the experience with the Phi-creatures has lifted the scientists to a new level of understanding about the planet. No longer is there no "single indisputable conclusion"; the scientists know now that they are dealing with a living creature, that, as Kelvin says, the "ocean lived thought and acted. The 'Solaris problem' had not been annihilated by its very absurdity. We were truly dealing with a living creature. The 'lost' faculty was not lost at all. All this seemed proved beyond doubt" (p. 179). In the penultimate chapter, Snow rehearses some of the other indisputable conclusions that can be drawn from the affair; the ocean, he says, "has given a demonstration of considered activity. It is capable of carrying out organic synthesis on the most complex level, a synthesis that we ourselves have never managed to achieve. It knows the structure, microstructure and metabolism of our bodies . . . " (p. 200). Because of this progress, however partial and tentative, he says, "from now on we stand a chance" (p. 200) at establishing contact with the creature, and he decides to stay on at the station.

To maintain that the ocean acted in some sense deliberately in creating the Phi-creatures is not to maintain that its intention can be fathomed by its investigators. As Robert Philmus warns, the ocean

> remains especially unintelligible in terms of the binary opposition between "conscious will" and pure accident. Assigning a telos to its intricately patterned ballet of forms involves an exercise in fantasizing; but it is just as fantastic to imagine that its responses to a human presence are sheerly random. If its acts have no ultimate purpose and certainly none that is humanly discoverable, they nevertheless appear to be purposive.[17]

In the final paragraph of the novel, Kelvin even calls into question the extent to which the ocean's purposes might be unfathomable: "Yet its activities did have a purpose," he muses, and then immediately adds, "True, I was not absolutely certain, but leaving would mean giving up a chance, perhaps an infinitesimal one, perhaps only imaginary" (p. 211). And so, he too decides to remain at the station, hoping against hope that Contact with the ocean will be reestablished. By ending the novel this way, Lem reaffirms "his faith in the repeatedly wrongheaded and unverifiable attempts of science to take the measure of the external universe."[18]

In the narratology of the speculative Self/Other encounter, taking the measure of the external universe, delineating the dimensions of the Other, more often than not entails defining the dimensions of the Self. This certainly holds true for *Solaris*. The appearance of the third term in the human/nonhuman polarity, the Phi-creatures, who are at once alien entities and extensions or projections of the most human aspects of the scientists, brings into sharp relief the notion that an encounter with an Other is at the same time an exploration of the Self; as one critic puts it, "the Solarists' obsession with the mysteries of Solaris dissolves into a broader struggle to understand human reflection and identity."[19] Indeed, Snow links our interest in otherness with a basic preoccupation with, and blindness about, our selves: "We think of ourselves as the Knights of Holy Contact. This is another lie. We are only seeking Man. We have no need of other worlds. We need mirrors." Solaris does provide a mirror on our souls, one that reveals "that part of our reality which we would prefer to pass over in silence" (p. 81). It may indeed "be worth our while to stay" on the planet, Snow suggests, because "we're unlikely to learn anything about *it*, but about ourselves . . . " (p. 86). The anthropomorphism that we foist upon other planets may well be a function of our inability or failure to know ourselves; self-ignorance, argues one critic, "is the principal barrier to the human understanding of 'other worlds.' "[20] Exposure to an other world, to an alien encounter, then, reveals to us hidden aspects of our secret selves and, in so doing, prepares us to meet that alien on its own terms.

This, of course, is exactly what happens to Kelvin in the novel. His exposure to his Phi-creature Rheya compels him to face up to the extent to which he was guilty of his young wife's death, a guilt he plays out again, first in his attempts to rid himself of his Phi-creature, later in his determination to hold fast to "Rheya," whatever she might be, and finally in his fear that, despite his conscious desire to save her, his unconscious mind, that "labyrinth of dark passages and secret chambers," might well want only her destruction (p. 165). In other words, he does everything possible "to stay human in an inhuman situation" (p. 159). As Snow warns him, they are trapped in a "situation that is beyond morality," in which it is not possible "to be anything but a traitor" (pp. 160, 161). But it is only after "Rheya" sacrifices herself, going willingly to her death, and his one anthropomorphic link with the ocean is dissolved, that Kelvin is able to encounter Otherness face to face, as it were. What Kelvin must put aside is his anthropocentric value system; he "is compelled to recognize that in a world defined by the encounter of the human with a non-human intelligence, the most noble human values may be only quixotic illusions."[21] He must become, as Stephen Potts puts it, "an empty slate ready to receive the universe on its own terms."[22]

It is only at this point that Kelvin is ready for Contact with the ocean. He leaves the station for the first time and explores a decaying "mimoid" formation on the ocean's surface, where he experiences a well-documented Solarian phenomenon. When he extends his hand to the ocean, a wave envelops it with a thin layer of gelatinous material, creating a glove separated from the hand by a minuscule layer of air. Kelvin repeats the "game" a number of times, until the ocean "tires" of it and does not respond to his hand. Although Kelvin has read about this phenomenon in the literature about the planet, the actual experience moves him more than expected: "I felt somehow changed," he says (p. 210). He senses in the ocean "a curiosity avid for quick apprehension of a new, unexpected form, and regretful at having to retreat, unable to exceed the limits set by a mysterious law" (p. 210). Strongly moved by an awareness of the ocean's presence, he is finally able to shed the last vestiges of his self and to identify with "the dumb, fluid colossus," during which time he decides once and for all to stay on the planet, to live, not in hope but "in expectation," to persist in "the faith that the time of cruel miracles was not past" (p. 211). Having achieved Contact, however tenuous and problematic, Kelvin has joined the ranks of "that generation of researchers who had been daring and optimistic enough to hark back to the golden age, and who did not disown their own version of a faith that overstepped the frontiers imposed by science, since it presupposed the success of perseverance" (p. 182).

Readers of *Solaris*, Istvan Csicsery-Ronay has perceptively noted, also join the ranks of dedicated Solarists, because they too undertake the study of the mysterious planet.[23] Since Kelvin's experience on the planet serves as a model for the reader's, what does the former tell us about the recuperation of speculative SF worlds? We noted in the previous section (see 2.2) that extrapolative SF is forged on tight links between the SF world and the basic narrative world. Given the contiguity between Here and There, the reader is well advised to bring to the reading experience certain axiological assumptions and/or forms of knowledge, which then will be interrogated or examined, found lacking or affirmed. They will not, however, be totally repudiated, since extrapolative SF assumes there is a linear relation between Here and There. Speculative SF is more radical in its cognitive demands. It requires that its readers begin at "absolute zero," jettisoning eventually all preconceptions or presuppositions. They must put in suspension, in particular, assumptions having to do with teleology and with morality. As Snow once says to Kelvin when the latter tries to assert the priority of romantic love, "It's touching, it's magnificent, anything you like, but it's out of place here—it's the wrong setting" (p. 162). In the alien settings of speculative SF, the reader must abandon the most basic "terran" preconceptions.

What an encounter with "true" Otherness calls for, in fact, is nothing less than uncritical identification with the novum; one participates in or experiences the "murky mystery" without preconceptions about its parameters, solution, solubility, or significance. Csicsery-Ronay has argued convincingly, in regard to *Solaris*, that Kelvin first achieves Contact with the ocean in chapter 12, suggestively titled "The Dreams." After a number of attempts to achieve contact by beaming X-rays modified by his own brain patterns into the ocean, Kelvin has sunk into a period of exhaustion and lethargy, exacerbated, he claims, "by an invisible presence which had taken possession of the Station" (p. 186). This presence makes itself felt during the scientists' nonwaking hours. Kelvin records one particularly "real" and disturbing dream in which he *becomes* an alien being clothed in a formless substance (like the ocean). This being is "touched" by a disembodied hand and becomes a human form which in turn brings into being another human form, perhaps female. The two beings combine into one, realize that the "caress" that created them has been transformed into a "presence of indefinable, unimaginable cruelty" (p. 187), and then undergo a period of excruciating suffering until they are dispersed in all directions. The whole dream is resonant, but for our purposes the most significant fact is that the series of incarnations blurs the distinction between Kelvin and the ocean, collapsing the two into a third entity (an amalgam of Kelvin, the ocean, and Rheya) which endures "a mountain of grief visible in the dazzling light of another world" (p. 188). These dream passages, then, "resist interpretation as anything other than moments of non-rational, non-conscious exchange—true moments of contact so surpassing the common run of human communication that they could well be taken for religious inspiration."[24]

These dream passages also suggest that speculative SF is a less linear and rational form than extrapolative SF. Where extrapolative SF asks that the reader work logically, speculative SF elicits a more "intuitive" reading, one capable of oneiric twists and transformations. Where extrapolative SF encourages the reader to work linearly, gradually refining the interpretive framework without discarding entire interpretive paradigms, speculative SF calls forth any number of interpretive models, some mutually contradictory, in no particular order. Where the trope that governs extrapolative SF is metonymy, the trope that subtends speculative SF is metaphor. In the Self/Other encounter of *Solaris*, for example, the main weapon in the Solarists' arsenal is analogy; the ocean is like a cosmic yogi or an autistic child. While the novel submits the process of analogy to a rigorous interrogation and foregrounds its inevitable anthropomorphism,[25] at the same time it (the novel) does suggest that the process can lead to insights about Otherness, bringing us closer to the alien, if only by approximation. In the last chapter of the novel Snow and Kelvin come up with a final theory to explain the ocean's behavior, that it is an "evolving" and imperfect God in its infancy. Now Ketterer is certainly right to remind us that this is "one more anthropomorphic hypothesis about the planet,"[26] but given that this is a completely new hypothesis, that it comes in the final chapter, and, most important, that it is a "better," more inclusive model, this reading earns a privileged status. As Kelvin says to Snow: "You've produced a completely new hypothesis about Solaris—congratulations! Everything suddenly falls into place: the failure to achieve contact, the absence of responses, various . . . let's say various peculiarities in its behavior towards ourselves. Everything is explicable in terms of the behavior of a small child" (p. 206). The theory of the evolving and despairing God affirms the ability of man to take the measure of the unknown while at the same time circumscribing the limits of human cognition in the face of that unknown.

Mark Rose has said of Lem's work that in it "cosmology, the traditional concern of science fiction in the space category, yields to epistemology, an exploration of the limitations inherent in any human frame of reference."[27] I would add that this is the thrust of speculative SF in general. Because it cannot be recuperated or naturalized using linear or extrapolative models, speculative SF tends to subvert such models.[28] Because it reveals that scientific theories are inevitably anthropomorphic and that scientific data are to some extent preselected by those theories, it "calls in question the entire set of assumptions underlying any naively positivistic thought."[29] Speculative SF investigates the extent to which science is a *human* discipline. In the case of *Solaris*, we might note that Kelvin was a psychological scientist, whose thesis rested on observed similarities between electronic readings of strong human emotions and the recordings of electrical discharges from the ocean (p. 183). By thus systematically interrogating science, by revealing its human face, speculative SF finally suggests the degree to which science's assumptions about the way the world works rest, not on any firm empirical footing but on faith alone. At the same time, by suggesting that we can somehow transcend our human limitations, it reaffirms our need for faith of some kind; indeed, it tends to explore the many forms that faith takes.

III

A TYPOLOGY OF SF

I consider the exercise of taxonomizing (classifications, genealogies) in Literature to be a harmful brand of scholastic activity (if it is meant to tell us how to pigeonhole a work), because the most interesting issues happen to be located at the borders of classes.

—Stanislaw Lem, Interview with Istvan Csicsery-Ronay, Jr.

A postulate has no need of proofs; but its effectiveness can be measured by the results we reach by accepting it.

—Tzvetan Todorov, *The Fantastic*

In this chapter we will explore the thematic fields of each of the four major SF types—alien encounter, alternate society, gadget, and alternate world SF—and examine in detail representative novels, extrapolative and speculative, of each type. In regard to the individual texts, in each case we have tried to select exemplary or paradigmatic texts, ones which have as their dominant novum the estrangement factor specified by the type and which confront and explore that factor in a cognitively rewarding manner. We have tried also to draw from a wide spectrum of SF, incorporating as much as possible representative texts from America, England, and the Continent. In most typological slots, however, there are any number of texts which might serve as exempla; in alternate society SF, for example, one could pick and choose within a spectrum of SF "classics." In cases such as these, we have deliberately passed over texts which have received attention elsewhere and selected texts which are relatively less well known but deserving of attention. In constructing and exploring this typology, we hope to circumscribe and define the thematic contours of SF in general, while at the same time providing the kind of close readings that respect each text's uniqueness and integrity.

3.1 Alien Encounters: Self and Other in SF

"Why are these sins permitted? What sins have we done? The morning service was over, I was walking through the roads to clear my brain for the afternoon, and then—fire, earthquake, death! As if it were Sodom and Gomorrah! All our work undone, all the work . . . What are these Martians?"

"What are we?" I answered, clearing my throat.

—H. G. Wells, *The War of the Worlds*

When science fiction uses its limitless range of symbol and metaphor novelistically, with the subject at the center, it can show us who we are, and where we are, and what choices face us, with unsurpassed clarity, and with a great and troubling beauty.

Ursula K. LeGuin, "Science Fiction and Mrs. Brown"

In order to make a point about the value of SF in his essay "Fiction about the Future," H. G. Wells indulges in the following "thought experiment": Let us suppose that sometime in the future biologists discover a way for females to produce only female children without any intercession by males; this hypothesis makes possible one legitimate SF world—a world without men. Wells goes on to point out that the idea informing an SF world is less important than the treatment of it, and then ranks some possible treatments in terms of their cognitive potentials. First, the writer could ignore "the fact that [this transformation] would change the resultant human being into a creature mentally and emotionally different from ourselves" and use the novum simply as a means for making fun of an all-woman world, thereby creating "the Futurist Story at the lowest level." Or the writer could create a "graver story," dealing with the social complications inherent in a world in which there was no courtship process and no marriage market, with the economic and political structures that would evolve in a manless world. The writer would then create, I suggest, an "alternate society" SF (see 3.2) which, Wells admits, might be loaded down with "dissertations" (as is the case with much utopic/dystopic SF) but would be a "much finer thing to bring off."

Wells offers as a third alternative the possibility that the writer focus on the struggle that would necessarily occur during the changeover period, narrowing the story "down to a small group of people" and dealing with the conflicts within the group; the product would then be a "futurist novel, the highest and most difficult form of futurist literature."[1] Implicit in Wells's definition of "novel" here is the assumption that the form deals on a personal and intimate basis with the psychological states of its actants, with conflict between well-rounded and real-ized characters. Wells thus gives highest place to "futurist fiction" which foregrounds actantial confrontations, which, to borrow LeGuin's phrase, keeps "the subject at the center." In terms of the typology outlined in this book, the SF type whose novum by definition speaks to the issue of the subject and its possible transformations is the alien encounter.

Alien encounter SF involves the introduction of sentient alien beings into the actantial system of the fictional universe; one or more of the actants are nonhuman or superhuman or subhuman. The encounter with the alien necessarily broaches the question of Self and Other. In general, the reader recuperates this type of fiction by comparing human and alien entities, trying to understand what it is to be human. One paradigmatic example of such an attempt occurs in Roger Zelazny's celebrated story "For a Breath I Tarry" (1966). Long after all humans have disappeared from the Earth, an orbital master computer named Solcom presides over the robots and machines that remain, and has divided supervision of the planet between two "lieutenant" machines, Frost in the North and Beta in the South. Frost, however, was created during an "unprecedented solar flareup"[2] and exhibits some unusual traits, among them a curiosity about the former inhabitants of Earth. Determined to discover the nature of Man, despite being forewarned that it is "basically incomprehensible" (p. 87), he becomes more and more absorbed in the study of the remaining artifacts and relics, until he is drawn into a seemingly unwinnable wager with Divcom, the subterranean renegade computer who wishes to wrest control of Earth away from Solcom; either Frost will *become* a Man, or he will employ his powers in the service of Divcom. The story centers on Frost's ongoing attempt to comprehend and appropriate the essence of what it is to be human.

Convinced at first that given "sufficient data" he can understand everything, Frost begins by devouring what remains of the library of Man, a process that takes a century. Afterward he scans the surviving films and tapes and analyzes in detail all the artifacts with which Divcom can supply him. Five years of processing and assimilating this data cannot unlock the mystery, so the indefatigable Frost rigs for himself the entire human sensory apparatus and sets off to visit Man's final abode and to witness the scenes and landscapes that gave Man pleasure. At one of these sites, the following dialogue with Divcom's emissary takes place:

> "What do you see, hear, taste, smell?" asked Mordel.
> "Everything I did before," replied Frost, "but within a more limited range."
> "You do not perceive any beauty?"
> "Perhaps none remains after so long a time," said Frost.
> "It is not supposed to be the sort of thing which gets used up," said Mordel. (P. 96)

Learning from this experience that the "senses do not make a Man" (p. 99), Frost undertakes an exhaustive study of remaining human works of art and then tries to create works of art—a sculpture, a painting—himself. But because he approaches these projects as he would when "designing a machine," his artifacts remain literal copies or mechanical reproductions. Realizing at last that he cannot "comprehend the Nature of Man" in "His works" because of an "element of non-logic" in them (p. 108), Frost determines to grow a human body from living cells taken from corpses buried beneath the North Pole and to transfer his awareness to the resultant human nervous system. It is only then that he is able to achieve his objective.

From the very beginning of the story, Frost manifests some peculiarly human traits. He is curious: "He wondered much . . . about being a Man" (p. 113). He is both proud and ambitious: "I still know I can do it [become a Man]" (p. 94). But he's convinced that all the transformation takes is logic and sufficient data; humanity can be attained incrementally. First he accumulates encyclopedias of knowledge, then he grafts on the human sensory system, and finally he copies human behaviors. Indeed, while he is not yet a genuine Man, he is nonetheless becoming more human, a condition reflected in the language that he uses, in the forms of address he employs. When questioned by Solcom about his actions, Frost responds with a very human question having to do with teleology: "Then let me ask you of your plan: What good is it? What is it for?" (p. 114). But, the ending of the story suggests, the essence of humanity lies not in curiosity, not in the intellect, not even in the imagination. To be fully human one must be incarnated, trapped within the prison of human physiology. It is only there that Frost experiences human emotions such as fear and despair, emotions which are themselves the only sure indices of the quantum step to becoming human: "[Frost] spoke to me through human lips. He knows fear and despair, which are immeasurable. Frost is a Man" (p. 117). The story ends with Frost incarnating Beta as his bride and beginning human history all over again.

In "For a Breath I Tarry," then, Zelazny employs a sentient alien actant, in this case an overreaching machine, to stage the exploration of the essence of being human. This is, I would argue, the model and the thematic thrust of all alien encounters, defining the Self from the estranged perspective of the Other. Since the alien Other can take a wide variety of forms, alien encounter SF includes a wide spectrum of fictions. The alien Other might take the form of a technologically transformed version of the Self, as in Frederik Pohl's *Man Plus* (1976), or of a mutant, as in Van Vogt's *Slan* (1940). Or it may appear as a monstrous alter ego, as in Shelley's *Frankenstein* (1818), Stevenson's *Dr. Jekyll and Mr. Hyde* (1886), or Wells's *The Invisible Man* (1897). In another place, *The Island of Doctor Moreau* (1896), Wells uses surgically altered animals as his dominant novum. Like Zelazny, Harlan Ellison uses a sentient computer to explore the nature of the Self in "I Have No Mouth, and I Must Scream" (1967). The most common form of the alien, of course, is the extraterrestrial, as in Lem's *His Master's Voice* (1968), Harry Bates's Golden Age classic "Farewell to the Master" (1943), and Clarke's celebrated *Childhood's End* (1953). Although some critics would assign these fictions to separate categories,[3] I would argue that they share a common dominant novum, an alien Other, which determines their type and circumscribes their thematic field to the examination of selfhood from the vantage point of alternity.

Some critics have argued that SF, given its grounding in the epistemology of science and its acceptance of an impersonal, value-neutral universe (both functions of its discourse; see 1.1), is generically inimical to the exploration of "character." Scott Sanders, for example, suggests that *"in the twentieth century science fiction is centrally about the disappearance of character*, in the same sense in which the eighteenth- and nineteenth-century bourgeois novel is about the emergence of character."[4] Putting aside the objection that naturalistic fiction, whose discourse shares the same assumptions as SF's, is nonetheless able to create some memorable and well-rounded characters (such as Leopold Bloom), I can say only that such a view ignores, overlooks, or is ignorant of alien encounter SF, which foregrounds the collision between Self and Other, in so doing exploring not only who we are (in the classic, liberal sense) but also what we might become in a future certain to be different from the present.

A related complaint is that, because SF frequently focuses on the ideational complications inherent in its novum, it tends to rely heavily on stereotypes in its portrayal of character. Robert Scholes says that "it is fair to say that the representation of unique individuality is not so much an end in itself in SF as it has been in some realistic novels."[5] And Kingsley Amis cites, with approval, the following comment by Edmund Crispin, a "leading British commentator on science fiction":

> The characters of a science fiction story are usually treated rather as representatives of their species than as individuals in their own right. They are matchstick men and women, for the reason that if they were not, the anthropocentric habit of our culture would cause us, in reading, to give altogether too much attention to them and altogether too little to the non-human forces which constitute the important remainder of the *dramatis personae*.[6]

Here again, the critic seems to have confused gadget SF, space opera, or alternate world SF with the totality of the genre. When evaluating SF, one must pay attention to the nature of the estranging novum. While I would admit that some SF (like other forms of fiction) resorts to stock characters and stereotypes in elaborating its roster of actants, alien encounter SF just cannot do that. The alien actant and its human counterpart occupy the center stage of the fictional universe, and an exploration of their respective unique qualities is the *sine qua non* of the fiction. It may well happen that the human serves as "representative" of his or her species, and the fiction focuses more on human selfhood than on a unique individual. In *Omnivore*, for example, Piers Anthony imagines a fungoid life form, the mantas from Nacre, in order to investigate what it means to be an "omnivore," an indiscriminately destructive species. In this case and in all such fiction, the encounter with the alien interrogates the "anthropocentric habit of our culture."

Another standard complaint about alien encounter stories has it that, whatever form the alien Other might take, it is never really "alien." The scientist Loren Eiseley, for example, claims, "In the modern literature on space travel I have read about cabbage men and bird men; I have investigated the loves of lizard men and the tree men, but in each case I have labored under no illusion. I have been reading about man, *Homo sapiens*, that common earthling."[7] He accuses SF writers of a failure of the imagination, of an inability to create an actant that is truly Other. But absolute Otherness is an artistic impossibility; that which is completely Other would be also completely incomprehensible to the reader, who is necessarily locked into an anthropocentric framework to an extent. As Csicsery-Ronay points out, "anthropocentric projection is not something a reader of SF can avoid; it is the basis for making sense of the fiction."[8]

In regard to the degree of strangeness of the alien, Gregory Benford makes the following discrimination: we can distinguish between "anthropocentric aliens," those which represent an exaggeration of recognizable human traits, and "unknowable aliens," those which retain an "essential strangeness."[9] In the former category, which I would term *extrapolative Otherness*, we would locate the Overlords from Clarke's *Childhood's End*, creatures who represent an extreme form of rationality. The same novel offers us an "unknowable alien" (an example of *speculative Otherness*) in the form of the Overmind, an irreducibly strange entity with a genuinely different way of looking at the universe. In this latter category, Benford would place two of his own novels, *If the Stars Are Gods* (1977) and *In the Ocean of Night* (1972). Benford's categories, based, I would argue, on the distinction between extrapolation and speculation, have a heuristic value, especially as long as they are not invested with a hierarchical valuation. For both extrapolative and speculative alien encounters can provide a degree of estrangement or displacement. As Benford has maintained elsewhere, "the alien in SF is an experience, not a statement or an answer to a question. An artistic—that is, fulfilling, multifaceted, resonant—rendering of the alien is a thing in the world itself, not merely a text or a commentary on the world."[10] I would add only that this kind of treatment necessarily carries with it a cognitive charge, challenging traditional conceptions of the nature of the Self and its possible relations to the Other.

Stanislaw Lem charges that alien encounter SF is not guilty of a failure of the imagination so much in the creation of its aliens as in its oversimplification of possible relations between human Self and alien Other. American SF in particular, Lem claims, has been guilty of reducing the human/alien encounter to a single, implausible option: "Rule them or be ruled by them."[11] In this version of the encounter, Lem points out, the authors are merely giving way to paranoia, projecting "their fears and self-generated delusions on the universe."[12] Now, while Lem's stricture certainly holds true for much alien encounter SF, it does not really do justice to the spectrum of shapes that the Self/Other encounter can take and has taken in SF in general.

At the lowest level, the alien actant may, as Eiseley claims, turn out to be an undisguised variant of the Self, more human than alien. The sentient robots in Asimov's *I, Robot*, for example, are all variations of human stereotypes; the telepathic robot in "Liar," to cite just one story, quite "naturally" develops an overriding interest in human psychology and becomes a counselor and confidant for the various human actants in the story. In Heinlein's *The Moon Is a Harsh Mistress*, Mike, the computer who awakens into consciousness, creates a number of stereotypical human alter egos—Michelle, Adam Selene, Simon Jester—while masterminding and orchestrating the moon's revolt against Earth. And the Mesklinites in Hal Clement's *Mission of Gravity*, while they do have unusual morphologies because of variable gravity on their planet, generally converse like people from Middle America and behave like shrewd petite bourgeoisie. Clearly these are cases in which the alien is not really alien at all. It should be noted, however, that none of these novels are typologically alien encounter SF but rather, respectively, gadget SF, alternate society SF, and alternate world SF. The "aliens," in these instances, serve as a kind of window dressing for a fiction whose cognitive thrust goes elsewhere.

Also falling into the gadget SF category would be those fictions in which the encounter with the alien is seen merely as an opportunity for exploitation. John Berryman's "Berom" (1951), for example, depicts the jockeying for advantage between Americans and Russians following an alien landing in Kansas. Each side wants to be the first to make contact in order to discover the technological and scientific secrets locked up in the alien spacecraft. In stories such as these, there is no real interest in Otherness per se, no exploration of alien psychology, no real confrontation between Self and Other, because the alien has no other reality than as a tool to be exploited, an object containing a number of valuable secrets.

If alien encounters depicting the Other as simple variant of Self or the Other as Object either fall into other typological niches or do not use their novums as a source of cognitive estrangement, what, then, are the true, and valuable, alien encounter stories? The vast majority, as Lem has pointed out, present the Other as Enemy, as a source of imminent danger, even extinction, for the human race. Murray Leinster's "First Contact" (1945) can serve as the paradigm for this type of encounter, because it thematizes this very idea. In the story, the first encounter takes place in outer space, in the Crab nebula, where alien and terran spacecraft have been drawn on similar missions of exploration. This chance meeting poses a singular problem for the respective skippers of the two ships, a problem seemingly admitting of only one solution:

> Each [of the skippers] insisted—perhaps truthfully—that he wished for friendship between the two races. But neither could trust the other not to make every conceivable effort to find out the one thing he needed most desperately to conceal—the location of his home planet. And neither dared believe the other was unable to trail him and find out. Because each felt it was his own duty to accomplish that unbearable—to the other—act, neither could risk the possible extinction of his race by trusting the other. They must fight because they could not do anything else.[13]

The logic here, as in other alien-as-enemy stories, is predicated upon rather limited assumptions about the encounter with the Other, assumptions based essentially upon questions of power. As the skipper of the terran ship says,

> "If we did manage to make friendly contact, how long would it stay friendly? If their weapons were inferior to ours, they'd feel that for their own safety they had to improve them. And we, knowing they were planning to revolt, would crush them while we could—for our own safety! If it happened the other way about, they'd have to smash us before we could catch up to them." (P. 335)

This Cold War mentality can envision the Other only in terms of conquest, of "us" versus "them." Given this sort of two-value logic, stories such as these usually devolve into space opera pyrotechnics.

Leinster, however, treats the situation as a problem to be solved and brings off the solution with a literal *deus ex machina*—the two races agree to swap ships, return to their home planets, and then rendezvous at the Crab nebula at a prescribed time, when they will presumably know more about each other and have a basis for trust. Whether this swap indeed solves their problem is moot; an examination of the respective ships might well increase levels of paranoia. But even this solution would not have been available had the aliens been more human than otherwise in the first place. Throughout the story, the aliens behave in ways which are highly congruent with human behavior, even if the story attributes to them a "completely alien thought-pattern" (p. 331). The aliens accept the two-value logic that the humans see as operative. Their actions are never mysterious or strange; they are always accessible to rational explanation. The aliens even discover simultaneously the same solution as the humans. They may breathe through gills, see by heat waves, and communicate through short-wave, but they think and act just like humans: "But their brains worked alike. Amazingly alike. Tommy Dort felt an actual sympathy and even something close to friendship for the gill-breathing, bald, and dryly ironic creatures of the black space vessel" (p. 337). The degree of likeness, of congruence, is so high that the story ends with representatives from the rival ships swapping dirty stories.

Alien encounter stories such as these tend to have limited cognitive value. As Gary Wolfe says, "it is in these first-contact stories that science fiction tends to be at its most obsessively paranoid, concerned with the potential danger to the race inherent in alien contact."[14] In the worst case, these stories do reveal that our first reaction to an encounter with the unknown may well be a reversion to a reflexive xenophobia. Leinster's story, in addition, suggests that we can counteract that reflex if we keep our wits about us and rely on our ingenuity. But in general alien-as-enemy SF, just because it necessarily assumes that the Other is just a form of the Self, does not take advantage of the thematic potential of a confrontation with real Otherness.[15]

In terms of themes of Self and Other, the best alien encounter SF is that which deals with true Otherness, where the story focuses on the human attempt to come to terms with an alien actant whose selfhood, developed in some detail, deviates significantly from human norms. Such Otherness need not be speculative in mode, as Benford's division of alien beings into "anthropocentric aliens" and "unknowable aliens" perhaps suggests. The "anthropocentric alien," the human in another form, can embody the kind of Otherness which sheds light on questions of the Self, as Ursula K. LeGuin's story "Nine Lives" (1969) proves.

"Nine Lives" opens with the standard encounter motif: two terrans, the Welshman Pugh and the Argentinian Martin, are awaiting the arrival of reinforcements on the isolated mining planet to which they have been assigned. "I'll be glad to see a human face," Pugh says, to which Martin rejoins, "Thanks," the brief interchange suggesting the kind of healthy camaraderie the men share, even after many months in space."[16] They discover that the new arrivals are human-with-a-difference, when a tenclone—five men and five women, all genetically identical except for sex—disembarks. At this point the narrator explicitly circumscribes the thematic field of the story: "It is hard to meet a stranger. Even the greatest extrovert meeting even the meekest stranger knows a certain dread, though he may not know he knows it. Will he make a fool of me wreck my image of myself invade me destroy me change me? Yes, that he will. There's the terrible thing: the strangeness of the stranger" (p. 387). Martin and Pugh, after two years on a dead planet, isolated from others of their kind, no longer comfortable with "the habit of difference" (p. 387), will, it seems, encounter strangeness, in the form of the tenclone, and will be changed by the encounter. In part this is just what happens, as the two humans struggle to deal with the interchangeability of the clone members, their incestuous sexual practices, and especially the group's absolute self-sufficiency. But midway through the story LeGuin reverses the terms of the encounter, in so doing shifting emphasis from the general theme of tolerance to a more explicit treatment of Self and Other. Nine of the clone members are killed in an earthquake, and the remaining one, Kaph, after suffering empathetically nine deaths, must learn how to go on as a separate individual, as a Self. The focus of the story switches to the alien's attempt to become *human*.

Immediately after the traumatic event, Kaph is little more than a breathing corpse, "nine-tenths dead," totally oblivious to the existence of others, because the very concept of Otherness is unfamiliar to him. As Pugh notes, "He [Kaph] doesn't see us or hear us, that's the truth. He never had to see anyone else before. He never was alone before. He had himself to see talk with, live with, nine other selves all his life. He doesn't know how to go it alone" (p. 400). To learn how "to go it alone," he must first learn about the existence of others, or else he is condemned to the "child's dream": "There is no one else alive in the world but me. In all the world" (p. 404). In the days that follow, Kaph manages to survive and function, but not really as a human being. He begins to eat and to perform routine tasks, but he does nothing that calls for initiative, and in neither speech nor action does he acknowledge the existence of the other two men. Pugh suggests to Martin that Kaph is recuperating and elicits this retort: "He's not. He's turning himself into a machine. Does what he's programmed to do, no reaction to anything else. He's worse off than when he didn't function at all. He's not human any more" (p. 402).

The point is, however, that, because he's never known anyone but himself, Kaph has never been really human; being human is a function of awareness of the Other. The relation between Martin and Pugh serves eventually as the channel through which Kaph becomes aware of Otherness. On the day before their departure from the planet, Martin goes out to inspect a trench and is caught in a severe quake. Without hesitation, Pugh risks his own life by rushing out to save his friend, despite Kaph's logical protest that it's an "unnecessary risk" (p. 404). After Martin is rescued and put to bed, Kaph addresses a key question to Pugh:

> "Do you love Martin?"
> Pugh looked up with angry eyes: "Martin is my friend. We've worked together, he's a good man." He stopped. After a while he said, "Yes, I love him. Why did you ask that?"
> Kaph said nothing, but he looked at the other man. His face was changed, as if he were glimpsing something he had not seen before; his voice too was changed. "How can you . . . ? How do you . . . ?" (P. 406)

The elided question here is surely "How can you love an Other?" Pugh answers that he does not know, but that since each of us is alone, "What can you do but hold out your hand in the dark?" Pugh then figuratively holds out his hand by suggesting that Kaph remain with him and Martin, as part of their team. "Pugh's quiet voice trailed off. He stood unbuttoning his coat, stooped a little with fatigue. Kaph looked at him and saw the thing he had never seen before: saw him: Owen Pugh, the other, the stranger who held out his hand in the dark" (p. 406).

The story ends with Kaph acknowledging Pugh's existence by saying goodnight, thus suggesting that he has learned an essential aspect of being human: that each of us is alone, solitary, in the dark; and that the only way to break that solitude and become fully human is to reach out to the Other, who is also alone and in the dark. In the case of LeGuin's Kaph, then, an extrapolative alien is employed to illuminate the general question of the Self and Other and to explore thereby what it means to be human. This, I would argue, is the accomplishment of all alien encounter SF in which the alien is imagined as something truly Other.

3.1.1 Extrapolative Alien Encounter: Silverberg's *Dying Inside*

> The story of transformation is the correlative of the story of alien confrontation. Instead of meeting the alien across a barrier of otherness, man discovers himself to be in some sense alien.
>
> —Mark Rose, *Alien Encounters: Anatomy of Science Fiction*

> You don't need to go to Sirius to find an alien; the aliens are inside.
>
> —Ian Watson *The Martian Inca* (1977)

That the encounter with the alien can take on a great number of different forms should be made clear by the number of ways we can run into alienity here on Earth. The alien may appear on Earth by accident, in need of assistance, as in the movie *E.T.* or in Raymond F. Jones's short story "Correspondence Course" (1945). The alien may come here by design, either to save humanity from itself, as in Clarke's *Childhood's End*, or to subjugate or annihilate the human race, as in Wells's *The War of the Worlds*. The alien may appear here and attach itself to the human body, either as a parasite (Heinlein's *The Puppet Masters*) or as a symbiont (Clement's *Needle*), in so doing converting a human Self into an alien Other. Humans can themselves create or invent an alien being, either benevolent,as in George Alec Effinger's *The Wolves of Memory*, malevolent, as in Ellison's "I Have No Mouth and I Must Scream," or ethically neutral, as in Shelley's *Frankenstein*. Or a human may be transformed into something alien, either by design, as in Pohl's *Man Plus* and Joseph McElroy's *Plus*, or by Nature herself, in the form of mutants, as in Van Vogt's *Slan*. It is into this last category that Robert Silverberg's *Dying Inside* falls; *Dying* recounts the story of one David Selig, born with the "gift" of telepathy but gradually losing it. By depicting what it is to have such a power, to lose it, and to be without it, the novel incorporates a spectrum of perspectives on the question of the Self and the Other.

The very first page of the novel makes it clear that the encounter between Self and Other in this case takes an unusual form. Having quoted the first line of Eliot's "The Love Song of J. Alfred Prufrock," first-person narrator Selig muses about the references of the two deictic pronouns in that sentence:

> You and I. To whom do I refer? I'm heading downtown alone, after all. *You and I.*
>
> Why, of course I refer to myself and that creature which lives within me, skulking in its spongy lair and spying on unsuspecting mortals. That sneaky monster within me, that ailing monster, dying even more swiftly than I. Yeats once wrote a dialogue of self and soul; why then shouldn't Selig, who is divided against himself in a way poor goofy Yeats could never have understood, speak of his unique and perishable gift as though it were some encapsulated intruder lodged in his skull? Why not? Let us go then, you and I.[1]

This schizophrenic form of address is perfectly appropriate because Selig is literally a split personality, with a telepathic self and a nontelepathic self, the former giving way in the course of the novel to the latter. Given the focus on the waning of the power, the novel can be read as a realistic fiction dealing metaphorically with the loss of powers brought on by middle age, a reading that the novel foregrounds by equating the power with potency and creativity,[2] but such a reading fails to explore the Self-and-Other and Self-as-Other dynamics that the motif of telepathy imparts to the novel. By making Selig in some sense both superhuman and subhuman, telepathy foregrounds and interrogates the issue of what it is to be human in the first place.

When asked by his sister, Judith, how he feels about losing his power, Selig gives the following revealing response: "I'm of two minds. I'd like it to vanish completely. Christ, I wish I'd never had it. But on the other hand, if I lose it, who am I? Where's my identity?" (p. 89). Like Selig himself, the novel is "of two minds" about the power, trying to figure out whether it is a "curse, a savage penalty for some unimaginable sin," or a "divine gift" (p. 74). At various points, Selig refers to himself as an eavesdropper, a voyeur, a peeping tom, a mutant, a genetic sport, a bloodsucker, a leech, and a vampire; he is cursed with a power that enables him to feed off of the experiences of others, "ripping off the intimacies of innocent strangers to cheer his chilly heart" (p. 66). From his earliest days, Selig has thought of the power as "something apart from [himself], something intrusive," as a worm wrapped around his cerebrum (p. 67).

At the same time, the power is "the central fact of [his] life" (p. 38), that which distinguishes him from others; it is a form of divine blessing, as his sister reminds him: "It made you someone special. It made you unique. When everything else went wrong for you, you could always fall back on that, the knowledge that you could go into minds, that you could see the unseeable, that you could get close to people's souls. A gift from God" (p. 88).

This ability to get close to the souls of others, to "tune in to the deepest layers of the mind—where the soul lives" (p. 18), supplies Selig with an experience he can describe only as "ecstasy," an experience that makes up for all the misery and isolation he has to put up with. David's final moment of such contact, during his interview with a former Columbia classmate, epitomizes the nature of the experience:

> This is ecstasy! This is contact! Other minds surround his. In whatever direction he moves, he feels their presence, welcoming him, supporting him, reaching toward him. Come, they say, join us, be one with us, give up those tattered shreds of self, let go of all that holds you apart from us. Yes, Selig replies. Yes, I affirm the ecstasy of life. I affirm the joy of contact. I give myself to you. They touch him. He touches them. It was for this, he knows, that I received my gift, my blessing, my power. For this moment of affirmation and fulfillment. (Pp. 229–30)

This same experience, however, also brings with it "a numbing sense of guilt" (p. 19) because it represents an ultimate form of voyeurism.

Selig's whole life is shaped, then, by his power, about which he has decidedly mixed feelings. The power compels or enables him to live alone, with "myself whom I can't get away from" (p. 35), in a total isolation that is, from time to time, total communion. His power, and the attendant schizophrenia it generates, determine to some extent his vocation, that of "ghost writer" for student term papers;[3] he literally feeds himself by reading the minds of others, by taking advantage of his ghostly other self. The schizophrenia produced by his power even manifests itself in his narrative discourse; at least eight of the novel's twenty-six chapters are narrated in the third person, as if Selig were undergoing "forcible dislocation of personality" (the phrase comes from Pynchon's Herbert Stencil in *V.*) in the process of narrating his story.[4] All of these chapters deal with incidents in which Selig's power or his identity is being called into question or tested in some way. It is also significant that the number of these third-person chapters tends to increase in the second half of the novel.[5]

By the end of the novel, Selig has entirely lost his power and become a mere mortal again. But before that happens, the novel explores the nature of telepathic otherness by presenting encounters between the still-telepathic Selig and a series of Other human beings, both normal and abnormal, encounters which shed light on the nature and responsibilities of telepathic selfhood and at the same time cover the spectrum of possible relations between the Self and the Other. At one point, for example, Selig taps into the deepest feelings of Yahya Lumumba, an angry black student who is hiring Selig to do a term paper: *"Fucking Jew bigbrain shithead Christ how I hate the little bald mother conning me three-fifty a page I ought to jew him down I ought to bust his teeth the exploiter the oppressor he wouldn't charge a Jew that much I bet special price for niggers . . ."* (pp. 71–72). Lumumba represents not only the black radical mindset but also that form of selfhood which can see the Other only in racist or xenophobic terms. That Selig is himself capable of a similar sort of pathological response is made clear in his reaction to the arrival of his sister, to be discussed in more detail shortly. Selig also violates the selfhood of the promiscuous Lisa, a student who sees him as a "suffering" poet—just, in fact, as Selig would like to be seen by other women. When Lisa arranges an afternoon liaison with Selig, he callously uses his power to "mindfuck" her, ransacking her mind to find out her secrets and hang-ups. Here Selig is clearly guilty of treating the Other as Object, of using his power in a parasitic way, of being a voyeur out for cheap thrills.

Another revealing pairing in the novel involves Selig's two serious relationships with women. The relationship with Toni, which comes second in terms of chronology but which is described first in the narration, involves the drug-induced creation of a telepathic connection between Self and Other. One day, after the two of them have been living together for several weeks, Toni tries to convince David to take LSD with her. David refuses, in large part because he is concerned about what the drug will do to his power. David has been careful to this point not to eavesdrop on Toni's thoughts, because he cares for her, but while she is hallucinating, for some reason an open-ended telepathic connection is created between them. David finds himself reading Toni's thoughts, and thus sharing her hallucinatory experience, against his will. He thinks that he sees himself as she sees him, as a "hairy vampire bat, a crouching huddled bloodsucker" (p. 60). He recoils from her, from her sordid past, from her image of him.

But the actual situation is not as one-directional as that. As Toni explains later, "It was like our minds were linked, David. Like a telepathic channel had opened between us. And all sorts of stuff was pouring from you into me. Hateful stuff. Poisonous stuff. I was thinking your thoughts" (p. 135). The fact that the images that David supposedly finds in Toni's mind—the vampire bat, the bloodsucker—are those that he had used previously suggests that she has indeed been reading him and rebroadcasting thoughts colored by his own obsessions. As David himself wonders during their mutual "trip," "is that merely David Selig's own image of David Selig, bouncing between us like the reflection in a barber shop's parallel mirrors" (p. 60)? The point is that a truly open, two-way telepathic channel between Self and Other carries with it the risk of distortion and deformation, the chance that the thoughts one is reading are twisted versions of one's own thoughts. Thus the marriage of true minds becomes "that terrible gateway between us" (p. 136), which, once it is opened, dooms the relationship between David and Toni. A direct channel between Self and Other actually destroys the relation between Self and Other.

Selig's relationship with Kitty Holstein begins on an obverse state of affairs but over time develops a parallel set of themes. Selig is first attracted to Kitty in part because he is unable to "read" her; her mind is totally closed to him. In effect, she thus represents the Other as Other, as something fundamentally unknowable, separate, discrete. David, twenty-eight years old but still emotionally immature when he meets Kitty, tries to do what many people do with their first loves—make them over. Convinced, illogically, that Kitty's uniqueness, her being closed to him, is a sign that the power of telepathy is latent in her, David subjects her to a grueling set of experiments and exercises designed to bring out the power. At the same time, he tries to make over her interest in reading, her feeling for the arts, even her career, to be more compatible with his own, in the stubborn belief that such a transformation can only strengthen their love. As David remarks in an imaginary letter to Kitty, *"because you were different from any person I had ever known, truly and qualitatively different, I made you the center of my fantasies and could not accept you as you were"* (p. 151). Confronted by real Otherness, Selig tries to transform it into Sameness because he mistakenly feels that therein lies the way to make the connection stronger: "Different worlds, different kinds of mind. Yet I always had hope of creating a bridge" (p. 209). Making the Other into a pale copy of the Self is not the way to create a real bridge,[6] Selig learns, a lesson he inscribes in the form of an axiom: "It's a sin against love to try to remake the soul of someone you love, even if you think you'll love her more after you've transformed her into something else" (p. 206).

The core of David's problem is best spelled out in the character of the only other real telepath he meets, Tom Nyquist. Nyquist is a telepath without guilt, without anxiety, without any hang-ups about the power at all. Unlike Selig, he likes himself and the life he leads. In this respect, he seems healthy, sane, normal. When David refers to the "intruder" in his brain, Nyquist responds, "That's schizoid, man, setting up a duality like that. Your power is you. You are your power. Why try to alienate yourself from your own brain?" (p. 68). He himself uses the power to make a comfortable living on the stock market, to single out vulnerable women for easy sexual conquests, and eventually to take Kitty Holstein (whom he can read) away from David Selig. As Selig notes, Nyquist is a "predator" who employs the power to take what he needs when he needs it. The power enables Nyquist to be completely self-sufficient and, in so doing, converts him into something less than human. Selig warns Kitty in a rambling and incoherent letter that Nyquist is "a machine, self-programmed for maximum self-realization, . . . a manipulative man, incapable of giving love, capable only of using" (p. 219). Selig's letter may be motivated by spite, but his indictment seems totally just.

The character of Nyquist thus figures the real dangers of being a telepath, of being a Self who has one-way access to the essence of Others. As Selig notes early in the novel (p. 30), the power paradoxically cuts him off from humanity, by marking him as different, strange, and at the same time joins him to humanity, by giving him total access to its inner life. Over a period of time, as the power wanes, David comes to feel that the estrangement, alienation, and isolation attendant on possession of the power outweigh the joys inherent in the access it gives him. At an early stage in his life, he confesses to Nyquist, "The problem is I feel isolated from other human beings" (p. 113). He gradually comes to see that this isolation not only is a function of his being "marked" but is inherent in the power itself. "What if," he asks in an essay on entropy, "a person a human being *turns* himself, inadvertently or by choice, into an isolated system?" (p. 204). As Selig well knows, the result is an increase in entropy, resulting eventually in "heat death." David has turned himself into just such a system, a human being who has "fun just being by [him]self" (p. 15), someone who is "dying inside."

One way to resist or reverse entropy at the human level is to exchange information with other humans, to communicate. Communication is based on a two-way feedback loop, something for which a telepath has no need. Selig notes early on in the novel that he is able only to receive the thoughts of others, never to transmit his own thoughts. The telepath is essentially a passive receiver of the transmissions of others, the reception of which obviates the need or the desire to make transmissions of one's own, a condition necessarily resulting in progressive isolation and an increase in entropy. In time, Selig comes to fear contact in general, "any sort of contact" (p. 117), just because his power enables him to do without it.

Telepathy, in effect, converts the Self into a self-contained, self-maintained, self-centered system. And it is for this reason that David finds his moments of ecstatic communion so gratifying, so justifying; they tend to obliterate the Self. As Peter Alterman puts it, "This condition of ecstasy is the one true gift David has gleaned from his telepathic power—an orgasm of selflessness, the joy of losing one's ego in something larger than one-self. . . . At bottom, David's transcendental ecstasy is a way of getting outside himself, of being part of someone or something else."[7] This being part of something larger than the self is exactly what David remarks during his final ecstatic experience: "No longer is he David Selig. He is part of them and they are part of him, and in that joyous blending he experiences loss of self . . ." (p. 230).

Another way to become part of something larger than the self is to be able to love, and it is just this capacity that telepathy undermines. Nyquist is "incapable of giving love," Selig warns Kitty, without perhaps realizing the same might be said of him. Elsewhere he acknowledges, in a somewhat self-pitying way, just how the power affects his love life:

> The nature of my condition diminishes my capacity to love and be loved. A man in my circumstances, wide open to everyone's innermost thoughts, really isn't going to experience a great deal of love. He is poor at giving love

because he doesn't much trust his fellow human beings: he knows too many of their dirty little secrets, and that kills his feelings for them. Unable to give, he cannot get. His soul, hardened by isolation and ungivingness, becomes inaccessible, and so it is not easy for others to love him. The loop closes upon itself and he is trapped within. (P. 52)

Total accessibility leads, paradoxically, to total inaccessibility. In this respect, the loss of Selig's gift should be seen as a blessing, as a second chance to learn to love, to embrace the world across a barrier of difference.

The second-chance motif figures most in David's relation with his lone surviving family member, his sister, Judith. When David was ten years old, Judith had been adopted by David's parents on the advice of a psychologist, who suggested that a sibling might be just the thing to bring David outside himself. But David can see her only in terms that reveal the extent of his self-centeredness: "I saw her as a rival from the word go. I was the first-born, I was the difficult one, the maladjusted one. I was supposed to be the center of everything. Those were the terms of my contract with God: I must suffer because I am different, but by way of compensation the entire universe will revolve about me" (p. 97). Since he conceives of his new sister only as enemy, as intruder, he first tries to use his power to destroy her by literally absorbing her mind, an effort the baby girl repels with a self-defending "look of frosty malevolence" (p. 47). Subsequently he treats her as a piece of furniture, an inconvenience to be endured. But Judith *is* family, his only living relative, and the only normal human who knows about his power to read minds, a situation brought about by a malicious slip on David's part. That slip, David realizes in the very center of the novel, had been in some way deliberate, a way of giving his sister "a weapon with which she could destroy me. . . . I had given her a weapon. How strange that she never chose to use it" (p. 105). The fact that she has never used that weapon, in the almost twenty years she has possessed it, reveals to David that to give the Self over to the Other is not necessarily a form of suicide.

By the end of the novel, David Selig has completely lost his power, become a mere mortal, no longer superhuman. Part of him has indeed "died inside," and he must in part reinvent himself: "Now that the power's gone, who am I? How do I define myself now? I've lost my special thing, my wound, my reason for apartness. . . . How do I relate to mankind, now that the difference is gone and I'm still here?" (p. 242). The power had been, ironically, a sign of difference and a "reason for apartness." Now David is at once no longer different and yet still separate, alone, apart. He must be reborn, learn anew how to relate by creating bridges across the distances that separate all human beings. Admitting to his sister that he is indeed beginning a "new life," David begins by trying to forge one such bridge, that of love: "How strange that is, to watch Judith cry. For love of me, no less. For love of me" (p. 245). The greatest loss might well be the greatest gain.

The novel begins with the invocation to "let us go then, you and I." In context, the "you" here is defined as David's other self, the intruder in his mind. But the "you" has another conventional referent, namely, the reader of David's confessional memoirs. Selig reinforces this possibility by directly addressing the reader in places, either in an ingratiating way—"I'll tell you about Kitty some other time" (p. 35)—or even in a hostile way—"What the hell are you doing reading someone else's mail? Don't you have any decency? I can't show you this" (p. 151). The ambiguity in the pronoun reference is perfectly appropriate,[8] since reading a confession such as Selig's is indeed a kind of mind reading, as Selig makes clear in another passage of direct address to the reader: "I need you to bolster my grip on reality by looking into my life, by incorporating parts of it into your own experience, by discovering that I'm real, I exist, I suffer, I have a past if not a future" (p. 149). At one point, David confesses to the desire to become a novelist (p. 192), and *Dying Inside* can naturally be seen as the product of that desire. It is an attempt to break the ring of silence and isolation that encloses David once he loses his power, an attempt to make contact with the Other, the reader as Other. At the same time Selig reminds us that reading is a form of voyeuristic eavesdropping, that, like Selig himself when he had the power, we are reading someone "like a book," that reading may be as close to telepathy as ordinary humans can come. In light of Selig's personal history, the moral would seem to be that this power can be either a blessing or a curse, depending on whether we use it to bridge the gap between the Self and the Other, or to convert the Other into just another Self.

3.1.2 Speculative Alien Encounter: Watson's *The Martian Inca*

For me, the most interesting aspect of the alien lies, not in its use as a fresh enemy, an analog human, or a mirror for ourselves, but rather in its essential strangeness. Remarkably few science fiction works have considered the alien at this most basic level.

—Gregory Benford, "Aliens and Knowability: A Scientist's Perspective"

"But I'm an expert on alien psychology, Ned. I know more about it than any other human being, because I'm the only one who ever said hello to an alien race. Kill the stranger: it's the law of the universe. And if you don't kill him, at least screw him up a little."

—Robert Silverberg, *The Man in the Maze*

Arthur C. Clarke's *Childhood's End* is an exemplary alien encounter fiction, in that it deals with both extrapolative and speculative Otherness, in the respective forms of the Overlords and the Overmind. The Overlords are creatures of pure intellect, rationality extrapolated and perfected, and are therefore "knowable" despite the mystery surrounding them and their actions. The Overmind, however, whom the Overlords serve, is a virtually omnipotent entity of extreme Otherness. The degree of Otherness is suggested by the glimpse of the Overmind that Jan Rodericks gets on the Overlords' planet. Jan sees on the horizon what he takes to be a mountain, dull red, of immense proportions. As Jan watches transfixed, the mountain comes alive, sending off streams of vivid yellow lava that move upward, exhaling a huge ruby-colored ring, and finally metamorphosing into a massive golden cyclonic funnel. Jan cannot account for the phenomenon, but he intuitively grasps its significance: "it was then that he guessed, for the first time, that the Overlords had masters, too."[1] And when the Overmind comes to Earth to absorb the metamorphosed children of the race (whose various actions also bespeak a radical form of Otherness), it appears again as a "great burning column, like a tree of fire" (p. 215), but it is apprehended and "known," not in its essence but mainly through its awesome effects, which Jan Rodericks, the last human alive, faithfully records for the Overlords:

> "Now it looks like the curtains of the aurora, dancing and flickering across the stars. Why, that's what it really is, I'm sure—a great auroral storm. The whole landscape is lit up—it's brighter than day—reds and greens and golds are chasing each other across the sky—oh, it's beyond words, it doesn't seem fair that I'm the only one to see it—I never thought such colors . . . "
> (P. 215)

Although the encounter with speculative Otherness is indeed "beyond words," Rodericks does manage to suggest its strangeness, its magnitude, its wonder.

As depicted by Clarke, the Overmind is not at all susceptible to rational explanation, not even that of the hyperrational Overlords. It needs the Overlords as mediators, as "advance men," but they have no inkling of its motivation, its purposes, its essential nature. The Overmind bears "the same relation to man as man [bears] to the amoeba" (p. 205). Potentially infinite and apparently immortal, it wanders the universe absorbing the energies of select races, those with parapsychological power (itself a nonrational phenomenon), thus affording those races a kind of terrible apotheosis. In imagining this entity which is "as much beyond life as [life] is above the inorganic world" (p. 215), Clarke has attempted to create a kind of pure Otherness, something quintessentially alien.

Clarke's example demonstrates that it is possible for an SF writer to create alien entities with an irreducible strangeness. Because that which is totally alien would be literally unspeakable, Clarke is forced to depict not the being itself but the effect it has on our familiar world. Other writers—Lem in *Solaris, The Invincible,* and *His Master's Voice,* Gregory Benford in *If the Stars Are Gods* and *In the Ocean of Night*—have tried to capture that quintessential strangeness more directly, using a variety of strategies, all of which share one feature: the insistence on an element of mystery. Clarke's example also indicates the common denominator of all speculative alien encounter SF— the assumption that the encounter with essential Otherness necessarily entails the possibility of the transcendence of man, of passing beyond the merely human. Benford and Eklund's *If the Stars Are Gods*, for example, presents its readers with a spectrum of actants—humans, giraffe people, cyborgs, the sphere beings of Jupiter, the lattice creatures of Titan—who have but one thing in common, the need to discover something larger than the Self, something transcendent. One speculative alien encounter fiction which explores its alien actant from the inside and which deals directly with the theme of transcendence is Ian Watson's *The Martian Inca*.

As the title makes clear, the alien actant here is an Inca Indian who is exposed to a sample of Martian soil that an unmanned Russian space probe has brought back from the red planet. The probe malfunctions on its return and crashes somewhere in the Bolivian Andes, where its contents infect some thirty Inca peasants in the middle of a fiesta. All thirty fall into a deep coma; all but two are treated by modern medicine and die. The two not treated are Julio Capac and Angelina Sonco, who eventually emerge from the coma transfigured and assume the roles of "reborn" Inca king and queen. As Julio proclaims soon after his awakening, "We have a world to remake. The Inca has been waiting all this time—in me."[2]

Watson renders the nature of the Incas' transformation in terms drawn from Jungian psychology and myth. During the coma period, which is later described as a kind of "mummification" (p. 97), Julio dreams of the "many selves that made up a man" (p. 63), both in terms of biography—the youth who participated in village rituals and who later copulated with Angelina, the man who labored in the mines and drowned his misery and power- lessness in drink—and in terms of archetypes—the condor man, the giant parrot, the bewigged toad (p. 77). All of these "hidden selves within him- self" (p. 70), Julio realizes, contribute to that larger being which is Julio Capac. But during the dreams, Julio is also aware of another, even "larger, enclosing self" (p. 75), a "later different person from the dream-boy" (p. 70), a self which sees these prior selves as so many puppets manipulated by invisible strings, a God-like self which can take control of those strings and become its "own puppet-master" (p. 78). When Julio awakens from the coma, his first words are, "I return to speak to you! I am reborn. I am the Son of the Sun. The Inca" (p. 80).

At the same time that Julio is experiencing his conversion on Earth, the first manned expedition, in the American spacecraft *Frontiersman*, is on its way to Mars. Soon after the landing there, one of the crewmen, Eugene Silverman, cuts himself in an accident, is exposed to Martian soil, and undergoes the same process of death-in-life and rebirth. He, however, is able to describe the transformation in "scientific" terms. The Martian soil apparently contains an "activator" substance, a "biochemical trigger for organization" (p. 262), which "pulls things together in the human brain" (p. 254), setting off "something genetically laid down in Man" (p. 131). The most important consequence is a "doubling of consciousness," organized hierarchically, involving awareness and awareness of awareness. Silverman explains this double vision as follows:

> "What happens when the brain 'sees' the world? A topological model of filtered reality is produced in the n-space within, by interacting, interfering electro-chemical wavefronts. What happens when I *see* the forms that constrain and sustain the thought-system? . . . I don't mean that I'm developing a double brain or anything! I mean that out of one model—of the world around me in my brain—is being generalized a secondary model of the topology relationships permeating the first model: using memory as the 'virtual' building blocks, because you can *remember* and see the real world at the same time." (Pp. 239–40)

The result, then, is that the reborn ones see simultaneously "two separate depths of reality" (p. 202): in mythic terms the experience and the archetype informing it; in computer terms, the "programmes" and the "metaprogrammes," "the programmes that govern our own thinking programmes" (p. 134). To be capable of this kind of *seeing* feels like making "contact with beings other than ourselves," with "higher beings," with "Gods" (p. 134). In primitive terms, one has been "reborn a God" (p. 100); in scientific terms, one has taken the next evolutionary step to a higher consciousness level, that of "Future Man" (p. 248).

The use of parallel sets of transformation and contrastive linguistic registers to describe that process enables Watson to naturalize the transfiguration while at the same time maintaining the essential Otherness of its end product. To reinforce and foreground the enigmatic nature of this transformation, Watson, at the very end of the novel, renders the Martian life form that the activator substance brings into being—the "supergrex." Driven by the patterning agent in the activator, the microorganic grex form advances itself by clumping with other grex forms to create a higher-order structure, which then feeds on bacteria and lower-order grex forms until ready for the next stage of clumping. The process continues until the "supergrex" comes into being, a "complex thinking creature" (p. 265) capable of communication, in other words, a Self:

> And then it sees the domed tower of another Grex-47. *Itself*—distanced from it!
> Not itself! Another—in its own self-image!
> It stands frozen in adulthood, alienated, realizing the existence of another being equal to it out there in the world. The World becomes Object and Subject. Itself—and the World. (P. 289)

This passage articulates a basic existential theme, the idea that awareness of Self is contingent upon the existence of the Other, and that such awareness necessarily alienates that Self from the World. But this particular Self sees the World in its own unique way, for the supergrex is a "being for whom awareness was primarily of morphogenetic forms present as its real environment, then only secondarily of the world that it mapped itself on to, the canvas beneath the paint" (p. 292). The vision of the supergrex, in other words, because of the influence of the activator substance, is dominated by the "metaprogramme," a circumstance which causes the being to impose its own grex form on everything it sees, reducing the real world to the "canvas" beneath the "paint."

As the inclusion of the supergrex experience makes clear, Watson is attempting, in this novel, to portray a radical kind of Otherness and its mode of vision and, in so doing, to explore the relation between subject and object, the mind and reality. In an essay, Watson makes the following rather startling claim about the latter relation: "We are in the sort of universe we are in *because* we are here to observe it; what, then, is the connection between thought and reality, cosmologically?"[3] This theme is basic to alternate world SF, which concerns itself with relations between Self and World. The theme dominates Watson's SF, but in *The Martian Inca* he comes at it more indirectly, with the encounter between Self and Other as narrative dominant. The novel systematically foregrounds various interpersonal relationships—between Julio and Angelina, between Silverman and his wife, Renate, between Silverman and fellow astronauts Oates and Weaver, between Oates and wife Kathy and mistress Milly-Kim, between CIA agent Inskip and the Mars crew, between Inskip and the Martian Inca—in order to explore the ways in which the Self seeks to control, dominate, or reshape the Other for its own ends.

The novel suggests that the relation between Self and Other can be seen as a subset of the relation between Self and World by linking the two over and over. Julio Capac awakens into a kind of divinity, and his first idea is that, once he has taken Angelina as queen, together they will "begin to alter the world" (p. 111). His new selfhood gives him power over the world. In point of fact, it was the world itself, in the form of Martian soil, that brought about his "deification." Silverman's field of expertise is "transforming worlds" (p. 51), and the Mars expedition's primary goal is to set up a solar reflector with which to melt the carbon dioxide frozen in the polar ice caps, thereby creating a greenhouse effect which will warm and fertilize the entire planet. Silverman's vision is of a "blue" Mars, of "Mars remade as a Second Earth" (p. 26). He and Renate name their child Gaia, in part because the name reflects "the idea of a world as a living being" (p. 60). And Silverman boasts to his wife that the Mars expedition will, in effect, make over Mars into "part of our body" (p. 57).

The notion of "terraforming" thus serves as a cautionary model for the relation between Self and Other in the novel. Terraforming consists in making over the Other (in this case, other world) until it conforms to the needs or desires or image repertoire of the Self, or in simply appropriating or absorbing the Other into the Self, making it an extension of the body. Silverman's wife, Renate,is a sculptor who creates holographic human forms that can be remodeled or reshaped by viewers; her exhibition is entitled *Transforms & Deforms*. When her daughter Gaia is born, Renate

> sculpted Deforms and Transforms of her daughter, who was thus sur-rounded from early days by transitory playmates that were images of herself, twisted out of true along twin axes of perfection and deformity. It was as though Renate was intent on running through the whole chromosomal ga-mut of possible daughters she might have had. At times she seemed in danger of losing the knowledge of her real flesh and blood daughter amidst all the range of alternatives she evoked. (P. 60)

Renate's work, Silverman realizes, plays with the same double vision with which those infected by Martian soil are endowed:

> She was working right at this frontier. On the one side, perfection, the idea of the perfect human body; on the other side, actual imperfect bodies in the real world. Her art mirrored the whole idea of the underlying forms—me-taprogrammes—and the real, imperfect structures—the programmes they give rise to. Renate wanted to get back across the divide from the one to the other. To find how a real world body could seize control of its own shaping, reshape itself. . . . (P. 137)

Renate's art figures prominently in the novel just because it provides both a parallel and a contrast to the experiences of her husband, Eu-gene,and the Martian Inca. Eventually Renate returns to sculpting natural shapes, "rejecting the whole idea of transforming nature—bodies or worlds" (p. 61). Julio Capac and Eugene Silverman, the two supermen of the novel, repudiate neither. Capac leads an Indian revolt against the leftist government of Bolivia, seeking to return his people to the customs and life style, to the very world, of his Inca ancestors. But it is a hermetically sealed world, without access to the outside world, without free speech, with a rigid hierarchical structure. Hemmed in by an antagonistic world without, Capac dreams of constructing an unbreachable wall by making "a masonry of people" (p. 197). Eventually the revolt turns on Capac, and he is captured and executed in a ritualistic manner that literalizes and parodies his dreams of divinity and the idea of transcendence. Silverman, meanwhile, despite being warned about the "wholesomeness, the permanence of deforming Mars" (p. 61), proceeds blindly with the terraforming of the planet, in the process deliberately infecting Oates with the Martian soil and eventually falling victim to the storm created by the melting of the Martian ice caps. Both men, Capac and Silverman, willfully attempt to make over nature—

human beings and environments—to conform to the distorted inner visions they see; they prove to be gods "with clay feet" (p. 206). And both men see those worlds turn on them and destroy them.

Like Silverman's mate, Renate, Julio's mate, Angelina, tries to provide her husband with a corrective vision. Reawakening from the coma, she too feels that "this was how it had to be if you were reborn a God" (p. 100), but she knows that this is a self-serving delusion of grandeur. She tells Julio flatly, "You didn't wake up a God! You woke up a human being—or what human beings might be if they had this double vision we have of the World and the Thought-World" (p. 112). She realizes that Julio is aggrandizing himself partly out of self-defense and partly out of will to power. She herself feels that the transformation has cleared her mind but has caused Julio's to be obsessed with dreams of power (p. 149). Julio sees other human beings as puppets and himself as puppeteer, failing to see that the strings he supposedly controls are projected by him onto the world. Angelina tells him, "You think you see the whole truth of the world, yet you're only seeing what your own thoughts are. They needn't be the *right* ones. I too felt clarified. Yet only *within me*. This limited person, me—" (p. 156). The point is that Julio's transformation has made him feel larger than he actually is, caused him to impose the Self upon the World, to make the Self into a World of its own. When Julio refuses to give up on his "Reconquest" of the Inca empire, Angelina can only say wistfully, "you're a prisoner of yourself again. The puppet of your own mind dolls. How sad" (p. 156).

The Martian Inca is a novel in which people see the Other only in terms of use value. The Americans are terraforming the planet Mars to make it into a second Earth; the Russians are doing the same thing with Venus. Julio is using the Incas to re-create a world of the past; Silverman is making over Oates in his own likeness; and Inskip and the CIA are using both the Inca revolt and the Martian expedition to advance their vision of the global political situation, "to bring it in line with what they saw" (p. 121). The transformation brought about by the activator substance only intensifies or reinforces this syndrome. The Martian Inca claims to have given birth to himself (p. 94), a claim which hints at the solipsistic view of the world that his apotheosis brings into being. Failing to recognize that his vision of the world is partial, limited, circumscribed, he becomes the puppet of his "own mind dolls." Eugene Silverman feels that control of his "metaprogramme" enables a "real world body" to "seize control of its own shaping, reshape itself" (p. 137), but fails to see how such control cuts him off from the real world. The reawakened Oates asks, near the end of the novel, "what did [the metaprogrammes] really tell him about the world out there: the universe which Gene felt so confident they modelled, or represented to him? If a model—the world understood in the human brain—only models itself on to another (memory) model inside the *same thought system*, what then?'' (p. 293). The Martian life form, the supergrex, is not even aware of the landscape over which it moves; it "does not see itself anywhere—because itself is everywhere" (p. 289).

The novel suggests that the act of predation is built into the relation between Self and Other, that the Self sees the Other only as something to be apprehended or appropriated. Transcending the human state, becoming a God or Future Man, only exacerbates this predation. Silverman comes to believe that the "act of grasping prey in space," of "*capturing*," is constitutive in the creation of the Self, that "*Ego*, the sense of self, was born" when the Self becomes aware that there is another Self out there to capture and feed on, that "all life was predatory in one way or another" (p. 243). In such a world the grex process of incorporating the external world, appropriating the Other, is the natural state of affairs, the universal condition.

Watson's point is that consciousness itself entails alienation from the world, and that one solution to that alienation is the forcible reappropriation of the world. As Angelina explains to Julio, "humans are separate as soon as they start to think about the world. Humans are opposite—which means that we know the great opposite of all: evil. Because evil is absence, loss, and separation" (p. 175). The wrong way to overcome loss and separation is to appropriate Otherness, to assimilate it. The right way is to respect it. Like that other example of speculative Otherness, *Solaris*, *The Martian Inca* thus uses its novum in order to interrogate the relation between consciousness and its objects, between mind and world. Like *Solaris*, Watson's novel addresses the limits of knowledge and the dangers of solipsism. Yet both novels insist that consciousness brings with it its own blessings. Silverman says at one point that the "real wonder is that the human mind should evolve along lines so that it can *know* itself" (p. 135). Ian Watson has said elsewhere that SF should serve as an "evolutionary tool,"[4] and *The Martian Inca* contributes to that ongoing evolution by using speculative Otherness to help us know our own minds better.

3.2 Alternate Society SF: Utopias, Dystopias, and the Rest

[SF's] most important use, I submit, is a means of dramatising social inquiry, as providing a fictional model in which cultural tendencies can be isolated and judged.

—Kingsley Amis, *New Maps of Hell*

Science fiction . . . is really concerned with the fictitious society it pictures. It becomes not merely a lesson to us, a text from which to draw a moral, but something that bears the possibility of importance in its own right.

—Isaac Asimov, "Social Science Fiction"

In his essay on "Fiction about the Future," H. G. Wells claims that the most significant "futurist" fiction, and the most difficult to bring off, would be that sort which uses as its novum an estranged social order—Wells uses the example of a world populated entirely by women—and then focuses on the struggle of a few individuals to come to terms with that social order. Kingsley Amis devotes much of his influential book on SF to those fictions which serve as an "instrument of social diagnosis and warning." And Isaac Asimov baldly states that what he terms "social science fiction" is the "most mature" and the "most socially significant" form that SF can take.[1] All three writers seem to be privileging or valorizing one particular SF form, alternate society SF, the dominant novum of which is an estranged or alternative social order. The paradigm here typically involves the visit to a utopic or dystopic society, during which the visitor (and, of course, the reader) is invited to compare that society with his or her own. Alternate society SF poses a wide assortment of questions, including the following: What constitutes a good or bad society? What is the proper relation between the individual and the community? To what extent are freedom and order mutually antagonistic? What are the main determinants of "social reality"? What is the relation between language and the social order? These fictions, many of which are considered SF "classics,"[2] mediate the proper relation between Self and Society and in general elicit a normative reading, the establishment of a framework of value.

We have chosen the phrase *alternate society SF* because we feel that it serves as an all-inclusive rubric without previous semantic freight. The term *social science fiction*, as defined by Asimov, is at once too broad and too narrow. He designates as "social SF" "that branch of literature which is concerned with the impact of scientific advance upon human beings."[3] This definition would make into SF any "mainstream" novel dealing with the impact of science or technology upon people. Elsewhere in the same essay he refers to social SF as "that branch of literature which deals with a fictitious society, differing from our own chiefly in the nature or extent of its technological development."[4] This definition takes into account the need for a factor of estrangement ("differing from our own"), and it does locate that factor at the level of the social order, but the essence of that difference is linked to technology. The essay makes clear that Asimov intends by "social SF" that kind of SF which introduces a technological novum and then explores its impact on human beings. Such fiction, it will be seen (see 3.3), can be either "gadget SF" or "alternate society SF," but it by no means constitutes either the entire spectrum of SF (it leaves out alien encounter SF, for example) or even the subset alternate society SF, not all of which is predicated upon technological developments. Similarly, to rely on the utopia/dystopia polarity would also be to circumscribe the subset, as the recent proliferation of competing "topias" (heterotopia, meta-utopia, critical utopia, ambiguous utopia, anti-utopia, to name a few) suggests. In addition, the term *utopia* (and perhaps *dystopia* as well) connotes a certain degree of planning, the willed transformation of society according to a deliberate design. But many of the alternate societies of SF come into existence by contingency, as the haphazard products of fate (as in the post-holocaust world of Walter Miller's *A Canticle for Liebowitz*), or by circumstance, as the product of their surroundings (as in the anarchic lunar colony in Heinlein's *The Moon Is a Harsh Mistress*).

The rubric utopia/dystopia also tends to pass over that whole class of SF which uses a new language as its dominant novum and explores the ways in which language is constitutive of social reality. I am thinking here not of a fiction such as Orwell's *1984*, where the governmental "Newspeak" reinforces totalitarian control within the dystopic society, but of fictions such as Delany's *Babel-17*, Jack Vance's *The Languages of Pao*, and Ian Watson's *The Embedding*, all of which deal with the invention of languages with the power to transform social reality. These fictions use an artificial language as their dominant novum in order to investigate the nature of language, the relation of language and reality, and the possibilities of linguistic otherness. A similar case could be made for Orson Scott Card's *Songmaster*, which posits a society in which narrative singing wields a political force in order to explore the relation between art and politics.

The point is that alternate society SF takes in more than just those fictions which use their societal novums as a critique of the existing social organization. At the highest level of generality this subset includes that SF which examines the nature of humanity as a species, "human nature," as it were. Another of Card's novels, *The Worthing Chronicle*, deals with the deliberate dismantling of a utopic world, a world without pain or tragedy, by the very beings who brought that world into existence. These beings come to realize that eliminating suffering was really "stealing from [humans] all that makes them human," that "men and women would only become human again with the possibility of pain."[5] The novel is less concerned with possible forms of social organization than with human nature and human existence in general. Of course, it should be added that utopias and dystopias share the same concern and deal with similarly "ultimate" questions. But they approach those questions from the standpoint of a specifically realized social order; not all alternate society SF needs to come at the issue from that vantage point.

Most alternate society SF, it must be admitted, deals with the cognitive import of the contrast between the estranged social order and the author's social order, the imagined society over and against historical society. In some cases, most particularly utopic fictions, the contrast between the two societies becomes the primary focus of the work. As Tom Moylan notes, "in utopia, the social structure, and what it represents and encourages, is traditionally seen as the main protagonist."[6] The fiction typically consists of a visit to the "no-place" by a representative of the basic narrative world, who is chaperoned through the estranged society by a serviceable and articulate guide. The main plot complication consists in whether or not the visitor will choose to stay. Much of the work is reduced to dialogues between representatives of the two societies, dialogues which tend to fill the "cognitive space" between the two worlds, to overdetermine their relation, and thus to push the fiction in the direction of the *dogmatic* (see 2.1). A representative example would be Wells's *In the Days of the Comet*. A recent study, however, argues that in the contemporary "critical utopia," a form which appeared in the 1960s and 1970s, "the primacy of the social alternative over character and plot is reversed, and the alternative society and indeed the originary society fall back as settings for the foregrounded political quest of the protagonist."[7] It may well be that the most compelling utopic fiction must focus on the struggle of the Self to find a place in the estranged Society, that only in so doing can it address "universal hopes and fears, complexes of emotion that arise not from the intellectual contemplation of group alternatives but from the personal experiences of living."[8] Such personal experiences are best articulated in conditions of conflict, which helps to explain why dystopias, where conflict is built into the relation between protagonist and society, are inevitably more memorable than static, conflict-free utopias.

The best alternate society SF, then, is that which involves not merely the dialogue between alternate society and originary society but also the personal struggle of an individual Self to find a place for itself in the estranged Society.[9] The interplay between Self and Society can at times cause typological confusion. The question becomes, Does this fiction foreground themes of the Self, in which case it should be considered a permutation of alien encounter SF, or is it dominated by themes of Society, in which case it is indeed alternate society SF? In these instances, the typological character of the fiction is dictated, as our model indicates, by the element of the fiction that has been estranged, transformed, mutated. If the novum occurs at the level of actant, as in Van Vogt's *Slan*, then the fiction is typologically alien encounter; if at the level of society, as in Herbert's *The Santaroga Barrier*, then the fiction is alternate society by type. Both types frequently share a great deal of thematic overlap, if only because themes of the Self are necessarily intertwined with conceptions of Society.[10]

A frequently noted characteristic of much alternate society SF is the presence of the barrier, the physical dividing line separating the estranged society from the originary society (as in Herbert's *The Santaroga Barrier*) or marking the boundary of that society and the adjoining natural world (as in Zamiatin's *We*). Now the barrier clearly figures significantly in the *story* of the fiction; the narrative is necessarily generated by penetration of the barrier (an actant moves from one topological space to the other), and the outcome of the story frequently hinges on the possible elimination of the barrier.[11] But the barrier also serves as a thematic marker; as one critic says, "the function of these barriers . . . is twofold: seen from the inside, they function to keep disorder and chaos out; seen from the outside, they function to keep docile and unknowing inhabitants within and can be read as an unambiguous sign of utopian desire to escape the uncertainties and contingencies of time and history."[12] The barrier, the dividing line, the slash, represents the most salient feature of alternate society thematics— its organization around, or foundation in, polarities, contradictions, or antinomies. Whether a work be utopic or dystopic or a mix thereof, it generates its semantic field around the oppositions which inhere in the Self/Society axis: individual vs. community, anarchy vs. order, freedom vs. security, nature vs. civilization, irrationality vs. rationality, change vs. stasis, and so on. Alternate society SF not only marshals these oppositions, it also tends to create a normative framework with which the reader can make judgments about them.

If we look at the two main categories within the field—utopias and dystopias—we can make some general discriminations about their respective axiological grains. Utopias are predicated on, among other things, the belief that humans can work together rationally to shape their social life; these works therefore valorize qualities such as community, cooperation, and collectivity. Northrop Frye has suggested that the spectrum of possible utopias has been rendered for us in the Bible, in the choice presented by the arcadian paradise of the Garden or the urban paradise of the New Jerusalem, "the two myths that polarize social thought, . . . the myth of origin and the myth of telos."[13] These utopias are brought into being either through atavistic reversion to "an earlier humankind in closer and happier relation to necessity and nature and self,"[14] or through the progressive amelioration of the human condition contingent upon the technological mastery of nature. In either case, they tend to locate their ideal societies outside time; their no-place is a "no time," located outside the historical matrix and resistant to the incursion of historical time. Dystopias, on the other hand, are rooted in "a basic distrust of all social groups,"[15] which can envision self-realization only in terms of alienation, conflict, and the surplus of consciousness attendant upon the former. Gordon Beauchamp defines the "central mythos" of dystopia as " 'natural man' in revolt against the rigid and reductionist rationalism of utopia."[16] This formulation, however, holds only for the technological utopia, the one achieved by the complete subjugation of nature. The more general dystopian move consists in asserting the rights of the individual, breaking the barrier separating the "ideal" society from its surroundings, and attempting to reinsert that society into historical time and the process of becoming.

It should be clear that the above distinctions patently oversimplify the dialectic of Self and Society in utopian and dystopian SF. Peter Ruppert, for example, has demonstrated the extent to which utopia is not a monolithic or unilateral form, how it is "dialogic in nature," inherently self-contradictory and riddled with inconsistencies. Utopia, he claims, is synonymous with a desire for social change but constructs a system that denies any further changes; it sets out to liberate us from forms of social manipulation and containment but provides us with a system that, in its constraints and manipulations, also becomes oppressive, is itself constraining and manipulative; it unmasks existing ideology as contradictory but then masks the significance of this recognition with an ideology that pretends to be the end of ideology.[17]

Dystopias, on the other hand, can be either reactionary or progressive, depending upon the nature of the monolithic society that the protagonist opposes and attempts to subvert. And yet one can safely say that dystopia privileges the rights of the Self at the expense of those of Society, while utopia elevates the needs of Society at the expense of those of the Self. What the forms have in common is the function of rendering the society of the basic narrative world as contingent and historical, and therefore subject to the possibility of change. As Ruppert points out, "Even though utopias project a desirable world, while anti-utopias project a nightmare world, both make use of a dialectical structure that juxtaposes contradictory possibilities to create a cognitive tension between what is and what might be, a tension designed to induce a critical attitude toward the existing historical situation."[18] Both forms, in other words, set themselves up against the status quo.

As a number of critics have noted, the twentieth century has witnessed the appearance of ambiguous, hybridized, and self-reflexive "topias," alternate society narratives which have generated an assortment of new typological rubrics—the anti-utopia, the meta-utopia, the critical utopia, the ambiguous utopia and the heterotopia.[19] These texts have several features in common, including the multiplication of alternate societies within the fictional world, a self-conscious awareness of the utopian/dystopian literary tradition, open-ended narrative structures, and profound ambivalence about final normative pronouncements. In regard to the final feature, axiological ambiguity or open-endedness, Ruppert has shown, in *Reader in a Strange Land*, how competing values are built into the dialogic structure of alternate society fiction, a structure which compels the reader to take an active role in mediating the contradictory claims made by the estranged society and the originary society. But the relativization of values is perhaps more pronounced in postwar alternate society fiction, which seems more comfortable imagining a spectrum of competing societies, the conflicting ideals of which cannot necessarily be negotiated or mediated.

In *The Santaroga Barrier*, for example, Frank Herbert creates, in a northern California valley, an isolated society which embodies many of the values of the 1960s counterculture—ecological awareness, rejection of commercialization and mass culture, faith in heightened states of consciousness, reversion to a simpler, arcadian life style, a social order which respects the individual but puts the community first, and so on. The society is able to enforce these values by means of a mycological hallucinogen, Jaspers, which grows only in the caves of the valley. The Santaroga community, especially as compared to the crass, venal, and manipulative world outside, seems to have much to say for itself. But the community is, by necessity, isolated, static, and monolithic. More incriminating, the fear of the outside world generates in Santarogans an unconscious group violence which causes them to arrange the "accidental" deaths of all who come to investigate the community. The novel ends when the intruder from the outside world, Dasein ("being there"), himself engineers the murder of his employer and then is exculpated in a rigged inquest. At once drawn to and repulsed by Santarogan life, Dasein perches on the barrier between the two worlds: "It was a hateful world. *Which world?* he asked himself. *Was it Santaroga . . . or the outside?*" On the final page a dazed and drugged Dasein alternates between radically opposed feelings: "Dasein had the sudden feeling that he was a moth in a glass cage, a frantic thing fluttering against his barriers, lost, confused." The novel ends, however, with Dasein remembering that Santaroga takes "care of its own": "*It'll be a beautiful life,* he thought."[20] The novel, by depicting contrastive dystopias separated by an impermeable barrier, suggests that the best society would be one which combines features from both, the ecological awareness and the communality of Santaroga and the pluralism and individual initiative of the outside world. It is the barrier between the worlds which is artificial and must come down. As one critic concludes, "the image of the barrier is the image of the destructive separation of the vital aspects of human consciousness and social life."[21]

We began the discussion of the themes of alternate society SF by identifying the barrier as the boundary line marking the thematic antitheses that make up the semantic field. The best alternate society SF is aware that that marker is artificial, unmotivated, or even nonexistent. In a remarkable passage in Zamiatin's celebrated dystopian novel *We*, the narrator observes:

> Human history ascends in circles, like an aero. The circles differ—some are golden, some bloody. But all are equally divided into three hundred and sixty degrees. And the movement is from zero—onward to ten, twenty, two hundred, three hundred and sixty degrees—back to zero. Yes, we have returned to zero—yes. But to my mathematical mind it is clear that this zero is altogether different, altogether new. We started from zero to the right, we have returned to it from the left. Hence, instead of plus zero, we have minus zero. Do you understand?
>
> I envisage this Zero as an enormous, silent, narrow, knife-sharp crag. In fierce, shaggy darkness, holding our breath, we set out from the black night side of Zero crag. For ages we, the Columbuses, have sailed and sailed; we have circled the entire earth. And at long last, hurrah! The burst of a salute, and everyone aloft the masts: before us is a different, hitherto unknown side of Zero crag, illumined by the northern lights of the One State—a pale blue mass, sparks, rainbows, suns, hundreds of suns, billions of rainbows. . . .

What if we are but a knife's breadth away from the other, black side of the crag? The knife is the strongest, the most immortal, the most brilliant of man's creations. The knife has been a guillotine; the knife is the universal means of solving all knots; along the knife's edge is the road of paradoxes—the only road worthy of a fearless mind.[22]

Here we have encapsulated the central utopian mythos—the journey to the uncharted land across the seas, a brave new world, where human beings have perfected their social relations. This world, however, is separated from where we began by the Crag, the barrier between the two worlds. The barrier is figured as a knife, which historically has served to execute all non-believers and mythologically represents the solution to the most insoluble problems. Elsewhere in the novel the knife is also referred to as at once the surgeon's tool and the highwayman's weapon, an instrument which can preserve life or take life. The knife is an indestructible barrier, dividing plus zero from minus zero. But, from a mathematical standpoint, those two figures are equivalent, if not identical. And time and again in the novel, two contrastive values, apparently antithetical, are shown to be equivalent, if not identical; the novel obscures conventional polarities, reverses traditional equations. The glass city of *We*, for example, clearly belongs to the New Jerusalem type of "paradise" that rests upon the domination of nature in a postlapsarian world. But the story of D-503, the protagonist, is clearly that of the Fall into knowledge and strife. At the same time the arcadian "paradise" that surrounds the glass city, the Green World, is shown to be populated by those who are unfallen (they live in harmony with nature) but at the same time fallen (they belong to the party of the devil, as is shown by the way they use D-503 for their own ends).[23] The best alternate society SF reveals over and over to what extent that immortal knife is shown to be simply a creation of man, an easy solution to a complex problem. Such SF acknowledges the ineluctability and desirability of historical change and insists that "there can no longer be any question of social perfection, of closed systems, of fixed boundaries, of an absolute cognition of the good society."[24] Such fiction rides the edge of the knife, the road of paradoxes, "the only road worthy of a fearless mind."

3.2.1 Extrapolative Alternate Society SF: Wilhelm's *Where Late the Sweet Birds Sang*

America and Western Europe were interested first in the individual human life, and only secondarily in the social whole. For these peoples, loyalty involved a reluctant self-sacrifice, and the ideal was ever a person, excelling in prowess of various kinds.

—Olaf Stapledon, *Last and First Men*

After what has been said about SF in general, the related proposition on the nature and the political function of the utopian genre will come as no particular surprise: namely, that its deepest vocation is to bring home, in local and determinate ways, and with a fullness of concrete detail, our constitutional inability to imagine Utopia itself, and this, not owing to any individual failure of imagination but as the result of the systemic, cultural, and ideological closure of which we are all in one way or another prisoners.

—Fredric Jameson, "Progress versus Utopia;
Or, Can We Imagine the Future?"

Kate Wilhelm's *Where Late the Sweet Birds Sang* opens with a domestic scene which both establishes the thematic fields of the novel and serves as a model for the subsequent actions in the story. The Sumner family adults are holding a family council on their farm in the hills of northern Virginia, discussing, among other things, the well-being and future of son David. The discussion takes place "as if he were not there,"[1] and David self-consciously dissociates himself from it, imagines himself floating above the group, taking pot shots at those he especially dislikes. The session ends for him when his father asks him to go out and play with the other children, at which time the members of the extended family turn "their collective mind to one of the other offspring" (p. 8). Here we have, then, some of the key parameters of the novel: a decision-making group (the family) responsible for the welfare of its members; the partial exclusion of one member, such exclusion resulting in the birth of self-consciousness and an antagonistic posture on the part of the excluded; and the final exclusion of that member so that the group can carry on with its business.

David's childhood and adolescence, however, are not unhappy, as this scene might suggest. As a matter of fact, his is the last generation to come of age relatively unscarred by the changes occurring in the late twentieth-century America that serves as the setting of the novel. Wilhelm imagines a world more and more beset by ecological problems of its own making: worldwide famine, wholesale pollution of the environment, higher radiation levels in the atmosphere resulting in increasing sterility and new forms of disease, climatological changes which produce widespread drought and flooding, and national conflicts created by the global crisis. In a single generation the population of the world is virtually wiped out. The resilient Sumner family resists the catastrophe by drawing together in the valley which it owns, creating from its diverse and provident members a self-sufficient little world, complete with a mill to provide power, dormitories, schools, a hospital, and research laboratories buried in caves. Once the community has resisted invasion by marauders from the outside world, its only real problem is the increasing sterility of all its members, a problem which the resourceful family solves by perfecting the process of cloning. Cloning, however, proves to be only a short-term solution since, from the third generation on, the clones manifest a sharp decline in potency. The first third of the novel, which borrows its title from the novel, relates the attempt by David and his generation to create a viable community with the first few clone generations.

At first the community thrives, fashioning in the valley the kind of serene and homely village that from a distance reminds David of a "sentimental card titled 'Rural Life' " (p. 44). But the clones, who were spawned in groups, are somehow different from the human "elders" of the society. As David notes, the designation "elder" itself marks a breach within the society: "When had they started calling themselves that? Was it because they had to differentiate somehow, and none of them had permitted himself to call the others by what they were? Clones! he said to himself vehemently. Clones! Not quite human. *Clones*" (p. 48). Actually, the "inhuman" clone enclave is in many respects superior to the society of the elders. They, for example, do not turn on one another, as happened in the human society when the cloning solution was first proposed. Since they share an em-pathetic network with their brothers and sisters, and a pain endured by one is suffered by all, the very idea of violence is repugnant to them. Their sense of belonging makes them immune to the hopelessness and despair that periodically wrack the "human" society, makes them certain that a future does exist if they work together. They do exceptionally well in their studies, grasping in their teens what David mastered only in his twenties, and they apply themselves to assigned tasks cheerfully, diligently, inter-changeably. They suffer no sexual tension or jealousy and mate promis-cuously, such arrangements being encouraged in order to confirm the individual's potency or lack thereof. They constitute, as David wistfully observes, the "first really classless society" (p. 45).

But *et in Arcadia* there are undercurrents of dissension and difference. The clones are, for the elders, not only interchangeable but also indistin-guishable. David sees these newcomers, some of whom look just like him at earlier ages, as both "familiar and alien, known and unknown," as re-juvenated images of himself and his family but "with something missing" (p. 49). And they, for their part, come to see the elders as superfluous holdovers from a past world, as self-contained and secretive children who need to be managed and coddled. Understandably, after a time the first generation of clones, whom David can refer to only as the "Ones," begin to assume responsibility for the community. "They're taking over," David complains to his uncle Walt (p. 46). Two episodes trigger the foreshadowed rupture in the community. First, the cloning of subsequent generations proves that after the fourth generation, potency gradually returns, and sexual reproduction could result in a new generation of "humans." Then an accident at the mill injures a number of workers, both human and clone, but the clone doctors, Walt One and Two, refuse to treat the critically injured original Walt until they have taken care of the minor injuries suffered by the clones. When confronted by David, Walt One, who strikes David as a "Walt with something missing, a dead area," informs the elder that they (the clones) "won't go back to what you are." He refers to the clones as a "higher species," one which enjoys empathetic communion and a feeling of togetherness. Since they prefer not to return to the state of aloneness and apartness that the elders endure, they have chosen to use the fertile women among them only to replenish their supply of cloning material. The first section concludes when David tries to end the cloning process by destroying the mill; he is stopped and brought before the community tribunal. For the safety of the community, he is permanently ostracized, and he wanders out into the wilderness to die.

The first section establishes a number of thematic oppositions which are pursued in the subsequent two sections. First and foremost among these is the division of the actantial field into family and nonfamily members. The Sumner family is able to survive the initial ecological disaster by isolating itself from the external world and resisting incursions from that world. When the rest of the world's population is eventually wiped out because of its failure to organize itself into self-sufficient communities, this us-versus-them strategy is vindicated as the only possible one, given the extent of the crisis. The crisis also results in another antithesis, technological versus "natural" means of reproduction. In an increasingly sterile world, the only means of ensuring the survival of the human race is by cloning. This process, however, produces small groups of virtually identical members who are somehow different from the original human members, this difference signaled, significantly enough, by the notion of absence or lack ("something missing"). Given their allegiance to their fellow clones and their ability to work together efficiently, these new generations are able to consolidate the community and reinforce the concept of family, but only through the marginalization of the individual. This consolidation activates or generates another antithesis, that of stasis versus change. The discovery that subsequent generations of clones regain their sexual potency makes possible a return to natural reproduction, a condition that would disrupt the now smoothly running clone society. The clones reject such a return, specifically choosing uniformity over diversity and risking therefore entropic decline; as they inform David before exiling him, "You [humans] pay a high price for individuality" (p. 53).

The section thus marshals an interrelated series of antithetical fields—family/nonfamily, technology/nature, clones/humans, community/individual, stasis/change, uniformity/diversity—and applies to them a shifting axiological marker which identifies the first member of each pair as positive only insofar as that value is necessary for survival. Once survival is ensured, the second member asserts priority. Unfortunately, the community, a kind of group mind (a "unit consciousness" [p. 106]), is unable to acknowledge that priority and is forced to isolate any individual who stands up for it.

Subsequent parts of the novel elaborate on these thematic fields and the process of exclusion that is implicit in them. The second part, "Shenan-

doah," picks up the story of the community several (unspecified) generations after the ostracism and death sentence of David Sumner. The old
human species is entirely extinct, and the groups of clones making up the
new social order each function as a "single organism" (pp. 63, 98). The
society has become literally an extended family, consisting of subfamilies
of virtually identical and interchangeable brothers and sisters. Each member of these subfamilies is indissolubly linked to the other members by
chains of empathy. No one is ever alone, or separate, or lonely. The group's
needs have been elevated far above those of the individual. As one brother
says, "We all know and agree it is our duty to safeguard the well-being of
the unit, not the various individuals within it. If there is a conflict between
those two choices, we must abandon the individual. That is a given" (p.
100). Elsewhere the notion of the sacrifice of the individual for the good
of the group is referred to as the single most important "law" of the community (p. 92).

At first glance, "Shenandoah" presents an idyllic world without division,
without strife, without walls. But there is a dark underside. The above
"law," for example, entails not simply isolation or exile of the individual
but execution: "Early on, the family had decided that no community threat
could be allowed to survive" (p. 72). Nor is the community any longer a
"classless society," a world without walls or secrets or exploitation, since
there is a separate "breeders' compound" for the fertile women on whom
the community's survival depends. The community needs these women
to regenerate itself, to produce the nonclone children who are necessary
to forestall the gradual decline affecting those children who are "pure"
clones. As will be seen, these breeders form an inferior class which is set
apart and brutally exploited.

The most important "wall," however, is that which divides the community from the external world. The main action of this section consists
in the attempt to breach that wall temporarily for purposes of reconnaissance and salvage. A party of six, five men and a woman, each from
separate units, take a boat down the Shenandoah River to Washington D.C.,
to see what remains of the city and to look for materials and supplies which
the community needs. The key figure is the woman Molly, who is chosen
for the expedition because of her ability to remember and reproduce in
drawings everything that she sees. More important, she has the imagination to alter subtly what she reproduces, in so doing to "capture" its
uniqueness or essence, and to create images and landscapes with no empirical correspondent. In these traits, she is different from her five sisters,
and her trip down the river exacerbates that difference; she literally and
figuratively drifts away from them, "until she float[s] away from them
entirely" (p. 66).

The initial experience of separation from those sisters is excruciating for
Molly:

It was being alone for the first time in her life, she told herself. Really alone, out of reach, out of touch. It was loneliness that made her hurry through the undergrowth, now crushed down, hacked out of the way. And she thought, this was why men went mad in the centuries gone by: they went mad from loneliness, from never knowing the comfort of brothers and sisters who were as one, with the same thoughts, the same longings, desires, joys. (P. 70)

But, as one of the other expedition members notes, this same loneliness was at times deliberately sought out by humans: "And yet those other men of the distant past had sought isolation, and Ben couldn't think why" (p. 79).

Molly subdues her fears by clinging to her brothers on the boat, but the prolonged separation ultimately changes her entirely. On her return trip she comes to feel that breaching the wall of the outside world has ironically created another "thick clear wall [which] separate[s] her from every living thing on earth" (p. 82). She comes to feel that the natural world, initially experienced as an ominous, threatening, whispering presence, is actually a consoling being "that seem[s] to have a voice, and infinite wisdom" (p. 83). When she finally returns to the settlement, she realizes that her sisters are "strangers" to her.

What has happened, it is clear, is that Molly has undergone belatedly the experience of ego formation, the creation of a separate, autonomous self, a process that transforms her relation to the community: "The sisters hadn't changed. The valley was unchanged. And yet everything was different. She knew something had died. Something else had come alive, and it frightened and isolated her in a way that distance and the river had not been able to do" (p. 86). She becomes alienated from her sisters, whom she sees as somehow superficial and inconsequential, as "empty" (p. 84). The various groups of brothers and sisters all look alike to her, like animated and conspiratorial "dolls" (p. 93). She realizes that during her seven-week absence nothing at all had happened, that nothing had changed in the valley, and that this is a sign of stagnation. Her sisters and the other members of the community find her paintings disturbing; they find her very presence unnerving, in part because they feel that Molly is "watching all the time, watching her sisters as they work and play" (p. 89). This uncanny ability to step outside the group and observe it is a function of *self*-consciousness, the awareness of self as a locus of subjectivity. She is different from the others, Molly explains to one of her brothers, because her eyes see both outward and inward. And though the existence of this separate self brings her pain and isolation, eventually even breaks the empathetic bond she once shared with her sisters, she nonetheless feels that "there was something that had come to live within her, something that was vaguely threatening, and yet could give her peace as nothing else could" (p. 86).

The community chooses finally not to destroy her but to isolate her for purposes of study; they hope to "use" her, to find out what made her separate herself from her sisters and to forestall such happenings in the future. During what is for her an idyllic six-year period of isolation at the old Sumner house, she cultivates her selfhood by exploring the satisfactions of art and by communing with the natural world, and gives birth in secret (the father is the doctor who was selected to study her) to a son, Mark, to whom she passes on the joys and abilities of individuality. Her idyll ends when Mark's existence is discovered, at which time she is removed to the breeders' compound. There, over a two-year period, much of which she is insensible to because of extensive drugging, she is turned into a breeding machine, strapped to a table on a monthly basis for artificial insemination, and subjected to chemical conditioning that makes doing any kind of art-work nauseating and leaving the compound psychologically unbearable. She discovers what the real condition of the breeders is: "it was not the separation, it was the humiliation of being treated like an object, of being drugged and then used, forced to cooperate in that procedure unques-tioningly" (p. 113). She is treated like a "thing, an object, press this button and this is what comes out, all predictable, on cue" (p. 117).[2] Eventually, through a superhuman exertion of individual will, Molly is able to break the chemical conditioning and leave the compound. She arranges a brief rendezvous with her son, whom she tells to preserve carefully that "other self" who whispers to him, because it is more important than anything the community can give to him or take from him. She then gathers a few belongings and wanders away from the community to join the boy's father, who had earlier drowned in the Shenandoah River. "Shenandoah" ends, like part one, with the exclusion and death of the individual who opposes the community.

The second part, then, builds on the thematic oppositions that structured part one. The conflict between the individual and the community is height-ened; the existence of the latter entails the elimination of the former. The technology of the hermetically sealed community of families creates a buffer zone that separates it from the natural world, more and more seen as something alien and threatening. The community itself shows signs of cracking and decline: its members are unable to handle any forms of iso-lation or separation; it has become intolerant of difference; its existence depends upon the ruthless exploitation of an inferior breeder class, which it keeps docile with drugs and conditioning. Correspondingly, the indi-vidual is shown to enjoy qualities that the group lacks or has lost, among them self-consciousness (a locus of both pain and satisfaction), self-reliance, an affinity with the natural world, and imagination. This last quality may well be the most important of all, since one needs imagination in order to deal with change, and change, though it may be resisted or denied, cannot be obviated.

The final section of the novel, "At the Still Point," relates the coming of age of Molly's son Mark during a period of threatening change for the community, change brought about by the coming of a new ice age. This part adheres to the same model as the first two—the progressive exclusion of the exceptional individual from an increasingly uniform and rigidified community. It ends, however, on a more positive note, with Mark stealing away from the community, taking with him breeders, clones, livestock, and supplies in order to create a countercommunity farther south. At the same time, part three heightens the thematic oppositions that structure the novel by extending them to their logical conclusions.

An examination of the resolution of those oppositions should clarify the essentially conservative ideology of Wilhelm's novel. From the community's standpoint, nature has become something more and more fearful and threatening. Even the eldest members, the most individuated and resourceful, cannot spend more than a few moments in the woods without feeling panic and becoming disoriented: "They couldn't send their people out to live in the forests, he knew. This was a hostile environment, with a spirit of malevolence that would stifle them, craze them, kill them. He could feel the presence now, pressing in on him, drawing closer, feeling him. . . . Abruptly he stood up and started to follow Mark" (p. 141). Since the community has eliminated Otherness within its ranks, it can conceive of the Otherness of nature only as something hostile, to be systematically destroyed. The leader of the community flatly states, "The best thing we can do with the woods is clear them as quickly as possible" (p. 142). The general posture of the community is to use its advanced technology to create a future that is perfectly planned, to do away with contingency. The irony is that nature has fashioned a dramatic "contingency plan" of its own, in the form of the advancing glacier of a new ice age. Compounding the irony, the novel describes the advancing glacier as "a great white wall," obliterating differences as it moves, "grinding everything to powder" (p. 169). The two forces, then, technology and nature, have mustered conflicting walls, each designed to do away with Otherness.

The community also intends to use its technology to eliminate nature in the reproductive process. As one of the teachers tells his class of clones, "Our goal is to remove the need for sexual reproduction. Then we will be able to plan our future. If we need road builders, we can clone fifty or a hundred for this purpose, train them from infancy, and send them out to fulfill their destiny" (p. 132). As the example makes clear, the community is evolving from a class society (clones and breeders) into a caste society, with the most intelligent clones making all the decisions, using the breeders to ensure "a continuing population of capable adults to carry on affairs" (p. 187), while cloning en masse virtually mindless hordes of expendable workers. This sort of outcome, the novel suggests, inheres in a social order which sees biological nature as something to be overcome and which systematically purges itself of individual difference.

The appearance of a caste of exploited workers reveals that the real threat to the social order comes not from the outside world but from within. Control of reproductive forces, the cloning of generation after generation, entails its own heavy price in the form of lost talents and abilities: "Each generation lost something; sometimes it couldn't be regained, sometimes it couldn't be identified immediately" (p. 191). The extent of the loss is brought home most forcefully when Andrew, one of the leaders of the community, announces triumphantly that a solution has been found to the problem of decline in generations after the fourth at the very moment that the community has reached the "still point," when "none of the new people would ever think of altering anything" (p. 188). Mark's peers, for example, have lost the ability to invent narrative; the very fact that he can "tell stories that no one ever heard" (p. 180) makes him a figure of awe. More disturbing, the children have lost the ability to recognize symbolic representations; they see the remarkable snow sculpture that Mark creates as "just snow." The loss of the symbolic function signals a wholesale decline in the psychic economy; subsequent testing reveals that "children under nine or ten could not identify the line drawings, could not complete a simple story, could not generalize a particular situation to a new situation" (pp. 157–58). As a result, they must memorize everything they need to know to survive.

The breakdown in imaginative, symbolic, and inductive functions means, of course, that they will be unable to anticipate unforeseen circumstances or to originate innovative solutions to those circumstances. Indeed, members of the community internalize to some degree the extent of their losses. As one of the sisters confides to Mark, "If you turned me inside out, there wouldn't be anything at all there" (p. 190). This "emptiness" invades even their affective faculties. They seem incapable of feeling strong emotions; Mark is the only one who cries when six of the clones die during a reconnaissance foray, the only one who feels guilt about his complicity in their deaths, the only one able to feel love for another individual. All of these factors—the progressive de-differentiation and rigidification of clone society, the members' loss of intellective and affective faculties, the exigencies posed by an increasingly harsh natural environment—of course doom the clone community, a fact which Mark is the only one to recognize. His foresight results in the creation of an alternate community, based on different principles, the establishment of which ensures the survival of the human race.[3]

Mark, the solitary individual of part three, carries all of the traits which the novel's thematic field privileges: he foments discord in the community; he is able to live in harmony with nature; in his sculpture and storytelling he embodies the principle of imagination; he retains affective ties to individual members of the community, while acknowledging his loyalty to the community as a whole; he demonstrates foresight and exercises individual initiative by creating a countercommunity and thus saving the human race. His eventual triumph—in the novel's epilogue, set twenty years after his departure, he returns to the clone community to find it destroyed by natural forces—settles once and for all the contest between the conflicting principles of Self and Society in favor of the former. Any society which fashions the individual self as its "enemy" carries within it the seeds of its own destruction.

What sort of society, then, does Mark create in the wilderness? The brief epilogue does not go into great detail, but clearly his new order is an atavism of sorts. It is a communal and egalitarian society in which individual members work together on group projects, such as the bathhouse, water wheel, and community fireplace. It is essentially agrarian, since the technology it has retained predates the Industrial Revolution. It lives both in and off of nature; crops are tilled, but there is also foraging (done, typically enough, by tribes of naked children). It is, in effect, the product of the pastoral/arcadian step outside history, into mythic time, as Mark is well aware:

> Mark had led his people into a timeless period, where the recurring seasons and the cycles of the heavens and of life, birth, and death marked their days. Now the joys of men and women, and their agonies, were private affairs that would come and go without a trace. In the timeless period life became the goal, not the re-creation of the past or the elaborate structuring of the future. The fan of possibilities had almost closed, but was opening once more, and each new child widened its spread. More than that couldn't be asked. (P. 207)

In a mythic world outside time, where one is not haunted by the nightmares of the past or tempted by the dreams of the future, more than that *need* not be asked. Wilhelm can imagine a utopian world only in a "no time," for only there can the conflicting demands between individual and society be, in effect, ignored; only there are values such as individual initiative, cultural diversity, and personal satisfaction seen as not at all at odds with group survival or harmony. Only there can one smile, as Mark does at the very end of the novel, at the new generation of children just because "all the children were different" (p. 207).

3.2.2 Speculative Alternate Society SF: Russ's *The Female Man*

> The task of an oppositional utopian text is not to foreclose the agenda for the future in terms of a homogeneous revolutionary plan but rather to hold open the act of negating the present and to imagine any of several modes of adaptation to society and nature based generally upon principles of autonomy, mutual aid, and equality.
>
> —Tom Moylan, *Demand the Impossible*

A dozen times between my door and Washington Street I had to stop and pull myself together, such power had been in that vision of the future to make the real Boston strange.

—Edward Bellamy, *Looking Backward*

A conventional SF motif that lends itself to speculative treatment is the premise that there exist alternate probability time lines or alternate futures predicated upon choices we make in the present.[1] If we make such and such a decision, the premise goes, then one resultant future comes into being; another decision results in a correspondingly different future. Fictions employing such a premise usually juxtapose and explore their respective alternate probabilities, treat them as coexisting, in this way foregrounding their respective structures and the kind of decisions that brought them into being. Because these alternate futures exist in separate time lines, they are to some degree divorced from historical time, outside the parameters of conventional extrapolation, a situation which allows for considerable imaginative latitude on the author's part. He or she is able to deform the basic narrative world radically in such futures, thereby bringing into being any number of possible speculative worlds. This is exactly what Joanna Russ does in *The Female Man*, a novel which juxtaposes four different alternate societies, two of them versions of the present, two of them possible futures.

At an early point in the novel, Russ provides the scientific rationale for her intersecting universes. "Every choice begets at least two worlds of possibility," her narrator says, one in which you choose one course of action, and one in which you choose the other. If we consider, then, that each lifetime is made up of an infinite number of such choices, "there must be an infinite number of possible universes": "with each decision you make (back there in the Past) that new probable universe itself branches, creating simultaneously a new Past and a new Present, or to put it plainly, a new universe."[2] Russ imagines two such alternate futures, each of which has mastered "probability mechanics," has learned how to pass from one probability to another, and is actively seeking out women from alternate pasts for different, if related, purposes. The combined efforts of the agents from these futures bring together four very different women from four different societies, each representative of the mode of being available to women given the nature of that society.

At the same time, these women represent four different aspects of one female self; as Jael, one of the women from the future, says, "It came to me several months ago that I might find my other selves out there in the great, gray might-have-been, so I undertook . . . to get hold of the three of you." Because the women share "essentially the same genotype, modified by age, by circumstances, by education, by diet, by learning, by God knows what," Jael can rightfully conclude that she is "looking at three other myselves" (pp. 160–62). The fact that these women represent "four versions of the same woman" (p. 162),[3] and that the differences between them are mainly a function of the societies they come from, when added to the fact that the novel's form is fragmented and its plot minimized,[4] serves to foreground the interrelationships and interactions of these women and the worlds from which they come. In order to examine these fields of intersection, we must first look at each world and its representative separately.

The first person to make her appearance in the text is Janet Evason, who announces in the first sentence that she was born on a farm on the world of Whileaway. Her precedence in the text signals the privileged place that Whileaway occupies; it is a near-utopic world located on a small-probability time line some one thousand years in the future. It is utopian, we gather, mainly because it is a world without men, a world, Janet explains, which lost all its men to a plague some eight hundred years earlier and which reproduces parthenogenetically. Since the focus of the novel is on Janet's relation with the women from the other time lines, an exhaustive description of Whileawayan society is not really necessary.[5] In general, it is a decentralized, pastoral society which combines family-based farms and advanced technology, including biological engineering, matter-antimatter reactors, and labor-saving induction helmets which connect the human nervous system with machinery and computers. Whileaway provides, one critic concludes, "a way of life that combines a post-industrial, cybernetic technology with a libertarian pastoral social system. Fulfillment of each person, not accumulation of profit and centralization of power, is the goal of the economy."[6] Central government and hierarchical organization are institutions that seem to have disappeared with the men, and the society places its highest values on hard work, personal freedom, privacy, creativity, and ecological awareness. The credo of the community is best figured in the aphorism of one of its philosophers: "If not me or mine, O. K. If me or mine—alas. If us and ours—*watch out!*" (p. 55). This credo stresses tolerance first, a rejection of possessiveness next, and loyalty to the community above all. As is implicit in the name, Whileaway is at once a pleasant diversion, a way to pass time, and something in the remote future, a while away.

Janet has been chosen as emissary from this society not because she is exceptional but because she is expendable. By vocation a police officer, she is not much needed in her world; in fact she was chosen for her profession because, as compared to her peers, she is "stupid" (with an IQ of 187). And yet, in comparison with the women and men she meets in other time tracks, she is exceptional. She embodies the best of the world of Whileaway—self-reliance, strength, affection, loyalty, adaptability, and common sense. During her extended stay in Joanna's world ("our" own world of 1969), she reveals again and again its shortsightedness, its chauvinism, its sexual hang-ups, its superficiality. At the end of part seven, just before the four women are united for the first time, each of the initial trio (Janet,

Jeannine, and Joanna) articulates her fundamental values. Janet's statement begins as follows:

> "Life has to end. What a pity! Sometimes, when one is alone, the universe presses itself into one's hands: a plethora of joy, an organized plenitude. The iridescent, peacock-green folds of the mountains in South Continent, the cobalt-colored sky, the white sunlight that makes everything too real to be true. The existence of existence always amazes me. You tell me that men are supposed to like challenge, that it is risk that makes them truly men, but if I—a foreigner—may venture an opinion, what we know beyond any doubt is that the world is a bath; we bathe in air, as Saint Theresa said the fish is in the sea and the sea is in the fish." (P. 153)

In the face of our inevitable mortality, Janet articulates a womanly perspective that rejects the idea of existence as a challenge and exalts the mystery and plenitude of being.

The second woman to make an appearance in the novel is Jeannine Dadier, who lives in an alternate present, a 1969 world still caught up in the Great Depression, in part because Adolph Shicklgruber died in 1936 and there was no Second World War, and no postwar economic boom. Jeannine's world is antithetical to Janet's, a male-dominated world in which the only conceivable future for a single woman is a man and marriage. Jeannine is a twenty-nine-year-old part-time librarian who drifts through life waiting for the right man to find her; her ultimate goal, Joanna says, is to be "relieved of personality at last and forever" (p. 93). Her first response to Janet's initial appearance in her world is denial; when she herself is transported to other time lines she insists that she doesn't belong there. When she is transported to Whileaway, she can only imagine scenarios in which that world might be destroyed. So frightened is she by Whileaway that, when she returns briefly to her own world, she tries to escape into a loveless marriage with her self-centered boyfriend. When she is confronted by different mores, including Janet's lesbian relation with Laura, her first reaction is to retreat into the background; her boyfriend laughingly refers to her as the "vanishing woman" (p. 4). Her general strategy is to resist the unusual and to preserve the status quo. Her virtual nonexistence is best figured in the fact that she is the only "J" character who does not appear in the first person; as Catherine McClenahan notes, "the narrative of Jeannine is always someone else's."[7]

The contrast between Jeannine's and Janet's view of romantic love is indicative of the positions they occupy. Jeannine sees such love as the only salvation from the dreary life she leads. She daydreams continually about a "tall, dark, and handsome" man entering her life, singling her out because of her beauty, her figure, or her clothes, and carrying her off to indulge her in an endless romance of candlelit dinners and moonlit balls. Romantic love is for her a way to escape the burdens of personality. Janet, for her part, sees romantic love as narcissistic, as a way of imposing one's self on the world; it is a "dreadful intrusion, a sickness," that turns one into a sleepwalker convinced that the external world is but "an eruption of one's inner life" (p. 75). It is a "parasite" that imbues the host with feelings of "self-consequence" (p. 79). "Romance is bad for the mind," she flatly declares, because the very idea of it results in any number of "images, ideals, pictures, and fanciful representations" that serve to divorce the lover from reality. If Jeannine hopes that one day her prince might come, Janet can only respond, "Princes and princesses are fools. They do nothing interesting in your stories. They are not even real" (pp. 153–54). Her advice: better that one go and embrace a frog.

Although Jeannine at first rejects Whileaway and everything it represents, she is nonetheless profoundly affected by her visit there. Upon her return she dreams of Whileaway, awakening from the dreams with the feeling of something lost, of being cheated by her own world. She begins to wish she had the courage to change her life, to ask herself questions that were previously unthinkable: "who am I, what am I, what do I want, where do I go, what world is this?" (p. 122). She predictably reacts to this disturbing quandary by retreating to the unreal dream of romance and agrees to marry her repellent boyfriend, Cal. She wishes to remain "Sleeping Beauty," the princess who can be awakened only by the prince's kiss.

Throughout most of the novel Jeannine is depicted as someone asleep; she sleeps late, she dawdles, she sleepwalks through life. Joanna, the woman from our "own" world of 1969, has, by comparison, experienced an "awakening." Thirty-five years old, an academic, and a publishing writer (just like the author at the time of *The Female Man*), Joanna lives in the more volatile, affluent, "liberated" world of late '60s America. Although she enjoys a certain amount of personal autonomy and freedom, she is well aware that in this world she must

> dress for The Man
> smile for The Man
> talk wittily to The Man
> sympathize with The Man
> flatter The Man
> understand The Man
> defer to The Man
> entertain The Man
> keep The Man
> live for The Man. (P. 29)

She has awakened to the fact that she is a second-class citizen and a sexual commodity in a patriarchal society, but she is cautious, reluctant to give up the liberal humanism which counsels reconciliation and gradual reform.

Janet's arrival in her world creates a "new interest" in her life (p. 29), gradually transforming her, improving her health and her outlook, making

her more outspoken about the oppression of women, the socialization process, female stereotyping, and the stupidity of men. After spending more
than half a year with Janet, Joanna is able to ask how she can reconcile the
demands of this society of hers "with my human life, my intellectual life,
my solitude, my transcendence, my brains, and my fearful, fearful ambi-
tion" (p. 151). During a visit to Jeannine's world, she sees the latter trying
to close off her future by rushing into marriage with Cal and comments as
follows: "At one stroke she [Jeannine] has amputated her past. She's going
to be fulfilled. She hugs herself and waits. That's all you have to do if you
are a real, first-class Sleeping Beauty. . . . And there, but for the grace of
God, go I" (p. 131). Jeannine's world is forever closed to Joanna, a world
of sleepwalkers and zombies, but Janet's is, at the same time, out of reach,
unattainable, un-*real*-izable; Janet herself, "whom we don't believe in,"
represents the "Might-be of our dreams, living as she does in a blessedness
none of us will ever know" (pp. 212–13). Having experienced both sides
of the social coin, Janet's utopia and Jeannine's dystopia, oppressed by her
own world, Joanna feels trapped "between worlds" (p. 110), unable to
reconcile her visions or transform her own world.

It is the fourth self, Jael, who serves as a catalyst for Joanna, suggesting
to her a possible course of action. Jael comes from a near-future world, one
in which the war between the sexes has become just that, a pitched battle
pitting the Have-nots against the Haves (to be understood in both economic
and physiological terms), Us against Them, women against men (p. 165).
Her world is divided into two zones, Manland and Womanland, at the
moment enduring a truce period during the prolonged war. She is the one
who has been "collecting Js" (p. 155); she brings the other three women
into her time line to recruit them as allies in that war. She tells the women:
"We want bases on your worlds; we want raw materials if you've got them.
We want places to recuperate and places to hide an army; we want places
to store our machines. Above all, we want places to move from—bases
that the other side doesn't know about" (p. 200). With the help of the
others, she intends to end the truce and bring the war to a successful
conclusion, eliminating men from her world.

During their visit the three women witness Jael's violent assassination
of a Manlander higher-up; Jeannine watches calmly, Joanna is ashamed,
and Janet weeps. When questioned about the necessity of the action, Jael
responds, "I don't give a damn whether it was necessary or not. . . . I liked
it" (p. 184). Murder, she says, is her "one way out" (p. 195), her only way
to counteract the guilt society imposed upon her for being a woman, for
growing up with a "lack." Jael tells the women that she is the "grand-
daughter of Madam Cause," that everything she does is done "*by cause*,
that is to say *Because*, that is to say out of necessity" (p. 192). She thus
argues that anger, organized resistance, and violence are legitimate and
necessary responses to the brutal oppression experienced by women in a
male-dominated society.

As critics have noted, Jael's world in some ways mediates between Jeannine's and Janet's; it combines "the worst case environment we connect with Jeannine and the freedom and energy we identify with Janet."[8] Like Janet, Jael comes from a future world and refuses to be intimidated by men. Unlike Janet, however, she is an "old-fashioned girl" (a phrase she herself uses several times), who accepts the logic of male domination and oppression but simply inverts it. She reveals her old-fashionedness in her relation to Jeannine; she deliberately "woos" the retiring girl from alternate 1969, whispering in her ear like "the Devil in the fable tempting the young girl" (p. 163), using the diminutive "Jeannie" just like the men in Jeannine's world. That this strategy succeeds is shown when Jeannine proves to be the only one of the three who agrees to "do business with Womanland" (p. 211). In Jeannine's world, the only way to say "goodbye to all that [her second-class status and dependence on men]" (p. 209) is to invert the logic of male domination by waging war against men. For Joanna, on the other hand, Jael represents a more authentic and satisfying response to the stifling and oppressive patriarchy—anger. In a lecture Russ has said that "it is Anger that mediates between Oppression and Freedom."[9] Jael's world and actions open Joanna's eyes to the legitimacy and usefulness of anger and enable her to mediate the gap between the oppression of Jeannine's world and the freedom of Janet's.

If we consider each woman and her world in synchronic relationship, drawing upon a number of explicitly articulated polarities, we can construct the following square:

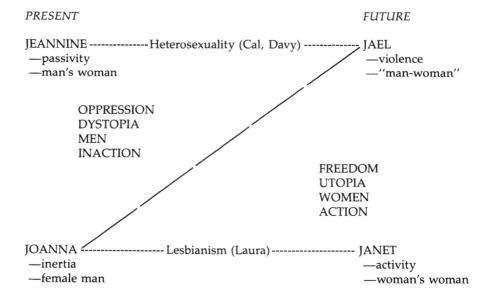

Throughout the novel, Russ has stressed the differences between men and women and played with forms of mediation of those differences. Jeannine, after meeting Janet, states flatly, "I won't be a man" (p. 86), but her exposure to Jael converts her into a warlike woman. In Jael's world, there exist in Manland the "changed" and the "half-changed," transsexual and homosexual men who act out female stereotypes and thus parody the notion of mediation. Jael herself says that she has been raised as a "man-woman" (p. 188), the order of the pairing suggesting the masculine value system that she has embraced. But it is Joanna who discovers the most fruitful negotiation between the polarity, the "female man." The only way, she says, to overcome the "perception of experience through two sets of eyes, two systems of value, two habits of expectation, almost two minds," the only way to "resolve contrarieties," is to "unite them in your own person" (p. 138). By willed transformation, she turns herself into a "female man," a person who assumes all the privileges and priorities pertaining to the male sex, while retaining her essential femaleness.

Both women from the future, Jael and Janet, contribute to her transformation. Before Jael's appearance late in the novel, Joanna is trapped between two worlds, "unable to detach herself from Jeannine or to become Janet."[10] Jael catalyzes Joanna into action, by revealing to her both the necessity of organized resistance and the usefulness of anger in generating that resistance. In part nine, the "Book of Joanna," Joanna claims to have committed her first "revolutionary act," by shutting the door on a man's thumb (a neat inversion of the code of male chivalry). Later she confesses that she likes Jael best of all, that she would like to "be Jael, twisted as she is on the rack of her own hard logic, triumphant in her extremity" (p. 212). Janet, on the other hand, reveals to Joanna the possibility of fulfillment in relationships with women. Joanna had at first rejected lesbianism as "unnatural," but in the same ninth book, she describes her seduction of Laura and the satisfaction it gives her. In that seduction she acts out the role of the "female man."

The schematization on page 98 depicts the women's synchronic sets of relations. Their diachronic relation is also revealing. If we take into consideration the women's ages and the nature of their respective worlds, we get the following order:

J1 = Jeannine, 29, living in a world of the past
J2 = Joanna, 35, living in "our" world of the present
J3 = Jael, 42, living in the near future
J4 = Janet, late 40s, living in a future that is a "while away"

The novel itself authorizes such an order when Jael suggests to Janet that the all-women world of Whileaway was not created by a plague which wiped out all the men, but rather by the all-out war which Jael's world is waging. The linking of the two futures converts the whole system into a historical chain, in which the women represent four phases of an ongoing historical process. The linking also argues that the utopian Whileaway "is the product not of natural creation but of willed human transformation of society."[11] Such a reading valorizes the kind of willed changes that the two women from the present undergo. By committing her first revolutionary act of violence and establishing a lesbian relation with another woman, Joanna takes steps along the axes which connect her with Jael and Janet. By transforming herself into the female man, she moves out of the present into the future. Likewise Jeannine, who moves along the axis connecting her and Jael by enlisting in the latter's war, undergoes a transformation of sorts; she becomes, in effect, a man-woman. Exposure to other worlds has changed these two women's lives. As one critic says, "the novel has, it seems, brought about changes; profound experiences of different probabilities can do that for people who are open to possibilities in life."[12] The same logic, of course, obtains for readers of *The Female Man* who are "open to possibilities in life."

Tom Moylan has identified as follows three venues or loci of change which *The Female Man* advocates: the ongoing socialization which teaches sisterhood and self-love, best represented by Janet; the anger and violence necessary "to strike back and destroy the coercive powers of the current system," best represented by Jael; and the "ideological resistance to the present dominant discourse," best represented in the book that Joanna writes, *The Female Man*.[13] Joanna herself makes several references to her act of composing the novel, an act apparently catalyzed by the appearance of Janet and Jael in her life. At one point she says that the work is being written in her blood and tears, but that they are a thing of the past, because "the future is a different matter" (p. 95). The future is indeed a different matter, just because in it there will exist a book called *The Female Man*.

The very act of composing the novel is that of a "female man," as Joanna makes clear from the very beginning. After introducing readers to Janet and Jeannine, she introduces herself, "me, Joanna," and announces that she had just that moment changed into a female man, before the encounters and exchanges that make up the novel (p. 5). She reminds readers of her unusual status at various places in the novel (e.g., p. 19, pp. 133–40). Only a female man could produce *The Female Man*, the composition of which is itself a revolutionary act.

At various places in the novel Joanna (or someone) makes reference to a fifth "I," one not linked to any of the protagonists. When Joanna, Jeannine, and Janet visit Whileaway, for example, this other "I" records the experience as follows: "I have never visited Whileaway in my own person, and when Janet, Jeannine, and Joanna stepped out of the stainless steel sphere into which they had been transported from wherever the dickens it was that they were before (etcetera), they did so alone. I was there only as the spirit or soul of an experience is always there" (p. 89). Elsewhere this voice refers to itself as "the spirit of the author" (p. 167). And when the four women gather for a final lunch at Schrafft's on Thanksgiving Day (1969, presumably), they have to pay up a "quintuple bill" (p. 212). Moylan argues that it is Joanna who becomes this fifth "I" and who is responsible for the self-reflexive passages, the ones drawing attention to the text as text.[14] I would argue that the pronoun's referent is the book itself, the entity that is *The Female Man*.

At the very center of the synchronic relation diagrammed on p. 98, there exists that fifth entity, the only one that mediates the novel's polarities—male/female, utopia/dystopia, present/future, activity/passivity—the novel itself, *The Female Man*. It represents a willed act of organized resistance that fosters the socialization of women while at the same time contesting the dominant ideology. It gives us in Whileaway the "dream that challenges our insufficient present," "the vision that provokes change."[15] It gives us in Jael the notion that we can bring Whileaway into existence only through conscious acts of resistance. By bringing "fantasies into the real world," by trying to "make Real what was Unreal," it contends with Reality itself (p. 208), while at the same time reminding us that it is just a fiction. It tears a hole in the fabric of Reality, thereby revealing to what extent that apparently self-evident entity is a social construct, a fiction itself. The very existence of alternate time lines depends on the premise that decisions we make now create any number of possible futures. The decision to read *TheFemale Man*, Russ suggests, helps to bring into being a better future for all of us. On the final pages, she sends her "little book"—the "real" female man—off into the real world, to do its work until the day that we are all free.

3.3 Gadget SF: Hardware and Software

> Science fiction is as trivial as all artistic forms that deal with phenomena rather than people.
>
> —Fritz Leiber, *The Wanderer*

> Tomorrow's Machines Today!
>
> —Hugo Gernsback, advertising blurb for *Amazing*

In his editorial for the July 1926 edition of *Amazing*, Hugo Gernsback makes the following heady claim for the "scientifiction" he is promoting: "If only five hundred years ago (or little more than ten generations), which is not a long time as human progress goes, anyone had come along with a story wherein radio telephone, steamships, airplanes, electricity, painless surgery, the phonograph, and a few other modern marvels were described, he would probably have been promptly flung into a dungeon. . . . There are few things written by our scientifiction writers, frankly impossible to-day, that may not become a reality tomorrow."[1] Gernsback is not simply justifying SF here; he is making two related claims for it, both of which have been generally discredited. He suggests first that SF can be a prophetic genre, anticipating today discoveries that science will make tomorrow. He also intimates that SF can act as a positive incentive to such discovery, by inspiring some lonely genius to invent what he or she has only read about. Both claims are figured in Gernsback's slogan for his magazine: "Extravagant Fiction Today—Cold Fact Tomorrow." For our own purposes, however, what is most significant about his editorial is that it identifies what Gernsback sees as the primary novums of SF—hardware, machines, the products of technology. Gernsback thus champions the most elementary SF type, gadget SF, in which the factor of estrangement is an alien object or "thing." The introduction of a new object—gadget, process, discovery—into the fictional world enables the author to explore the relation between humanity and "things," between Self and Technology.

Gadget SF probably is also the SF type that is most maligned, by both SF writers and critics. Writers can abuse this type if they present the object as an end in itself, either as a "modern marvel" or as a literal *deus ex machina*. This kind of SF, as Brian Aldiss says, "exists as propaganda for the wares of the inventor."[2] It tends to promise that there is a technological "fix" for everything that ails humankind. But before we write off gadget SF *in toto*, we must distinguish between various levels of the gadget story and investigate the problematics of gadget SF.

Perhaps the most rudimentary use of a gadget novum is as vehicle for a series of adventures, as in much "space opera," where a spaceship is introduced mainly to transport the hero to one conquest after another. In this case, the gadget takes a back seat to the adventures themselves; the gadget is merely a *device* subtending the plot, and the cognitive thrust of the story is minimal. A similar case can be made against stories in which the gadget figures primarily as a puzzle or a problem. In "The Time Locker" and "The Proud Robot," both by Lewis Padgett (Henry Kuttner), the titular inventions—respectively, a compartment which transports its contents a week into the future and a robot created during a drunken stupor—serve mainly the function of mystification; the stories pivot on the hero's figuring out what it is these machines do. In Padgett's "The Twonky," a "temporal snag" deposits a futuristic machine into 1940s Mid-America, a mysterious console which controls human behavior, turning its owners into docile, obedient, brainwashed "zombies." In all of these stories, a great part of the pleasure of the text has to do with discovering what these machines do and whether the human actants will regain control of them. But as the last clause makes clear, collectively these stories call into question the proper relation between humanity and its technologies. Gadget stories, in other words, tell us something about the dangers and delights of gadgets.

SF stories involving robots constitute a problematic case which at once helps to define the limits of the gadget story and to sketch out its thematics. At first glance all stories involving robots would seem to be gadget SF, since the informing novum is a machine specifically designed to assist humanity in some way. But what happens, as is the case in Shelley's *Frankenstein* and Ellison's "I Have No Mouth and I Must Scream," when the machine is endowed with sentience or achieves selfhood and establishes a personal relation with its creators? Then, clearly, the story changes type; it becomes an alien encounter SF. But the addition of sentience to a robot does not automatically transform the typological character of a fiction. In one of the most heralded robot collections of all, Asimov's *I, Robot*, "positronic" robots evolve from mere machines to sentient beings who eventually take on human form (Stephen Byerley) and take control of human affairs. Yet, because their behavior is rigidly circumscribed by the famous "three laws" of robotics, they remain in essence machines, and *I, Robot* remains gadget SF, mediating the correct relation between humanity and its technological creations. A diametrically different view of this relation is presented in Jack Williamson's "With Folded Hands" (made into *The Humanoids*, 1950), in which "rhodomagnetic" humanoid robots, originally designed to wage war and then "perfected" in order "to save men from themselves,"[3] imprison humanity in a perfect but stagnant world, free of "war and crime, of poverty and inequality, of human blundering and resulting human pain" (p. 74). Here again, although the humanoids are extremely intelligent, they adhere slavishly to their "Prime Directive: *to serve and obey, and guard men from harm*" (p. 73) and are without emotions, so that their actions are those of a machine. *I, Robot* and "With Folded Hands," then, represent robot fictions which fall within the gadget category because their respective novums remain undifferentiated technological creations. At the same time, these two fictions define in general terms the axiological spectrum of gadget SF. This spectrum runs from the wholesale endorsement of technology, as in some "Golden Age" gadget SF which assumes that the solution to whatever ails us is more and better technology, to a kind of technophobia, as in Fred Saberhagen's *Berserker* series, in which interstellar machines—berserkers—are shown to have only one directive, the extinction of sentient life. The middle case would be monitory or cautionary gadget SF, which accepts the place of technology in postindustrial society but is well aware of its possible abuses.

As should be clear from Gernsback's promise to deliver "tomorrow's machines today," much gadget SF is extrapolative in nature. Technology itself, the application of discoveries in the "hard" sciences to industrial uses, tends to develop in a linear fashion which lends itself to extrapolative logic. But an author can indeed imagine gadgets that are so speculative as to frustrate human comprehension. In "Mimsy Were the Borogroves," for example, the master of the form, Lewis Padgett (the name itself puns on the informing novum), conceives of a set of alien toys, accidentally deposited in our own world, which transport the children who find them into another dimension. As this example makes clear, SF featuring speculative gadgets frequently shifts its thematic focus from the gadget itself to the human reaction to the alien novum. This is the case with Philip José Farmer's *Traitor to the Living* and Algis Budrys's *Rogue Moon*, both of which feature "death machines" in which those who die are brought back to life, with Frederik Pohl's *Gateway* series, whose titular novum is a very dangerous alien gadget which makes interstellar flight possible, and with Poul Anderson's *Tau Zero*, where a spaceship able to approach the speed of light and thus enjoy the time dilation effect makes it possible for its passengers to witness the death and rebirth of the universe. In these fictions the gadget figures as a vehicle for an exposure to alternity *in extremis* (e.g., death), an experience which necessarily foregrounds themes of the Self and moves the fiction in the direction of alien encounter. Speculative gadget SF, like speculative SF in general, tends to assault hard and fast boundaries between SF types, to probe the human response to Otherness per se. But at the same time these fictions take for granted that "there are more things in heaven and earth than are spoken of" in our technology and in so doing try to open readers' eyes to the possibilities of technology.

Brian Aldiss has said of the "Golden Age" writers of gadget SF that "they did not question the basic value of technology. They saw that technology would bring big troubles . . . , but they were secure in the belief that more massive, more organised, doses of technology would take care of the problem."[4] Such a view does not pertain, it should be clear, to gadget SF in general. But it is also unfair to "Golden Age" gadget SF, which explores the limits, the pitfalls, and the drawbacks of technology at the same time that it endorses the technological ethos. Aldiss seems to think that gadget SF is the product of a more naive, even "benighted" era, in which some people at least believed that technology held all the answers to the problems facing humanity, an era no longer with us. But Aldiss perhaps forgets that technology is always, now even more and more, "with us," and that technological developments can and will stimulate forms of gadget SF. Indeed, at this time gadget SF is making a comeback of sorts, in the form of "cyberpunk" (e.g., William Gibson's *Neuromancer*, 1984), which uses as its dominant novum technologies spawned by the incredible advances in cybernetics. In this way, it, like all valuable gadget SF, explores the "interface" between humanity and its technologies.

3.3.1 Extrapolative Gadget SF: Clarke's *Rendezvous with Rama*

There are a certain class of people, and we hear continually from them, who condemn the policy of this magazine because we exploit the future. These good people never realize that there can be no progress without prediction. It is impossible to have in mind an invention without planning it beforehand, and no matter how fantastic and impossible the device may appear, there is no telling when it will attain reality in the future.

—Hugo Gernsback, editorial for *Predicting Future Inventions*

The year is A.D. 2130. The vigilant SPACEGUARD computers register the appearance of an "intruder" in the solar system, a heretofore undetected object of at least forty kilometers in diameter. Presumably an asteroid, the object displays a number of anomalous features. For one thing, it is unusually large for a previously undetected body. Also, its orbit and velocity are such that it will flash inward to the sun and out again, never to return. Astronomers decide that the object deserves a name and christen it Rama. Additional data add to the mysteries surrounding Rama; light curve readings reveal that the object is apparently perfectly symmetrical and spinning at the rate of more than a thousand kilometers an hour. One astronomer jumps to the conclusion that Earth might be witnessing the appearance of a collapsed sun, a neutron star, the only possible celestial object with that size and rotation period. Finally, space probe reconnaissance photos prove conclusively that Rama is not a natural object, that it is "a cylinder so geometrically perfect that it might have been turned on a lathe,"[1] a cylinder twenty kilometers in diameter and fifty in length, with a mass of ten trillion tons. Gravitational readings reveal that it is hollow, and there is only one possible conclusion: "The long-hoped-for, long-feared encounter had come at last. Mankind was about to receive the first visitor from the stars" (p. 12).

Rendezvous with Rama details the subsequent exploration of this "visitor," which turns out to be an apparently uninhabited space cruiser of monumental proportions. It is, in other words, an artifact, a tool, a "gadget." Using "sophisticated techniques of estrangement based on rigid extrapolation,"[2] Clarke has fashioned an overwhelmingly huge, but scientifically consistent, technological object, designed to serve a specific purpose. As a scientist in the novel points out, "there's nothing conceptually novel about Rama, though its size is startling. Men have imagined such things for two hundred years" (p. 43).

The very size of the object serves to enhance its strangeness; the size creates effects and spectacles that defy or confound analogies drawn from Earth. When Norton, leader of the exploration team, enters Rama through the hub and sets off a flare to get a view of the interior, he first sees himself at the bottom of a crater whose walls rise up to become the sky, but he checks himself abruptly: "No—that impression was false; he must discard the instincts both of Earth and of space, and re-orientate himself to a new system of coordinates" (p. 35). Patterns of perception or reference frames brought from Earth are just not adequate within the giant space enclosed by Rama. For one thing, the disk rotates very rapidly (radial velocity of one thousand kilometers an hour) around its central axis, creating within it a variable gravity that goes from zero at the axis to 0.6G at the perimeter (i.e., along the Raman "plain"). The middle of the cylinder is marked by a cylindrical sea. Standing on the plain and looking along the axis, one sees an ordinary expanse of water, but looking directly up, one can see it rise up in a curving arc that continues over one's head. In some ways, as one critic says, "Rama is a reversal of the Earth, an enclosed and concave rather than a convex and exposed world, a world where weightlessness is at the centre rather than at the periphery."[3] The spectacle provided by Rama continually forces the explorers (and the readers of the novel) to adopt new reference systems in regard to up and down, in and out, big and little, to see the enclosed space of Rama with a new set of eyes. The net result is, as Norton notes, a "sense of awe and mystery" (p. 65) that comes from an object whose very dimensions disorient us and whose workings stretch our powers of apprehension and comprehension.

The awe provoked by Rama is a function of its size; the mystery, a function of its nature. From its first appearance in the solar system, Rama poses a series of questions or problems for the people exploring it and studying it. The answer to one question leads only to another, more puzzling one; as regards Rama, "surprise was the only certainty" (p. 14). The mysteries surrounding Rama follow a logical progression, from "What is it?" to "Is it working?" to "How does it work?" to "What is it doing?" to "Why is it doing what it is doing?" This aspect of the text is deliberately foregrounded by Clarke. He explicitly embeds these questions within the novel's discourse—"Is this world alive? they asked themselves, over and over again. Is it dead? Or is it merely sleeping?" (pp. 19–20; see also pp. 40, 203)—as if to invite readers to participate in the mystery's solution. As Nicholas Ruddick says, the "novel's energy lies not in plot or character, but in the posing of a riddle, followed by the discovery of an apparent solution, followed by the realization that a deeper riddle is implied by this solution—and so on until the very structure of the universe seems to founder."[4]

The structure of the universe seems to founder, not only because the Raman space drive controverts Newton's Third Law (p. 266) but, more important, because Rama has taken no notice of its human visitors while at the same time confounding their understanding. We are left, according to Ruddick, with a vision of "an insignificant human race, still crudely homocentric, suddenly gaining a glimpse of the unknowability of the cosmos."[5] Another critic claims that the departure of the ship leaves humankind in the position of "stupid tourist before the mysteries of the universe."[6] And C. N. Manlove asserts that the ship presents both its explorers and readers with "objects and events so incomprehensible as to tell us we are getting nowhere." "The whole book," Manlove concludes, "is organized along the lines of a steady tapering into the unknown," in part because the successive enigmas surrounding Rama act out the uncertainty principle: "The uncertainty principle is fundamental to the way ideas concerning Rama shift throughout the story, and to the way Rama itself changes aspect. It is perhaps fitting that man in Rama should be in a weightless environment where he cannot get his bearings: the ground is in every way taken from under him."[7] Since, as the narrator tells us, an "element of total uncertainty" (p. 18) is something which no one can readily tolerate, the experience with Rama is ultimately frustrating, a situation reflected in the novel by Norton's final feelings about Rama: "the rest of his life he would be haunted by a sense of anticlimax and the knowledge of opportunities missed" (p. 274).

The above readings emphasize the extent to which the human encounter with Rama frustrates human understanding, but they pass over the very real successes that Norton and his crew enjoy during the exploration process. At one point in the novel, during an uncanny *déjà vu* experience, Norton speaks of being "face to face with the fundamental mystery of Rama" (p. 73), of having the feeling that "his well-ordered universe had been turned upside down," giving him "a dizzying glimpse of those mysteries at the edge of existence" (p. 74). But Norton soon remembers the original for the *déjà vu* experience, and he is relieved and heartened: "There was mystery here—yes; but it might not be beyond human understanding" (p. 75). Episodes such as this (Jimmy Pak has a similar experience during his exploration of the South Pole) suggest that, given perseverance and insight, human beings can decipher at least some of the enigmas of Rama. As Ruddick points out, throughout the novel "Clarke is continually urging the reader to distinguish between those enigmas which are capable of being solved and those which are not."[8]

From a "global" perspective, the novel records, not humanity's continual frustration at the object's inscrutability but a series of cognitive triumphs, as its human explorers master a sequence of puzzling phenomena and/or events. The novel presents us with many more mysteries that are solved than left unsolved (or declared insoluble, for that matter). Norton and his team are puzzled by the three valleys that run the length of Rama, interrupted only by the Circular Sea; they at first take them to be irrigation ditches, but soon discover (in the significantly titled chapter "Dawn") that they provide illumination for the vessel. After the melting of the Circular Sea, there is a substantial and mysterious rise in the oxygen level inside Rama; the crew quickly learns that it is caused by photosynthesis taking place in the sea. Everyone is puzzled by the five-hundred-meter cliff on the southern edge of the Circular Sea. But an exobiologist is able to figure out that such a wall is necessary to hold the water in during periods of acceleration, and from the height of the wall to determine the maximum feasible rate of acceleration of the vessel.

The Southern Plain and the South Pole are at first a complete blank on the human's map of Rama, but Jimmy Pak's courageous flight to the nether end brings back knowledge of its topography, a single sample of Raman life in the form of a flower, and confirmation that the great spires are somehow part of the ship's space drive. A last-minute exploration of one of the "cities" on the Raman plain reveals that they are not abandoned or deserted metropolises at all but rather huge hermetically sealed storehouses containing templates for the manufacture of various Raman tools and materiel. Even the mystery of Rama's strange course is solved in the end, when the humans realize that the ship is passing incredibly close to the sun in order to increase velocity and to refuel. There *are* some unsolved mysteries in the novel, and, as John Hollow notes, the "book has much to say about the difficulties of humans learning anything about the universe." But "difficult" and "impossible" are not synonymous, and "the point is that humans can still discover the truth. They are often wrong—short-sighted and set in their ways—but there is enough truth in their categories and analogies to enable them to make several correct conjectures about the huge cylinder they call Rama."[9]

The mysteries that remain at the end of the novel are substantial. One, of course, is the secret to the space drive, a technology which, in effect, obviates or circumvents basic Newtonian physics. But knowledge that such a drive is possible is itself a positive step for humanity. More disconcerting, at least for Commander Norton, is the fact that "the nature and the purpose of the Ramans was [sic] still utterly unknown" (p. 273). For this reason alone, he considers his mission a failure. In fact, however, the explorers have deduced a number of facts about Raman physiology, namely, that they are humanoid oxygen-eaters, standing about two meters tall, with trilateral symmetry. But the twin questions of if the Ramans still exist and where they might be found remain problematic. And the question of the purpose of their mission is shrouded in mystery. So Norton's frustration is perhaps well founded: "As Rama speeds out of our system," Eric Rabkin summarizes, "Norton is sad that he was unable to crack open the mechanical world and find its secret, for whatever mission Rama was on it must have been supremely important."[10]

But we must distinguish here between Norton's decodings and our own, "for the reader, unlike Norton, may gain access to the key to Rama's enigmas, even though Clarke . . . is not prepared simply to hand this key over on a plate."[11] In regard to the enigma of the Ramans' existence, it might be helpful to begin with the creatures who do populate the vessel during its passage past the sun, the "biots." Jimmy Pak encounters the first of these creatures when he regains consciousness after his crash landing on the Southern Plain. He opens his eyes and discovers a "large crablike creature" apparently dining on his wrecked vehicle (p. 168). Observing from a safe distance that the creature is not eating the vehicle but demolishing it, he tries to figure out whether it is an animal acting on instinct or a being of "fairly high intelligence." He then notices that it has a seemingly metallic carapace, and he wonders if it could be a robot. Even after a careful inventory of the creature's anatomy, he cannot be sure as to its nature: "The animal-or-robot question remained in perfect balance in his mind" (p. 169).

The subsequent appearance of other such creatures—the anthropomorphically named "spiders" and "sharks" and "window cleaners"—fails to resolve this question. It is impossible to tell whether they are animals or machines, even though it is clear that they "came from the same line of evolution, or the same drawing board" (p. 195). Even an autopsy of one of the spider creatures cannot solve the question once and for all. The creatures are organic, like animals, but electrically powered, like machines. Perera, the exobiologist, summarizes the problems presented by them as follows:

> "Could such creatures evolve naturally? I really don't think so. They appear to be *designed*, like machines, for specific jobs. If I had to describe them, I would say that they are robots—biological robots—something that has no analogy on Earth.
> "If Rama is a spaceship, perhaps they are part of its crew. As to how they are born—or created—that's something I can't tell you." (P. 209)

As their name indicates, the "biots"—biological robots—constitute a middle or mediating term, one which blurs the usually hard and fast distinction between animal and machine, biology and technology, evolution and creation, Life and Art. Their appearance means that "life, with all its infinite possibilities, had come to Rama. If the biological robots were not living creatures, they were certainly very good imitations" (p. 214).

After admitting that the "born" vs. "created" question is at present insoluble, Perera offers as a hunch the idea that "the answer's over there in New York" (p. 209), there being the Manhattan-like island in the Circular Sea. Time and again, New York is singled out as somehow special, different from the other Raman "cities." Norton and his team go to some lengths to explore the city—"If they did nothing else, they must reach New York"— because they sense that it is "the real heart of this world" (p. 129). While passing over the island, Jimmy Pak is careful to take elaborate photos of the edifice, because "one day—perhaps years hence—some student might find in them the key to Rama's secrets" (p. 151). And the Hermian Ambassador singles out the island as the possible "queen" for some sort of quasi–insect colony (p. 229).

What really sets New York apart from other Raman cities, of course, is the fact that it is the only one located on the Circular Sea, itself one of the more mysterious entities on Rama. During the Raman "spring" that follows the melting of the ice, the sea, an "organic soup" that has been "shaken into life" (p. 126), recapitulates in a few hours a process which took 375 million years on Earth, the creation of single-celled oxygen-producing microorganisms. The sea is the place from which the biots apparently come, and to which they return once they have performed their assigned functions. Most important, the sea, the proverbial mother of life, is linked to the island of New York.

Just a few minutes of exploration of the island confirm for Norton what had been his first impression of the structure, that it is not a city but a machine, albeit a puzzling one:

The closest analogy to this place that he had ever seen on Earth was a giant chemical-processing plant. However, there were no stockpiles of raw materials, or any indications of a transport system to move them around. Nor could he imagine where the finished product would emerge—still less what that product could possibly be. It was all very baffling, and more than a little frustrating. (P. 136)

Norton may be baffled, but crewmate McAndrews is not. Noting that the sea surrounding the island "contains just about anything you can think of," and may be the source of raw materials, he says, "I believe New York is a factory for making . . . Ramans." Indeed, "that's the way it all happened on Earth, though in a different way" (p. 137). The appearance of the biots a short time later tends to confirm McAndrews's extravagant theory, as does the fact that the sea is able to accelerate life-formation processes exponentially. Before leaving the island, Norton speculates that the machines are sleeping and wonders if they will ever wake again and, if so, for what purpose. Observing that everything seems to be in perfect condition, he muses that "it would be easy to believe that the closing of a single circuit in some patient, hidden computer would bring all this maze back to life" (p. 138). The answer to the question "Where are the Ramans?" is, it seems to me, pretty simple: "Nowhere . . . yet." When the vessel reaches its ultimate destination (and the passage through the solar system suggests that Rama is still on course), the computer circuit will close, and the island of New York will set about its main business—producing Ramans.

The speculation that Rama is a "space ark" (p. 41) and the reference to it as a "cosmic egg" (p. 116) thus prove more accurate than is supposed, a fact which suggests that humans can take the measure of Rama.[12] The fact is, as one critic complains, that Rama is "perfectly logical."[13] If there's one thing that Norton learns, it's that the Ramans seem "to have planned for everything" (p. 139). They have created the technological means whereby they can master the immensity of the universe. By fashioning a technology which obliterates the clear-cut distinction between natural and artificial, between "born" and "created," by mastering the process whereby life is created from an "organic soup" virtually overnight, the Ramans have defied the limits that the universe has tried to impose upon them; they have overcome both time and space. The paradigm Clarke employs here is a linear extrapolation from recent technological successes; there is no inherent limit to what technology can do, not even the limit between nonlife and life. *Rendezvous with Rama* thus celebrates the possibilities of technology; Rama comes to represent, as Ruddick says, "what a human civilization might look like that has embraced technology, used it to achieve unity through refashioning its world, and taken upon itself a patient yet purposeful quest for meaning across the gulfs of interstellar space."[14]

Some critics have interpreted the fact that Rama takes no notice of its human investigators as a blow to human pretensions, as a sign that the universe is utterly indifferent to the existence of humanity, a reading which the text seems to corroborate. "Such monumental indifference," thinks Commander Norton, "was worse than any deliberate insult" (p. 273). Eric Rabkin tries to turn this reading to humanity's advantage: "The universe may not care to be understood by us, but we care to understand the universe."[15] But Rama represents, not the universe at large but an artifact constructed by another race of beings confronted by that same vast and indifferent universe, a *machine* created, in fact, to counteract the limitations imposed by the vastness and indifference of that universe. John Hollow offers a more balanced reading of the ending of the novel:

> Insofar as Rama sails away, as it does, without in any way acknowledging the existence of the human race, it remains a symbol of the universe's indifference. Insofar, however, as it is itself a magnificent achievement, a triumph over the vast depths of time and space, it is a symbol of the power of intelligence to deal in and perhaps even *with* the universe.[16]

Rendezvous with Rama is a novel which affirms the possibilities of our technological creations, while at the same time reminding us of our insignificance in the larger scheme of things. Indeed, it suggests that the former can compensate for or counteract the latter.

3.3.2 Speculative Gadget SF: The Strugatskys' *Roadside Picnic*

> Suppose you had a machine that would enable you to fix everything that's wrong in the world. Let's say it draws on all the resources of modern technology, not to mention the powers of a rich, well-stocked imagination and a highly developed ethical sense. The machine can do anything.
>
> —Robert Silverberg, "Ms. Found in an Abandoned Time Machine" (1973)

> "For me the Visitation is primarily a unique event that allows us to skip several steps in the process of cognition. Like a trip into the future of technology. Like a quantum generator ending up in Isaac Newton's laboratory."
>
> —Arkady and Boris Strugatsky, *Roadside Picnic*

The premise informing the Strugatsky brothers' *Roadside Picnic* is pretty conventional—namely, that the Earth is "visited" in the latter part of the twentieth century by aliens from another star system. But the Strugatskys handle this standard SF motif in a unique manner. They set the novel some twenty years *after* the "Visitation," about which we learn very little at all, in part because the event is shrouded in mystery—no one seems to know what form the alien visit really took. The only "hard" evidence of that encounter is the six "Visitation Zones"[1] that the aliens have left behind, well-defined, self-enclosed areas characterized by strange atmospheric phenomena and even stranger objects. In the course of the novel a couple of theories are propounded to account for these Zones. It is suggested, for example, that they represent a kind of testing ground, a place in which a supercivilization has deposited a number of its artifacts for humanity to study, and thereby "to make a giant technological leap, and send a signal in response that will show we are ready for contact" (p. 108). A more compelling theory, given the nature of the Zones, is that they are simply the dumping grounds left over from a chance alien visit, areas of trash and refuse left behind after an interstellar "roadside picnic."[2] Critics of the novel sometimes argue that the "central mystery of *Picnic* is the identity of the Visitors,"[3] thus indicating that we are dealing with an alien encounter, but the novel deflects interest from the aliens to the *objects* they have left behind in the Zones. It focuses not on the aliens themselves but on the "rubbish" they've apparently discarded, more particularly on the impact of one of these Zones and its objects upon the inhabitants of Harmont, a small Canadian town which has been "blessed" by one of the Visitations.

What the visitors have deposited or discarded in the Zones is not traditional alien hardware (matter transmitters, ray guns, transponders, etc.); it consists of some very strange and puzzling "stuff." The stalkers, ordinary townspeople who sneak into the Zones at night to steal objects and sell them on the black market, are forced to resort to poetic terms to describe the phenomena there—"burning fluff," "spitting devil's cabbage," "witches' jelly," "mosquito mange," "lobster eyes," "rattling napkins." Their vocabulary is evocative or suggestive without being explanatory. The fact is that even the simplest item there, the "empty," "really is something mysterious and maybe even incomprehensible" (pp. 7–8). As some of the names suggest, many of the objects are extremely dangerous, even deadly. As a result, the Zones are fearful and treacherous places, and experienced stalkers feel that anyone who thinks he knows the Zone is going to die soon (p. 10). Even those objects recovered from the Zones that have been put to some sort of beneficial use—the inexhaustible supplier of energy, the life-process stimulator—are completely misunderstood and are probably being misused. "I am positive," says one scientist, "that in the vast majority of cases we are hammering nails with microscopes" (p. 111).

But even more puzzling, and finally terrifying, than the objects are the effects of the Zone upon the inhabitants of Harmont. During the Visitation period, those in or near the Zone fell ill, died (perhaps from fright), or were "blinded from a loud noise" (p. 20) that no one else heard. The aftermath of the Visitation witnesses other inexplicable "horrors born of the Zone" (p. 124). There is the resurrection of corpses from the cemeteries, resulting in the return of mute "zombies" to their stupefied families. There is the uncanny "mutagen effect" (p. 114), which brings about changes in the phenotype and genotype of those who spend time in the Zone and causes their children to be nonhuman. The Zone itself, however, does not emit radiation of any sort. Most disturbing is the "emigrant effect." It seems that those who experienced the Visitation somehow become bearers of bad luck, victims of the "evil eye." When they leave the vicinity of the Zone and relocate, their new surroundings become subject to a disproportionate number of catastrophes, deaths, natural disasters, and the like. As the scientist Pilman explains, "such cataclysmic events take place in any city, any area where an emigrant from a Zone area settles. The number of catastrophes is directly proportional to the number of emigrants who have moved to the city" (p. 113). This phenomenon violates not simply common sense but the notion of cause and effect, and "the violation of the law of causality is much more terrifying than a stampede of ghosts" (p. 114).

Roadside Picnic, then, has as its dominant novum a set of strange objects and the mysterious Zone they occupy. Noting that these "magic tools" "come without operating instructions," Csicsery-Ronay summarizes their status as follows: "Because they are objects without subjects, they have no intentional value. They are deprived of any signs that might give humanity an idea of their purpose and moral charge in a cultural system—even if only in the alien culture of the Visitors. . . . But 'gifts' deprived of purpose are only signs of otherness."[4] As pure objects, these gifts might be only "signs of otherness," but as uncanny objects inserted into the human economy and taking their effect upon human consciousness and human lives, they become vehicles for an exploration of the human encounter with speculative hardware, with advance technology cut loose from an intending subject.

The novel presents us with a spectrum of positive and negative attitudes toward the Zone, attitudes which entail both courses of action in regard to the Zone and possible uses of the Zone. Introduced first is the naive scientific posture of Kirill Panov, the Russian scientist who sees in the wonders of the Zone the possibility of knowledge which can bring about "a new world" (p. 46), a utopian world of plenty. The novel undercuts this posture when Panov dies from an accident caused by his own carelessness during his first visit to the Zone. His attitude is linked formally (by proximity) and thematically with that of Gutalin, the religious enthusiast who sees those who study the Zone as "Satan's children" and the stalkers as "Satan's servant[s]," who, with each trip, bring "another devil's artifact into the world" (pp. 39, 40). Gutalin drowns his apprehensions in alcohol. The religious man wants to make the Zone off limits; the scientific man wants to open it up.

A slightly different scientific view is offered by Pilman, the theoretical scientist. About serious matters such as the Zone, he says, he maintains a "healthy careful skepticism" (p. 110). Thus, though he is the one who theorizes that the Zones might be remnants from a roadside picnic, he is of the opinion that the objects from them may well be unknowable. He represents, as one critic says, the "irremediable alienation of cognition and theory" from the post-Visitation world.[5] Unlike Panov, he is careful to stay away from the Zones. He has, in effect, given up on science, and he can only salute what he sees as the great human virtue, the will to survive.

His attitude is linked structurally with that of stalker Redrick Schuhart; of the five chapters in the novel, Schuhart narrates and dominates three of them, while Pilman figures largely in the other two. Unlike Pilman, Redrick goes again and again into the Zone, searching for "swag" that he can sell on the black market so that he can support himself and his family. His attitude to the Zone is at once practical and optimistic, not theoretical and pessimistic like Pilman's. While Pilman represents the cognitive dimension, Schuhart occupies the emotional heart of the novel; he comes to stand for the value of affective relationships. In the course of the novel his approach toward the Zone and its objects tends to displace Pilman's. As Csicsery-Ronay puts it, "the Zone has left theoretical reason, represented by Pilman, impotent and baseless, while human affections, represented by Red, are driven more and more intensely to find a justification in the world."[6] By focusing on Red's approach to the Zone, the Strugatskys are able to foreground and isolate the key issue in the novel, the uses to which the Zone is put. As one character inquires of Pilman in the novel, "Are you hoping for something fundamental to come out of the Zone, something that will alter science, technology, our way of life?" (p. 110). It is Redrick Schuhart who is concerned with bringing things "out of the Zone" and using them to alter his "way of life." He thus serves as the moral center of the novel, and his own relation to the Zone recapitulates the history of the ways the Zone is put to use.

At a relatively early point in the novel, the ultimate fate of the Zones is made clear. They will become not laboratories of scientific investigation and discovery but storehouses to be pillaged and exploited. When he learns of Panov's death, a drunken Red turns on Ernest, the owner of the bar, accusing him of "dealing in death" (p. 45). Ernest, it seems, is a key middleman in the thriving black market which has grown up around the objects taken by the stalkers from the Zone. In the second chapter, set five years later, we find that Red has become a full-time stalker, someone who, when he is arrested, proves willing to sell the deadly witches' brew in order to protect his family from economic ruin. The town of Harmont is enjoying an economic boom, built primarily on the black market, which has become, Red realizes, a "lousy fungus that was growing on the Zone, drinking on the Zone, eating, exploiting, and growing fat on the Zone" (p. 71). The Zone is doomed to a parasitic commercialization. As Lem says, "the Zones succumb to being domesticated; for what one can neither understand nor ignore, one can at least consume piecemeal. Accordingly, the Zones, rather than being the subjects of eschatological thought, are the goal of bus tours."[7]

While the Zone is being commercialized, its objects are being commodified. "Because there is no new structure of values to accompany the Visitation's objects," Csicsery-Ronay notes, "nothing prevents them from being absorbed by the structure already in place."[8] Rather than being a source of "advances and discoveries of a technological nature . . . that our earth scientists and engineers could use" (p. 5), the Zone has been transformed into a stockpile of commodities for exchange on the open market. The overall perversion of the Zone is perhaps best exemplified in the case of the doctor Red consults in chapter 2:

> He [the doctor] had gotten mixed up with the stalkers not for the money, of course. He collected from the Zone: he took various types of swag, which he used for research in his practice; he took knowledge, since he studied the stricken stalkers and the various diseases, mutilations, and traumas of the human body that had never been known before; and he took glory, becoming famous as the first doctor on the planet to be a specialist in non-human diseases of man. He was also not averse to taking money, and in great amounts. (P. 58)

His entire relation with the Zone is tainted by greed and egocentrism; the doctor has become a veritable bloodsucker on the Zone.

Early in the novel, Redrick comments that the Zone is an area beyond moral considerations: it "doesn't ask who the good guys are and who the bad guys are" (p. 23). That may well be true, but one *can* make moral discriminations as to the uses of the Zone. Indeed, Schuhart occupies the center of the novel just because his life is most intimately wrapped up in the things that come out of the Zone and the uses to which they are put. The novel documents three of his visits to the Zone to bring back treasure, each involving loss and frustration, each more dangerous, each more and more desperate. Just what is it that motivates Schuhart to risk his life time and again, especially since there are other jobs he could get?

The common assumption is that stalkers are motivated by greed (p. 14), but Schuhart's case is more complicated than that. His first trip to the Zone is motivated by his desire to help his friend Panov recover a "full empty." He is responding, in other words, to the mutually supportive claims of affection and idealism; like Panov, he believes that "knowledge comes through this hole," that it is a "hole into the future" where "everyone will have everything that he needs" (p. 37). In this chapter, then, Red stands (up) for the values of the heart and links them to the possibility of a better social order. Indeed, he has become a stalker in large part because opportunities for meaningful and rewarding work are nonexistent in a world which has become uniformly grey, dreary, routinized: "Our Zone, the bitch, the killer, was a hundred times dearer to me at that second than all of their Europes and Africas. And I wasn't drunk yet, I had just pictured for a minute how I would drag myself home in a herd of cretins just like myself, how I would be pushed and squeezed in the subway, and how I was sick and tired of everything" (p. 38). The reasons for Red's involvement with the Zone are complex, having to do with idealism, the need for excitement, loyalty to family and friends, the opportunity for rewarding and satisfying employment, and, increasingly, despair and frustration.

In the course of the novel, Red's relationship to the Zone changes, such change constituting the ethical axis of the novel; as Csicsery-Ronay puts it, "the backbone of the story is the ambiguous Pilgrim's Progress of Red Schuhart."[9] In chapter 1, Red makes a legal trip into the Zone, trying to help his friend Panov find the object the latter needs for his studies. Even though Schuhart is more cynical than Panov, he shares his idealistic vision. When Panov dies, Red is truly bereft: "Kirill, my buddy, my only friend, how could it have happened? How will I get on without you? You painted vistas for me, about a new world, a changed world" (p. 46).

In chapter 2, set five years later, Red is married and a father, with "no permanent occupation" (p. 49). In order to feed and clothe his family, he has become a full-time stalker. He has, in other words, "sold out" to the underground commercial interests that are controlling the Zone. In this chapter, Red risks his life to save the life of a morally bankrupt fellow stalker, in so doing reaffirming his commitment to the value of life. But later the "bloodsucker" Ernest turns him in to the security police, and Red faces a crisis of conscience. Knowing that he will be going to prison for several years, he agonizes about the fate of his family. In case of just such a contingency, he had previously secreted a container of the extremely dangerous witches' brew. Caught between his moral scruples and his need to protect his family, he looks at the "porcelain container and the invincible and inevitable death" it contains. He knows that "they can kill us all with this thing," but in the end he decides, "Every man for himself, only God takes care of everybody. I've had it" (p. 85), and he turns the stuff over to black marketeers in exchange for economic security for his family. Since we discover in chapter 3 that the experiment with witches' brew backfires, killing thirty-five and crippling more than a hundred (p. 109), we realize that Red inhabits a world where the needs of the family unit and those of the social order inevitably and explosively conflict, where everyone must look out for himself because God is looking out for no one.

By chapter 4, set soon after his release from prison, Red Schuhart has become a lone operator,[10] increasingly desperate and concerned only with the fate of his horror-beset family. His daughter suffers from the "mutagen effect" and has become nonhuman. His resurrected father, one of the mute "zombies" reanimated by the Zone, haunts the household. Red returns to the Zone with only one objective, to get to the fabulous and mysterious Golden Ball, which, like something from a fairy tale,[11] is reputed to grant the wishes of those who "capture" it. The Zone has become Red's last resort, his only hope for a "miracle": "And now this hope—no longer a hope, but confidence in a miracle—filled him to the brim, and he was amazed at how he could have lived for so long in the impenetrable, exitless gloom" (p. 132). His desire to save his family overrides all other moral considerations; he takes with him the son of the man whose life he saved in chapter 2, only in order to use that son as a "minesweeper" to get Red past the "meatgrinder" that guards the Golden Ball. He watches impassively as the boy dances up to the ball, blithely and unsuspectingly incantating a wish for everyone's happiness, watches unmoved as a "transparent emptiness" seizes the boy and breaks him in two. As he rationalizes earlier, it is "either this boy, or my Monkey [his daughter]" (p. 138). At last he approaches the ball, thinking at first only of his family and of revenge: "All right. Monkey, my father. . . . Make them pay for that, steal the bastards' souls, let the sons of bitches eat what I've been eating . . . " (p. 151).

All of a sudden, however, Red draws himself up: "No, that's not it, Red" (p. 151). He begins to rehearse a train of thought which has been nibbling at his resolve throughout this final trip to the Zone. He realizes that life has reduced him, literally and figuratively, to wallowing in "filth," that "there isn't a single clean place left," and that it is the "system" that is somehow at fault (pp. 143–44). He realizes that his "me" against "them" attitude is not even an oversimplification but rather a symptom of moral shortsightedness: "Everything had to be changed. Not one life or two lives, not one fate or two—every link in this rotten, stinking world had to be changed" (p. 149). As he approaches the ball, he realizes that he cannot so readily distinguish between the good guys and the bad guys ("Let all of us be happy and let all of them drop dead. Who is us and who are they?" [p. 152]), but he is sure the socioeconomic order is, at bottom, at fault: "I don't want to work for you, your work makes me puke, do you understand? This is the way I figure it: if a man works with you, he is always working for one of you, he is a slave and nothing else. And I always wanted to be myself, on my own, so I could spit at you all, at your boredom and despair" (p. 152). Determined to put an end to such a system, armed with faint utopian dreams, he addresses the Golden Ball, asks it to look into his heart, to examine his still-human soul, and then utters his "wish": "HAPPINESS FOR EVERYBODY, FREE, AND NO ONE WILL GO AWAY UNSATISFIED!" (p. 153). That is the last line of the novel, so we are not sure whether his wish is granted.[12]

Throughout the novel Red acts as a moral counterweight to the Zone and to the apparatus set up to take advantage of the Zone. Unlike Pilman and Panov, he is not a scientist; he admits that he's not even much of a "thinker" (p. 151). Unlike the people he "hangs out" with (Noonan, Buzzard, etc.), he's a dedicated family man, most of whose actions can be directly related to a desire to serve his family. And unlike the Zone itself, which is indifferent to questions of value, and unlike life in general, which seems to him an "indifferent chaos" (p. 132), Red confronts again and again the issue of good and evil, deals with the problematics of choice. As one critic has noted, Red figures so largely in the novel just because it, like Red himself, is concerned with an attempt to capture "value-centered-ness."[13]

This brings us full circle to the question of *Roadside Picnic* as speculative gadget SF. In the creation of a self-enclosed and mysterious Zone occupied by incomprehensible and frightening objects, the net effect of which defies laws of causality, the Strugatskys have fashioned an image of impersonal technology run wild, of a mentality which divorces moral questions from the instruments it creates. The aliens are "absent" in the novel for good reason; they represent a race of beings that denies any responsibility for its technologies, that sees those technologies as impersonal, value-neutral, beyond good and evil. Csicsery-Ronay has argued convincingly that "the identity of the Visitors is left a mystery primarily because they are not only like us, *they are us*: they are our image of our own future,"[14] a future in which technology has been cut loose from the "subjects" it was designed to serve. In such a future, the very fabric of society will be rent, familial relations sundered, the very stability of the world called into question, as questions of value give way to questions of comfort and acquisitiveness. It may well seem, the Strugatskys suggest, like an alien invasion.

At the same time, through the character of Red, the Strugatsky brothers intimate that such a fate inheres not in science and technology themselves but in the human use of such instrumentalities. Pilman and others may wash their hands of the Zone, claiming that it only goes to show that "we are not alone in the universe" (p. 5), but Red refuses to do so. In the end he approaches the Golden Ball, originally intending to use it to serve his own personal ends, and discovers that what is at the bottom of his heart is the happiness of his fellow humans. He begins by listening to his head, but he ends by following his heart. The Golden Ball episode thus represents the "ultimate expression of the need to compel the tools [of technology] to serve the deepest human desires."[15]

Speculative gadget SF, since it frequently deals with the uses of technology, with the insertion of technology into a social order and the subsequent repercussions, tends to blur the distinction between simple gadget SF and alternate society SF. Such blurring, we have seen, is characteristic of much speculative SF, which tends to be wholistic in its vision and execution. In the case of *Roadside Picnic*, we are shown how the "super" technologies of the future can destroy society as a whole if they are divorced from axiological questions. At one point in the novel, the scientist Pilman makes a distinction between "knowledge" and "understanding" in order to belittle the latter. The "average man," he claims, has no real interest in knowledge, because knowledge entails hard intellectual work. On the contrary, he continues,

> "there is a need to understand, and you don't need knowledge for that. The hypothesis of God, for instance, gives an incomparably absolute op-

portunity to understand everything and know absolutely nothing. Give man an extremely simplified system of the world and explain every phenomenon away on the basis of that system. Any approach like that doesn't require any knowledge." (P. 106)

He thus links "understanding" with anticognitive systems such as religion[16] and dismisses them as an adequate approach to the postindustrial world. But the novel's treatment of Pilman suggests that he represent someone who "knows" everything and "understands" absolutely nothing. Understanding involves the application of a value system to the objects of cognition. In *Roadside Picnic* it is the "average man" Redrick Schuhart who articulates the basis for, and demonstrates the need for, such a system.

3.4 Alternate World SF: Alien Landscapes

Ultimately, of course, it is environment that matters to science fiction, to us, and to the human race.

—James Gunn, cited in Casey Fredericks, *The Future of Eternity*

Science fiction is that class of fiction that focuses upon man's relationship with his environment rather than upon individual psychology.

—Thomas H. Keeling, "Science Fiction and the Gothic"

But though the mere navigation of space was thus easily accomplished, the major task was still untouched. It was necessary either to remake man's nature to suit another planet, or to modify conditions upon another planet to suit man's nature.

—Olaf Stapledon, *Last and First Men*

Our typology of SF transformations involving the "things" of a fictional universe (see chapter 1) identifies two possible levels at which an estrangement can be effectuated—at the micro level of objects in that universe (gadget SF), or at the macro level of the world itself (alternate world SF). Although there seems to be a difference in order of magnitude between the novums of gadget SF and those of alternate world SF, the distinction between the two types is not always so clear. Some critics have, for example, considered the interstellar cruiser Rama in Clarke's novel as an example of a self-contained "world apart" and have tended to read the novel in terms of the encounter between Self and World. I have tried to show (in 3.3.1) how this reading does not do justice to the novel. Rama is, first and foremost, a *tool* designed to perform a specific function, and *Rendezvous with*

Rama is best understood as gadget SF. But how does one categorize a novel such as Larry Niven's *Ringworld*, where the dominant novum is an artificial world, a ring with a radius of the earth's distance from the sun encircling a star, the inner surface of which constitutes an area millions of times greater than Earth's? Clearly, Ringworld is a tool, designed to maximize the amount of habitable space. But the novel *Ringworld* focuses not so much on the "gadget" itself as on the series of adventures that a group of explorers has on its surface. The novel treats its novum as a *world* to be experienced, foregrounds the Self/World encounter, and thus is best approached as alternate world SF.

The prototype for alternate world SF is the *voyage extraordinaire*, the journey to a mysterious and miraculous hidden land, such as Doyle's *The Lost Continent* or Verne's *Mysterious Island*. The emphasis in such fictions is less upon the social order of the new land or the individual psychology of the actants than upon the encounter between trailblazing explorer and the unknown and fabulous terrains. Alternate world SF frequently features a series of adventures unfolding in an alien locale where "no man has gone before." But alternate world SF need not entail a voyage or journey or exploration. Our own Earth can be transformed into an estranged terrain, as happens in some "catastrophe" fiction. In *Lucifer's Hammer* (1977), for example, Larry Niven and Jerry Pournelle recount the struggle of a hardy band of survivors to remake an Earth totally transformed by the impact of a comet which has spawned cataclysmic earthquakes and massive tidal waves. Catastrophe fictions involve the struggle to overcome vicissitudes created by disasters inflicted by the cosmos, nature, or humanity upon our terran environment. What all these fictions have in common is an encounter between an embattled self and a hostile and/or mysterious terrain; they deal with the human attempt to master or come to terms with that terrain. The thematic locus of such fiction is thus the relation between Self and Environment. Alternate world SF explores the possible relations which humans can establish with the environments in which they find themselves.

The fact that many such fictions consist of a series of adventures in which the actants basically struggle to survive perhaps suggests that in terms of thematics not much is really at stake, that these new worlds are designed to provide a number of thrilling challenges, the successful negotiation of which serves primarily sublimative ends. Readers are looking for the satisfactions that derive from all adventure stories, the pleasure of seeing the protagonists survive anything the world "throws" at them. Or, some would argue, the fiction, like other noncognitive SF, can be reduced to an exercise in problem solving. The pleasure of the text resides in anticipating or discovering the solution to a puzzle posed by the alien planet. An example might be Clifford D. Simak's much-anthologized story "Desertion" (1944). The story deals with the attempt to colonize Jupiter, to find some way to make it possible for humans to withstand the incredible pressures on the giant planet's surface and to resist the poisonous and corrosive effects of the planet's methane atmosphere. The solution seems to be the so-called converter, a device able to convert humans into alien forms. Fortunately there exists a native Jovian form capable of handling the pressure and the atmosphere, something that the colonists have called a "loper" because of its shape and movements. So the explorers use the converter to transform humans into lopers and then send them off into the Jovian world. The rub is that they never return. When the story begins, five such "converts" have been mobilized and have disappeared. The mystery, of course, is what happens to them. The implication is that somehow Jupiter is killing them, and Fowler, the leader of the expedition, is accused of using his volunteers as expendable guinea pigs: "You're going to keep on sentencing them to death. . . . You're going to keep marching them out face to face with Jupiter. You're going to sit in here safe and comfortable and send them out to die."[1] Fowler finally decides to be converted himself and to find out once and for all what's happening to his men.

Thomas Clareson refers to "Desertion" as a "classic example of one of the basic sf structural patterns: the solution of a specific problem."[2] This should not be taken to mean that it is merely an intellectual puzzle story (as can be said for many of Asimov's robot stories, considered separately), for the very terms of the puzzle and its solution do entail real cognitive consequences. As Gary Wolfe has tellingly pointed out,[3] at the very heart of "Desertion" lies a serious examination of the proper relations between humanity and the environments of which it seeks to make use. Borrowing his terms from Geza Roheim's anthropological study of primitive and technological cultures, Wolfe identifies two contrastive models for relating to one's environment or for gaining rewards from that environment—"autoplastic" and "alloplastic." By autoplastic adaptation, he refers to the attempt to accommodate one's self to the environment through the modification or manipulation of the human body; this adaptation can take the form of personal disfigurement (as in primitive scarification rites) or simply the protection of the body from the elements (as in the wearing of clothes).

Advanced technological societies, by way of contrast, are generally characterized by "alloplastic" relations with the environment, involving the manipulation of the environment itself (through architecture, engineering, or technology) to make it more amenable to human habitation, as in the construction of heat-generating homes or deforestation for the purposes of agriculture. In terms of SF, autoplastic adaptations manifest themselves in the form of surgical or biogenetic reconstruction of human beings, in the fields of bionics and cyberorganics; alloplastic adaptations figure in the concepts of world-cities, controlled environments, artificial worlds, the question of terraforming, and so on. In simplified terms, these two antinomial sets of relations pose a basic question: Does one alter one's self in order to function or survive in a given environment, or does one transform that environment to conform to the needs of the self? Some people who mistakenly identify SF with a perspective which wholeheartedly endorses the technological appropriation of the universe may well think that the genre answers this question in only one way, but such is not the case, as a return to the story "Desertion" reveals.

It should be clear that the story deals directly with the conflict between autoplastic and alloplastic relations with the external environment. The terran expedition has come to Jupiter in order to make use of the planet's vast resources. If the conversion process works, "the resources of the giant planet would be thrown open. Men would take over Jupiter as they already had taken over the smaller planets" (p. 196). The ultimate objective, then, is alloplastic in nature, the wholesale exploitation of a planet's environmental wealth. In order to accomplish this end, however, the humans must resort to autoplastic means; they must undergo a process of individual metamorphosis simply to survive on the planet. But the solution to the mystery of the five disappearances subverts this hierarchy of values. Determined to find out what has happened to his previous recruits, Fowler has his dog Towser and himself converted into lopers and sent out into the maelstrom of Jupiter. He is not at all ready for what he discovers out there:

> It was not the Jupiter he had known through the televisor. He had expected it to be different, but not like this. He had expected a hell of ammonia rain and stinking fumes and the deafening, thundering tumult of the storm. He had expected swirling clouds and fog and the snarling flicker of monstrous thunderbolts.
> He had not expected that the lashing downpour would be reduced to drifting purple mist that moved like fleeing shadows over a red and purple sward. He had not even guessed the snaking bolts of lightning would be flares of pure ecstasy across a painted sky. (P. 203)

Jupiter, as seen through the loper's eyes, is, in short, a perceptual paradise, full of breathtaking colors, shapes, smells, breezes, and so forth. Fowler discovers also that his loper body is stronger, his loper mind clearer and sharper, than their human counterparts. Since he is using all of his brain (not the measly 10 percent that humans can draw on), he soon comes up with the formula for a metal that can withstand the rigors of Jupiter and thus make purely alloplastic development of the planet possible. But the joy of being fully alive that he experiences in his new body makes going back unthinkable, and so he joins the ranks of the other five "deserters." The story ends with this conversation between Fowler and his dog (with whom Fowler has discovered he can communicate telepathically):

> "I can't go back," said Towser.
> "Nor I," said Fowler.
> "They would turn me back into a dog," said Towser.
> "And me," said Fowler, "back into a man." (P. 208)

Simak suggests that changes to the body, adaptations of the self, can result in a real "conversion" experience, that one can find in such changes a "superior means of achieving integration"[4] with the external world, that it is healthier to adapt the Self to the Environment than to insist upon the wholesale physical appropriation of that Environment.

Alternate world SF which foregrounds the relation between humans and their environment frequently sees that relation in ecological terms, as a system of interlocking and interacting systems, in which changes in one system entail changes in the others, in which there is a real give-and-take between humans and their environments. But alternate world SF also includes those fictions which look at the relation between humanity and its environment in more cosmic terms, focusing on the encounter between humanity and the universe. An example would be Wells's famous short story "The Star" (1897), a catastrophe fiction in which a wandering planet enters the solar system, colliding with Neptune to create an incandescent mass, which then plunges toward the Earth. The near-passage of this body wreaks havoc upon the Earth, the resultant earthquakes, floods, eruptions, and storms killing millions and reducing civilization to a primitive stage. The coda to the story is supplied by Martian astronomers who, tracking the encounter from the perspective of Mars, are truly amazed at "what a little damage the earth, which [the star] missed so narrowly, has sustained." The narrator makes explicit the "moral" for those who've missed it: "Which only shows how small the vastest of human catastrophes may seem, at a distance of a few million miles."[5]

A similar case can be made for another SF classic, Tom Godwin's "The Cold Equations" (1954), in which a girl who stows away aboard an interstellar cruiser must finally be jettisoned because of fuel constraints; Newton's laws of motion dictate that there is just not enough fuel to bring the craft to its destination, given the girl's added mass, and, in such a case, "the laws of the space frontier must, of necessity, be as hard and relentless as the environment that gave them birth."[6] Asimov's classic story "Nightfall" also falls into this category, portraying as it does a planet which experiences total darkness only once a millennium. The novum in each of these stories is an "alternate world" more loosely conceived, an alien terrain governed by natural law with which humans must come to terms. Fictions such as these step back from the "hands-on" encounter between Self and Environment to examine from a cosmic perspective the relation between humanity and the larger universe. As these stories make clear, this form of alternate world SF emphasizes the insignificance of humanity in the larger scheme of things and the impartiality of natural law. These themes, I would argue, are built into the discourse of SF which assumes a value-neutral universe as given (see 1.1).

David Ketterer has argued that most alternate world SF reflects a poverty of the writer's imagination: "As a thousand or more science-fiction writers have demonstrated, our moon or the planets, Mars, Venus, Dune, or Winter, are all envisaged as aspects of Earth. Until quite recently, Venus and Mars, to take the two most clichéd examples, were most typically presented as mirrors of Earth's prehistoric past or catastrophic future."[7] Although much alternate world SF does rely on forms of chronological displacement (extrapolative in mode), not all such worlds are modeled on terran prototypes. In *Mission of Gravity* (1954), for example, Hal Clement posits a disk-shaped planet with a variable gravity from one to seven hundred times Earth normal and then rigorously extrapolates the life forms and the psychology that would be needed to survive on such a planet. The inhabitants of the planet, the Mesklinites, are indeed two-dimensional caricatures of human stereotypes (one good reason why the novel should not be typed as alien encounter SF), but the environment they are situated in offers challenges that are very different from any faced here on Earth.

The case of alternate worlds that are speculative in nature is extremely problematic. At one level, we encounter the example of "living environments" (as in Eric Frank Russell's "Symbiotica" [1938] or Piers Anthony's *Omnivore* [1968]), in which the alien life forms blur the distinction between environmental Other and sentient Other; these fictions can often be read as alternate world SF, as alien encounter SF, or as alternate society SF, depending on how the novum is treated, as a living environment, an individual being, or a group being. Such ambiguity, I would argue, is built into any fictional universe which erases the lines between Self, Society, and World in the creation of its novum.

At another level we have those fictions in which the external universe figures at one and the same time as environment to be encountered and as a projection of the self that does the encountering. The "New Wave" fictions of J. G. Ballard, for example, present us with landscapes which are apparently extrapolative in nature—a "drowned" world, a "crystal" world, and so on—but which "turn" speculative in the course of the fiction. These landscapes become analogues for states of mind under duress, metaphors for psychic realities, extensions of the human mind; in this way these fictions convert the naturalistic encounter with the environment into a surrealistic encounter with the buried Self. Linked with such worlds are the "split reality" novels of writers such as Philip Dick, in which the worlds projected by drugs, dreams, or death are given the same ontological status as the empirical world; they have their own reality and their own rules. These novels feature the ontological collision between one world and the next and thus undercut the assumption that "reality" is monolithic; they suggest that the distinction between subjective and objective realities is specious, that empirical science cannot comprehend the whole picture. The dream landscapes of Ballard and the split-reality novels of Dick thus tend toward "science fantasy" (see chapter 4). Indeed, speculative alternate world SF, built as it is on new assumptions about the nature of a world itself, continually frustrates easy classification. Since these worlds are built on a wholesale re-vision of the relation between Self and Environment, since they call into question the status of natural law, since they dwell on basic ontological questions, they occupy a middle ground between SF and science fantasy, confirming Lem's assertion that sometimes the most interesting cases are indeed those that resist classification.

3.4.1 Extrapolative Alternate World SF:
Benford and Brin's *Heart of the Comet*

Man's destiny was to modify his environment. To go on modifying it increasingly. Man must become his own environment.

—Ian Watson, *The Martian Inca*

But what about *changing* the Earthbreed animals . . . altering them to fit into this strange environment?
He knew it hadn't been attempted. Nobody else had the skill—or the arrogance—to try it. Already his mind was turning over ideas, genes of expression and regulation, ways of adapting creatures to work *with* an alien environment instead of against it.

—Gregory Benford and David Brin, *Heart of the Comet*

In *Heart of the Comet*, Gregory Benford and David Brin tell the story of some four hundred explorers who try to colonize Halley's comet during its next pass through the solar system in 2061. Like all those who seek out new worlds (including those who do so within the pages of a piece of fiction), these men and women are motivated by a number of reasons— escape, diversion, pleasure, and profit. More specifically, the explorers of Halley come out for the new knowledge which can be gained from a body created from the original matter of space; they come out to see if they can use the comet and its frozen water in the seeding of other planets; they come out to test the "sleep slots" which will enable them to survive their seventy-six-year cruise through the solar system; they come out for the financial rewards they will accrue during that period (most of which time will be spent sleeping); they come out just because the comet is *there*, luring men on; and they come out to show that by working together, humans can overcome the most daunting challenges, can "rise above superstition and prejudice" and in so doing overcome "the fundamental hostility of the universe."[1] What they experience during the expedition, however, while it doesn't negate these motivations, certainly frustrates the colonists' expectations.

Their main antagonists, they presume, will be those inhering in space itself, the "unremitting hostility of the hard empty cold" (p. 383) and the amounts of time necessary to negotiate its vast expanses. The cryogenic sleep slots are designed to handle the latter problem; the former will be dealt with by a system of "orderly tunnels and rooms" (p. 5) excavated within the comet's interior. That this remaking of the cometary environment for human purposes will be dangerous is made clear at the very beginning; the novel opens with the violent accidental deaths of two construction workers soon after rendezvous with the comet. Another forty members of the mission are at the same time lost forever to the depths of space when their ship *Newburn* fails to make that rendezvous. But the well-laid plans of the humans are most jeopardized and sabotaged by one factor they could not anticipate, the fact that Halley has lifeforms of its own, forms which thrive in the waves of heat generated by the human attempt to reshape the comet. The forms at first are limited to harmless mosslike "lichenoids" which cover the walls of the tunnels. But this "green gunk" (p. 131) serves as fodder for the more dangerous purple worms which penetrate crevices in the human habitation system and prove to feed on almost anything organic, including humans. Even more threatening, however, are the myriad Halley microorganisms which infiltrate the human body and interfere with the immune system. Halley turns out to be a honeycombed hive of lifeforms which are so compatible with terran lifeforms that they make for an extremely "hostile biological environment" (p. 259).

The original plan to remake Halley into a neat and sterile laboratory for human investigators gives way to an ongoing war between lifeforms competing for survival. The colonists' first reaction to Halley forms is predictably murderous, a simple function of "us" versus "them." But the Halley forms are both hardy and adaptable, and the humans seem fated to lose inevitably a lengthy war of attrition. The struggle is all the more complicated by the fact that certain members of the expedition have serious moral qualms about it. Saul Lintz, the biologist/doctor who ultimately "saves" the expedition, voices that position as follows: "A part of him wondered if it was morally legitimate to go looking for ways to fight the indigenous lifeforms that were causing the spacers such grief. After all, Earthmen were the invaders here" (p. 127). Some of the crew eventually go "over" to the Halley side, turning on their fellow humans: "Leave it, leave it, leave it *be*! You killers! *You're* the aliens here!" (p. 29).

It is on this issue, the question of the proper relation between humans and the Halley environment they have imposed themselves on, that the novel really turns. This issue is figured most forcefully in the factionalism that exists in the crew from the very start. The crew consists of two human "types": normal human beings, or "Orthos"; and "Percells," humans that have been genetically altered by a gene-correcting program invented by Simon Percell. On Earth, it seems that there is considerable hostility between the two groups, such that the Orthos, who hold the numerical upper hand, are systematically discriminating against the Percells in matters such as reproductive rights. Indeed, the Halley expedition, one-third of which is Percell, hopes to "prove to those on Earth that so-called Orthos and so-called Percells, living and working together on a long and dangerous mission, can rely on each other simply as fellow human beings, and bring home great discoveries to benefit all mankind" (p. 76). But the crew brings with it the resentment between the two groups, a resentment fueled by the fact that Orthos hold all the positions of command and the fact that the Percells prove more resistant to cometary diseases than unmodified human beings.

The Orthos and Percells are also divided by a difference of opinion in regard to the ultimate fate of the mission. The Percells, "living reminders of the arrogance of twentieth-century northern science" (p. 47), which squandered resources in its attempt to remake the world and refashion humanity, tend to take an activist position about the comet; they want to put it in orbit around Jupiter or use it as a source of water with which to "terraform" Mars. Their radical faction, the *Ubers* (short for *Ubermenschen*), who see themselves as "Nietzsche's supermen, evolution's ordained next step" (p. 69), and refuse to compromise with unmodified human beings, want to leave the inner solar system entirely and create a Percell colony of supermen in orbit around Neptune. Ironically, then, the Percells, themselves products of autoplastic adaptation, advocate alloplastic exploitation of the comet.

The Orthos, on the other hand, represent a much more conservative attitude toward the possibilities presented by Halley. On Earth they are associated with the "Movement to Restore and Reflect" (p. 19), an environmental group trying to offset the damage done to Nature during the previous "Hell Century," which witnessed the destruction of a third of the Earth's species (p. 48). Their radical members, the Arcists (drawn from the equatorial peoples in the "Arc of the Sun"), take a fanatical attitude against interference with the works of nature, shun the Percells because they (the Percells) are genetically "unclean," and want "above all costs to keep Earth pristine and safe from Halley contamination" (pp. 328–29). In order to preserve Earth's precious biosphere, they are willing, if necessary, to destroy the comet and commit suicide in deep space. The Arcists thus represent a commitment to autoplastic extinction if necessary to avoid alloplastic catastrophe. Caught in the middle between the two factions and their respective extremes are the experienced spacers, most of whom are interested mainly in achieving "Plateau Three," extensive exploration and exploitation of the solar system, through all available means, including wholesale terraforming using comets for their volatiles. When confronted with dangers presented by the Halley lifeforms, this group's main concern is simply to survive (p. 332), whatever that might take. In sum, then, the Halley expedition had hoped to rise above "those stupid Earthside fights" (p. 36) but fails; as Carl Osborn, the spacer Percell who in time becomes leader of the mission, thinks, "No, Halley was all too representative of humanity" (p. 263).

The Halley mission thus wages war on two fronts, one involving human lifeforms versus alien lifeforms, the other pitting humans against humans.

This state of antagonism is reflected in the very design of the comet, which calls for neat little human enclosures separate from the comet, for a set of walls and partitions between the humans and the phenomenon they are studying. In time these enclosed spaces become enclaves, isolated head-quarters for the various clans which develop out of the ongoing cometary debate: "Making her way here this afternoon, she [Virginia Herbert, the computer expert of the mission] had been struck by how the expedition was like this—separate rooms, immensely powerful ideas sealed off from each other, all contributing but each isolated. Men and women pocketed into cylinders and cubes and spheres" (p. 57). The main action of *Heart of the Comet* involves the breaking down of barriers previously conceived of as insurmountable. One of the pieces of technology that make the mission possible in the first place is the cryogenic sleep slots, which in effect bridge the gap between life and death. When entombed in the freezing-cold "cof-fins" stored in the excavated vaults, the "sleepers were as near to dead as you could get and still come back" (p. 66). These slots serve as a model in the novel for the kinds of mediation and forms of integration that develop between presumably antinomial sets of pairs—life and death, natural and artificial, biological and technological, human and alien.

The fate of Virginia Herbert, the computer specialist, serves as a model for this process of mediation. Herbert brings along with her, as part of her weight allowance, a "bio-organic computer," a machine "that might really think," a line of cybernetic development that had been spurned by "in-creasingly conservative twenty-first-century science" (p. 27). She has named her unit JonVon, after John Von Neumann, inventor of the theory of games. Through direct mind-machine interface, she is able to link up with JonVon, to add to his programming, even to transfer to the machine the motor skills she uses to control the "mechs" who do the mechanical work on the comet. Virginia develops a personal and intimate relationship with JonVon, who, she realizes, is "midway between humans and silicon computers in his information processing," a circumstance that leads to "unexpected capabilities" (p. 191). Finally, when an accident incurred dur-ing an armed conflict with radical *Ubers* threatens Virginia's life, her entire mind and personality are transferred into the computer, and the first mem-ber of the species Biocybernetic Man comes into being:

> To use the jargon of science, she was a new phylum, no longer a vertebrate but biocybernetic. She was a wedding of the organic and the electronic, with a dash of sapient consciousness. By strict definition, a phylum should emerge through evolution by sexual gene sorting and speciation. But once intelligence had appeared, that aeons-long process was outmoded. A new phylum could emerge and develop by design. (P. 476)

From one perspective, then, Virginia represents an extreme form of de-liberate autoplastic adaptation to the environment, the marriage of Self and

Machine and the creation of a new mode of being, something at once human and suprahuman:

> Yet she was more. The joy that Carl and Lani felt brought her occasional pangs; Saul's wistful nostalgia for her embodiment gave real pain. But though she understood and felt all this, she came to see it as a subset of the larger issues that confronted her. These frail people were bound up in the true passing life that the laws of natural selection had decreed—their deaths were written into their bones. . . . They felt deeply and thought upon the mortal questions. (P. 476)

Virginia's new phylum is no longer caught up in the "mortal questions." Indeed, her very existence proves that the laws of natural selection, the mechanisms that generate adaptive adjustments, no longer work entirely randomly. In Virginia's case they are directed by human intelligence, and the result is something that is "not strictly human any longer" (p. 476).

A parallel process, though one with a very different outcome, affects the other members of the Halley mission. The prime mover[2] of this other process is Saul Lintz, resident biologist of the mission and former colleague of Simon Percell. In order to deal with the levels of hydrogen cyanide to be encountered on Halley, Lintz had fashioned, back on Earth, the cyanute, "a wonder—a new human symbiont" (p. 15). The cyanute, which lives in the human bloodstream, has all the qualities that will make it possible for members of the expedition to survive on Halley: "*self-limiting reproduction, benign acceptance by the human immune system, pH sensitivity, a voracious appetite for other potential cometary toxins* . . . " (pp. 14–15, italics in original). Cyanutes are thus a form of autoplastic adaptation. But Saul is concerned not only with the health of humans but also with that of the human symbionts. He sees human beings "not as individuals . . . but as great synergistic hives of cooperating species" (p. 19). Confronted by the menacing Halley lifeforms, Saul responds at first in a schizophrenic manner; part of him wants to play the "caveman" and destroy on sight all xenological lifeforms, but the "philosopher" in him recognizes that the humans are the invading aliens here, "killing what they did not understand" (p. 180). There are, in effect, two options available to the colonists, one alloplastic, the other autoplastic. They can exterminate all forms of Halley life and "terraform" the comet into an Earth in miniature. Or they can allow Halley life to overwhelm them, either killing them in the process or transforming them into the crazed, subhuman "moss-men" (p. 186) who lurk in the nether caverns of the comet. Eventually Saul realizes, however, that there is a third alternative, one not predicated on two-value logic or forms of parasitism, one modeled on the very process that enables the colonists to survive on Halley—namely, symbiosis.

A key step in Saul's evolving view of the mission's relation to Halley involves his redefinition of the concept "disease": "Disease is not a *war* between species. More often, it is a case of *failed negotiation*" (p. 296). In order to facilitate such negotiation, he begins to tailor new sets of symbionts which absorb the Halley lifeforms and to put them to work for human beings, in the process enabling both species to survive and thrive. The colonists of Halley become quite literally that, colony organisms consisting of mutually supportive lifeforms. At the human level, the net result is the evolution of "cometary man" (p. 478), a creature who lives in a condition of "growing synergism" with its external environment. At the cometary level, we witness the conversion of an astral body into the "first starship" (p. 469), as the colonists realize that return to Earth is impossible, given their newly evolved forms, and pilot the comet out of the solar system toward the ice asteroids in the Oort Cloud. The hard and fast distinction between invader and invaded, human form and Halley form, Self and Environment, has been dissolved:

> [Carl] felt Virginia around them all, sensed the entire community of Halley as a matrix threaded through the ancient ice. They were no longer buried inside, going for a ride. No Percells, no Orthos. They were a new, beleaguered society, a new way for a versatile primate to stretch further, to be more than it was. They were not merely in the center of the old dead ice, they were the heart of the comet. (P. 458)

And when his wife Lani insists, "We're all Halley," Carl can only respond, "Yeah, I suppose we are" (p. 458).

Early in the novel, one of the more idealistic objectives of the mission is spelled out as overcoming "that fear of *otherness* that has caused such hatred and horror from time immemorial" (p. 76). At first the colonists almost completely fail at that undertaking. Fear of the other pits Orthos against Percells in a series of internecine wars that nearly destroy the mission. Fear of the other, in the form of Halley lifeforms, exacerbates the factionalism in the crew, creating an atmosphere of paranoia in which the Environment is seen mainly in terms of the dangers with which it threatens the Self. But in the course of the novel, terms of opposition are reconceived, the disease infecting the expedition is redefined as "failed negotiation," and forms of mediation between Self and Other, at both the human and the environmental level, take the place of unremitting hostility. In time a "new ecosystem" is evolved, and the "heart of the comet" comes into being.

Heart of the Comet assumes that it is not other environments or other lifeforms that humanity must fear and contend with, but rather "the unremitting hostility of the hard empty cold" of space (p. 383), that the main struggle involves "fragile, organic life against the enclosing chill" (p. 432). In such a conflict, lifeforms of all sorts are not natural enemies but natural allies. This is brought home most forcefully in the solution to the final Halley mystery, the source of Halley life and the reason for its miraculous compatibility with human lifeforms. The discovery of more and more basic protolife forms in the very center of the comet reveals that Halley coalesced around the fragments of another life-bearing planet from a system which had gone nova, the same planet which, Saul speculates, seeded life on Earth millions of years before:

> Or were the old stories of comet-borne disasters really true? Could it be that the Earth had always been "freshened," from time to time, with new doses of the ancient biology, floating down into the atmosphere each time a comet passed close by? That would help explain why the lifeforms were so compatible. Earth's life kept incorporating new bits and pieces from the storehouse of deep space. (P. 473)

At one point, Saul, overwhelmed by the multiplicity of Halley lifeforms, thinks to himself that "life might be a driver in the evolution of worlds, rather than a simple passive passenger, shoved about by the rude winds of astronomical fate" (pp. 202–203). The coincidental seeding of both Earth and Halley tends at once to subvert that theory, by turning the existence of life into an accident caused by the "rude winds of astronomical fate," and at the same time to support that theory, by making it possible for life to control its environment rather than remaining a "passive passenger." The point is that, once life is given a foothold on a world, it can indeed become the "driver," integrating itself with that world and other lifeforms. *Heart of the Comet* thus stands the evolutionary paradigm on its head by suggesting that life need not be at the mercy of either environmental conditions or competing species, that life, granted a bit of "sapient consciousness," can enter into symbiotic relations with its surroundings.

3.4.2 Speculative Alternate World SF: Ballard's *The Drowned World*

The only truly alien planet is Earth.

—J. G. Ballard, cited by Aldiss, "The Wounded Land: J. G. Ballard"

The setting is important only as it impinges upon the protagonist.

—Joanna Russ, "On Setting"

In the 1960s, J. G. Ballard wrote a series of catastrophe novels—*The Drowned World* (1962), *The Wind from Nowhere* (1962), *The Drought* (1965), and *The Crystal World* (1966)—each of which depicts an apocalyptic future based upon an imbalance triggered in an "elemental" force (respectively, water, air, fire, and earth). The four novels concern themselves less with the catastrophic forces involved than with the "psychic transformation"[1] brought about in the actants who must come to terms with the alien environments created by those forces. These novels have been criticized for their failure to supply a convincing scientific rationale for the phenomena on which they rely so heavily. As H. Bruce Franklin says, "there is often no consistent explanation of why the cataclysm is occurring other than some vague pseudo-scientific theory, presented like a magician's patter and perhaps offered to satisfy the conventional expectations of the readers of science fiction."[2] Ballard's work has also been castigated, by Lem among others, for its cognitive pessimism, for its absolute refusal to admit the possibility of change for the better, for its antiscientism: "Only in mankind's severe, resolute rejection of all chances of development, in complete negation, in a gesture of escapism or nihilism, do [writers such as Ballard] find the proper mission of all science fiction that would not be cheap."[3] Given Ballard's failure to motivate his worlds in any rigorously scientific way, given his systematic rejection of scientific progress and cognitive optimism, given his programmatic obliteration of the clear-cut distinction between external landscape and psychic mindscape, some critics question whether his work should even be considered "real" SF: "Such works may be apocalyptic in a psychedelic or surrealistic sense, but in many cases where the science-fictional landscape has the ontological status of metaphor, I would deny that they belong to the genre of science fiction."[4] These criticisms, though somewhat harsh, contain a measure of truth. And this is so, I would argue, because of the very nature or kind of world building Ballard does. The speculative re-vision of a landscape, the creation of a dramatically alien world, necessarily calls into question fundamental assumptions about the nature of the world and the relation between Self and World, assumptions that are integral to pure SF, the problematization of which results in the obliteration of neat generic boundaries. In order to explore this generic confusion, I propose to look in some detail at what most critics see as Ballard's strongest SF novel, *The Drowned World*.

The catastrophe which creates the "drowned world" rests on a firmer scientific footing than those in other Ballard novels (e.g., *The Wind from Nowhere* or *The Crystal World*). A period of unprecedented solar flares causes the mean temperatures on Earth to rise steadily over a period of years. The increase not only makes the equatorial regions uninhabitable, it also begins to melt the polar ice caps, the resultant flooding and silting reshaping the entire geography of Earth and turning the northern cities into flooded lagoons. The survivors of the catastrophe, who have relocated northward and southward and created settlements in the only habitable regions, the North and South Poles, now explore these drowned regions, recording climatological changes and the appearance of new life forms. The solar storms, it seems, have burned away parts of the ionosphere, and the resultant higher levels of radiation have increased the rate of occurrence of mutated life forms. Mammalian fertility has declined, reptilian and amphibian forms have thrived, and the Earth apparently is reverting to the "terrifying jungles of the Paleocene,"[5] the period when the great reptiles roamed the planet. As Kerans, the protagonist, sums up, "one could simply say that in response to the rises in temperature, humidity and radiation levels the flora and fauna of this planet are beginning to assume once again the forms they displayed the last time such conditions were present— roughly speaking, the Triassic period" (p. 41).

There is nothing particularly radical, or speculative, about a prehistoric world, which is, after all, the product of a backward extrapolation in time. Other writers (Verne and Doyle, for example) have employed such worlds as an arena for a series of heroic adventures. What makes Ballard's use of a prehistoric world distinctive is the relation he posits between that world and its human inhabitants. Ballard assumes, for the purposes of all his catastrophe novels, that geological and biological forces work in concert. Changes in the external environment bring about not only the appearance of primeval life forms but also, in humans, physiological changes and profound "psychic transformations." Kerans, for example, suffers from a "chronic lack of appetite" (p. 11) that gives him the look of an ascetic; in the course of the novel, he becomes more and more indolent, with fewer waking hours. He discovers that his metabolism slows down gradually, enabling him to deal with the overwhelming heat. But more important than the physical changes are the psychological changes. Kerans at first assumes that he is undergoing a personality change (p. 11), becoming more introverted and withdrawn, beginning to act without full awareness of his motives. He soon realizes that these are just symptoms of a more fundamental transformation:

> This growing isolation and self-containment, exhibited by other members of the unit . . . , reminded Kerans of the slackening metabolism and biological withdrawal of all animal forms about to undergo a major metamorphosis. Sometimes he wondered what zone of transit he himself was entering, sure that his own withdrawal was symptomatic not of a dormant schizophrenia, but of a careful preparation for a radically new environment, with its own internal landscape and logic, where old categories of thought would merely be an encumbrance. (P. 14)

The "radically new environment" brings about complex psychological changes in Kerans and others, a "metamorphosis" that is accounted for in chapter 3, significantly titled "Towards a New Psychology." In the chapter, one of Kerans's scientific colleagues explains that the movement backward in geophysical time has triggered a similar reversion or regression in psychic time, driving the subconscious mind back through the oldest memories and fears that are imprinted there: "we are now being plunged back into the archaeopsychic past, uncovering the ancient taboos and drives that have been dormant for epochs" (p. 43). The swamps and lagoons of the new landscape seem familiar just because they are imprinted on the "total memory" of the race:

"The innate releasing mechanisms laid down in your cytoplasm millions of years ago have been awakened, the expanding sun and the rising temperature are driving you back down the spinal levels into the drowned seas submerged beneath the lowest layers of your unconscious, into the entirely new zone of the neuronic psyche. . . . We really *remember* these swamps and lagoons." (P. 72)

This descent into "deep time" manifests itself in the form of "jungle dreams" (p. 49), which Kerans first experiences in chapter 5. In the recurrent dream, which all the "time-travellers" share, there is a gigantic drumming sun looming over a jungle-encircled lagoon. The drumming of the sun, which coincides with the dreamer's heartbeat, increases in intensity as the sun draws nearer, bringing enormous Triassic lizards to the lagoon's edge, where they roar in unison at the sun, the whole scene having a mesmerizing effect on the dreamer, drawing him into the lake, "whose waters now seemed an extension of his own bloodstream" (p. 69). The recurrence of the dream reinforces the descent into "neuronic time": "Guided by his dreams, [Kerans] was moving backwards through the emergent past, through a succession of ever stranger landscapes, centred upon the lagoon, each of which, as Bodkin had said, seemed to represent one of his own spinal levels" (pp. 82–83).

Kerans and the others thus experience a psychic descent through "total time" or "cosmic time" that serves to bring into being a one-to-one correspondence between external, physical landscapes and internal, mental landscapes. There are, in effect, at least two "drowned worlds"—the watery world of the environment and the submerged regions of the psyche—and adapting to the former entails descending into the latter, where the "archaic sun" burns in the mind, "illuminating the fleeting shadows that darted fitfully through its profoundest depths" (p. 29). As Franklin notes, the relationship between humanity and environment is reciprocal: "Just as the drowned planet projects an inner landscape, so the body and psyche of the protagonist recapitulate in microcosm the world of nature."[6]

This reciprocity justifies to some extent Ballard's oft-quoted claim that in his fictions the exploration of "outer space" is really an investigation of "inner space," a point that *The Drowned World* makes explicit in the scene in which Kerans, outfitted in diving gear, is said to resemble "the man from inner space" (p. 102).[7] This equation of "outer space" and "inner space," this equivalence between external and internal landscapes, if taken too far, tends to reduce the novel to that form of fantasy or horror fiction that deals with dreams and hallucinations, where there is no objective reality and everything must be read in metaphoric terms. This sort of reading eventually collapses all of Ballard's catastrophe novels into variations on a single theme, the idea that all catastrophes can be seen as literal or figurative projections of the deranged modern psyche. Or it invites the superimposition of allegory, as when *The Drowned World* is read as sug-

gesting that all civilization rests tenuously on the swamps of the unconscious. The point is that *The Drowned World* is best read as the limit case
of alien landscape SF, where a "radically new environment, with its own
internal landscape and logic," an environment which is ontologically present and chronologically prior, triggers a "major metamorphosis" (p. 14) in
the actants who inhabit it.

The novel makes an overt issue of the relationship between actant and
environment by presenting, in the form of the three main male actants,
three different responses to the external environment. Kerans is initially
paired with Colonel Riggs, his military colleague who is in charge of the
expedition. Riggs, an exemplum of "self-discipline and single-minded-
ness" (p. 61), proves to be immune to the "spell" exerted by the drowned
world, seeing the whole situation as something calling for "damage control." He, Kerans notes, apparently does not experience the jungle dream,
does not feel "its immense hallucinatory power," since all his actions reveal
that he is "still obeying reason and logic" (p. 73). He is the one who still
"dresses for dinner," who tries to prevent Hardeman from moving south
to the heart of the drowned world, who arranges for the expedition's retreat
northward when rising temperatures and impending storms make staying
unfeasible, who rescues Kerans from certain death at the hands of the
freebooter Strangman in the second half of the novel. A man of action who
advocates coping with the external world, Riggs comes to represent, ironically enough, as Kerans's lover, Beatrice, says, "a total lack of adaptability"
(p. 78) to that world.

When Riggs and the rest of the expedition withdraw to the north, Kerans
and a couple of others similarly immersed in neuronic time cut their ties
with the group in order to remain behind in the "zone of transit," where
they are "assimilating [their] own biological pasts" (p. 90). This period of
introspection is interrupted by the arrival of the "pirate" Strangman, who
leads his black crew through the lagoons of the drowned world looting
and pillaging the abandoned cities. Although repelled by this man, his
white toothy smile and unnaturally white skin (which together create a
skeleton effect), Kerans is nonetheless drawn to him, sensing that the pirate
serves some kind of "neuronic role, . . . holding a warning mirror up to
Kerans and obliquely cautioning him about the future he had chosen" (p.
114). As Strangman himself says to Kerans later, "I'm obviously bringing
you back to the present" (p. 117). This he tries to accomplish in part by
arranging to have one of the lagoons drained, inverting Kerans's "normal
world" and "turning the once limpid beauty of the underwater city into a
drained and festering sewer" (p. 119). If Riggs represents a (twentieth-
century) frame of mind that seeks to contain the environment, cohabit with
Nature, then Strangman represents a (nineteenth-century) posture that
seeks to dominate the environment in order to plunder it; Strangman is,
as Franklin observes, "an avatar of the man of power, pride, will, and
egoism who seeks to conquer nature."[8] Both men represent the old order,

one which is not equipped to confront the "real realities" of the drowned world. Strangman is, as his crew members superstitiously believe, a dead man; Riggs becomes, as Kerans notes, the real "time-traveller" (p. 155), the intruder in a world he never made.

Kerans, it should be clear, occupies another position on the spectrum of possible relations with the environment, one that compounds the problem of keeping the inner and outer landscapes distinct. For Kerans, the drowned world comes to fill "a complex of neuronic needs that were impossible to satisfy by any other means" (p. 127). Strangman explains Kerans's near-drowning in the submerged planetarium as a failed suicide: "[Kerans] *wanted* to become part of the drowned world" (p. 110). In a figurative, and perhaps literal, way, this is true. Jolted out of his indolence by his encounter with Strangman, Kerans realizes that he must now abandon the cities entirely and go south, the "only direction," he informs Riggs, into the heart of this new world:

> His time [in the city] had outlived itself, and the air-supplied suite with its constant temperature and humidity, its supplies of fuel and food, were nothing more than an encapsulated form of his previous environment, to which he had clung like a reluctant embryo to its yolk sac. The shattering of this shell . . . was the necessary spur to action, to his emergence into the brighter day of the interior, archaeopsychic sun. Now he would have to go forward. Both the past, represented by Riggs, and the present contained within the demolished penthouse, no longer offered a viable existence. His commitment to the future, so far one of choice and plagued by so many hesitations and doubts, was now absolute. (Pp. 144–45)

The novel ends with Kerans on the move, "following the lagoons southward through the increasing rain and heat, attacked by alligators and giant bats, a second Adam searching for the forgotten paradises of the reborn sun" (p. 170).

As the last two quotes indicate, the ending of the novel to a certain extent invites a positive reading, one stressing the recurrent motif of rebirth, or the image of Adam and new paradises. Kerans's journey south has been seen as a "kind of holy pilgrimage," the quest for a "magical zone in which the distinction between man and nature, between Kerans' tortured consciousness and the abyss of the infinite that is at once inside and outside mankind, ceases to exist."[9] Since, as Kerans's colleague notes, the "uterine odyssey of the growing foetus recapitulates the entire evolutionary past," to move backward in geophysical time is to enter the "amnionic corridor," to return, in effect, to the womb in order to be reborn as a second Adam in the "forgotten paradises of the reborn sun." But, at the same time, Kerans's odyssey to the south is clearly suicidal, and so must be seen as a function of the "death instinct, masked as a desire to return to the amniotic state of pre-natal consciousness."[10] Kerans poses this possibility to himself in the form of a question: "Was the drowned world itself, and the mysterious quest for the south . . . no more than an impulse to suicide, an unconscious acceptance of the logic of his own devolutionary descent, the ultimate neuronic synthesis of the archaeopsychic zero?" (p. 111). In the note that he leaves behind at the very end of the novel, Kerans says that he is "moving south" and that "all is well" (p. 171), but he himself acknowledges that he "might not long survive the massive unbroken jungles to the south" (p. 171). Is his a quest for suicide or salvation? The ending of the novel refuses to answer this question, holding the two possibilities in solution, as it were, "in a manner which does not permit them to be disambiguated from one another, or (in that sense) resolved."[11]

Ambiguities proliferate in *The Drowned World.* The fact that Kerans's final journey might be either a quest for transcendence or a submission to the death instinct, that dream worlds have more ontological presence than empirical worlds, that the resurrected city of the drained lagoon is in some sense a "nightmare world" (p. 156), that the entire novel confuses the distinction between internal and external landscapes—these facts serve to foreground the whole issue of sanity, of the proper or correct or "normal" way of perceiving reality. When Kerans insists that the drained lagoon must be reflooded, the "sane" Riggs can only respond, "Robert, you really are out of touch with reality" (p. 155). Conversely, Riggs's behavior seems mad to Kerans. *The Drowned World* does indeed offer to its readers the spectacle of conflicting realities, of worlds in collision, of "two interlocking worlds apparently suspended at some junction in time" (p. 10). Kerans admits that he is withdrawing from "the normal world of space and time" (p. 15). From this perspective, the "single plane of time on which Strangman and his men existed seemed so transparent as to have a negligible claim to reality" (p. 95). The novel stages for us the collision between "the shifting planes of dissonant realities millions of years apart" (p. 127). In so doing, it calls into question the idea that reality itself is single, monolithic, or matter-of-fact. For Ballard, then, as Robert Platzner notes, "the psychophysical conditions of life we term 'reality' are just so many fortuitous arrangements," and the "proper function of catastrophe . . . is to expose the essential arbitrariness of those arrangements and of the certitudes they have spawned."[12]

This questioning of reality, this ontological probing, is necessarily built into alternate world SF. Alternate world SF in the speculative mode tends to explore what it is that constitutes world-ness, where it is that the Self stops and the World begins, what rules or laws obtain in the operations of that world; in this respect it is very like science fantasy (see chapter 4), which is not really surprising since both forms "play" with or invert essential components of a fictional universe. And so, as we have seen, speculative SF in general tends to blur, obliterate, or cross over the lines separating the "pure" SF types. This "mongrelization," I would argue, is inherent in the very act of speculation which, because it is based on metaphoric substitution at the "deep structure" level, acts upon the worlds it transforms in a radically wholistic way.

As we have seen in other cases of speculative SF, this mode of world building tends to call into question some of the basic assumptions informing both the scientific epistemology and the discourse of SF. Turning back to *The Drowned World*, we see that Kerans's journey to the forgotten paradises of the reborn sun, his attempt to become *part* of the drowned world, to merge with that world, obviates the usefulness of the autoplastic/alloplastic distinction. In *The Drowned World* there is no question of willfully acting on or adapting Self and World. Here we experience the radical submission of Self to World, a submission that interrogates the instrumentality of the human will in relation to the external environment. In this way Ballard repudiates the distinction between subject and object on which the scientific method rests. The novel thus challenges one of the fundamental tenets of empiricism and positivism. By harking back to the possibility of a more "primitive" relation with the external world, one in which boundaries are not fixed but fluid (cf. title), the novel at once problematizes science and proposes the desirability of a more "mystical," one might say religious, relation with the world outside. In this respect, the novel has much in common with science fantasy, to which we now turn our attention.

IV

SCIENCE FANTASY

Without faith that nature is subject to law, there can be no science.

—Norbert Wiener, *The Human Use of Human Beings*

"But I was leading up to the subject of 'natural law.' Is not the invariability of natural law an unproved assumption? Even on Earth?"

—Robert Heinlein, *Glory Road*

In chapter 3, we considered the various SF types generated by the insertion of a novum into the system of actants, social order, or topography making up the fictional world. Actants, social system, and topography all presuppose an operative system of natural laws. These laws remain consistent and universal in all SF proper. Indeed, a belief in their existence and discoverability is built into the genre's ontology; the discourse of the genre is rooted in an acceptance of natural law and faith in the scientific epistemology. The final form of world transformation, involving as it does the universal natural laws subtending the genre and the assumptions informing its discourse, results in an "impure" SF form called *science fantasy*. Science fantasy is predicated upon an estrangement of the "laws" upon which an SF world rests, upon the reversal of natural law or the contravention of the scientific epistemology. Since faith in natural law and the scientific epistemology is a distinguishing feature of SF, this sort of estrangement converts the form into *fantasy*.

If there is a critical consensus about the nature of fantasy, it is that fantasy in some way violates the conventional norms of possibility.[1] As S. C. Fredericks says, fantasy writers "take as *their point of departure* the deliberate violation of norms and facts we regard as essential to our conventional conception of 'reality,' in order to create an imaginary counter-structure or counter-norm."[2] It should be stressed that this contravention of possibility is deliberate and conscious; fantasy is informed by an attitude that "admits fabulous and supernatural beings (other than God) have no objective existence while at the same time insisting that art has the right to invoke and describe such beings."[3] The worlds of fantasy are under no obligation to be faithful to a scientific epistemology. In such worlds various forms of magic can govern relations between human and natural realms, without any scientific motivation or rationale. Science fiction, on the other hand, because it accepts the dictates of scientific necessity, attempts to make its worlds conform to the norms of scientific possibility. As Mark Rose has noted, "by invoking the scientific ethos to assert the possibility of the fictional worlds it describes, science fiction differentiates itself from fantasy."[4]

These two genres, SF and fantasy, do have a locus of intersection, science fantasy, an unstable hybrid form combining features from each subgenre. Authors, critics, even booksellers acknowledge that this hybrid form exists, but they have been at a loss to define it in any systematic way. The most substantial definition is Brian Attebury's contribution to the *Dictionary of Literary Biography*. He sees science fantasy as a heterogeneous category composed of anomalous cases which don't quite fit into the "two well-defined categories, science fiction and fantasy,"[5] and proceeds to examine those anomalous cases. Gary Wolfe's entry in his SF and fantasy glossary admits that the term is "rather imprecise" but refers to it as a genre "in which devices of fantasy are employed in a 'science-fictional' context."[6] The science fantasy author Gene Wolfe says that "a science fantasy story is one in which the means of science are used to achieve the spirit of fantasy."[7] William Atheling, Jr. (SF author James Blish), sees the form in a negative light; he calls it "a kind of hybrid in which plausibility is specifically invoked for most of the story, but may be cast aside in patches at the author's whim and according to no visible system or principle."[8] Echoing Atheling's position is SF theoretician Darko Suvin, who doesn't define the genre but refers to it as "misshapen" and accuses it of capriciously dispensing with plausibility and rejecting "cognitive logic."[9] All these writers see the form as mixing features from SF and fantasy, but they don't really specify the nature of the mix. For our own purposes, the most pertinent definition of the form is L. David Allen's: "Under this heading would go those stories which, assuming an orderly universe with regular and discoverable laws, propose that the natural laws are different from those we derive from our current sciences."[10]

Science fantasy, then, is an unstable hybrid form combining features of SF and fantasy.[11] An SF world introduces a factor (or factors) of estrangement into its system of actants and topoi (which themselves presuppose an operative set of natural laws), but neither that factor nor the world in which it is inscribed violates natural law or the scientific epistemology. A fantasy world, on the other hand, is free to contravene both natural laws and the scientific epistemology in creating and concatenating its actants and topoi. A fantasy world is distinguished by a "full 180-degree reversal of a ground rule,"[12] a contravention of the conventional norms of possibility; the discourse of fantasy never naturalizes its fantasy elements and sometimes paradoxically affirms both their existence and their impossibility. The introduction of a fantasy actant (such as a ghost, witch, demon, sorcerer, ghoul, or dragon) signals the fact that in that world certain laws or assumptions of physical science have been suspended.

A science fantasy world, then, would be one in which the actants or topoi presuppose at least one deliberate and obvious contravention of natural law or empirical fact, but which provides a scientific rationale for the contravention and explicitly grounds its discourse in the scientific method and scientific necessity. Science fantasy, like SF, assumes "an orderly universe with regular and discernible laws,"[13] but, like fantasy, it contains at least one violation of the laws that we derive from the current state of science. A science fantasy world has all of the predicates that we associate with SF worlds—logical consistency, predictability, regularity, accountability, comprehensibility. In such a world, an organized or "scientific" explanation can be formulated for whatever happens. The source, validity, cogency, or plausibility of that explanation is not at issue; indeed, frequently the explanation draws on questionable analogies, imaginary science, far-fetched gadgets, or counterfactual postulates. Regardless, science fantasy is rooted in a discourse which takes for granted the validity of the scientific episteme, and which therefore provides a quasi-scientific rationale for its reversals of natural law. As a matter of fact, the scientific discourse of science fantasy serves to validate the counterscientific element, convincing us of its plausibility. The "science" in science fantasy represents "an attempt to legitimize situations that depend on fantastic assertions."[14]

4.1 Two Test Cases: Leiber's *Conjure Wife* and Lem's *The Investigation*

INQUISITOR: Bring in the witch-woman, Brother.
FAMILIAR: Such are they all—though some are worse than others.

—Gene Wolfe, *The Claw of the Conciliator*

The poet should prefer probable impossibilities to improbable possibilities.

—Aristotle, *The Poetics*

In order to elaborate a bit on the discourse of science fantasy, I would like to look in some detail at two science fantasy "metatexts," texts which interrogate the boundaries of the genre, namely, Fritz Leiber's *Conjure Wife* (1953) and Stanislaw Lem's *The Investigation* (1959; English translation, 1974). Leiber's novel is of interest because it thematizes the contradiction inherent between science and magic as ways of understanding and dealing with the human condition; that is, it incorporates the tension and conflict between the two into both its story and its discourse. The hero, Norman Sayler, is a sociology professor at a small, exclusive, snobbish New England college. His field of study is ethnology, and he has specialized in feminine psychology in relation to magic and the parallels between primitive superstition and modern neuroses. In other words, his life's work has been to document the extent to which primitive customs and beliefs survive and to put them into an explanatory scientific framework. He firmly believes in "the systematic use of the scientific method."[15]

His ordered and orderly universe unravels one day when, snooping through his wife, Tansy's, possessions, he discovers that she herself has been practicing conjure magic. When confronted, she admits that she has been using spells and charms, but only to protect him and to advance his career. In one "session" that lasts an entire evening, Norman convinces his wife that she must repudiate entirely these superstitious beliefs and practices, and together they burn all her charms and totems. Not surprisingly, in the next few days Norman suffers a series of minor and major disasters and reversals. A former student who feels that Norman was responsible for his dismissal from school makes a pathetic attempt on Norman's life; a sexually frustrated coed accuses him of having seduced her; a colleague discovers an obscure manuscript which seems to have anticipated Norman's own scholarship, thus implicating him in an act of plagiarism; the college offers the departmental chair to an inept colleague; even in his private life Norman falls prey to a number of accidents and mishaps. Naturally he is tempted to connect these setbacks with the destruction of his wife's protective charms, but he rejects the possibility out of hand, because that way lies madness: "Thoughts are dangerous, he told himself, and thoughts against all science, all civilized intelligence, all sanity, are most dangerous of all" (p. 96).

His personal and professional fortunes continue to deteriorate, and he begins to entertain the notion that all women are to some degree and with varying aptitudes witches:

> Why not carry it a step further? Maybe all women were the same. Guardians of mankind's ancient customs and traditions, including the practice of witchcraft. Fighting their husbands' battles from behind the scenes, by sorcery. Keeping it a secret; and on those occasions when they were discovered, conveniently explaining it as feminine susceptibility to superstitious fads.
> Half the human race still actively practicing sorcery.
> Why not? (P. 66)

He discovers, moreover, that three women in particular, wives of influential colleagues, are conspiring to sabotage his career and destroy him and his wife. But he categorically refuses to admit that he is dealing with *real* witchcraft, instead attributing the aberrant behavior to the neuroses and hysteria of suggestible women.

The conflict between the parties escalates, until Norman is thrown into a situation where he is quite literally battling this diabolical trio for the possession of his wife's soul. His wife leaves him the instructions for a counterspell, but he is reluctant to carry them out—to do so is "to compromise with magic" (p. 120). Even at the crucial moment, as the clock moves on toward midnight, he hesitates: "But to tackle it in dead seriousness, to open your mind to superstition—that was to join hands with the forces pushing the world back to the dark ages, to cancel the term 'science' out of the equation" (p. 132). At the last moment he goes ahead with the counterspell, arguing to himself that he must do everything to save his wife, in order to keep faith with a loved one. As he struggles to put the spell together, he comes to a startling realization:

> Then, in one instant of diabolic, paralyzing insight, he knew that *this* was sorcery. No mere puttering about with ridiculous medieval implements, no effortless sleight of hand, but a straining, backbreaking struggle to keep control of *forces summoned*, of which the objects he manipulated were only the symbols. . . .
> He could not believe it. He did not believe it. Yet somehow he *had* to believe it. (P. 134)

In the denouement that follows, Norman not only devotes himself to the mastery of sorcery (eventually defeating his adversaries with their own weapons), he begins to put the discipline on a scientific footing. By theorizing and rationalizing magic, he turns it into a kind of bastardized science, for which "the basic formulas and the master-formulas have never been discovered" (p. 158). Indeed, a mathematical analysis of the symbolic logic of a number of spells gives him the master formula with which he defeats his enemies. In other words, the scientific method produces the equivalent of super-magic. All the while Norman tries to convince himself that he is acting out an elaborate charade for his wife: "What strangeness pressing on the heels of strangeness it was, Norman thought dreamily, not only to pretend to believe in black magic in order to overawe three superstitious, psychotic women who had a hold on his wife's mental life, but even to invoke the modern science of symbolic logic in the service of that pretended belief" (p. 173). And yet in the next moment he admits to himself that these are "stuffy rationalizations" (p. 174), that his wife's soul has indeed been stolen.

In terms of our own discussion of science fantasy as a genre, we can say that *Conjure Wife* plainly draws on actants and forces and motifs that we associate with traditional fantasy; that, like the protagonist, the reader is "wrench[ed] . . . away from rationality" (p. 196) in a short period of time. Leiber does turn the novel in the direction of science fantasy by naturalizing magic in the final chapters, more specifically by converting it into a "soft" science (like psychology, according to Tansy).[16] The scientific paradigm is modified so as to make room for magic. In this way Leiber draws attention to the compulsive need of the scientific mentality to domesticate or master the most anomalous phenomena. The work thus foregrounds and interrogates the scientific episteme in general. As will be seen, this kind of interrogation constitutes science fantasy's central theme. The scientific explanation of magic is based on analogy and is not particularly convincing, but by dramatizing the tension between magic and science and by inserting magic into a naturalizing discourse, Leiber has created a science fantasy novel.

It is instructive to pair *Conjure Wife* with another novel which explores the tensions between scientific and unscientific explanations for supernatural phenomena, but which avoids any reference to occultism or magic: Lem's *The Investigation*. Like *Conjure Wife*, *The Investigation* interrogates the very terms of its narrative identity, exploring the limits of the scientific method in the face of an inexplicable universe; its focal point is "what its title announces to be: not . . . the phenomena being investigated, but the process of investigation itself."[17] Moreover, as George Guffey points out, in the novel Lem takes on both nineteenth- and twentieth-century scientific paradigms, both Newtonian and quantum physics, both inductive/deductive reasoning and statistical analysis.[18]

When dead bodies begin to disappear from various morgues in England, apparently of their own volition—a series of resurrections, as it were—Scotland Yard, in the person of the untried Lieutenant Gregory, is called in to investigate. He is assisted in the investigation by the brilliant but eccentric statistician Dr. Sciss. Although their approaches are radically different, both men share a faith in the inviolability of "facts" and in the ability of reason to explain the apparently inexplicable. Gregory is looking for a human perpetrator of the body snatchings; Sciss is looking for some mathematical correlation between the disappearances and the circumstances surrounding them, because between the two phenomena "there is always a definite correlation, a valid basis for a discussion of causes and effects."[19] Indeed, Sciss discovers a mathematical pattern, a regularity, to the incidents of "resurrection," one involving factors of time, space, and temperature; that is, the product of the distance and the time between the consecutive incidents, multiplied by the temperature differential, is a constant. The implications of Sciss's findings are summarized as follows by Gregory's boss, Chief Inspector Sheppard: "The pattern that emerges from our series of incidents is impersonal. Impersonal, like a natural law of some kind. . . . The mathematical perfection of this series suggests that there is no culprit" (p. 43). Gregory recoils instinctively from this line of reasoning, insisting that there must be a human agent behind the episodes.

But Gregory admits that the case is peculiar, paradoxical. At face value the disappearances seem to be the work of a psychopath, a maniac, but this hypothesis is contradicted by the planning and methodicalness of the alleged perpetrator. "Nothing very good. Nothing very good at all," he complains. "A series of acts without a single slipup, that's pretty bad. . . . In fact it appalls me, it's absolutely inhuman" (p. 39). The mystery of the case is compounded by the fact that there seems to be absolutely no motive. The criminal has simply gone out of his way "to make it look like the bodies had come back to life" (p. 43), perhaps with the intent to confound the police and/or to create a "new myth" or a "new religion" (pp. 44, 47). In his desperate need to have a human culprit, perhaps a very intelligent one, Gregory absurdly focuses his suspicions first on his boss, the chief inspector, and later on Dr. Sciss. In fact, he goes so far as to harass the latter, frequently making a fool of himself. Trying to explain his unorthodox methods to his chief, he says, "You're right, sir . . . I acted like an idiot. And I have no excuse at all, except that I absolutely refuse to believe in miracles, and nothing is going to make me, even if I go crazy" (p. 120).

In the course of his investigation, Gregory very nearly does lose his sanity, plunging deeper and deeper into a world which loses definition and clarity, becomes more and more surreal. Everything about his life—his colleagues, his landlords, the random people he encounters—begins to seem mysterious, enigmatic, unfathomable. He comes to inhabit a Kafkaesque world peopled by freaks, dwarves, eccentrics, and the like; at one point he confuses his mirror image with that of a suspicious stranger. He gets a break in the case when a morgue stakeout turns up another "bodysnatching," but the constable on patrol is knocked unconscious in a car accident (he was apparently running blindly from the scene of the incident), and all the evidence seems to point to a "natural" resurrection. As Gregory tells his chief, "The situation is much worse" (p. 95).

Dr. Sciss, meanwhile, continues his statistical analysis of the incidents and comes up with a solution of sorts. First he states his scientific credo: "Science progresses by discovering the connection between one phenomenon and other phenomena, and this is exactly what I succeeded in doing. . . . I was assigned to determine the cause of this seemingly abnormal series of phenomena, and, its uniqueness notwithstanding, to connect it with some other series of phenomena that was already familiar" (p. 108). For him the "operative causes" are indeed "forces of nature" (p. 106). It turns out that the region in which the disappearances have occurred happens also to have the lowest incidence of death from cancer in the last twenty years. The implication, as Gregory explains to his chief, is that a mutated organism of some sort, perhaps a virus, is responsible for the "miracles":

> The reasoning goes this way; cancer manifests itself in an organism as chaos; the organism itself, representing order as it is found in the life processes of a living body, is the antithesis of chaos. Under certain conditions, this chaos factor—that is, cancer, or more accurately, the cancer virus—is mutated, but it remains alive, vegetating in whatever medium is its host. . . . Ultimately it undergoes such a complete transformation that it develops

entirely new powers; it changes from a factor that causes chaos to one that tries to create a new kind of order, a posthumous order. In other words, for a specific period of time it fights against chaos represented by death and the decomposition of the body that follows death. To do this, this new factor tries to restore the life process in an organism whose body is already dead. (P. 122)

Sciss also offers an alternative explanation, as if in passing: that this order-microbe or virus might have been planted by extraterrestrials who are curious about the mechanics of the human organism but wisely do not wish to interfere with living beings. In this account, the cancer correlation is complicated but has to do with the fact that those who are relatively immune to the cancer organism are proportionately susceptible to the alien organism.[20]

As might be expected, Gregory rejects both solutions out of hand, because to accept them would be to repudiate everything in which he believes. For one thing, solution number one would call into question Christianity, and, by extension, Western civilization in general. Suppose, Gregory says, there was a similar drop in cancer mortality in the Near East about two thousand years ago, that "there was a series of alleged resurrections then also—you know, Lazarus, and . . . the other one" (p. 124). In addition, his profession and his sanity rest ultimately on the firm belief that the world he inhabits, while not always sane, nonetheless is orderly and therefore subject to systematic explanation. As the novelist Black says to Gregory, "It's a matter of faith. You believe in a perpetrator because you have to" (p. 143). In this way, the novel suggests that matters of empirical fact are at bottom matters of faith.

When the constable who had witnessed the "resurrection" during the morgue stakeout finally regains consciousness and in his final moments testifies that there was no human culprit, that the corpse got up of its own accord and stumbled drunkenly around, Gregory does approach the limits of his sanity. He begins to suspect that "Chaos is the law of nature" (Henry Adams), that the world is a kind of "soup with all kinds of things floating around in it and from time to time some of them get stuck together by chance to make some kind of whole" (p. 179). In such a world absolutely anything is possible, and "blind chance, the eternal arrangement of fortuitous events" (p. 180), governs all phenomena.

Chief Sheppard knows that such speculations are dangerous for "investigators," and so he fabricates for Gregory an elaborate and patently improbable "out," involving a demented lorry driver driven to irrational acts, such as coffin robbing, while working night shifts in the pea soup of the English fog. When Gregory asks if that is *really* how it happened, the chief replies in the negative, but adds, "it can become the truth" (p. 186). And when Gregory wants to know why Sheppard has concocted such a contrived but plausible explanation, the latter's response is just as significant:

"Well, in the final analysis . . . well, because I work for Scotland Yard, also" (p. 187). With a deliberate fiction he is able to give "a semblance of order to disorder" and to ensure that the two of them are not "left crying in the wilderness" (p. 188).

It should be clear from the interpretive summary above that Lem is quite explicitly interrogating the bases upon which scientific explanations of the world rest. He is calling into question "both the mechanistic models that science latterly subscribes to and the teleological ones that man tends to fall back on when confronted with the inadequacy of a purely mechanistic scheme of things."[21] In so doing, he finally demystifies science itself, exposing it as a kind of enabling fiction, one which makes it possible for us to "do" things with the world while blinding us to the strangeness of the *suppenwelt* we inhabit. But at the same time Lem inscribes this interrogation of science in a text which relies on the conventions and procedures of the scientific method and which incorporates a number of quasi-scientific explanations into its discourse. Because the basic ground situation—the premise that corpses might resurrect themselves—contravenes some basic natural laws and scientific givens, *The Investigation* must finally be described as a science fantasy.

4.2 Forms of Science Fantasy

> I never spent much time thinking carefully about the term, Scientific Fantasy, because various definitions and genological arguments meant to divide SF from Scientific Fantasy always seemed to me so much scholastic irrelevance, and of no benefit to either the authors or the readers.
>
> —Stanislaw Lem, Interview with Istvan Csicsery-Ronay, Jr.

> "Those who cannot see devils, cannot see angels!"
>
> —Joanna Russ, "The Man Who Could Not See Devils"

To return to the task of definition, then, we can say that science fantasy inscribes a *counternatural* world within a naturalizing and scientific discourse. The forms that this counternaturalness can take are several; in fact, we can distinguish a number of science fantasy types according to the nature of the contravention or violation that the author assumes in the creation of the fictional world.

Let us consider first a most problematic case, that of the time-travel story, since this case unfolds for us the fuzziness of science fantasy's contours. A conservative and conventional estimation of the current state of scientific knowledge rules that it is impossible to travel through time without violating several very basic physical laws. In "The Theory and Practice of Time Travel," Larry Niven spells out just what laws must be suspended or ignored, including conservation of matter, conservation of energy, and laws of motion in general. Since for him time travel is thus "impossible on any level,"[22] Niven refuses to write SF that employs it as an estrangement device. But he admits that time travel would be admissible in a fantasy fiction, and he employs and foregrounds it in his collection of stories *The Flight of the Horse* (1973). In these stories, a time traveler named Svetz from the distant future travels into the past to bring back extinct species for a zoo. When he is told to bring back a horse, he brings back a unicorn; when he tries to capture a wolf, he gets stuck with a werewolf. In other words, Svetz travels not into the past but into never-was, the land of fantasy. Because time travel "violates too many of the laws of physics and reason,"[23] Niven can use it only within a fantasy format where he says that it serves purposes of wish fulfillment, enabling him to stage, for example, a fight between a human and a dragon.

Niven's theory and practice suggest that since time travel is impossible, time-travel stories must be fantasy. Indeed, some writers (LeGuin and Lem, for example) have conscientiously ruled it out of their serious SF. I would argue, however, that most time-travel stories are *not* science fantasy, and not simply because time travel is "probably impossible but difficult to disprove."[24] A key text here is the most famous time-travel story of them all, Wells's *The Time Machine*, a "pure" science fiction. Niven argues that *The Time Machine* is SF simply because it uses only travel to the far future and thus avoids the paradoxes of time travel,[25] but more important are the facts that within the grapholect or writing practice of Wells's time, such a machine did not so clearly violate contemporary scientific possibility, and that Wells provided for his machine a (now-unconvincing) scientific rationale.

Once Wells had firmly embedded a time machine within an SF story, that gadget entered into the accumulating conventions of the genre, where it could be appropriated and utilized by other SF writers. Any SF novum (such as a time machine, FTL travel, and ESP) can become part of the repertoire of SF conventions and therefore a device or tool for other authors. It should be noted that conventionalized novums are indeed *devices*, that they serve as means to an end, namely, the introduction of the dominant or foregrounded novum in the fiction.[26] In other words, the conventionalized novum has in fact lost its status as novum and now serves simply as a device subtending the "real" or dominant novum (as when an FTL drive is used to stage an alien encounter). In addition, as Scortia points out,[27] time travel can be engineered in "pure" SF when its scientific rationale accords with the realm of possibility. In *Timescape* (1980), for example, Gregory Benford bases time travel of a sort on the tachyon, a hypothetical faster-than-light particle not excluded by relativity theory. And the protagonists of Poul Anderson's *Tau Zero* travel in time to the end of the universe and beyond by virtue of the time-dilation effect that occurs at speeds close to the speed of light. In short, despite the fact that time travel would seem to be the kind of impossibility associated with fantasy, it can be a purely SF motif when it is used as an enabling device or when it is inscribed in a naturalizing and scientific discourse.

A science fantasy, then, must have as its dominant novum an entity or motif which explicitly violates standards of scientific possibility or empirical fact. There is a form of time-travel story which intrinsically violates reason, science, and common sense, and which therefore qualifies as science fantasy. I refer here to the "time-loop" story, in which an actant journeys via a time machine into his own past, meets up with himself at an earlier point in time, and supplies that former self with assistance based on future technologies or future events, thus solving the main conflict of the story. An extreme example is Heinlein's "All You Zombies," in which a traveler in time impregnates himself and gives birth to himself—the same actant is at once father, mother, and child. As Lem points out, time-loop stories frequently involve an act of *creatio ex nihilo* and violate basic notions of cause and effect and before and after; these narrative structures are "internally contradictory in a causal sense."[28] Although these stories can be read allegorically (for example, "All You Zombies" can be read as the literalization of philosophical solipsism and thus as a parody of that notion), the time-loop story more frequently devolves into a kind of intellectual game in which the fictionist is free to play with logical contradiction and pseudological hypotheses or to parody the conventions of SF itself. As Niven says, this kind of story is a "form of fantasy superbly suited to games of logic." And these "games of logic" serve cognitive ends to the extent to which they call into question epistemological assumptions, empirical givens, or literary conventions.[29]

Science, in its largest sense, consists not only in a set of natural laws and a set of procedures based on a certain epistemology but also in a respect for empirical givens, in a faith in the inalterability of accepted fact. It follows that one can create science fantasy by deliberately reversing or denying a given historical fact.[30] This is the case in "alternative history" science fantasies. In *Pavane* (1966) Keith Roberts imagines an alternative time stream in which the Spanish Armada defeated the English fleet in 1588, resulting in a 1966 world dominated by a monolithic Catholic church. *Tunnel through the Deeps* (1972) by Harry Harrison is set in an alternate present in which the United States are still colonies of Great Britain because Americans lost the Revolutionary War.

The most celebrated of alternate fictions is Dick's *The Man in a High Castle* (1962). Dick imagines a 1960s United States which lost World War II to the Axis powers and which has been partitioned (à la East and West Germany) into two rival zones, the West Coast under the comparatively benign occupation of the Japanese, the East Coast under the brutal domination of pathological Germans. Alternate present worlds such as these necessarily call into question received notions of history and progress and at the same time point out that cultural values are not absolute, that they are very much shaped by historical forces and events. They suggest the degree to which our view of things is a function of factors out of our control. Moreover, readers are encouraged to compare the alternate present with the actual present and see what the two worlds have in common. Dick's novel, for example, suggests that, like the characters in his counterfactual present, we live in a world in which madmen are in power, because those in power see themselves as agents not victims of history, because they believe they are godlike. An alternate present world, then, is science fantasy because it is created by extrapolation from a counterfactual postulate involving the reversal of a given historical fact. The extrapolated present of this "what if" world, though entirely imaginary, nonetheless may address significant thematic concerns dealing with questions of history, progress, values, and assumptions.

If one way to create a science fantasy is to extrapolate from a reversal of historical fact, then a similar way would be to postulate a deviation from scientific fact and thus to envision a counterscientific world. The fictionist deliberately ignores the current state of scientific knowledge about a phenomenon in order to create a world that serves particular aesthetic ends. Frequently this contravention of scientific fact involves the planets of the solar system, such as Mars and Venus. C. S. Lewis, for example, admits that he put canals on Mars in his "Space Trilogy" despite the knowledge that such canals were an "optical delusion."[31] The stories in Bradbury's *The Martian Chronicles* (1950) all take place on a Mars populated by the ghosts and artifacts of a noble race that never was or ever could be. As Eric Rabkin points out, "by giving Mars a breathable atmosphere . . . , Ray Bradbury announces that his work is not to be taken entirely as science fiction—and held exclusively to that genre's aesthetic criteria—but rather is to be read at least in part as a kind of fairy tale set in a realm miraculously hospitable to humanity."[32] A deliberate contravention of this sort changes the generic identity of the fiction, moves it in the direction of fantasy, and calls forth from its reader slightly different reading protocols. The inscription of counterscientific worlds, these impossibly hospitable planets, sometimes serves no apparent cognitive ends; these fabulous worlds are their own justification. As Lewis says, "Nor need the strange worlds, when we get there, be at all strictly tied to scientific probabilities. It is their wonder or beauty or suggestiveness that matter."[33]

A final form of science fantasy involves the introduction of a counternatural entity into the system of actants, but, in contrast to pure fantasy, in a world grounded in both scientific discourse and scientific necessity. An actant is posited whose morphology, powers, or existence contravenes scientific possibility, but it appears in a world otherwise compatible with scientific necessity and inscribed in a scientific discourse. Robert Silver-berg's *Majipoor* trilogy (1981, 1983, 1984), for example, recounts the epic struggle for global power on a sprawling planet colonized and governed for many centuries by humans sometime in the distant future. Although these humans have forgotten much of the science bequeathed to them by an earlier "golden age," their home planet, Majipoor, obeys the basic dic-tates of an extrapolative or speculative SF world. The two native Maji-poorian species, however, the protean Metamorphs and the telepathic giant sea dragons, are sets of counterscientific actants who "turn" the fiction toward science fantasy.

Similarly, in Anne McCaffery's Dragonrider series, the reader encounters a fictional world which conflates SF and fantasy elements. The dragons of Pern have the ability to breathe fire and to fly, but both abilities are given scientific rationales. The image of fire-breathing dragons in flight certainly recalls traditional fantasy, an impression that is reinforced by the fact that the dragons possess other "magical" powers, including precognition, te-lepathy, race memory, and time travel. These fantasy elements, however, are embedded in a discourse predicated upon the validity of the scientific method and scientific necessity. In hybridized science fantasies such as these (and those by Bradley, Moorcock, Anthony, and Wolfe), it is the tension between apparently contrastive elements—magic/science, super-nature/nature, mysticism/empiricism—that structures and informs the themes and the plot. These fictions demonstrate that "man is not satis-fied . . . with reason and science. He desires myth and magic, and if they do not exist, he will use science to create them."[34]

We can imagine a spectrum of "hybridized worlds"—worlds whose ac-tants and events combine scientific and fantasy elements—along which we can locate the above examples and other problematic cases. At the SF end we would find *Dune*, a novel whose fantasy elements are systematically naturalized and accounted for.[35] At the other end we would find those novels which approach pure fantasy, such as Zelazny's Amber series or Norton's Witchworld series. At this end we would also find the fictions of E. R. Burroughs, A. Merritt, and E. E. "Doc" Smith, borderline science fantasies which rely on "unbridled, swashbuckling fantasy while retaining the terminology of science fiction."[36] Occupying the center of the spectrum would be a novel such as LeGuin's *Lathe of Heaven*, in which the protagonist discovers that his dreams have the power to change reality. This kind of power is extremely counterscientific (so much so that it cries out for met-aphorical and metaliterary readings), but in the novel the scientist Haber goes to some lengths to account for it in scientific terms.

We can also locate the other forms of science fantasy along such a spec-trum. At the SF end would be situated those alternate histories, such as *The Man in the High Castle*, which entail the reversal of a single historical fact. Toward the fantasy end we would find such alternate histories as

Randall Garrett's Lord Darcy stories of the Anglo-French empire (collected in *Too Many Magicians*), in which the reversal of historical fact brings about an alternate present in which magic is the operative science. Lem's *The Investigation* would be near the center, on the SF side, whereas Leiber's *Conjure Wife* would be more toward the fantasy end. Even within such a spectrum there would be problematic cases. I would argue, however, that the narrative discourse can, in most cases, determine where on the spectrum the work belongs. We must examine the way in which the work presents and accounts for its fantasy elements. If the discourse rigorously and systematically naturalizes those elements, then the work approaches SF; if it does not, then the work approaches fantasy.

The last category—hybridized science fantasy—is certainly the "mainstream" of science fantasy and includes certain novels that have eluded typological definition. Sturgeon's *More Than Human*, for example, won the International Fantasy Award in 1954 but generally is treated as an SF novel of the "Golden Age." But SF "purists" have always been a little bit uncomfortable with the novel, perhaps because of the way it brings together a group of urchins and strays with extraordinary, and counterscientific, psi-powers. If we recognize, however, that these children are really transformed fantasy actants inserted into the prosaic and ordinary world of postwar America, then we see that Sturgeon was writing science fantasy, at a time when "hard" SF was generally the rule.

Joanna Russ has said of fantasy that it "very often imitates the structure of the pastoral; one escapes from the familiar into the strange or fantastic only to return to the familiar at the end of the story."[37] Science fantasy frequently appropriates the same structure. A representative of the world of science, of rationality and empiricism, journeys forth to encounter the world of fantasy, mysteries beyond science's purview, the kind of phenomena which A. Merritt prefigures in the opening paragraphs of *The Metal Monster*:

> In this great crucible we call the world—in the vaster one we call the universe—the mysteries lie close packed, unaccountable as the grains of sand on ocean's shores. They thread gigantic, the star-flung spaces; they creep, atomic, beneath the microscope's peering eye. They walk beside us, unseen and unheard, calling out to us, asking if we are deaf to their crying, blind to their wonder.
>
> Sometimes the veils drop from a man's eyes, and he sees—and speaks of his vision.[38]

The central action of such novels involves a struggle between the world of science and that of fantasy, sometimes an armed conflict or physical agon, but always a struggle to comprehend and to explain, for a belief in the possibility of understanding lies at the heart of the scientific enterprise:

"All of [these mysteries] I was certain lay in the domain of the explicable, could be resolved into normality once the basic facts were gained" (Merritt 48). The protagonist may indeed be able to put some sort of scientific gloss upon the phenomena he witnesses, but he returns to the normal world chastened, more credulous, wiser:

> But to me—to each of us who saw those phenomena—their lesson remains, ineradicable; giving new strength and purpose to us, teaching us a new humility.
> For in the vast crucible of life of which we are so small a part, what other shapes may even now be rising to submerge us?
> In that vast reservoir of force that is the mystery-filled infinite through which we roll, what other shadows may be speeding upon us? Who knows? (Merritt 203)[39]

This encounter/return pattern is used in a number of science fantasies. In Merritt's *The Metal Monster*, botanist Walter Goodwin confronts the counternatural metal being and its quasi-human child Norhala in the remote regions of the Himalayas. In Elgin's *Yonder Comes the Other End of Time*, Trigalactic Federation agent Coyote Jones, an advocate of "pscience," meets and is defeated by the magical world of Ozark. In C. S. Lewis's *Out of the Silent Planet*, Ransom, Devine, and Weston discover that Sol's fourth planet is not Mars, a world to be exploited, but Malacandra, a world presided over by Oyarsa, a powerful spiritual being. In Lindsay's *A Voyage to Arcturus*, the adventurer Maskull is drawn into a journey from drawing-room London to the protean and fabulous planet of Tormance, a world tied into spiritual and metaphysical realities. In Piers Anthony's *Split Infinity*, the protagonist moves back and forth between SF and fantasy worlds—Proton and Phaze—in alternating chapters, each chapter labeled either *SF* or *F*, depending on the nature of the world involved. In each case the scientific mentality or approach or world-view is shown to be limited, and the representative of science returns from his encounter with his horizons expanded.

It is also interesting to note that many hybridized science fantasy novels adhere to the traditional romance archetype, perhaps because of the natural affinity between their respective worlds.[40] For one thing, the fantasy actants of hybridized science fantasy presuppose a "world elsewhere," a marvelous or exotic topos in which one or more constraints of empirical reality or scientific necessity are suspended. In this world the protagonist is endowed with certain counternatural powers or attributes, which give his or her adventures a larger-than-life quality. And those adventures frequently involve some sort of quest, either for a clearly defined object of desire or for the restoration of a shattered equilibrium. Most important, the recourse to fantasy allows the fictionist to stage the story in a universe with value, as opposed to the value-neutral universe of SF. C. S. Lewis depicts this movement from one universe to another in *Out of the Silent Planet* when Ransom, aboard the spaceship, becomes aware of the true nature of the interplanetary "void":

> But Ransom, as time wore on, became aware of another and more spiritual cause for his progressive lightening and exultation of heart. A nightmare, long engendered in the modern mind by the mythology that follows in the wake of science, was falling off him. He had read of "Space": at the back of his thinking for years had lurked the dismal fancy of the black, cold vacuity, the utter deadness, which was supposed to separate the worlds. He had not known how much it affected him till now—now that the very name "Space" seemed a blasphemous libel for this empyrean ocean of radiance in which they swam. He could not call it "dead"; he felt life pouring into him from it every moment. How indeed should it be otherwise, since out of this ocean the worlds and all their life had come? He had thought it barren: he saw now that it was the womb of worlds. . . . No: Space was the wrong name. Older thinkers had been wiser when they named it simply the heavens.[41]

It is this conversion of "Space" into "the Heavens" which signals the movement from SF to science fantasy, from a phenomenal universe to a noumenal universe. Like fantasy, science fantasy is free to invest its actants and motifs with a power or a pattern that is lacking in the purely phenomenal world of the senses and the value-neutral universe of SF. Mark Rose has noted that "at the core of all romance forms appears to be a Manichaean vision of the universe as a struggle between good and bad magic."[42] Fantasy, a subset of romance, frequently appropriates both the realm of magic and the Manichaean axis informing that realm; indeed, LeGuin argues that "most great fantasies contain a very strong, striking moral dialectic, often expressed as a struggle between the Darkness and the Light."[43] Diane Waggoner suggests that this ethical or moral dimension is critical for fantasy, that the genre is based on a faith in some kind of supernatural moral order, an order which "is important not because it offers excitement and fun and escape, but because it provides laws and moral values."[44] Hybridized science fantasy frequently borrows from fantasy its ethical framework, its distinctions between good and bad magic. These distinctions are not always clear (one thinks here of Wolfe's *The Book of the New Sun*; see 4.4), but they can be made. In such fictions the outcome is seldom in doubt; at the end the goal is secured, the forces of evil are defeated or thwarted, order is restored. Because of their formal shapelessness (a function of the romance archetype), these fictions satisfy sublimative needs; they speak to our desires and dreams. As Gene Wolfe says, they achieve "the spirit of fantasy," revealing "the mystery of things."[45]

4.3 Themes of Science Fantasy

> Science, one might well argue, is the real myth of our culture, and science fiction is merely the codification and expression of beliefs in that myth.
>
> —Gary Wolfe, *The Known and the Unknown*

The problematics of hybridized science fantasy worlds reveal to some extent what an unstable, dynamic, and polymorphic subgenre science fantasy is. Questions of historical context, the current state of knowledge, discursive strategies, and dominant features must all be taken into account in identifying this elusive (not to say illusive) subgenre. Why go to all that trouble? One might answer quite simply that it is important to be able to name a distinction which exists, that the possibility of making distinctions lies at the heart of genre theory. Or one might be more pragmatic than dogmatic, pointing out the use value of such a distinction. In terms of literary history, this distinction enables us to locate certain problematic literary texts, to identify Poe's *The Narrative of Arthur Gordon Pym* and Verne's *Journey to the Center of the Earth* as science fantasies within the contexts of their respective cultural grapholects. It also enables us to name certain trends in contemporary fantasy and SF, namely, the movement from SF to science fantasy by writers such as Silverberg, Moorcock, and Anthony.

But still the question might be asked, What's in a name? Granted that science fantasy is a valid and thriving subgenre, why go to some lengths to define and particularize it? But distinctions become very important if different narrative genres mobilize different reading protocols; then to name a type is to know how to read. At least one critic argues that fantasy and SF are "natural enemies" in terms of reading strategies:

> Two kinds of art [fantasy and science ficton] instruct us to respond with two different parts of ourselves, the emotional and the rational, and each kind sees responding to the alien with the other side of the self to be counterproductive. And the status of objects in the two universes is correspondingly different. In "fantasy," objects have primarily figurative status, whereas in "science fiction," the thing is *a thing*, a literal object. And again, each genre presents the alternative as a fundamental error: in "fantasy," people have to be taught that the object is an externalization of their internal reality—it is, in short, a metaphor—whereas, in "science fiction," to see the object as a projection of the self is akin to madness.

Several pages later, the critic summarizes as follows: "In fantasy, reason cuts us off from the instinctive wisdom of the irrational. In science fiction, reason liberates us from the narrowness of our humanity."[46] The distinctions being made between SF and fantasy in regard to reason and emotion, internal and external reality, literal and figurative status of objects, are too absolute and simplistic, but the notion that the genres call for different reading strategies is a good one. Fantasy deals with the unreal,[47] SF with the unknown; this basic difference naturally affects the way in which these genres are recuperated or naturalized.

And science fantasy, located as it is at the intersection of these two genres, is uniquely situated to speak to both our heads and our hearts, to provide both cognitive and sublimative satisfaction. The fact that science fantasy is grounded in the discourse of scientific necessity and adheres to the scientific method guarantees that its world will have an internal consistency or logical explicability that is intellectually satisfying. But the contravention of natural law or empirical fact that defines the genre makes possible the introduction of actants, motifs, and topoi which play upon a wide range of human emotional needs while at the same time suspending the mimetic contract and its attendant responsibilities. C. S. Lewis argues that therein lies the fascination of science fantasy:

> The last sub-species of science fiction [by which he intends what we have termed science fantasy] represents simply an imaginative impulse as old as the human race working under the special conditions of our own time. It is not difficult to see why those who wish to visit strange regions in search of such beauty, awe, or terror as the actual world does not supply have increasingly been driven to other planets or other stars.[48]

Like "magic realism," another narrative subgenre enjoying a burgeoning interest, science fantasy is an oxymoronic form. In the counternatural worlds of science fantasy, the imaginary and actual, the magical and the prosaic, the mythical and the scientific meet and interanimate. In so doing, these worlds inspire us with new sensations and experiences, with "such beauty, awe, or terror as the actual world does not supply," with the stuff of desires, dreams, and dread.

But perhaps the most important reason for identifying the genre is that because it mobilizes different reading protocols, it tends to circumscribe areas of thematic concern different from the thematics of either fantasy or SF. The cognitive dimensions of science fantasy are fuzzy and problematic, in part because the subgenre can take on very different forms and pose a wide variety of questions, in part because it approaches its thematic fields obliquely and in an exploratory way. Perhaps it is best to come at those fields by examining the respective world-views inherent in SF and fantasy. SF takes for granted a phenomenal world of contingency, to be known through the application of "right reason," using empirical methods. Fantasy, on its part, assumes a noumenal universe, informed by unseen presences, presences which exert some control over destiny, must be accepted on faith, but can be apprehended through intuition. Science fantasy, perched between these two universes, can appropriate, reject, or interrogate any and all of these assumptions. By reversing natural law or empirical fact, science fantasy questions their absoluteness and givenness; by asserting the primacy of an invented and counternatural world, it questions the nature of reality; by taking on the principles and conventions and facts which we take for granted, it tends to broach ultimate philosophical questions having to do with metaphysics, theology, cosmology, ontology, metatheory (both scientific and literary), and mythopoeia. But most of all, because it stands poised between two opposing ways of conceiving the world, it addresses itself to the relation between ontology and epistemology. As David Ketterer says,

> the intrusion of the fantastic into what appears a science fiction text or a naturalistic text often simply alters the function of the fantastic material. Instead of being encouraged to think about questions of psychology and mortality, the reader is being encouraged to consider matters of epistemology: how do we know what we think we know is accurate? It is the function of epistemology to relate any debate about the "real" and the "unreal" to the relationship between the known and the unknown.[49]

In simplistic terms, SF deals with the known and unknown, fantasy with the real and unreal. Science fantasy then mediates these two philosophical axes and explores their interrelationships. It explores the epistemological assumptions of SF by interrogating "science" in its broadest sense, i.e., systematic and methodical ways of apprehending, comprehending, and appropriating the physical world.[50] It plays on the ontological assumptions of fantasy by calling into question the impossibility and unreality of the spectral horrors and beautiful desires that haunt the value-laden worlds of our dreams. It suggests that "magic" may well be an explicable phenomenon if it is inserted into the right kind of epistemological paradigm. It asks whether the universe is indeed ethically neutral and totally contingent. If "the real crux of the difference between fantasy and science fiction lies in the writer's attempt to present his ideas within the context of new assumptions about the way the world works,"[51] then the mixed genre of science fantasy is perfectly situated to interrogate those very assumptions, and it does, as a celebrated work of science fantasy, Gene Wolfe's *The Book of the New Sun*, clearly demonstrates.

Before we examine in detail Wolfe's tetralogy, we should take note of the fact that within the scientific community itself, certain fundamental assumptions are being called into question, in large part because of recent developments in science. Prigogine and Stengers argue, in *Order Out of Chaos: Man's New Dialogue with Nature* (1984), that a postmodern science is in the process of emerging, a science based on a new alliance between humanity and the world. The new alliance links humanity to a natural world reconceived as perpetually changing, incredibly diverse, inexhaustibly inventive, one "in which reversibility and randomness are the rules."[52] The attempt of "modern science" to master the world, a world of fixed and immutable laws, has given way to a postmodern "reenchantment of the world," in which humanity rediscovers a respect for nature's mystery. Because natural processes involve complex, rapidly evolving systems which are highly sensitive to the minutest fluctuations, the smallest changes can make a difference, and "individual activity is not doomed to insignificance." This leads Prigogine and Stengers to conclude that "we can no longer accept the old *a priori* distinction between scientific and ethical values."[53] If they are right, then it seems probable that this redefinition of nature and our relation to it, this reenchantment, will produce a cultural climate in which counterscientific forms such as science fantasy will flourish. In the long run, of course, it may turn out that these narratives are no longer counterscientific, and we will have to continue the process of naming.

4.4 Wolfe's *The Book of the New Sun*

It was, in fact, a fine and enviable madness, this delusion that all questions have answers.

—Larry Niven and Jerry Pournelle, *The Mote in God's Eye*

The mystery of life is not a problem to be solved but a reality to experience.

—Frank Herbert, *Dune*

Gene Wolfe's tetralogy *The Book of the New Sun*[54] is, in many respects, an exemplary and all-inclusive science fantasy. For one thing, it incorporates a spectrum of science fantasy motifs and elements, including a wide assortment of counternatural actants and objects. For another thing, it parades and examines the genre's basic themes—including the tension between magic and science and their common basis in faith; the natural and the physical over against the supernatural and the metaphysical; the limitations of two-value logic systems; the mystery beneath or within the commonplace; the relation of imagination and reality; the problematic grounds of knowledge; and ontological multiplicity. In this work Wolfe has undertaken a thorough and systematic demonstration of the ways in which the apparently conflicting narrative assumptions of fantasy and SF can be made to coexist.

The tetralogy is set on a fallen "Urth" of the far-distant future, a "posthistoric world" (*ST* 262), when the sun has so weakened that stars can be seen during the day and the moon has moved much closer to the Earth.

The social order of this future world is, as is usual in "sword and sorcery" science fantasy, feudal, with a hierarchical class system, headed by a powerful monarch (the "autarch"), who presides over an aristocratic class of administrators (the "exultants"), a military class (the "armigers"), a merchant class (the "optimates"), a set of guilds, and the commonality. That this world is "posthistoric," a future world that is not simply a reversion to the feudal past, is made clear by references to the accomplishments and hand-me-downs of earlier, more scientifically advanced eras—a green moon (the product of extensive irrigation), colonization of the solar system, "biogenetic manipulation" of extrasolar breeding stock (*ST* 261), and interstellar flight. Urth is a world that has known a storied and accomplished past but has gradually undergone an entropic process of decline and decay that has brought about a new Dark Age, an age which awaits, superstitiously it would seem, the coming of the New Sun.

At the center of the tetralogy is the story of the coming of age of one Severian, at first a member of the guild of torturers that serves the Autarch, in the end the Autarch himself and the hero who sets out to bring back the New Sun. Severian narrates the series of adventures and accidents which bring him from his lowly position within the torturer's guild, through a year of exile which exposes him to the wider world of Urth, back to the House Absolute and the throne itself.

During his travels Severian encounters a series of actants drawn from the worlds of fantasy and SF. Those which are terrestrial in origin are the kind of preternatural monsters associated with SF. There are the Morlock-like man-apes of the caves of Saltus, with fangs and saucer eyes and flap ears, all natural adaptations to years of living in darkness. There are the surgically humanized animals (à la *The Island of Doctor Moreau*) who inhabit the Great Wall of Nessus and serve as fierce guardians of the capital city's outer wall. There are the zoanthropes who live in the wilderness, humans who have deliberately given up their humanity by having their locus of identity and consciousness surgically removed from their brains. At one point Severian has his fortune told by a green man from the future, a man whose body chemistry has been altered so as to enable him to photosynthesize sunlight. Later, Severian discovers that his companion and friend, Jonas, is not a man at all but a robot, a relic from bygone eras who had human parts grafted onto his frame after an accident. Severian even encounters a two-headed man, created by grafting the head of a dying autarch onto the shoulders of a healthy peasant man. As should be clear, all of these fantastic actants are accounted for by scientific glosses that draw upon conventional SF paradigms. The undines, however, native humanoid water behemoths with almost supernatural powers who are plotting to enslave the human race and to gain mastery of Urth, are drawn not from SF but from myth. Because their existence is not given scientific motivation, and their "power surpasses understanding" (*CA* 285), they remain unrecuperated fantasy actants who impart an element of the uncanny to the work.

If the humanoid actants that Severian encounters are, for the most part, taken from the repertoire of SF, then the various horrific extraterrestrial creatures that pursue Severian during his travels have their roots in fantasy. The "notules" which attack him are batlike creatures which cannot be slain and which seek to bury themselves in human tissue and absorb warmth. The burning salamander that pursues Severian in Thrax, a "reptilian flower" that "burn[s] in a way never known on Urth" (*SL* 56, 57), recalls both reptilian nightmares and traditional dragons. Most frightening of all is the alzabo, an actant conflating features of werewolves and zombies. The alzabo devours humans whole but retains neural vestiges of the memories and personalities of its victims and thus can approach its next victim using a human voice and making a personal appeal. Indeed, if one partakes of human flesh treated by the brain of an alzabo, then one can absorb the personality, the neural network, of that human. This process of psychic appropriation Severian experiences more than once. These various nightmare creatures, fantasy actants which contravene conventional science, are explained, however, as having an extraterrestrial origin, as having been "brought from the stars long ago, as were many other things for the benefit of Urth" (*CC* 80). Fantastic they might be, but only from a limited geocentric and anthropomorphic perpective.

These basic science fantasy premises—a posthistoric world, fallen from the high science of long ago, infested by monsters created by that science, terrorized by demons imported from the stars, and visited by mysterious sentient extraterrestrials ("cacogens") whose purposes are unknown—allow Wolfe to introduce a wide assortment of traditional fantasy motifs and yet to inscribe them within a naturalizing discourse, to provide them with scientific motivation. He gives us a common barmaid transformed overnight into a voluptuous beauty through biochemical and surgical alteration. He gives us a giant in a lonely tower who is also a mad scientist. He gives us a form of resurrection of the dead, by means of chemically enhanced necrophagy. He gives us the spectacle of magical mirrors, which, by reflecting light back upon itself, create a warp in the universe and thus master space and time, making instantaneous travel possible. Such travel, however, violates the space/time continuum, a violation which results in travel through time. Those who travel in this way, "running up and down the corridors of time"—the green man, Master Ash, various cacogens—present themselves to Severian as legitimate or "natural" prophets, seers, oracles. Given such premises, one can accept even the "truly uncanny" (*CA* 118), a house whose lower stories are in the present and upper stories in the (possible) future.

On the world of Urth, the distinction between magic and science as mutually exclusive ways of mastering one's environment no longer obtains. The tower of the torturers' guild lies next to that of the witches. Severian is taken prisoner by a band of sorcerers and participates in a trial by magic. He accepts matter-of-factly the existence of "dark things everywhere" and the distinction between white and black magic (*SL* 152, 153). In his world magic is just another "science," another form of knowledge. As one of the seers that Severian meets says, "There is no magic. There is only knowledge, more or less hidden" (*CC* 243).

In the tetralogy there are a number of talismans, but the most magical is the Claw of the Conciliator, a gem with marvelous powers that falls into Severian's possession during his travels. The gem enables him to perform what seem to be miracles. With it he is able to heal wounds incurred by himself, his friend Jonas, and the man-ape who attacks him. With it he is able to resist the dark magic of the sorcerers. With it he brings the little girl in the jacal back from the very abyss of death, "as though some unimaginable power had acted in the interval from one chronon and the next to wrench the universe from its track" (*SL* 52). The Claw saves an uhlan who has been attacked by a notule, resurrects a dead soldier, and brings Dorcas back from the Garden of Endless Sleep. Drawing on its power, Severian is made over into a "witch indeed in everything except knowledge" (*SL* 48).

Dorcas explains the jewel's powers by insisting that it has the same power over time that Father Inire's mirrors have over space. When the Claw brings the uhlan back to life, it "twist[s] time for him to the point at which he still live[s]" (*SL* 68). For his part, Severian can only affirm that the Claw is "incommensurable," that it is "a thing from outside the universe" (*SL* 252), that it somehow taps into metaphysical dimensions and reveals profound truths:

> Whenever I looked at [the Claw], it seemed to erase thought. Not as wine or certain drugs do, by rendering the mind unfit for it, but by replacing it with a higher state for which I know no name. Again and again I felt myself enter this state, rising always higher until I feared I should never return to the mode of consciousness I call normality; and again and again I tore myself from it. Each time I emerged, I felt I had gained some inexpressible insight into immense realities. (*SL* 254)

The Claw is the most fabulous artifact in a fantastic world, and its powers are never really accounted for. At one point Severian examines in some detail the mystery of the Claw's powers (*CA* 282–86), but he is unable to solve it. The existence and powers of the Claw introduce into the tetralogy the possibility of a superordinated world, a world ordered from above.

Severian's world, then, is a hybridized admixture of actants and motifs drawn from SF and fantasy. In such a world, science and magic (and, by extension, religion) stand on the same footing because they "have always been matters of faith in something" (*CA* 131). This equation not only calls into question the empiricist assumptions of hard science; it problematizes the entire relation between humanity and the external world. As a physician who treats Severian says,

"The past's sterile science led to nothing but the exhaustion of the planet and the destruction of its races. It was founded in the mere desire to exploit the gross energies and material substances of the universe, without regard to their attractions, antipathies, and eventual destinies. Look! . . . Here is light. You will say that it is not a living entity, but you miss the point that it is more, not less. Without occupying space, it fills the universe. It nourishes everything, yet itself feeds on destruction. We claim to control it, but does it not perhaps cultivate us as a source of food? May it not be that all wood grows so that it can be set ablaze, and that men and women are born to kindle fires? Is it not possible that our claim to master light is as absurd as wheat's claiming to master us because we prepare the soil for it and attend its intercourse with Urth?" (CA 218)

This argument inverts the basic instrumentality of the world, in so doing decentering humanity in a radical and startling way. It problematizes fundamental assumptions about our relation to the external world, invests that world with a dimension of strangeness and mystery.

In similar fashion, the tetralogy sets about interrogating the very basis of our encounter with the external world, how we perceive and how we know. As C. N. Manlove has noted, The Book of the New Sun is at pains to remind us how little we know for sure, to what extent our experience of reality is local and hypothetical.[55] At one point Severian wonders "how much any of us see of what is before us" (CA 262). So much of seeing, he knows, is a function of models and constructs imposed upon reality by the human mind. Indeed, the "mystes" who maintain "that the real world has been constructed by the human mind, since our ways are governed by the artificial categories into which we place essentially undifferentiated things" (ST 3), provide a real insight into the nature of Severian's world, a world in constant dialectic with the human mind. Severian emphasizes the dynamic between mind and world by analyzing the relation between humans and their symbols (ST 8), by foregrounding the issue of his own sanity ("I realized for the first time that I am in some degree insane" [ST 24]), and by obscuring at times the distinction between memories, dreams, and actualities.

The Claw of the Conciliator, for example, opens with Severian dreaming of the woman he is to execute the next day, waking from that dream into one of himself as a little boy, waking from that dream into one involving the apprentices' dormitory, and then finally coming awake in the "real world." In such a Chinese box structure, who can say what is dream and what reality? This sort of disorienting collapse of ontologically separate realms Severian experiences frequently: "I woke again, and sat up. For a moment I truly thought I was in our dormitory again, that I was captain of the apprentices, that everything else, my masking, the death of Thecla, the combat of the averns, had been only a dream. This was not the last time this was to happen" (ST 205). If perception is itself filtered by the categories of the mind, if the mind itself is subject to delusion, hallucination, or madness, if the seemingly clear-cut distinctions between dream and reality and past and present are obscured if not obliterated, how, then, can Severian possibly *know* anything for certain? And, as Severian reminds us near the end of the tetralogy, "What is meant by *know*, in an appropriate sense?" (*CA* 283).

As is suggested by the Mind/World, Dream/Reality confusion above, the tetralogy appropriates familiar hierarchical polarities—such as Humanity/ Nature, Matter/Spirit, Science/Religion—and explores or inverts them, in so doing interrogating fundamental ontological and epistemological assumptions. At one point Severian speculates that "all two-valued systems are false" (*CA* 148), and the tetralogy systematically subverts a great number of them, including axiological antinomies.[56] For much of the tetralogy, Severian seems to be moving in a Manichaean world in which it is simple to assign predicates of good and evil. There is the party of the Autarch, which seeks to preserve the decadent status quo and preside over the inevitable death of Urth. Opposing them are the exultant Vodalus and his rebels, who hope to return Urth to its former greatness, to return mankind to the stars. Later, Severian learns that Vodalus is more concerned with personal power than with the destiny of humanity and that the Autarch himself is working for the real rebirth of Urth, that the Autarch has even sacrificed his manhood in a vain attempt to bring about the coming of the New Sun. At first, the cacogens are mysterious, menacing presences, who maintain the Autarch in power and must wear masks to cover their hideous visages. Later, Severian learns that that visage is itself a mask, beneath which there is an ineffable beauty, and that the cacogens are really "hierodules"—holy slaves—who have come to assist in the rebirth of Urth. At first, Severian can readily distinguish between white and black magic, but later he wonders if both might not ultimately serve the Increate.

The same argument can be made for the other enemies—the Ascians, even Abaia and the undines—against whom Severian finds himself pitted. He begins by believing, with Dorcas, that the "world is filled half with evil and half with good" (*ST* 179), and that it should be easy to avoid the one and serve the other. By the end of his journey, Severian knows that such distinctions are too simple. He is informed by the Autarch that he who serves as Autarch must stand "for so much that is wrong" because "until the New Sun comes, we have but a choice of evils" (*CA* 239). A cacogen suggests to him that the very categories of Good and Evil are inadequate:

> I drew a deep breath. "I don't know what you mean. But somehow I feel that though you and your kind are hideous, you are good. And that the undines are not, though they are so lovely, as well as so monstrous, that I can scarcely look at them."
>
> "Is all the world a war of good and bad? Have you not thought it might be something more?"
>
> I had not, and could only stare. (*SL* 233)

By the end of the final volume both reader and Severian come to suspect that there is "something more" involved, an order of being that transcends the categories of good and evil, that all those who "appear to differ so widely and indeed to wage a species of war upon one another . . . were nevertheless under the control of an unseen individual who operated the strings of both" (SL 187). In general, then, the world in which Severian lives tends to slide through an axiological spectrum, from purely contingent, through Manichaean, to providential.

The notion of a divinity that shapes our ends figures also in Severian's own life story. Severian begins his story with his encounter with Vodalus, because that night "was to mark the beginning of my manhood" (ST 4). His story, then, is one of coming of age, of initiation and maturation. It begins when he is locked out of the Citadel; the locked and rusted gate, he realizes, was a "symbol of [his] exile" (ST 1). His journey takes him from the naive belief that he is a true and faithful "journeyman of the Order of the Seekers for Truth and Penitence" (the torturers' guild), to the vague suspicion that he is a "pilgrim bound for some vague northern shrine" (ST 134), to the understanding that torturer is only one of many roles he must play (SL 53), to the realization that, in the final analysis, "I was an actor and no torturer, though I had been a torturer" (CA 109). Appropriately, he begins his exile by donning a mask, an emblem at once of his calling, a torturer or agent of Death, and of his essence, an Actor.

Throughout the tetralogy Severian plays many roles—apprentice, journeyman, torturer, lictor, prisoner, "wanderer," "adventurer," sorcerer, warrior, finally autarch—but most of all, as is foreshadowed when he joins Dr. Talos's company, that of actor in a larger drama, a player in a script written by another, a script contrived with a beginning and an end by a force beyond Severian's ken. The signature of that force can be seen throughout the tetralogy. The force intervenes early in his life, in the form of the undines, to save him from drowning in the river Gyoll; it leads him to the encounter with Vodalus that changes his life; it puts the Claw in his possession, the charm that saves his life and dictates many of his actions; through various prophecies and dreams, it reminds him that he has a greater destiny to fulfill. The apparently random journey that Severian makes, the one that backs him into the throne, as he informs us from the very start (ST 9), seems to some degree orchestrated or managed. His is a journey with a shape and a teleology, from Nessus north as journeyman to Thrax and beyond and back in a circle to Nessus as Autarch. At one point Severian compares himself to a "fly in amber" (CC 15) who could not have escaped his fate no matter what he did.

If Severian's history suggests that his actions are overseen and guided by the hand of fate, it does not specify just to whom that hand belongs. At various times in the tetralogy, Severian professes a hesitant belief in the Increate, who "commands the entirety and is served equally (that is, totally) by those who would obey and those who would rebel" (SL 186). This "all-pervasive power in the universe" (*SL* 214) has chosen Severian to hold the Claw for a time and make use of it. The Increate, it would seem, directs the actions of all—the Autarch, the cacogens, the undines, the Ascians, and so on.

But the ending of the tetralogy adds a twist to this idea, by suggesting that Severian may well have been acting as puppeteer for himself. After consolidating his rule as Autarch, Severian is to be taken by the cacogens out to the stars as a representative of Urth, there to be tested to see if Urth is deserving of a New Sun. If he passes the test, he will be returned to Urth as the Conciliator come again, so named because he would have the power "to reconcile the universe with humanity, and humanity with the universe, ending the old breach" (*CC* 213). Like the Claw itself, a relic of the first Conciliator, the Conciliator come again would have power over time, as the feverish Severian explains to the wounded soldier: "I don't know if you believe in the New Sun—I'm not sure I ever have. But if he will exist, he will be the Conciliator come again, and thus *Conciliator* and *New Sun* are only two names for the same individual, and we may ask why that individual should be called the New Sun. What do you think? Might not it be for the power to move time?" (*CA* 22). The reborn Conciliator will, in effect, be able to fold time over to a time when the sun is new.

The work ends with Severian about to leave for his testing, but he supposes that he will succeed and thus become the New Sun. This prospect leads him to a couple of speculations. First, he assumes that he is not the "first Severian." The first Severian led a more ordinary existence that by chance brought him to the Autarchy. Once he had been singled out in this way, "those who walk the corridors [of time] walked back to the time when he was young, and my own story—as I have given it here in so many pages—began" (*CA* 321). He also speculates that, after his apotheosis as New Sun, he himself becomes a runner through time, perhaps even one of those who give assistance to the "first Severian." In making his voyage to the stars, Severian steps outside time, because of the space/time dilation effect. As the tetralogy's "translator," G. W., speculates in his final appendix, "the ability to traverse hours and aeons possessed by these [star] ships may be no more than the natural consequence of their ability to penetrate interstellar and even intergalactic space, and to escape the death throes of the universe; and that to travel thus in time may not be so complex and difficult an affair as we are prone to suppose." If that is the case, the translator concludes, then it is possible that Severian becomes a traveler in time and "that from the beginning Severian had some presentiment of his future" (*CA* 328). This, the last line of the tetralogy, echoes almost verbatim Severian's first words in volume 1, underscoring the necessity that shapes his life and at the same serving as a resonant coda for the work. The time-travel hypothesis also explains Severian's strange attraction to the man from the past called Head of Day—he himself was/will be Head of Day, during a visit to the past that will take place in the future. Thus the ending of the tetralogy introduces another science fantasy motif—the time loop—which solves some mysteries and compounds others, while at the same time confounding fundamental assumptions about before and after and cause and effect.

If the shape of Severian's adventures can in part be explained by reference to the time runners, and their existence can also be "scientifically" accounted for, so too may the apparently religious reference to salvation through the intercession of the "New Sun" be given a "scientific" gloss. The "New Sun" will be not a spiritual being but a material thing—a White Fountain (the obverse of a "black hole")—a locus "from which matter and energy rejected by a higher universe flow in endless cataract into this one" which will be created in the heart of the dying sun, thus bringing the "epic penance of mankind" to an end (CA 253, 255).

As a young boy, Severian would retreat to his favorite tomb in the necropolis next to the torturers' guild (a tomb which apparently, by virtue of time looping, turns out to be his own, or at least the first Severian's) and be consumed by two "impossible" dreams: that "at some not-distant time, time itself would stop" and that "there existed somewhere a miraculous light . . . that engendered life in whatever it fell upon" (ST 11–12). By traveling to the stars and passing to a higher universe to undergo his testing, Severian does, in effect, bring time to a halt, opening up the past and the future to him. By coming into possession of the Claw, he is able to fold time for others and thus to restore them to life. Time, it seems, is simply a function of our lower universe, and the Conciliator, by virtue of access to extramundane reality, by the "transcendence of reality," is capable of the "negation of time" (ST 143).

But what is this higher reality, this "Yesod, the universe higher than our own" (CA 288–89)? It too is given a scientific gloss. Emissaries of the cacogens inform Severian that the universe itself has a divine year, during which it expands, then contracts, then blossoms forth again. During one such divine year, the humans from the analogue of Urth created a race of beings "such as humanity wished its own to be: united, compassionate, just" (CA 288). This race of beings—the Hierograms—escaped the birth/death cycle of the universe by opening a passage to Yesod, where they created worlds suitable for themselves. From this vantage point outside ordinary time, the hierograms looked forward and back until they discovered Severian's Urth. Now, Severian is told, "they shape us . . . as they themselves were shaped; it is at once their repayment and their revenge" (CA 289). They engineer this shaping by sending their servants—the cacogens, the green man, Severian himself—hurtling down the corridors of time, which themselves exist outside the universe.

Diane Waggoner has distinguished between fantasy and SF in the following way: "where fantasy's change of assumptions is metaphysical, science fiction's is only physical, since it must conform to an idea of scientific plausibility."[57] *The Book of the New Sun* demonstrates that scientific plausibility may be so stretched as to call into question or erase neat distinctions between the physical and the metaphysical. At one point Severian is accused of being a "materialist, like all ignorant people." He is told that, in the final analysis, it is "spirit and dream, thought and love and act that matter" (*CA* 76). By the end of his journey, Severian has abandoned his naive materialism. Walking along the beach, he discovers a thorn exactly the shape and size of the Claw buried within the gem he had carried so long. He experiences that likeness as a revelation:

> What struck me on the beach—and it struck me indeed, so that I staggered as at a blow—was that if the Eternal Principle had rested in that curved thorn I had carried about my neck across so many leagues, and if it now rested in the new thorn (perhaps the same thorn) I had only now put there, then it might rest in anything, and in fact probably did rest in everything, in every thorn on every bush, in every drop of water in the sea. The thorn was a sacred Claw because all thorns were sacred Claws; the sand in my boots was sacred sand because it came from a beach of sacred sand. The cenobites treasured up the relics of a sannyasins because the sannyasins had approached the Pancreator. But everything had approached and even touched the Pancreator, because everything had dropped from his hand. Everything was a relic. All the world was a relic. I drew off my boots, that had traveled with me so far, and threw them into the waves that I might not walk shod on holy ground. (*CA* 258)

In that moment Severian experiences the conversion of the material into spiritual, the profane into sacred, space into the heavens, that is one of the hallmarks of science fantasy.

The overall thrust of science fantasy, with its fantasy actants and motifs, conflation of magic and science, erasure of distinctions between material and spiritual or physical and metaphysical, is to call into question what most SF takes for granted—empirical reality. At one point, Severian maintains that we are all on a mission "to discover what is real" (*ST* 75). *The Book of the New Sun* seeks to expand our intuition of what is real, to make us accept within our conception of reality the spectrum of counternatural actants and motifs that haunt our dreams. It encourages us to refashion our ontological maps to allow for both magic and metaphysics. In an essay, Wolfe argues that science fantasy "uses the methodology of science fiction to show that [impossible creatures and things] are not only possible, but probable."[58] By convincing us of that probability, the tetralogy multiplies for us the possible layers of reality, until reality reveals itself as the ineffable mystery that it is.

Discussing semantics with Dorcas, Severian explains that everything has three meanings—a meaning in and of itself, a meaning in relation to the things around it, and a "transsubstantial meaning" through which it expresses the will of the Pancreator (*ST* 233). At one level, the tetralogy stresses the first meaning, the one Dorcas says is "impossible" to find. As

Manlove says, the "whole book can be said to be founded on the notion of taking away our certainty as to what a thing is,"[59] thereby revealing for us the "mystery of things."[60] At the same time, the tetralogy reminds us continually of the possibility of that third level, "the level of meaning above language, a level we like to believe scarcely exists, though if it were not for the constant discipline we have learned to exercise upon our thoughts, they would always be climbing to it unaware" (SL 46). *The Book of the New Sun* is "shot through with the numinous."[61] Like the Claw of the Conciliator itself, like science fantasy in general, it encourages the mind to ascend and to gain "some inexpressible insight into immense realities" (SL 54) by calling into question the monolithic and value-neutral nature of reality itself.

V

LOOKING BACKWARD AND FORWARD AT WORLDS APART

Significant modern SF . . . presupposes more complex and wider cognitions: it discusses primarily the political, psychological, and anthropological *use and effect of knowledge, of philosophy of science.*

—Darko Suvin, *Metamorphoses of Science Fiction*

But we do not quite believe in this prosaic world. Continually we are reminded of the strangeness of birth and death, the vastness of time and space, the unknowability of ourselves. One would like to live differently, more significantly. One would like to participate in events more meaningful than our daily round, feel sensations more exquisite than is our usual lot. One reads science fiction in order momentarily to transcend the dull quality of everyday life.

—Robert Sheckley, "The Search for the Marvellous"

Throughout this study it has been understood that the acronym *SF* stands for *science fiction*, not for any of the alternate rubrics that other writers and critics have proposed, such as speculative fiction (the choice of both Heinlein and Delany) or structural fabulation (Scholes's short-lived suggestion). It should be clear that I consider the standard designation to be the right one. It is appropriate that an anomalous genre have a two-word name, one word of which is the etymological derivative of a Latin word for knowledge, the other of which comes from a past participle form of a Latin verb meaning "having been feigned, invented, or contrived." As Gregory Benford has noted, "the science in SF represents knowledge—exploring and controlling and semisafe." Correspondingly, the fiction in SF promises alienity, "balancing this desire for certainty with the irreducible unknown."[1] Science and fiction, knowledge and imagination, cognition and sublimation (Scholes), thinking and dreaming (Aldiss), reason and wonder—these are the various polarities that the genre mobilizes. As Gary Wolfe puts it, SF "lets us have it both ways; it shows us that rationality can be made consistent with the wildest imaginings of new environments and new forms of life. It lets us experience the wonder that was once available only through fantasy and fairy tales, but without sacrificing the hard edge of reason that connects us to this world."[2] This "letting us have it both ways" is not only the reason for SF's fascination and popularity but also the basis of its value.

In various times and places, different claims about the central value of SF have been made. Some (Asimov comes to mind here) would argue that in its questioning of technology, its probing of the proper relation between man and machine, of the dangers of dehumanization in an increasingly mechanized, "technetronic" society, in this area lies SF's real contribution to our present world; the literature of technology, SF necessarily investigates technology and its applications. Some (Amis, for example) would generalize this notion to embrace the larger interrogation of power relations in postindustrial society, including relations between humanity and its technologies, between the two sexes, between contrastive social orders, between races, between humanity and the larger cosmos. As we have seen, these sets of relations do constitute some of the thematic fields of SF, with particular sets serving as the focus for separate SF types. But these kinds of interrogations are not the sole province of SF, nor do they make up its entire cognitive value.

Other writers have dwelled on the "science" in SF in a different way, arguing that the genre familiarizes readers with developments in science that would otherwise be inaccessible or incomprehensible. Donald Lawler summarizes this view succinctly: "For many readers, science fiction became the only way that theoretical and applied science was accessible to their emotional, imaginative, and therefore to their moral lives. In this way, science fiction has made science and its application both understandable and a vital part of the experience of the masses." Through the mediation of SF, he concludes, "modern scientific ways of knowing and thinking have become part of the imagined life of the people."[3] Heinlein makes a related claim for the genre by putting emphasis upon the fictive part of SF. In SF, he says, one can try out imaginary thought experiments that would be "too critically dangerous to try in fact. Through such speculative experiments science fiction can warn against dangerous solutions, urge toward better solutions."[4] His position is closely connected with that which stresses the futurological orientation of much SF, the most naive form of which holds that SF has prophetic value, that it gives us "tomorrow's machines (and news) today." Few would still make this claim, but they do assert that SF teaches us that tomorrow is not just "another day," that it will be an *other* day, one inextricably linked with today. In this view SF serves a monitory function, exhorting us to prepare today for what will inevitably come tomorrow. One could perhaps raise the objection that "futurology" in general serves this function in a more efficient and comprehensive, if less satisfying, fashion. One might also add that this line of argument privileges that mode of SF which Heinlein in general advocates and practices—

namely, extrapolative SF—and therefore undercuts the value of the imaginative leaps that speculative SF undertakes.

It can be said, however, that SF, unlike some other contemporary narrative forms, does take as given the ineluctable fact of change, and that in so doing it acculturates readers to that fact. Heinlein puts this case most strongly. "Change . . . change . . . endless change," he says, "that is the keynote of our times, whether we face it or run away from it. The mature speculative novel is the only form of fiction which stands even a chance of interpreting the spirit of our times." SF, in other words, is actually the most mimetic of fictional forms, the one that best reflects the spirit of the times, in so doing providing an invaluable service for its readership:

> In a broader sense, all science fiction prepares young people to live and survive in a world of ever-continuing change by teaching them early that the world does change. Since that is the only sort of world we have, science fiction leads in the direction of mental health, of adaptability. . . . In short, science fiction is preparing our youngsters to be mature citizens of the galaxy . . . as indeed they will have to be.[5]

As another critic says, "science fiction engenders a *positive adoptive attitude* in the minds of its readers."[6] It cultivates intellectual flexibility and open-mindedness and emphasizes the integral role of knowledge for those preparing for the future. But the same can be said for a number of other narrative forms, including the "mainstream" realistic novel.

One can claim for SF, then, that it is a narrative form which calls into question the uses (and abuses) of technology and power relations in general; that it provides venues for "thought experiments" which can have cautionary value; that it acknowledges and appropriates the fact of change and thereby fosters adaptability and tolerance in its readers. To an extent and in particular cases, SF addresses these themes and serves these functions, but as a genre it ultimately stages more fundamental and far-reaching questions.

As we have shown in chapter 1, the appearance of modern SF is predicated upon the establishment of the scientific episteme as the definitive and hegemonic way of envisioning and explaining the human condition and humanity's place in the larger universe. Although rooted in the scientific epistemology, SF has not reflected its assumptions and tenets in any simple, straightforward way; rather, since the pioneering example of *Frankenstein*, SF's relation to its epistemological base has been problematic. In part just because it begins with science as first principle, it has interrogated the assumptions, procedures, and objectives of the scientific way of knowing the world, an undertaking which grants it a privileged place in modern discourse. As Thomas Wymer points out, "because of its concern with science, SF has centered its attention on the problems of perception and knowledge, and it has derived its sense of value from these concerns. In one sense this puts SF in the mainstream of Western thought, which has, since the seventeenth century, placed its primary emphasis on the epistemological branch of philosophy, theory of knowledge."[7] This concern with epistemology is, I would argue, built into the genre, an inevitable part of its narrative ontology. SF necessarily stages a confrontation with the unknown, but it inscribes that confrontation in a discourse which assumes that what is unknown can be known. SF thus by definition deals with the problems, possibilities, and limits of knowledge; it is the epistemological genre *par excellence*. In one way or another, reading SF entails using, analyzing, critiquing, or subverting scientific paradigms of knowledge and their application to human life.

Wymer goes on to qualify his claim for SF by noting that in its most unsophisticated forms, SF has tended to accept unquestioningly a "rather narrow empiricism" which equates an increase in knowledge with the accumulation of facts and the accumulation of facts with the march of progress.[8] This kind of SF has quite properly been stigmatized as having embraced a naive and literalistic materialism, as having confused empirical facts with real knowledge, as having been seduced by a superficial understanding of the scientific method and its results, as having indulged a "cheap" cognitive optimism that ignores the darker side of the scientific enterprise. But the cognitive optimism that characterizes much SF need not be cheap or superficial; such a view can lead to a reactionary anti-scientific attitude, equally as superficial and perhaps more dangerous. Such an attitude informs what Heinlein calls "anti-science fiction," "another symptom of the neurotic, sometimes pathological, anti-intellectualism all too common today."[9] Stanislaw Lem, in a similar vein, accuses "fantasists" such as J. G. Ballard and Ray Bradbury of having deserted the proper domain of SF by rejecting out of hand the "programmatic rationalism of SF in favor of the irrational": "one is not allowed to entertain any cognitive hopes—that becomes the unwritten axiom of their work." Lem proposes by way of rebuttal that optimism of a special sort lies at the heart of SF:

> Cognitive optimism is, first of all, a thoroughly non-ludic premise in the creation of science fiction. The result is often extremely cheap, artistically as well as intellectually, but its principle is good. According to this principle, there is only one remedy for imperfect knowledge: better knowledge, because more varied knowledge. Science fiction, to be sure, normally supplies numerous surrogates for such knowledge. But, according to its premises, that knowledge exists and is accessible.[10]

The generic protocols of SF, in particular the grounding of its discourse in the scientific episteme, to some degree dictate that the genre presuppose a basic faith in the power of reason and the value of empirical knowledge. But, as Wymer points out, this need not lead to a narrow empiricism and a superficial optimism. The best SF is acutely aware that there is, built into Western (male) discourse, a tendency to equate science with knowledge and knowledge with power, and it ruthlessly interrogates both these equations. The best SF accepts the fact that science has bequeathed to us a deterministic and value-neutral universe but affirms the value of "the paradoxical and limited ways in which human freedom manages to exercise itself" in that universe.[11] The best SF endorses empiricism but recognizes that there is a personal, creative element in perception, and consequently explores the limits of empiricism or alternately investigates other modes of consciousness. This kind of SF, Wymer argues, bears the imprint of a romantic overlay on an Enlightenment world-view.

This argument recalls the fact that SF is generically a form of romance, a narrative form whose fictional world differs from the basic narrative world. We can thus come at the value of SF not only from its epistemic assumptions but from consideration of its literary form. As Rose has noted, the deep structure of SF involves the confrontation between the human and the nonhuman: "this opposition defines the semantic space, the field of interest, within which SF as a genre characteristically operates. It constitutes what we might call the genre's paradigm."[12] This encounter, between human and nonhuman, familiar and unfamiliar, known and unknown, contributes in large part to that "sense of wonder" the genre inspires:

> The sense of wonder in science fiction may well be a sense of the tension set up between the familiar and the unfamiliar, the known and the unknown. In experiencing the sense of wonder, we experience a feeling of endless possibilities, like standing at the edge of a vast abyss that is close enough to us to be real, yet great enough to be unfathomable.[13]

The fully real-ized novums of SF and the sense of wonder they invoke remind us that "there are more things in heaven and earth, than are dreamt of in our philosophy," and explain in part why the genre has been linked with mythology and even with religion (one thinks here of such SF film classics as *2001: A Space Odyssey* and *Close Encounters of the Third Kind*). These novums justify in part Rose's claim that "whereas in literary form SF may be understood as a displacement of romance, in content it may be understood as a displacement of religion."

The tension between SF's unfathomable wonders and its empiricist epistemology, its "essentially religious material" and its "materialistic ideology," Rose refers to as an "unresolvable incompatibility."[14] For him SF's story and discourse are necessarily at odds, the former embracing the incommensurability of the universe, the latter rejecting it. The encounter between the known and the unknown does have a religious dimension, particularly when the unknown is explicitly otherworldly. But SF typically depicts not just the encounter (God speaking to Moses from a burning bush, Kelvin shaking hands with the ocean of Solaris) but the human attempt to assimilate that encounter, to put it in a frame of reference that gives it meaning and significance, to locate it in a larger context in which reason has its place and knowledge and understanding are possible. It might be argued, in fact, that SF is less the literature of the unknown than the literature of the attempt to understand the unknown, that the story of SF is its discourse. In this respect, it can indeed be said that "even the inexperienced SF writer is working with materials that often cut very deep. This is why, in my view, it is pre-eminently the modern literature not of physics, but of metaphysics. It is in science fiction that we are now asking the deepest questions of meaning and causation."[15]

Our survey of the two modes of SF—extrapolative and speculative—reveals that the former tends to emphasize the science in SF, the latter, the fiction in SF. Extrapolative SF assumes a line of filiation between fictional world and basic narrative world, a metonymic relation between there and here. It also presupposes that that line, however sketchy and obscured, may be traced out through the systematic application of the scientific method. It may well qualify, as one writer has claimed for SF in general, as "the most rigorously rational form of literature we have ever had."[16] Extrapolative SF, for the most part, assumes that its novums are ultimately knowable or explicable within existing scientific paradigms or models or theories.

Speculative SF, on the other hand, is built on novums which exist "alongside" contemporary science, in a nether region that science neither repudiates nor embraces. The worlds of speculative SF exist in analogical relation with the basic narrative world, and they therefore elicit metaphorical or even allegorical readings, readings that are not predicated upon "if this goes on" logic, readings which stray into metaphysical or transcendental dimensions. Speculative SF is less cautionary and pragmatic and utilitarian than extrapolative SF; it strives to go to the "heart" of the matter, a move which frequently entails a wholesale re-vision of the human condition. Operating at the deep structural level of reality, speculative SF's transformations tend to blur the clear-cut distinctions between SF types. Gadget SF slides into alternate society SF; alternate world SF merges with alien encounter SF. Speculative SF immerses its readers in Otherness per se, in so doing resisting recuperation through sanctioned models of vraisemblance or existing scientific paradigms. It frequently deflects interest from its novum to the human encounter with that novum, or reverses relations between humanity and the external world, or converts the known into the unknown. It goes so far as to say that "the universe may be unknowable, and its 'moral' structure might forever lie beyond humanity's ken."[17]

If extrapolative SF asserts that the universe is ultimately knowable, while speculative SF calls this assertion into question, both modes share an epistemological dominant. That is, both modes focus on the nature and forms of knowledge, asking the same sorts of questions even if supplying slightly different answers: How can I know this world in which I find myself? How much can I know about it? How can I know that I know? Science fantasy, on the other hand, because it calls into question the very laws that govern and inform everyday reality, overlays that epistemological concern with an ontological dominant.[18] That is, it asks readers if the world is indeed everything that is the case, if reality is as monolithic, as given, as science would have it. Its questions include, how many worlds? how ordered? how superordinated? and how can we be sure?

We have tried to show how SF is necessarily tied to the dominant scientific paradigms of the day, to the ideational climate in which it is written. From a historical perspective, we can say, as Suvin has noted, that the nineteenth century witnessed a "historically crucial shift of the locus of estrangement from space to time,"[19] a shift that at once opened the future to the narrative imagination and provided that imagination with various time-centered paradigms on which it could draw. It is no accident that one phrase for such fiction was the "romance of the future," or that one of the first SF classics, Wells's *The Time Machine*, uses evolution and entropy as its informing paradigms. The dawning of the space age in the twentieth century, I would argue, restored space to SF as a locus of estrangement as writers realized that it might indeed be possible for humans to negotiate and navigate the expanses of space. In large part, space, and not time, is the dominant locus of estrangement for post–World War II SF, and the genre itself may well be a space-oriented narrative form. SF's displacements in time function to make available to the narrative imagination new spaces, new frontiers, new topoi, new worlds, either here or elsewhere.

But now new scientific paradigms—those detailing the immensity of the universe, the "silence" of the universe, the impossibility of an FTL drive—have taken space away again, eliminated it as a truly viable locus of estrangement for "pure" SF. We are stuck, it seems, with the Here of today and tomorrow. To be faithful to its scientific epistemology, such SF must turn its attentions to the frontiers of the solar system (as has been the case in recent work by Delany and Benford), to recent developments in technology (as has been the case in the appearance of cyberpunk), or to alternate society SF situated in the near future (as has been the case in recent fiction by Margaret Atwood and Suzette Haden Elgin). At the same time, other developments in science (I am thinking here of the work of Prigogine and Stengers) have called into question some of the basic givens of the scientific world-view, including the nature of change and the explicability of the universe (at both the macro and micro levels). As a result, the narrative imagination has also begun to take another look at the nature of the Here. Such reexamination has taken the form of oxymoronic genres such as science fantasy and magic realism, both of which probe the limits of reality. Reimagining the nature of reality, this sort of fiction is free to subvert the most basic assumptions of "realistic" fiction, including, most tellingly, the idea that the universe is axiologically neutral. If this process continues, then, as Patrick Parrinder says, "gone . . . would be the large body of popular writing which, in the last fifty years, has simply endorsed and propagated scientific values on the assumption that they embodied a coherent, challenging and imaginatively satisfying world-view. Such a development would probably mean the disappearance of SF as a separate genre."[20] The fields of estrangement may be shifting away from space, and SF may be redefining itself, but it is only a process of relocation for estranged fiction, not the beginning of the end.

NOTES

I. Worlds Apart

1. For excerpts from Reeve's argument, see *Novelists on the Novel*, ed. Miriam Allott (New York: Columbia UP, 1959), pp. 45, 47, 86–87.

2. Brian Aldiss, for example, refers to the novel as the "origin of the species." See *Billion Year Spree: The True History of Science Fiction* (New York: Schocken, 1973), chapter 1. Darko Suvin, in *Victorian Science Fiction in the United Kingdom: The Discourses of Knowledge and Power* (Boston: G. K. Hall, 1983), dates the beginning of the genre from May 1, 1871, the day of the appearance of Bulwer-Lytton's *The Coming Race* and Chesney's *The Battle of Dorking*, and the day Butler delivered *Erewhon* to his publisher. This date, Suvin argues, marks the time when "the sense of a secure society began to be openly and frequently doubted within the wide upper and middle-class consensus itself" (p. 387). Perhaps one could say that 1871 witnessed the birth of "social science fiction."

3. Robert Scholes and Eric S. Rabkin, *Science Fiction: History, Science, Vision* (New York: Oxford UP, 1977), p. 6.

4. Brian Stableford, unpublished manuscript, quoted in Samuel R. Delany, "Orders of Chaos: The Science Fiction of Joanna Russ," in *Women Worldwalkers: New Dimensions of Science Fiction and Fantasy*, ed. Jane B. Weedman (Lubbock: Texas Tech P, 1985), p. 104.

5. James Gunn, "Science Fiction and the Mainstream," in *Science Fiction, Today and Tomorrow*, ed. Reginald Bretnor (New York: Harper & Row, 1974), p. 187.

6. For a more thorough treatment of this issue, see Jerome Hamilton Buckley, *The Triumph of Time: A Study of the Victorian Concepts of Time, History, Progress, and Decadence* (Cambridge, Mass.: Harvard UP, 1966).

7. Hans Meyerhof, *Time in Literature* (Berkeley: U of California P, 1955), p. 97.

8. Suvin, *Victorian SF*, p. 407.

9. Buckley, p. 29.

10. Buckley, p. 20. Buckley defines the Historic Method as follows: "the comparison of the forms of an idea, or a usage, or a belief, at any given time, with the earlier forms from which they were evolved, or the later forms into which they were developed, and the establishment, from such a comparison, of an ascending and descending order among the facts" (p. 20).

11. Frank McConnell, *The Science Fiction of H. G. Wells* (New York: Oxford UP, 1981), p. 45.

12. Darko Suvin, *Metamorphoses of Science Fiction: On the Poetics and History of a Literary Genre* (New Haven, Conn.: Yale UP, 1979), p. 7.

13. Cf. Albert Wendland, *Science, Myth, and the Fictional Creation of Alien Worlds* (Ann Arbor, Mich.: UMI Research Press, 1985), p. 17: "the shared ontological grounds underlying SF's 'agreed upon' common reality are the currently accepted scientific laws, the supposition that the galaxies are united by concepts and rules that are objective, unchangeable, and understandable (if not now then someday)." Scholes and Rabkin date the universality of natural law back to Newton:

> Newton's Law of Gravitation not only succeeded in predicting how gravity worked on Earth, as in the fall of his famous apple, but also provided an identical means for predicting planetary motion if one assumed that the suns and planets had mass and

that the forces of relation were gravitational. This essential refinement of Kepler gave science its first *universal* law and changed the entire thinking of the world. Suddenly there was no Heaven different from Earth, but rather a uniform universe, all governed by the same simple laws, all amenable to intellectual examination. (P. 121)

14. Quoted in Buckley, p. 26.
15. L. David Allen, *Science Fiction: A Reader's Guide* (Lincoln, Nebr.: Centennial P, 1973), pp. 13–14. Cf. Thomas N. Scortia, "Science Fiction as the Imaginary Experiment," in *Science Fiction, Today and Tomorrow*, ed. Bretnor, pp. 136–37:

Implicit in such stories is the humanistic assumption that the laws of nature are amenable to the interpretation of human logic and, more than this, amenable to logical extrapolation. It is this tacit assumption that nature will yield her secrets by the application of logic and extrapolation that underlies all of science fiction, even that science fiction which at first glance appears to be anything but hard-core technological fiction.

16. Mark Rose, *Alien Encounters: Anatomy of Science Fiction* (Cambridge, Mass.: Harvard UP, 1981), p. 98.
17. Stanislaw Lem, *Microworlds: Writings on Science Fiction and Fantasy*, ed. Franz Rottensteiner (San Diego: Harcourt Brace Jovanovich, 1984), p. 250.
18. Donald L. Lawler, "Certain Assistances: The Utilities of Speculative Fiction in Shaping the Future," *Mosaic* 13, 3–4 (1980): 2. Cf. the comment by novelist W. H. Hudson, in his preface to *The Crystal Age* (1887), cited by Suvin, *Victorian SF*, p. 389: "Romances of the future, however fantastic they may be, . . . are born of a very common feeling—a sense of dissatisfaction with the existing order of things combined with a vague faith or hope of a better one to come." Cf. also the comment by contemporary SF writer Harry Harrison in his "Inventing New Worlds I," in *Future Imperfect: Science Fact and Science Fiction*, ed. Rex Malik (London: Francis Pinter, 1980), p. 78: "Science fiction is the only sort of fiction that, like science, knows the future exists. . . . Science fiction, like science, will admit that the future exists. And it will do an even more important thing, it will admit that there is change. And, a final thing it will do is admit that you can change change."
19. Rosemary Jackson, *Fantasy: The Literature of Subversion* (London: Methuen, 1981), p. 62.
20. Wells, "Preface to *The Scientific Romances*," rpt. in *H. G. Wells's Literary Criticism*, ed. Patrick Parrinder and Robert Philmus (Sussex: Harvester P, 1980), p. 241.
21. See, for example, Wendland's treatment of this issue, pp. 14–16.
22. According to Suvin, fidelity to the scientific episteme is the generic key to SF (*Metamorphoses*, p. 65): "what differentiates SF from the 'supernatural' literary genres (mythical tales, fairy tales, and so on, as well as horror and/or heroic fantasy in the narrow sense) is the presence of scientific cognition as the sign or correlative of a method (way, approach, atmosphere, sensibility) identical to that of a modern philosophy of science."
23. Thomas D. Clareson, "The Other Side of Realism," in *Science Fiction: The Other Side of Realism*, ed. Thomas D. Clareson (Bowling Green, Ohio: Bowling Green U Popular P, 1971), pp. 2, 3.
24. Gary K. Wolfe, *The Known and the Unknown: The Iconography of Science Fiction* (Kent, Ohio: Kent State UP, 1979), p. 4.
25. This granted, it must be added that the invented world of SF necessarily interacts with its story, generating its complications and confrontations and channeling its resolutions. The world has precedence, primacy, and priority, but once the world is postulated, an ongoing dynamic between world and story is set up.

26. Suvin, *Metamorphoses*, p. viii. Cf. Brian McHale, *Postmodernist Fiction* (New York: Methuen, 1987), p. 59: "What distinguishes science fiction is the occurrence of this *novum* not (or not only) at the level of story and actors but in the structure of the represented world itself."

27. Lubomir Dolezel, "Narrative Modalities," *Journal of Literary Semantics* 5, 1 (April 1976): 9–10.

28. Suvin, *Metamorphoses*, p. 11.

29. Eric S. Rabkin, *The Fantastic in Literature* (Princeton, N.J.: Princeton UP, 1977), pp. 20–21.

30. Reprinted in *SF: The Other Side of Realism*, ed. Clareson, pp. 130–45.

31. Cf. Northrop Frye, *The Anatomy of Criticism: Four Essays* (1957; rpt., Princeton, N.J.: Princeton UP, 1971), p. 49: "Science fiction frequently tries to imagine what life would be like on a plane as far above us as we are above savagery; its setting is often of a kind that appears to us technologically miraculous. It is thus a mode of romance with a strong inherent tendency to myth." Here Frye identifies SF as romance within his own theory of modes. I am using romance in its more generalized sense, as a narrative form which presents the reader with a world which departs in some way from the everyday, ordinary, prosaic world. Lionel Stevenson, in "The Artistic Problem: Science Fiction as Romance," in *SF: The Other Side of Realism*, ed. Clareson, pp. 96–104, links the form of the genre with nineteenth-century rationalism: "In an age when the mental attitudes of science had vitiated the traditional sources of romance, the alternative was to explore the romantic possibilities of science itself" (p. 101).

32. Ursula LeGuin, Preface to *The Left Hand of Darkness* (1969; rpt., New York: Ace, 1976), no page; Suvin, *Metamorphoses*, p. 63; Robert Scholes, *Structural Fabulation: An Essay on the Fiction of the Future* (Notre Dame, Ind.: U of Notre Dame P, 1975), p. 62.

33. Quoted in Patrick Parrinder, "Science Fiction and the Scientific World-View," in *Science Fiction: A Critical Guide*, ed. Patrick Parrinder (London: Longman, 1979), p. 67.

34. Parrinder makes a similar point in the essay cited above. See also Gerald Prince, "How New Is New?" in *Coordinates: Placing Science Fiction and Fantasy*, ed. George E. Slusser et al. (Carbondale: Southern Illinois UP, 1983), pp. 28–30. Prince argues that "scientific motivation" acts as an aesthetic constraint on SF.

35. Gregory Benford, "Science and Science Fiction," in *Science Fiction: The Academic Awakening*, ed. Willis E. McNelly (Shreveport, La.: CEA Chap Book, 1974), p. 33.

36. Robert A. Heinlein, "Science Fiction: Its Nature, Faults, and Virtues," in *The Science Fiction Novel: Imagination and Social Criticism*, ed. Basil Davenport (1959; rpt., Chicago: Advent, 1969), p. 19.

37. "Twenty-two Answers and Two Postscripts: An Interview with Stanislaw Lem," conducted by Istvan Csicsery-Ronay, Jr., trans. Mark Lugowski, *Science-Fiction Studies* 13 (1986): 255.

38. Alfred Bester, quoted in Paul A. Carter, " 'You Can Write Science Fiction If You Want To,' " in *Hard Science Fiction*, ed. George E. Slusser and Eric S. Rabkin (Carbondale: Southern Illinois UP, 1986), p. 143.

39. Cf. Rabkin, *The Fantastic in Literature*, p. 121:

What is important in the definition of science fiction is not the appurtenances of ray guns and lab coats, but the "scientific" habits of mind: the idea that paradigms do control our view of all phenomena, that within these paradigms all normal occurrences can be solved, and that abnormal occurrences must either be explained or initiate the search for a better (usually more inclusive) paradigm.

40. John Huntington, "Science Fiction and the Future," rpt. in *Science Fiction: A Collection of Critical Essays*, ed. Mark Rose (Englewood Cliffs, N.J.: Prentice-Hall, 1976), p. 161.

41. I borrow the term from Suvin, *Metamorphoses*, p. 3 and passim.

42. Steven Marcus, "The Novel Again," in *The Novel: Modern Essays in Criticism*, ed. Robert M. Davis (Englewood Cliffs, N.J.: Prentice-Hall, 1969), p. 284.

43. Jonathan Culler, *Structuralist Poetics* (Ithaca, N.Y.: Cornell UP, 1975), pp. 141–45.

44. Quoted in Suvin, *Metamorphoses*, p. 54.

45. Rose, *Alien Encounters*, p. 27.

46. Suvin, *Metamorphoses*, p. 4.

47. See, for example, L. David Allen, *SF: A Reader's Guide*, pp. 5–14.

48. Other critics have used other terms to identify this mental process. Suvin, in *Metamorphoses*, opts for *analogic* rather than *speculative*, but it is not a term that lends itself to a verb form, and his definition is redundant and unclear: "The analogic model of SF is based on analogy rather than extrapolation" (p. 29). Stanley Schmidt, in "The Science in Science Fiction," in *Many Futures, Many Worlds: Theme and Form in Science Fiction*, ed. Thomas D. Clareson (Kent, Ohio: Kent State UP, 1977), pp. 27–49, subsumes all of SF's thought experiments under the term *speculation* and uses the word *innovation* to designate the more creative process. I find this usage imprecise and vague.

49. Poul Anderson, *Earthmen and Strangers*, ed. Robert Silverberg (New York: Dell, 1966), pp. 78–79.

50. Quoted in Wolfe, *The Known and the Unknown*, p. 5.

51. Patrick Parrinder, "The Alien Encounter: Or, Ms Brown and Mrs LeGuin," in *SF: A Critical Guide*, ed. Parrinder, p. 150.

52. Cf. Donald A. Wollheim, quoted in Wendland, p. 34, on the conventionalization of novums: "Once the argument [for the novum] is made, the premise is at once accepted on its own word, enters the tool-shed of the science-fiction writer, and may be utilized thereafter by any craftsman without further repetition of the operational manual."

53. Walter E. Meyers discusses the argument for and against ESP in *Aliens and Linguists: Language Study and Science Fiction* (Athens: U of Georgia P, 1980), pp. 131–44.

54. These terms are not always construed in this way. See, for example, George E. Slusser, "The Ideal Worlds of Science Fiction," in *Hard Science Fiction*, pp. 214–46.

55. James Gunn, "The Readers of Hard SF," in *Hard Science Fiction*, p. 76. Cf. Slusser and Rabkin in their Introduction to *Hard Science Fiction*, p. vii: in hard SF,

> both setting and dramatic situation must derive strictly from the rigorous postulation and working out of a concrete physical problem. The method then of the hard SF story is logical, the means technological, and the result . . . objective and cold. What hard SF purports to affirm, therefore, is not the universality of human aspirations, for these are more often than not the "soft" products of our desires. Instead it asserts the truth of natural law, an absolute, seemingly ahuman vision of things.

56. Aldiss, *Billion Year Spree*, chap. 9.

57. Algis Budrys, "Paradise Charted," *TriQuarterly* 49 (Fall 1980): 24.

58. Roman Jakobson, "The Dominant," in *Readings in Russian Poetics*, ed. L. Matejka and K. Pomorsk (Cambridge: MIT P, 1971), p. 83.

59. See, for example, her essay "Science Fiction and Mrs. Brown," in *The Language of the Night: Essays on Fantasy and Science Fiction*, ed. Susan Wood (New York: G. P. Putnam's Sons, 1979), pp. 101–19.

60. Wolfe, p. 157.

61. For a tentative definition of science fantasy, see Brian Attebury, "Science Fantasy," in *Twentieth Century American Science Fiction Writers*, Part 2: M-Z, *Dictionary of Literary Biography*, Vol. 8, ed. David Cowart and Thomas L. Wymer (Detroit: Gale Research Co., 1981), pp. 236–42.

62. Allen, p. 7.

63. C. S. Lewis, "On Science Fiction," rpt. in *SF: A Collection of Critical Essays*, ed. Rose, p. 111.

64. Wolfe uses this term in *The Known and the Unknown*.

II. SF and the Reader

2.1 Reading SF

1. Menakhem Perry, "Literary Dynamics: How the Order of a Text Creates Its Meanings, with an Analysis of Faulkner's 'A Rose for Emily,' " *Poetics Today* 1, 1–2 (1979): 35–64, 311–61.

2. Marc Angenot, "The Absent Paradigm: An Introduction to the Semiotics of Science Fiction," *Science-Fiction Studies* 6 (1979): 10.

3. Albert Wendland, *Science, Myth, and the Fictional Creation of Alien Worlds* (Ann Arbor, Mich.: UMI Research P, 1985), p. 23.

4. For the notion of paradigm in relation to SF, and for parts of the analysis here, I am indebted to Marc Angenot, "The Absent Paradigm."

5. Angenot, p. 15.

6. C. S. Lewis, *Out of the Silent Planet* (1938; rpt., New York: Collier Books, 1965), p. 125.

7. Victor Shklovsky, "Art as Technique," in *Russian Formalist Criticism: Four Essays*, trans. and ed. Lee T. Lemon and Marion J. Reis (Lincoln: U of Nebraska P, 1965), p. 12.

8. Robert Scholes, *Structural Fabulation: An Essay on the Fiction of the Future* (Notre Dame, Ind.: U of Notre Dame P, 1975), p. 47.

9. H. G. Wells, "Fiction about the Future," in *H. G. Wells's Literary Criticism*, ed. Patrick Parrinder and Robert Philmus (Sussex: Harvester P, 1980), p. 248.

10. Darko Suvin, *Victorian Science Fiction in the United Kingdom: The Discourses of Knowledge and Power* (Boston: G. K. Hall, 1983), p. 308.

11. Suvin, *Victorian SF*, p. 309.

12. Suvin, *Victorian SF*, pp. 308, 309.

13. Suvin, *Metamorphoses of Science Fiction: On the Poetics and History of a Literary Genre* (New Haven, Conn.: Yale UP, 1979), p. 81.

14. Cf. Kingsley Amis, *New Maps of Hell: A Survey of Science Fiction* (New York: Harcourt Brace, 1960), p. 137: "*Idea as hero* is the basis of a great deal of science fiction." This sort of SF involves "the development of novelty without any . . . social or psychological implications" (p. 138). The conceptual basis of SF's estrangement explains in part why the genre is frequently described as a literature of ideas.

15. J. R. R. Tolkien, "On Fairy-Stories," in *Essays Presented to Charles Williams* (London: Oxford UP, 1947), p. 45.

16. Brian McHale, *Postmodernist Fiction* (New York: Methuen, 1987), p. 60.

17. Suvin, *Victorian SF*, p. 308.

18. Dieter Petzold has tried to do this for fantasy worlds in "Fantasy Fiction and Related Genres," *Modern Fiction Studies* 32, 1 (1986): 11–20. He offers his model with the following provision: "Aiming no higher than at heuristic usefulness, I make no claims for logical completeness" (p. 17).

19. Suvin, *Metamorphoses*, pp. 14–15.

20. McHale, p. 60.

21. Suvin, *Metamorphoses*, p. 79. If, however, the terran ambassador overinter-

prets or overdetermines that novum, making its connection to the basic narrative world too explicit or too particularized, then the fiction tends toward the dogmatic/didactic and loses its cognitive edge.

2.2 Wells's The Time Machine

1. Wells, "Fiction about the Future," in *H. G. Wells's Literary Criticism*, p. 246.
2. Wells, "Preface to *The Scientific Romances*," in *H. G. Wells's Literary Criticism*, p. 240.
3. Wells, "Preface to *The Scientific Romances*," p. 240.
4. Jean-Pierre Vernier, "*The Time Machine* and Its Context," trans. Frank D. McConnell, rpt. in *H. G. Wells:* The Time Machine *and* The War of the Worlds, ed. Frank D. McConnell (New York: Oxford UP, 1977), pp. 319, 318.
5. Amis, *New Maps of Hell*, p. 39.
6. Amis, pp. 39, 40.
7. Cited in McConnell, ed., p. 303.
8. Wells, "Preface to *The Sleeper Awakes*," in *H. G. Wells's Literary Criticism*, p. 238.
9. Wells, "Preface to *The Scientific Romances*," p. 242.
10. Samuel L. Hynes and Frank D. McConnell, "*The Time Machine* and *The War of the Worlds*: Parable and Possibility in H. G. Wells," rpt. in McConnell, ed., p. 349.
11. *H. G. Wells:* The Time Machine *and* The War of the Worlds, ed. McConnell, p. 62. All subsequent references will be to this edition and will be incorporated parenthetically in the text.
12. Gary K. Wolfe, *The Known and the Unknown: The Iconography of Science Fiction* (Kent, Ohio: Kent State UP, 1979), p. 8.
13. Cf. Frank D. McConnell, *The Science Fiction of H. G. Wells* (New York: Oxford UP, 1981), p. 84: "Faced with the implied question, 'What does the future of mankind hold in store?' the narrator, like a good scientific investigator, tries out explanation after explanation of the observed facts until he finally hits on the one explanation that suffices, that explains all the facts as observed and nothing but them." It should be noted here that nothing in the text (or the critical canon, for that matter) tends to call into question the validity of the Time Traveller's final reading of the relation between the Morlocks and the Elois.
14. John Huntington, *The Logic of Fantasy: H. G. Wells and Science Fiction* (New York: Columbia UP, 1982), pp. 42–43.
15. Each and every one of the Time Traveller's interpretations is ultimately validated by extrapolative logic or given an extrapolative coloration. Some of the other phrases he uses are: "We see some beginnings of this even in our own time" (p. 41); "For the first time I began to realize an odd consequence of the social effort in which we are engaged. And yet, come to think, it is a logical consequence enough" (pp. 42–43); "That is the drift of the current in spite of the eddies" (p. 43); "There is a sentiment arising, and it will grow . . . " (p. 44); and "Even now man is far less discriminating and exclusive in his food than he once was . . . " (p. 74).
16. In the analysis that follows, I am indebted to Suvin, *Metamorphoses*, pp. 230ff. Other critics have called attention to this aspect of *The Time Machine*. Cf. Mark Rose, *Alien Encounters: Anatomy of Science Fiction* (Cambridge, Mass.: Harvard UP, 1981), p. 102: "we have the traveller's intellectual movement through a series of hypotheses about the world of 802701 A. D." Frank McConnell, in *The Science Fiction of H. G. Wells,* claims that "three theories of society are in the end put forth by the Time Traveller, each of them cancelling out its predecessor, each of them a more complex view of the possibility of social evolution over an immense period of time, and each of them more grim" (p. 80). Like the Time Traveller himself, who also sees but three phases in his process of mastering the world of the future, McConnell

overlooks the first theory proposed (and only briefly maintained) of a perfect Communist Eden.

17. Huntington, p. 52.

18. Leo J. Henkin, *Darwinism in the English Novel, 1860–1910: The Impact of Evolution on Victorian Fiction* (New York: Russell & Russell, 1963), p. 197.

19. Henkin, p. 198.

20. Wells, "Preface to *The Scientific Romances,*" pp. 242–43.

21. Hynes and McConnell, p. 351.

22. Quoted in Suvin, *Metamorphoses,* p. 209.

23. Hynes and McConnell, p. 348.

24. Rose, pp. 101–102.

25. McConnell, *The Science Fiction of H. G. Wells,* pp. 70–71.

2.3 Lem's *Solaris*

1. Gregory Benford is the only critic who even obliquely calls into question the sentience of the ocean, in "Aliens and Knowability: A Scientist's Perspective," in *Bridges to Science Fiction,* ed. George E. Slusser et al. (Carbondale: Southern Illinois UP, 1980), p. 62: "I think a better understanding of *Solaris* might evolve from looking at it from the perspective of the social sciences. If in some sense the ocean were alive, then *Solaris* might, for example, be read as a reflection on the error of applying a mechanistic description to a social science, *not* to a physical one." In the analysis that follows, I will argue that Lem does indeed present us with an ocean that is at once alive, sentient, and incredibly alien in order to interrogate the empiricist assumptions of science in general.

2. Stanislaw Lem, *Solaris,* trans. from the French by Joanna Kilmartin and Steve Cox (1961; rpt., New York: Berkley, 1970), p. 26. All subsequent references will be to this edition and will be incorporated parenthetically in the text.

3. Rose, p. 82.

4. Rose, p. 83.

5. Angenot, p. 17.

6. Rose, p. 85.

7. Stephen Potts, "Dialogues concerning Human Understanding: Empirical Views of God from Locke to Lem," in *Bridges to Science Fiction,* p. 43.

8. One of the most forceful readings adopting this position is Istvan Csicsery-Ronay, Jr.'s, "The Book Is the Alien: On Certain and Uncertain Readings of Lem's *Solaris,*" *Science-Fiction Studies* 12 (1985): 6–21.

9. Wendland, p. 86.

10. Wendland, p. 90. Cf. Csicsery-Ronay, p. 6: "Science's answers reflect the questions scientists are impelled to ask of nature, and thus anthropomorphism is reintroduced at the level of hypothesis formation that preselects the data to be studied."

11. Rose, p. 89.

12. David Ketterer also makes this point, in *New Worlds for Old: The Apocalyptic Imagination, Science Fiction, and American Literature* (Bloomington: Indiana UP, 1974), p. 195.

13. Potts, p. 42.

14. Csicsery-Ronay, p. 17.

15. Kelvin later discovers that the other occupants of the station have used similar methods to verify their own sanity. Csicery-Ronay, who reads the novel in radically skeptical terms, argues that this test only foregrounds the sanity issue, without in any way resolving it. For him the fact that the figures match up could simply be the product of Kelvin's imagination as well. As a result, "never in reading *Solaris* can we establish a hierarchy of phenomena or significations stable enough for us to interpret events unambiguously. We can never tell what is the 'real' structure of

events and what are the deviations" (p. 13). I reject this reading for a number of reasons. For one thing, as I hope to show, it tends to overlook unambiguous assertions elsewhere in the text that progress is being made in the "Solaris affair." Also, it runs directly counter to the "cognitive optimism" that Lem has consistently spoken for in his essays and other writings. See, for example, his disparaging remarks about the SF of Ballard and Bradbury in "The Time-Travel Story and Related Matters of Science-Fiction Structuring," in his *Microworlds: Writings on Science Fiction and Fantasy*, ed. Franz Rottensteiner (New York: Harcourt Brace Jovanovich, 1984), pp. 157–60. Most important, this reading finally trivializes the novel, reducing it at one level to the totally unverifiable ramblings of a complete madman. I would argue that the novel blurs the line between sanity and insanity without erasing it.

16. Potts, p. 50.

17. Robert M. Philmus, "The Cybernetic Paradigms of Stanislaw Lem," in *Hard Science Fiction*, ed. George E. Slusser and Eric S. Rabkin (Carbondale: Southern Illinois UP, 1986), p. 187.

18. Ketterer, p. 188.

19. Csicsery-Ronay, p. 7.

20. Philmus, p. 201.

21. Csicsery-Ronay, p. 8.

22. Potts, p. 51. Potts links this idea to the protagonist's name: "like the scale of temperature that bears his name, Kelvin begins at absolute zero" (p. 51). He is thus able, one might add, in some way to take the measure of an absolutely alien quantity.

23. Csicsery-Ronay, p. 12.

24. Csicsery-Ronay, p. 12.

25. Cf. Wendland, p. 88: "The device of analogy is thus brought into question, or *objectified*, held up for examination and, in this case, found wanting."

26. Ketterer, p. 197. See Potts, p. 49, for a summary of critical opinion about this last theory. Snow, by the way, renounces "paternity" of the theory, a word which underscores the fact that humans "give birth" to theories that are inevitably of a human shape.

27. Rose, p. 82.

28. Speculative SF also tends to call into question other SF based on such models. As Ketterer says of *Solaris*, "Implicit in this basic assumption of Lem's is a critique of virtually all science fiction as hypocritically presenting images of radically new worlds based on anthropomorphic techniques of extrapolation and analogy" (p. 186).

29. Potts, pp. 51–52.

III. A Typology of SF

3.1 Alien Encounters

1. The example and the quotations can be found in "Fiction about the Future," in *H. G. Wells's Literary Criticism*, ed. Patrick Parrinder and Robert M. Philmus (Sussex: Harvester P, 1980), pp. 248–49.

2. Roger Zelazny, "For a Breath I Tarry," rpt. in *Alpha One*, ed. Robert Silverberg (New York: Ballantine, 1970), p. 80. All subsequent references will be to this anthology and will be incorporated parenthetically in the text.

3. Both Gary K. Wolfe, in *The Known and the Unknown: The Iconography of Science Fiction* (Kent, Ohio: Kent State UP, 1979), and Mark Rose, in *Alien Encounters: Anatomy of Science Fiction* (Cambridge, Mass.: Harvard UP, 1981), for example, divide alien encounters according to the nature of the alien (machine, monster, extraterrestrial) and thus tend to obscure the thematic congruence informing this type of SF.

4. Scott Sanders, "The Disappearance of Character," in *Science Fiction: A Critical Guide*, ed. Patrick Parrinder (London: Longman, 1979), p. 132.

5. Robert Scholes, *Structural Fabulation: An Essay on the Fiction of the Future* (Notre Dame, Ind.: U of Notre Dame P, 1975), p. 48.

6. Cited in Amis, *New Maps of Hell: A Survey of Science Fiction* (New York: Harcourt Brace, 1960), p. 128.

7. Cited by Robert G. Pielke, "Humans and Aliens: A Unique Relationship," *Mosaic* 13, 3–4 (1980): 30.

8. Istvan Csicsery-Ronay, Jr., "Towards the Last Fairy Tale: On the Fairy-Tale Paradigm in the Strugatskys' Science Fiction, 1963–72," *Science-Fiction Studies* 13 (1986): 28.

9. Gregory Benford, "Aliens and Knowability: A Scientist's Perspective," in *Bridges to Science Fiction*, ed. George E. Slusser et al. (Carbondale: Southern Illinois UP, 1980), pp. 53, 56.

10. Benford, "Effing the Ineffable," in *Aliens: The Anthropology of Science Fiction*, ed. George E. Slusser and Eric S. Rabkin (Carbondale: Southern Illinois UP, 1987), p. 15.

11. The quote is taken from Lem's novel *Solaris*, trans. from the French by Joanna Kilmartin and Steve Cox (1961; rpt., New York: Berkley, 1970), p. 167. For Lem's critique of American SF, see his *Microworlds: Writings on Science Fiction and Fantasy*, ed. Franz Rottensteiner (San Diego: Harcourt Brace Jovanovich, 1984), pp. 246–51.

12. Lem, *Microworlds*, p. 247.

13. Murray Leinster, "First Contact," rpt. in *Approaches to Science Fiction*, ed. Donald L. Lawler (Boston: Houghton Mifflin, 1978), p. 336. All subsequent references will be to this anthology and will be incorporated in the text.

14. Wolfe, p. 205.

15. This is not to say that such SF cannot have other merits or provide other satisfactions. Some of the "classic" SF stories—Campbell's "Who Goes There?" (1938) and Fredric Brown's "Arena" (1944), for example—fall into the alien-as-enemy type.

16. Ursula K. LeGuin, "Nine Lives," rpt. in *Approaches to Science Fiction*, p. 386. All subsequent references will be to this anthology and will be incorporated parenthetically in the text.

3.1.1 *Silverberg's* Dying Inside

1. Robert Silverberg, *Dying Inside* (1972; rpt., New York: Ballantine, 1976), pp. 1–2. All subsequent references will be to this edition and will be incorporated parenthetically in the text.

2. Silverberg himself has referred to the work as a "straight mainstream novel" with a science fiction motif added on. See *Hell's Cartographers*, ed. Brian Aldiss and Harry Harrison (London: Weidenfeld & Nicolson, 1975).

3. Peter S. Alterman points out in "Four Voices in Robert Silverberg's *Dying Inside*," in *Critical Encounters II: Writers and Themes in Science Fiction*, ed. Tom Staicar (New York: Frederick Ungar, 1982), pp. 90–103, that the papers Selig writes, two of which are incorporated in the text, tend to reflect the protagonist's overriding concerns. The Kafka paper deals with trying to achieve "grace in the acceptance of the inevitable" (p. 92). The Greek tragedy paper deals not only with relationships between siblings (cf. David's relation with his sister, Judith) but also with the hero's acceptance of a curse visited on him by the gods.

4. Alterman also draws attention to this aspect of the narration, pp. 101–102.

5. The chapters in the third person are 2, 9, 12, 16, 19, 20, and 22.

6. One is reminded here of that beautiful passage from another example of alien encounter SF, LeGuin's *The Left Hand of Darkness* (1969; rpt., New York: Ace, 1976), pp. 248–49:

> For it seemed to me, and I think to him, that it was from the sexual tension between us, admitted now and understood, but not assuaged, that the great and sudden assurance of friendship between us rose: a friendship so much needed by us both in our exile, and already so well proved in the days and nights of our bitter journey, that it might as well be called, now as later, love. But it was from the difference between us, not from the affinities and likenesses, but from the difference, that the love came: and it was itself the bridge, the only bridge, across what divided us.

7. Alterman, p. 95.
8. Alterman makes a similar point, p. 100.

3.1.2 *Watson's* The Martian Inca

1. Arthur C. Clarke, *Childhood's End* (1953; rpt., New York: Ballantine, 1976), p. 200. All subsequent references will be to this edition and will be incorporated parenthetically in the text.
2. Ian Watson, *The Martian Inca* (1977; rpt., New York: Ace, 1978), p. 98. All subsequent references will be to this edition and will be incorporated parenthetically in the text.
3. Quoted in Cy Chauvin, "Ian Watson's Miracle Men," in *Critical Encounters II: Writers and Themes in Science Fiction*, ed. Tom Staicar (New York: Frederick Ungar, 1982), p. 52.
4. Quoted in Chauvin, p. 44.

3.2 Alternate Society SF

1. Wells, "Fiction about the Future," p. 249; Amis, *New Maps of Hell*, p. 87; Asimov, "Social Science Fiction," rpt. in *Science Fiction: The Future*, ed. Dick Allen (New York: Harcourt Brace Jovanovich, 1971), p. 273.
2. A partial listing of "important" twentieth-century alternate society SF might include Wells, *A Modern Utopia*; Zamiatin, *We*; Stapledon, *Last and First Men*; Huxley, *Brave New World* and *Island*; Orwell, *1984*; Bradbury, *Fahrenheit 451*; Vonnegut, *Player Piano*; Kornbluth and Pohl, *The Space Merchants*; Heinlein, *The Moon Is a Harsh Mistress*; Fritz Leiber, *The Wanderer*; Burgess, *A Clockwork Orange*; Brunner, *Stand on Zanzibar*; Silverberg, *The World Inside*; Herbert, *The Santaroga Barrier*; LeGuin, *The Dispossessed* and *Always Coming Home*; Delany, *Triton* and *Dhalgren*; Russ, *The Female Man*; and Atwood, *A Handmaid's Tale*.
3. Asimov, p. 263.
4. Asimov, p. 269.
5. Orson Scott Card, *The Worthing Chronicle* (New York: Ace, 1983), pp. 258, 259.
6. Tom Moylan, *Demand the Impossible: Science Fiction and the Utopian Imagination* (New York: Methuen, 1987), p. 237. See also Martin Schaefer, "The Rise and Fall of Antiutopia: Utopia, Gothic Romance, Dystopia," *Science-Fiction Studies* 6 (1979): 287.
7. Moylan, p. 45.
8. Eric S. Rabkin, "Atavism and Utopia," in *No Place Else: Explorations in Utopian and Dystopian Fiction*, ed. Rabkin et al. (Carbondale: Southern Illinois UP, 1983), p. 1.
9. The lack of the personal, agonistic angle explains in part why Stapledon's *Last and First Men* reads more like eschatological philosophy than novelistic fiction.
10. An interesting border case is provided by John Wyndham's *The Chrysalids*, which features, in equal measure, the novum of a rigidified society brought about by nuclear holocaust and the novum of a mutated group of telepaths who are victimized by that society until they escape to join others of their race. The fact that neither novum is given dominance to some extent explains the novel's lack of focus.
11. For a discussion of the role of boundaries in the development of plot, see

Jurij Lotman, *The Structure of the Artistic Text*, trans. Ronald Vroon, Michigan Slavic Contributions, no. 7 (Ann Arbor: U of Michigan P, 1977), pp. 228–34.

12. Peter Ruppert, *Reader in a Strange Land: The Activity of Reading Literary Utopias* (Athens: U of Georgia P, 1986), p. 27. For a general discussion of the role played by barriers in SF, see Gary Wolfe, *The Known and the Unknown*, pp. 30–51. For a discussion of barriers in utopic fiction, see Fredric Jameson, "Of Islands and Trenches," *Diacritics* 7 (1977): 2–21.

13. Frye, "Varieties of Literary Utopias," in *Utopias and Utopian Thought*, ed. Frank E. Manuel (Boston: Houghton Mifflin, 1966), p. 34.

14. Rabkin, "Atavism and Utopia," p. 4.

15. Ruppert, p. 101.

16. Gordon Beauchamp, "Cultural Primitivism as Norm in the Dystopian Novel," *Extrapolation* 19, 1 (1977): 88.

17. Ruppert, p. 73.

18. Ruppert, p. 103.

19. These terms are used, respectively, by John Huntington, "Utopian and Anti-Utopian Logic: H. G. Wells and His Successors," *Science-Fiction Studies* 9 (1982): 124; Gary Morson, *The Boundaries of Genre: Dostoevsky's "Diary of a Writer" and Traditions of Literary Utopia* (Austin: U of Texas P, 1981), p. x; Moylan, p. 42; Ruppert, pp. 121–50; and Michel Foucault, *The Order of Things*, trans. Alan Sheridan-Smith (New York: Pantheon, 1970).

20. Frank Herbert, *The Santaroga Barrier* (New York: Berkley, 1968), p. 255.

21. Gary Wolfe, *The Known and the Unknown*, p. 50.

22. Yevgeny Zamiatin, *We*, trans. Mirra Ginsberg (1972; rpt., New York: Avon, 1983), pp. 116–17.

23. Huntington (pp. 129–34) and Ruppert (pp. 115ff.) examine some of the other knife-edge paradoxes in *We*.

24. Ruppert, p. 122.

3.2.1 Wilhelm's Where Late the Sweet Birds Sang

1. Kate Wilhelm, *Where Late the Sweet Birds Sang* (1976; rpt., New York: Pocket Books, 1977), p. 8. All subsequent references will be to this edition and will be incorporated parenthetically in the text.

2. For a similar critique of the treatment of the breeders, see Maureen S. Barr, *Alien to Femininity: Speculative Fiction and Feminist Theory* (New York: Greenwood P, 1987), pp. 129–31.

3. The ending of part three involves not exclusion but escape and serves as a coda to the novel's three-part structure. As should be clear from the summary of each section, they all share recurrent narrative motifs which impart to the novel a kind of inevitable rhythm, a "natural" necessity, in which the end echoes the beginning. The first part begins with a community of disparate individuals which grows more and more homogeneous until it necessarily ostracizes its sole remaining voice of the self. Part two begins with a harmonious and heterogeneous community, spawns the solitary individual, and then excludes her for its own safety. The final part begins with the community set over and against the unique individual, who eventually escapes the confines of that moribund group in order to start a community of separate individuals of his own. This pattern is reinforced by the shifting relation between humans and nature as worked out in the three parts. The first shows humanity at the mercy of nature; the second emphasizes the attempt to overcome nature; the third moves toward the peaceful accommodation between human society and natural forces.

3.2.2 Russ's The Female Man

1. Alternate histories, the creation of alternate pasts or presents based upon the reversal of historical fact, belong to the subgenre science fantasy. See chapter 4 for a detailed treatment of this narrative type.

2. Joanna Russ, *The Female Man* (1975; rpt., New York: Bantam, 1978), pp. 6–7. All subsequent references will be to this edition and will be incorporated parenthetically in the text.

3. The first-person narration of the novel reinforces this notion of identity by shifting the referent of the "I" quickly from one female actant to another (e.g., pp. 43–44) or by collapsing the "I" into a "we" (e.g., p. 62), as if a joint experience were being related. This collapsing of the "I" into "we" occurs most frequently with Janet and Joanna, a circumstance which links those two characters as, in some way, "soul-mates."

4. Moylan argues that the "alternative probability premise is the basis for the open and fragmented form of the novel itself" (*Demand the Impossible*, p. 62). The premise does allow for the abrupt shifting between time lines that fragments the text and does undercut "attitudes towards causality and progress that are restricted to simplified linear progression in one universal historical reality" (Moylan, p. 85), but it does not really account for the text's self-reflexivity. A formal analysis of *The Female Man*—one investigating its nine-part structure, its use of montage, its disrupted and even contradictory narrative line, its self-reflexive commentaries—is outside the scope of this work. For a partial treatment of these features, see Moylan, pp. 82–90.

5. One can find such a description in Moylan, pp. 65–75.

6. Moylan, p. 67.

7. Catherine L. McClenahan, "Textual Politics: The Uses of the Imagination in Joanna Russ's *The Female Man*," *Transactions of the Wisconsin Academy of Science, Arts, and Letters* 70 (1982): 117.

8. McClenahan, p. 121. Cf. Moylan, p. 74: "Womanland . . . is the place of action and mediation between utopia and dystopia, the front line of female freedom and fighting. . . . The anger and resistance generated out of Jael's world is the necessary step in the struggle, the necessary mediation between the oppression of Jeannine's and Joanna's '1969' and Janet's utopia."

9. Quoted in McClenahan, p. 121.

10. McClenahan, p. 120.

11. Moylan, p. 66.

12. Douglas Barbour, "Joanna Russ's *The Female Man*: An Appreciation," *Sphinx* 4, 1: 72. Cf. Natalie M. Rosinsky, "A Female Man? The 'Medusan' Humor of Joanna Russ," *Extrapolation* 23, 1 (1982): "we learn from *The Female Man* to step outside the frame of the 'cartoon' of our lives, just as Jeannine and Joanna step out of their lives into different realms of possibility" (p. 35).

13. Moylan, p. 76.

14. Moylan, p. 81.

15. Moylan, p. 57.

3.3 Gadget SF

1. Cited by Paul A. Carter, *The Creation of Tomorrow: Fifty Years of Magazine Science Fiction* (New York: Columbia UP, 1977), p. 4.

2. Brian Aldiss, *Billion Year Spree: The True History of Science Fiction* (New York: Schocken, 1973), p. 182.

3. Jack Williamson, "With Folded Hands," rpt. in *A Treasury of Science Fiction*, ed. Groff Conklin (New York: Berkley, 1948), p. 73. Subsequent page references to the story will be incorporated parenthetically in the text.

4. Aldiss, pp. 230–31.

3.3.1 *Clarke's* Rendezvous with Rama

1. Arthur C. Clarke, *Rendezvous with Rama* (1973; rpt., New York: Ballantine, 1988), p. 12. All subsequent references will be to this edition and will be incorporated parenthetically in the text.

2. Nicholas Ruddick, "The World Turned Inside Out: Decoding Clarke's *Rendezvous with Rama*," *Science-Fiction Studies* 12 (1985): 42.

3. C. N. Manlove, *Science Fiction: Ten Explorations* (Kent, Ohio: Kent State UP, 1986), p. 156.

4. Ruddick, pp. 42–43.

5. Ruddick, p. 42.

6. George E. Slusser, *The Space Odysseys of Arthur C. Clarke*, Milford Series of Popular Writers of Today, no. 8 (San Bernardino, Calif.: Borgo P, 1978), p. 61. Other critics who find that the novel thwarts our ability to understand its novum are Manlove, pp. 143–60; and Eric S. Rabkin, *Arthur C. Clarke*, Starmont Reader's Guide 1 (Mercer Island, Wash.: Starmont House, 1979).

7. Manlove, pp. 152, 153, 156. But the metaphor doesn't work. Rama presents a situation of variable gravity, in which it is possible, in places, to put one's feet firmly on the ground.

8. Ruddick, p. 43.

9. John Hollow, *Against the Night, the Stars: The Science Fiction of Arthur C. Clarke* (San Diego: Harcourt Brace Jovanovich, 1983), pp. 159, 160.

10. Rabkin, pp. 51–52.

11. Ruddick, p. 43.

12. Cf. Hollow, p. 160: "the fact that the cylinder turns out to be a sort of 'space ark,' carrying the disembodied patterns of its builders, makes the name Rama, the name of one of the incarnations of the Hindu god Vishnu the Preserver, more important than the humans who chose it anticipated."

13. Wendland, p. 105. Wendland points out elsewhere that the alien habitat of Rama "is seen primarily in terms of its rational functionalism. But not only is it *seen* that way, it also apparently was *created* with a focus solely on functionalism. . . . Clarke . . . makes a habitat that at times seems an extension of the people viewing it" (p. 100). Wendland goes on then to indict the novel because it privileges and supports SF's "special group" (p. 104), those who believe in the capabilities of science and technology. Wendland's position is that only SF which objectifies and calls into question this group and its assumptions is "experimental"; the rest is "conventional." Wendland, I think, is importing his own ideological orientation into his valuation of SF.

14. Ruddick, p. 47.

15. Rabkin, p. 52. Rabkin's misreading of the thrust of the text is a function, I would argue, of a failure to specify its novum, and thus an argument for the kind of typology articulated in this chapter.

16. Hollow, p. 164.

3.3.2 Strugatskys' Roadside Picnic

1. Arkady and Boris Strugatsky, *Roadside Picnic/Tale of the Troika*, trans. Antinina W. Bouis (1972; rpt., New York: Pocket Books, 1977), p. 4. All subsequent references will be to this edition and will be incorporated parenthetically in the text.

2. This reading is supported not only by the nature of the objects found in the Zone but also by the novel's title, and by references in the novel to "rubbish remaining after the Visitation" (p. 150). Stanislaw Lem proposes, in *Microworlds: Writings on Science Fiction and Fantasy*, ed. Franz Rottensteiner (San Diego: Harcourt Brace Jovanovich, 1984), a third possibility, a "new interpretation of the riddle presented by the landing" (p. 261):

> We maintain that there has been no landing after all. Our hypothesis, indeed, runs otherwise. . . . A spaceship filled with containers that held samples of the products of a highly developed civilization came into the vicinity of the earth. It was not a manned ship, but an automatically piloted space probe. . . . In the approach to earth,

the vessel sustained damage and broke into six parts, which one after another plunged from their orbit to earth. (P. 268)

Lem's line of reasoning, though ingenious, is ultimately irrelevant because it speculates about matters outside the text. Also, it suggests that the objects of the Zone should be seen as "gifts," a reading that the text does not support (and which, I think, impoverishes the text by naturalizing the objects).

3. Istvan Csicsery-Ronay, Jr., "Towards the Last Fairy Tale: On the Fairy-Tale Paradigm in the Strugatskys' Science Fiction, 1963–72," *Science-Fiction Studies* 13 (1986): 27. Lem makes a similar suggestion in *Microworlds*, p. 253. I am much indebted, by the way, to Csicsery-Ronay's analysis in the argument which follows.

4. Csicsery-Ronay, p. 28.

5. Csicsery-Ronay, p. 27.

6. Csicsery-Ronay, p. 25.

7. Lem, *Microworlds*, p. 259.

8. Csicsery-Ronay, p. 21.

9. Csicsery-Ronay, p. 21.

10. The titles of the chapters narrated by Schuhart reveal his progressive isolation and alienation from the social order. They are, successively, "Redrick Schuhart, Age 23, Bachelor, Laboratory Assistant at the Harmont Branch of the International Institute for Extraterrestrial Cultures"; "Redrick Schuhart, Age 28, Married, No Permanent Occupation"; and "Redrick Schuhart, Age 31."

11. All of the critics of the novel have commented on its fairy-tale structure. See Simonetta Salvestroni, "The Ambiguous Miracle in Three Novels by the Strugatsky Brothers," *Science-Fiction Studies* 11 (1984): 298–300; Lem, *Microworlds*, pp. 276–78; and Csicsery-Ronay, pp. 21–35. The last entry treats *Roadside Picnic* convincingly as an "inverted" and ambiguous fairy tale.

12. Csicsery-Ronay offers a subtle reading of the meaning of the novel's open-endedness. But I wonder if the novel is really open-ended, if indeed we finally do *not* know whether Red's wish is granted. There is textual evidence to suggest that the wish is not granted. Internal markers place Red's experience with the Zone as happening roughly thirteen to twenty years after the Visitation. The interview with Pilman that serves as the prologue to the novel occurs thirty years after the Visitation (p. 4). There is no evidence in that interview intimating that the world (or Pilman, for that matter) has undergone a drastic change of heart.

13. Csicsery-Ronay, p. 35.

14. Csicsery-Ronay, p. 30.

15. Csicsery-Ronay, p. 29.

16. There is much in the novel supporting a reading of it in religious terms. The word *visitation* itself carries religious connotations. And Red is continually connecting the Zone with religious experiences, even if only ironically. Cf. his comment to Panov, p. 17: "Pray on, pray. The further into the Zone the nearer to Heaven." See also pp. 17, 64.

3.4 Alternate World SF

1. Clifford D. Simak, "Desertion," rpt. in *Beyond Tomorrow*, ed. Damon Knight (Greenwich, Conn.: Fawcett, 1965), p. 197. All subsequent references will be to this anthology and will be incorporated parenthetically in the text.

2. Thomas D. Clareson, "Clifford D. Simak: The Inhabited Universe," in *Voices for the Future: Essays on Major Science Fiction Writers*, Vol. 1, ed. Thomas D. Clareson (Bowling Green, Ohio: Bowling Green U Popular P, 1976), p. 72.

3. Gary K. Wolfe, "Autoplastic and Alloplastic Adaptations in Science Fiction: 'Waldo' and 'Desertion,' " in *Coordinates: Placing Science Fiction and Fantasy*, ed.

George E. Slusser et al. (Carbondale: Southern Illinois UP, 1983), pp. 65–79. I am much indebted to Wolfe in the analysis which follows.

4. Wolfe, p. 77.

5. H. G. Wells, "The Star," rpt. in *Approaches to Science Fiction*, ed. Donald L. Lawler (Boston: Houghton Mifflin, 1978), p. 95.

6. Tom Godwin, "The Cold Equations," rpt. in *Approaches to Science Fiction*, p. 235.

7. David Ketterer, *New Worlds for Old: The Apocalyptic Imagination, Science Fiction, and American Literature* (Bloomington: Indiana UP, 1974), pp. 185–86.

3.4.1 Benford and Brin's Heart of the Comet

1. Gregory Benford and David Brin, *Heart of the Comet* (Toronto: Bantam, 1986), pp. 76, 254. All subsequent references will be to this edition and will be incorporated parenthetically in the text.

2. *Prime mover* is, in this case, an appropriate term. One of the major themes of the novel has to do with the joys, dangers, and responsibilities connected with "playing God" by radically altering lifeforms. See, for example, pp. 13, 14, 233, 269.

3.4.2 Ballard's The Drowned World

1. Ballard's phrase, cited by Lorenz J. Firsching, "J. G. Ballard's Ambiguous Apocalypse," *Science-Fiction Studies* 12 (1985): 298.

2. H. Bruce Franklin, "What Are We to Make of J. G. Ballard's Apocalypse?" in *Voices for the Future: Essays on Major Science Fiction Writers*, Vol. 2, ed. Thomas D. Clareson (Bowling Green, Ohio: Bowling Green U Popular P, 1979), p. 84. See also Brian Aldiss, "The Wounded Land: J. G. Ballard," in *Science Fiction: The Other Side of Realism*, ed. Clareson (Bowling Green, Ohio: Bowling Green U Popular P, 1971), pp. 124–26.

3. Lem, *Microworlds*, p. 159. Franklin gives a Marxist reading of this aspect of Ballard's work in "What Are We to Make of J. G. Ballard's Apocalypse?" pp. 100–105.

4. David Ketterer, *New Worlds for Old*, p. 187.

5. J. G. Ballard, *The Drowned World* (1962; rpt., New York: Penguin, 1976), p. 18. All subsequent references will be to this edition and will be incorporated parenthetically in the text.

6. Franklin, p. 91. Mark Rose makes a similar point in *Alien Encounters*, pp. 130–31.

7. Cf. Rose, p. 131: "The image of the sunken planetarium in this episode also makes explicit the way the familiar science-fiction icon of the starry infinite has been transferred to a watery world located below and within rather than above and outside."

8. Franklin, p. 91.

9. Rose, p. 137.

10. Robert L. Platzner, "The Metamorphic Vision of J. G. Ballard," *Essays in Literature* 10 (Fall 1983): 212.

11. Firsching, p. 306.

12. Platzner, p. 213. See also Firsching, pp. 307–308.

IV. Science Fantasy

1. Gary K. Wolfe argues, in "The Encounter with Fantasy," in *The Aesthetics of Fantasy Literature and Art*, ed. Roger C. Schlobin (Notre Dame, Ind.: U of Notre Dame P, 1982), pp. 1–2, that the "criterion of the impossible . . . may indeed be the first principle generally agreed upon for the study of fantasy." W. R. Irwin, in

The Game of the Impossible: A Rhetoric of Fantasy (Urbana: U of Illinois P, 1976), p. 4, defines fantasy as "a story based on and controlled by an overt violation of what is generally accepted as possibility; it is the narrative result of transforming the condition contrary to fact into 'fact' itself." Delany identifies the level of subjunctivity for fantasy as "*could not have happened*," in "About Five Thousand One Hundred and Seventy-five Words," rpt. in *SF: The Other Side of Realism*, ed. Thomas D. Clareson (Bowling Green, Ohio: Bowling Green U Popular P, 1971), p. 141. Russ, in "The Subjunctivity of Science Fiction," *Extrapolation* 15 (1973): 52, elaborates on Delany's idea as follows: "Fantasy . . . embodies a 'negative subjunctivity'—that is, fantasy is fantasy because it contravenes the real and violates it. . . . In Delany's words, fantasy is what *could not have happened*; i.e., what *cannot* happen, what *cannot* exist. . . . Fantasy violates the real, contravenes it, denies it, and insists on this denial throughout."

2. S. C. Fredericks, "Problems of Fantasy," *Science-Fiction Studies* 5 (1978): 37.

3. Dieter Petzold, "Fantasy Fiction and Related Genres," *Modern Fiction Studies* 32, 1 (1986): 16.

4. Mark Rose, *Alien Encounters: Anatomy of Science Fiction* (Cambridge, Mass.: Harvard UP, 1981), p. 20.

5. Brian Attebury, "Science Fantasy," in *Twentieth Century American Science Fiction Writers*, Part 2: M–Z, *Dictionary of Literary Biography*, Vol. 8, ed. David Cowart and Thomas L. Wymer (Detroit: Gale Research Co., 1981), p. 236.

6. Gary K. Wolfe, *Critical Terms for Science Fiction and Fantasy: A Glossary and Guide to Scholarship* (New York: Greenwood, 1986), p. 102.

7. Gene Wolfe, "What Do They Mean, SF?" *SFWA Bulletin* 75 (1981): 22.

8. William Atheling, Jr., *More Issues at Hand* (Chicago: Advent, 1970), pp. 99–100.

9. Darko Suvin, *Metamorphoses of Science Fiction* (New Haven, Conn.: Yale UP, 1979), p. 68.

10. L. David Allen, *Science Fiction: A Reader's Guide* (Lincoln, Nebr.: Centennial, 1973), p. 7.

11. The analysis which follows perhaps suggests a diachronic process, i.e., that first fantasy and science fiction existed as recognizable and distinct genres, and then someone came along and (deliberately?) combined features from each genre, creating a hybrid form. This is the way Gene Wolfe defines the genre. I must emphasize that I am describing a *synchronic system* in which, at a moment in time, science fantasy can be situated at a point of intersection between the two genres. The fact that certain fictions by Poe, Verne, E. R. Burroughs, and A. Merritt can best be identified as science fantasies attests to the genre's historical pedigree.

12. Eric S. Rabkin, *The Fantastic in Literature* (Princeton, N.J.: Princeton UP, 1977), p. 91.

13. Allen, p. 7.

14. Diane Waggoner, *The Hills of Faraway: A Guide to Fantasy* (New York: Atheneum, 1978), p. 19.

15. Fritz Leiber, *Conjure Wife* (1953; rpt., New York: Ace, 1984), p. 35. All subsequent references will be to this edition and will be incorporated parenthetically in the text.

16. Heinlein tries to rationalize magic in a similar way in two science fantasy novellas, "Waldo" and "Magic, Inc."

17. Robert M. Philmus, "The Cybernetic Paradigms of Stanislaw Lem," in *Hard Science Fiction*, ed. George E. Slusser and Eric S. Rabkin (Carbondale: Southern Illinois UP, 1986), p. 196.

18. George R. Guffey, "Noise, Information, and Statistics in Stanislaw Lem's *The Investigation*," in *Hard Science Fiction*, ed. Slusser and Rabkin, pp. 164–76.

19. Stanislaw Lem, *The Investigation*, trans. Adele Milch (1974; rpt., New York:

Avon, 1976), p. 22. All subsequent references will be to this edition and will be incorporated parenthetically in the text.

20. Philmus points out that Sciss's statistical and "probabilistic approach" is, like Gregory's Holmesian approach, also presented as problematic in the novel, in part because "any number of variables might yield the sort of correlation he posits between the disappearances in Norfolk and the (low) incidence of cancer in that region" (p. 195).

21. Philmus, p. 193. See also Guffey, p. 175.

22. Larry Niven, "Afterword," in *The Flight of the Horse* (New York: Ballantine, 1973), p. 211.

23. Niven, "The Theory and Practice of Time Travel," in *Looking Ahead: The Vision of Science Fiction*, ed. Dick Allen and Lori Allen (New York: Harcourt Brace Jovanovich, 1975), p. 366.

24. Gregory Benford, "Is There a Technological Fix for the Human Condition?" in *Hard SF*, ed. Slusser and Rabkin, p. 83.

25. Niven, "Theory and Practice," p. 363.

26. Cf. Attebury, p. 236:

> Such seemingly magical concepts as time-travel, telepathy, teleportation, precognition, and immortality are allowable [in SF] because they can be made to sound scientific. So many authors have proposed scientific rationales for such phenomena—warps in the space-time fabric, thought-wave amplifiers, anti-agathic drugs—that we now tend to accept them without second thought as a valid part of scientific extrapolation. They are conventions, which, like faster-than-light travel, open up the possibilities of the genre without seriously violating its rational basis.

27. Thomas N. Scortia, "Science Fiction as the Imaginary Experiment," in *Science Fiction, Today and Tomorrow*, ed. Reginald Bretnor (New York: Harper & Row, 1974), pp. 138–39.

28. Stanislaw Lem, *Microworlds: Writings on Science Fiction and Fantasy*, ed. Franz Rottensteiner (San Diego: Harcourt Brace Jovanovich, 1984), p. 142.

29. Niven, "Theory and Practice," p. 366. Algis Budrys argues, in "Paradise Charted," *TriQuarterly* 49 (1980), that another of Heinlein's classic time-loop stories, "By His Bootstraps," also parodies SF conventions, deriving "its underlying sagacity from the implicit truth that many of the enabling 'technologies' of Modern Science Fiction are only storytelling conventions, and scientifically absurd conventions" (p. 41).

30. Cf. Kingsley Amis, *New Maps of Hell: A Survey of Science Fiction* (New York: Harcourt Brace, 1960): "science fiction . . . maintains a respect for fact or presumptive fact, fantasy makes a point of flouting these" (p. 22).

31. C. S. Lewis, "On Science Fiction," rpt. in *Science Fiction: A Collection of Critical Essays*, ed. Mark Rose (Englewood Cliffs, N.J.: Prentice-Hall, 1976), p. 112.

32. Eric S. Rabkin, "The Rhetoric of Science in Fiction," in *Critical Encounters II: Writers and Themes in Science Fiction*, ed. Tom Staicar (New York: Frederick Ungar, 1982), p. 25.

33. Lewis, "On SF," pp. 111–12.

34. Attebury, p. 237.

35. *Dune* is an interesting case in point. I would argue that it is situated on the border between SF and science fantasy. I would use as evidence here the training of the protagonist Paul Atreides, which combines the magical witchcraft of the Bene Gesserit with the mathematical wizardry of the Mentats; the nature, size, and powers of the sand worms; and the parapsychological powers attributed to the main actants (Paul, his sister, his mother, the Bene Gesserit, and the Space Guild). Although these powers are scientifically grounded, they are invested with a mystical

or supernatural dimension that nudges *Dune* in the direction of science fantasy. In fact, the novel itself is built around sets of oppositions (science vs. religion, ecological science vs. mysticism) which may be loosely gathered within the science/ fantasy polarity. It might be argued that *Dune's* popularity, which foreshadows that which science fantasy enjoys today, was a function of the way in which it balanced science and magic within an SF format.

36. Attebury, p. 236.

37. Russ, "The Subjunctivity of Science Fiction," p. 55.

38. A. Merritt, *The Metal Monster* (1920; rpt., Westport, Conn.: Hyperion, 1974), p. 11. All subsequent references will be to this edition and will be incorporated parenthetically in the text.

39. It is this anticognitive aspect of some science fantasy which is responsible for Suvin's attack upon it. Although Suvin's objections do obtain for some science fantasy (especially space opera), I hope to show that he underestimates or passes over the cognitive possibilities of science fantasy in general.

40. Eric S. Rabkin, in "The Descent of Fantasy," in *Coordinates: Placing Science Fiction and Fantasy*, ed. George E. Slusser et al. (Carbondale: Southern Illinois UP, 1983), explains the link between fantasy and romance formulas as follows: "the less the particular, realistic content [of a narrative] the more its value rests on aesthetic considerations" (p. 22). Nonrealistic forms such as fantasy (and science fantasy), then, put a high premium on aesthetically pleasing shapeliness or form.

41. C. S. Lewis, *Out of the Silent Planet* (New York: Collier, 1965), p. 32.

42. Rose, p. 9. SF, however, would be a romance form rejecting such an ethical/ noumenal framework. Suvin distinguishes between two value-oriented "estranged literary genres," namely, "fantasy and folktale," both "anticognitive" forms:

> their world is actively oriented toward the hero. The folktale . . . world is oriented positively towards its protagonist; a folktale is defined by the hero's triumph: magic helpers and weapons are, with the necessary narrative retardations, at his beck and call. Inversely, the fantasy world is oriented negatively toward its protagonist; a fantasy is defined by its hero's horrible helplessness. . . . Thus, in the folktale and the fantasy, ethics coincides with physics—positive (hero-furthering) in the first case, and negative (hero-denying) in the second. (*Metamorphoses*, p. 19)

Most critics consider Suvin's "folktale" (the positively oriented world; cf. Tolkien's Faerie) a subset of fantasy. Like Suvin, Rosemary Jackson tends to belittle positively oriented fantasies; she considers them conservative, reactionary, and regressive because "they go along with a desire to cease 'to be,' a longing to transcend the human" (*Fantasy: The Literature of Subversion* [London: Methuen, 1981], p. 156). Unlike Suvin, however, she sees real value in negatively oriented fantasy, "post-Romantic fantasy (as opposed to faery)" (p. 81), a subversive literature of the nineteenth and twentieth centuries, in which supernatural or demonic motifs have been internalized and partially naturalized. This "secular" fantasy interrogates the category of the "real" and blurs the boundaries between good and evil, "the easy polarization of good and evil which had operated in tales of supernaturalism and magic" (p. 56). Although modern fantasy may problematize the moral dialect, the categories of good and evil to some extent inhere in fantasy, defined as it is by the notions of unreality, supernature, and Otherness. Cf. Fredric Jameson, *The Political Unconscious: Narrative as a Socially Symbolic Act* (Ithaca, New York: Cornell UP, 1981): "Yet surely, in the shrinking world of the present day, . . . it ought to be less difficult to understand to what degree the concept of good and evil is a positional one that coincides with categories of Otherness" (pp. 114–15).

43. Ursula LeGuin, *The Language of the Night: Essays on Fantasy and Science Fiction*, ed. Susan Wood (New York: G. P. Putnam's Sons, 1979), p. 65. Cf. Robert Scholes,

"Boiling Roses: Thoughts on Science Fantasy," in *Intersections: Fantasy and Science Fiction*, ed. George E. Slusser and Eric S. Rabkin (Carbondale: Southern Illinois UP, 1987): "Fantasy, until very recently, has always offered us a Manichean world in which values are polarized by absolutes of good and evil. Fictions grounded in such a matrix regularly present ultimate good and ultimate evil embodied in the fictional characters of the text" (p. 7).

44. Waggoner, p. 26.

45. Gene Wolfe, pp. 22, 23.

46. Jack P. Rawlins, "Confronting the Alien: Fantasy and Anti-Fantasy in Science Fiction Film and Literature," in *Bridges to Fantasy*, ed. George E. Slusser et al. (Carbondale: Southern Illinois UP, 1982), pp. 165, 168.

47, Cf. Jackson: "[Fantasy's] introduction of the 'unreal' is set against the category of the 'real'—a category which the fantastic interrogates by its difference" (p. 4); and "[Fantasy] *enters a dialogue with the 'real' and incorporates that dialogue as part of its essential structure*" (p. 36).

48. Lewis, "On SF," pp. 110–11.

49. David Ketterer, "Power Fantasy in the 'Science Fiction' of Mark Twain," in *Bridges to Fantasy*, ed. Slusser et al., p. 133.

50. For a playful examination of the scientific method, see Stanley Schmidt's science fantasy *Newton and the Quasi-Apple*.

51. Waggoner, p. 19.

52. Ilya Prigogine and Isabelle Stengers, *Order out of Chaos: Man's New Dialogue with Nature* (Toronto: Bantam, 1984), p. 8.

53. Prigogine and Stengers, pp. 313, 312.

54. The individual volumes are *The Shadow of the Torturer* (1980; rpt., New York: Pocket, 1981); *The Claw of the Conciliator* (1981; rpt., New York: Pocket, 1982); *The Sword of the Lictor* (1981; rpt., New York: Pocket, 1982); and *The Citadel of the Autarch* (1982; rpt., New York: Pocket, 1983). Hereinafter I shall refer to the individual volumes as, respectively, *ST*, *CC*, *SL*, and *CA*, and incorporate volume and page number parenthetically in the text.

55. C. N. Manlove, *Science Fiction: Ten Explorations* (Kent, Ohio: Kent State UP, 1986), p. 201.

56. Related to the strategy of inversion is that of reversal, which the tetralogy also employs and which Manlove discusses, pp. 208–11.

57. Waggoner, p. 19.

58. Wolfe, "What Do They Mean, SF?" p. 22.

59. Manlove, p. 210.

60. Wolfe, "What Do They Mean, SF?" p. 23.

61. Manlove, p. 208.

V. Looking Backward and Forward at Worlds Apart

1. Gregory Benford, "Effing the Ineffable," in *Aliens: The Anthropology of Science Fiction*, ed. George E. Slusser and Eric S. Rabkin (Carbondale: Southern Illinois UP, 1987), p. 13.

2. Gary K. Wolfe, *The Known and the Unknown: The Iconography of Science Fiction* (Kent, Ohio: Kent State UP, 1979), p. 224.

3. Donald L. Lawler, "Certain Assistances: The Utilities of Speculative Fiction in Shaping the Future," *Mosaic* 13, 3–4 (1980): 7, 8. Cf. Sir Richard Gregory's review of Wells's *The War of the Worlds*, rpt. in *H. G. Wells, The Time Machine and The War of the Worlds*, ed. Frank D. McConnell (New York: Oxford UP, 1977), p. 323: "In conclusion, it is worth remark that scientific romances are not without value in furthering scientific interests; they attract attention to work that is being done in

the realm of natural knowledge, and so create sympathy with the aims and observations of men of science."

4. Robert A. Heinlein, "Science Fiction: Its Nature, Faults, and Virtues," in *The Science Fiction Novel: Imagination and Social Criticism*, ed. Basil Davenport (Chicago: Advent, 1969), p. 45.

5. Heinlein, pp. 43, 46.

6. Alan E. Nourse, "Science Fiction and Man's Adaptation to Change," in *Science Fiction, Today and Tomorrow*, ed. Reginald Bretnor (New York: Harper & Row, 1974), p. 125.

7. Thomas L. Wymer, "Perception and Value in Science Fiction," in *Many Futures, Many Worlds: Theme and Form in Science Fiction*, ed. Thomas D. Clareson (Kent, Ohio: Kent State UP, 1977), p. 2.

8. Wymer, p. 3. Hard SF writer James Gunn argues, in "Science Fiction and the Mainstream," in *Science Fiction, Today and Tomorrow*, ed. Bretnor, p. 196, that the genre "tests mankind and the future against the principles of scientific positivism, a philosophy which rejects metaphysics and maintains that knowledge is based only on sense experience and scientific experiment and observation." The best SF, I would argue, interrogates scientific positivism. For a critique of "conventional SF," that which embraces scientism unquestioningly, see Albert Wendland, *Science, Myth, and the Fictional Creation of Alien Worlds* (Ann Arbor, Mich.: UMI Research P, 1985), esp. chapter 3.

9. Heinlein, p. 45.

10. Stanislaw Lem, *Microworlds: Writings on Science Fiction and Fantasy*, ed.Franz Rottensteiner (San Diego: Harcourt Brace Jovanovich, 1984), pp. 158, 159. Cf. Kingsley Amis, *New Maps of Hell: A Survey of Science Fiction* (New York: Harcourt Brace, 1960),p. 77: "The medium [of SF] is, if not optimistic, at any rate strongly activist in its attitudes. It may show, and often does show, human kind groaning in chains of its own construction, but nearly always with the qualification that those chains may be broken if people try hard enough."

11. Wymer, p. 11.

12. Mark Rose, *Alien Encounters: Anatomy of Science Fiction* (Cambridge, Mass.: Harvard UP, 1981), p. 32.

13. Wolfe, *The Known and the Unknown*, p. 24.

14. Rose, *Alien Encounters*, pp. 40, 44.

15. Peter Nicholls, "Science Fiction: The Monsters and the Critics," in *Science Fiction at Large*, ed. Nicholls (London: Victor Gollanz, 1976), p. 182.

16. Terry Carr, quoted in Jack P. Rawlins, "Confronting the Alien: Fantasy and Anti-Fantasy in Science Fiction Film and Literature," in *Bridges to Fantasy*, ed. George E. Slusser et al. (Carbondale: Southern Illinois UP, 1982), p. 164.

17. Benford, "Effing the Ineffable," p. 23.

18. For the distinction between the epistemological and ontological dominant, I am much indebted to Brian McHale, *Postmodernist Fiction* (New York: Methuen, 1987). See esp. part one, pp. 3–40.

19. Darko Suvin, *Metamorphoses of Science Fiction: On the Poetics and History of a Literary Genre* (New Haven, Conn.: Yale UP, 1979), p. 10. Cf. p. 89: "[SF's] central watershed is around 1800, when space loses its monopoly upon the location of estrangement and the alternative horizons shift from space to time."

20. Patrick Parrinder, "Science Fiction and the Scientific World-View," in *Science Fiction: A Critical Guide*, ed. Parrinder (London: Longman, 1979), p. 87.

BIBLIOGRAPHY

Aldiss, Brian. *Billion Year Spree: The True History of Science Fiction*. New York: Schocken, 1973.

———. "The Wounded Land: J. G. Ballard." In *Science Fiction: The Other Side of Realism*. Ed. Thomas D. Clareson. Bowling Green, Ohio: Bowling Green UP, 1971. 116–29.

———, and Harry Harrison, eds. *Hell's Cartographers*. London: Weidenfeld & Nicolson, 1975.

Aldridge, Alexandra. "Myths of Origin and Destiny in Utopian Literature: Zamiatin's *We*." *Extrapolation* 19, 1 (1977): 68–75.

Allen, Dick, ed. *Science Fiction: The Future*. New York: Harcourt Brace Jovanovich, 1971.

Allen, Dick, and Lori Allen, eds. *Looking Ahead: The Vision of Science Fiction*. New York: Harcourt Brace Jovanovich, 1975.

Allen, L. David. *Science Fiction: A Reader's Guide*. Lincoln, Nebr.: Centennial P, 1973.

Allott, Miriam, ed. *Novelists on the Novel*. New York: Columbia UP, 1959.

Alterman, Peter S. "Four Voices in Robert Silverberg's *Dying Inside*." In *Critical Encounters II: Writers and Themes in Science Fiction*. Ed. Tom Staicar. New York: Frederick Ungar, 1982. 90–103.

Amis, Kingsley. *New Maps of Hell: A Survey of Science Fiction*. New York: Harcourt Brace, 1960.

Anderson, Poul. "The Creation of Imaginary Worlds: The World Builder's Handbook and Pocket Companion." In *Science Fiction, Today and Tomorrow*. Ed. Reginald Bretnor. New York: Harper & Row, 1974. 235–57.

———. "Author's Note" to "Life Cycle." In *Earthmen and Strangers*. Ed. Robert Silverberg. New York: Dell, 1966. 77–78.

Angenot, Marc. "The Absent Paradigm: An Introduction to the Semiotics of Science Fiction." *Science-Fiction Studies* 6 (1979): 9–19.

Asimov, Isaac. "Social Science Fiction." In *Science Fiction: The Future*. Ed. Dick Allen. New York: Harcourt Brace Jovanovich, 1971. 263–99.

Atheling, William, Jr. *More Issues at Hand*. Chicago: Advent, 1970.

Attebury, Brian. "Science Fantasy." In *Twentieth Century American Science Fiction Writers*. Part 2: M-Z. *Dictionary of Literary Biography*. Vol. 8. Ed. David Cowart and Thomas L. Wymer. Detroit: Gale Research Co., 1981. 236–42.

Bainbridge, William Sims. *Dimensions of Science Fiction*. Cambridge, Mass.: Harvard UP, 1986.

Balcerzan, Edward. "Language and Ethics in *Solaris*." *Science-Fiction Studies* 2 (1975): 152–56.

Barbour, Douglas. "Joanna Russ's *The Female Man*: An Appreciation." *Sphinx* 4, 1: 67–75.

Barnouw, Dagmar. "Science Fiction as a Model for Probabilistic Worlds: Stanislaw Lem's Fantastic Empiricism." *Science-Fiction Studies* 6 (1979): 153–62.

Barr, Marleen S. *Alien to Femininity: Speculative Fiction and Feminist Theory*. New York: Greenwood P, 1987.

Barron, Neil. *Anatomy of Wonder: Science Fiction*. New York: Bowker, 1976.

Beauchamp, Gordon. "Cultural Primitivism as Norm in the Dystopian Novel." *Extrapolation* 19, 1 (1977): 88–96.

Benford, Gregory. "Aliens and Knowability: A Scientist's Perspective." In *Bridges to Science Fiction.* Ed. George E. Slusser et al. Carbondale: Southern Illinois UP, 1980. 53–63.

———. "Effing the Ineffable." In *Aliens: The Anthropology of Science Fiction.* Ed. George E. Slusser and Eric S. Rabkin. Carbondale: Southern Illinois UP, 1987. 13–25.

———. "Is There a Technological Fix for the Human Condition?" In *Hard Science Fiction.* Ed. George E. Slusser and Eric S. Rabkin. Carbondale: Southern Illinois UP, 1986. 82–98.

———. "Science and Science Fiction." In *Science Fiction: The Academic Awakening.* Ed. Willis E. McNelly. Shreveport, La.: CEA Chap Book, 1974. 30–33.

Berger, Harold B. *Science Fiction and the New Dark Age.* Bowling Green, Ohio: Bowling Green U Popular P, 1976.

Borman, Gilbert. "A New Look at Zamiatin's *We.*" *Extrapolation* 24, 1 (1983): 57–65.

Bretnor, Reginald, ed. *Science Fiction, Today and Tomorrow.* New York: Harper & Row, 1974.

Brooke-Rose, Christine. *A Rhetoric of the Unreal: Studies in Narrative and Structure, Especially of the Fantastic.* Cambridge: Cambridge UP, 1981.

Bruner, Jerome. *Actual Minds, Possible Worlds.* Cambridge, Mass.: Harvard UP, 1986.

Bruns, Gerald L. "The Formal Nature of Victorian Thinking." *PMLA* 90 (1975): 904–18.

Buckley, Jerome Hamilton. *The Triumph of Time: A Study of the Victorian Concepts of Time, History, Progress, and Decadence.* Cambridge, Mass.: Harvard UP, 1966.

Budrys, Algis. "Paradise Charted." *TriQuarterly* 49 (Fall 1980): 5–75.

Canary, Robert H. "Science Fiction as Fictive History." In *Many Futures, Many Worlds: Theme and Form in Science Fiction.* Ed. Thomas D. Clareson. Kent, Ohio: Kent State UP, 1977. 164–81.

Cannon, Walter F. "Darwin's Vision in *On the Origin of Species.*" In *The Art of Victorian Prose.* Ed. George Levine and William Madden. New York: Oxford UP, 1968. 154–76.

Carter, Paul A. *The Creation of Tomorrow: Fifty Years of Magazine Science Fiction.* New York: Columbia UP, 1977.

———. " 'You Can Write Science Fiction If You Want To.' " In *Hard Science Fiction.* Ed. George E. Slusser and Eric S. Rabkin. Carbondale: Southern Illinois UP, 1986. 144–51.

Chauvin, Cy. "Ian Watson's Miracle Men." In *Critical Encounters II: Writers and Themes in Science Fiction.* Ed. Tom Staicar. New York: Frederick Ungar, 1982. 44–59.

Clareson Thomas D. "The Fiction of Robert Silverberg." In *Voices for the Future: Essays on Major Science Fiction Writers.* Vol. 2. Bowling Green, Ohio: Bowling Green U Popular P, 1979. 1–33.

———. "The Other Side of Realism." In *Science Fiction: The Other Side of Realism.* Ed. Thomas D. Clareson. Bowling Green, Ohio: Bowling Green U Popular P, 1971. 1–28.

———. *Some Kind of Paradise: The Emergence of American Science Fiction.* Westport, Conn.: Greenwood P, 1985.

———, ed. *Many Futures, Many Worlds: Theme and Form in Science Fiction.* Kent, Ohio: Kent State UP, 1977.

———, ed. *Science Fiction: The Other Side of Realism.* Bowling Green, Ohio: Bowling Green U Popular P, 1971.

———, ed. *Voices for the Future: Essays on Major Science Fiction Writers.* Vol. 1. Bowling Green, Ohio: Bowling Green U Popular P, 1976.

———, ed. *Voices for the Future: Essays on Major Science Fiction Writers.* Vol. 2. Bowling Green, Ohio: Bowling Green U Popular P, 1979.

Clement, Hal. "The Creation of Imaginary Beings." In *Science Fiction, Today and Tomorrow*. Ed. Reginald Bretnor. New York: Harper & Row, 1974. 259–75.

Collins, Robert A. "Fantasy and 'Forestructures': The Effect of Philosophical Climate upon Perceptions of the Fantastic." In *Bridges to Fantasy*. Ed. George E. Slusser et al. Carbondale: Southern Illinois UP, 1982. 108–20.

Conant, James B. *Modern Science and Modern Man*. New York: Columbia UP, 1952.

Cowan, S. A. "The Crystalline Center of Zamyatin's *We*." *Extrapolation* 29, 2 (Summer 1988): 160–78.

Csicsery-Ronay, Istvan, Jr. "The Book Is the Alien: On Certain and Uncertain Readings of Lem's *Solaris*." *Science-Fiction Studies* 12 (1985): 6–21.

——. "Towards the Last Fairy Tale: On the Fairy-Tale Paradigm in the Strugatskys' Science Fiction, 1963–72." *Science-Fiction Studies* 13 (1986): 1–41.

——. "Twenty-two Answers and Two Postscripts: An Interview with Stanislaw Lem." Trans. Marek Lugowski. *Science-Fiction Studies* 13 (1986): 242–60.

Culler, Dwight A. "The Darwinian Revolution and Literary Form." In *The Art of Victorian Prose*. Ed. George Levine and William Madden. New York: Oxford UP, 1968. 224–46.

Culler, Jonathan. *Structuralist Poetics*. Ithaca, N.Y.: Cornell UP, 1975.

Davenport, Basil, ed. *The Science Fiction Novel: Imagination and Social Criticism*. 1959. Rpt., Chicago: Advent, 1969.

Davis, Robert M., ed. *The Novel: Modern Essays in Criticism*. Englewood Cliffs, N.J.: Prentice-Hall, 1969.

Delany, Samuel R. "About Five Thousand One Hundred and Seventy-five Words." In *Science Fiction: The Other Side of Realism*. Ed. Thomas D. Clareson. Bowling Green, Ohio: Bowling Green U Popular P, 1971. 130–46.

——. Critical Methods: Speculative Fiction." In *Many Futures, Many Worlds: Theme and Form in Science Fiction*. Ed. Thomas D. Clareson. Kent, Ohio: Kent State UP, 1977. 278–91.

——. Generic Protocols: Science Fiction and Mundane." In *The Technological Imagination: Theories and Fictions*. Ed. Teresa de Lauretis et al. Madison, Wis.: Coda P, 1980. 175–93.

——. "Orders of Chaos: The Science Fiction of Joanna Russ." In *Women Worldwalkers: New Dimensions of Science Fiction and Fantasy*. Ed. Jane B. Weedman. Lubbock: Texas Tech P, 1985. 95–123.

de Lauretis, Teresa. "Signs of Wonder." In *The Technological Imagination: Theories and Fictions*. Ed. Teresa de Lauretis et al. Madison, Wis.: Coda P, 1980. 159–74.

——, et al., eds. *The Technological Imagination: Theories and Fictions*. Madison, Wis.: Coda P, 1980.

Dick, Philip K. "Who Is an SF Writer?" In *Science Fiction: The Academic Awakening*. Ed. Willis E. McNelly. Shreveport, La.: CEA Chap Book, 1974. 46–50.

Dolezel, Lubomir. "Narrative Modalities." *Journal of Literary Semantics* 5, 1 (April 1976): 5–14.

Ebert, Teresa L. "The Convergence of Postmodern Innovative Fiction and Science Fiction: An Encounter with Samuel R. Delany's Technotopia." *Poetics Today* 1, 4 (1980): 91–104.

Eisenstein, Alex. "*The Time Machine* and the End of Man." *Science-Fiction Studies* 9 (July 1976): 161–65.

Federman, Raymond. "An Interview with Stanislaw Lem." *Science-Fiction Studies* 10 (1983): 2–14.

Firsching, Lorenz J. "J. G. Ballard's Ambiguous Apocalypse." *Science-Fiction Studies* 12 (1985): 297–310.

Franklin, H. Bruce. *Robert Heinlein: America as Science Fiction*. New York: Oxford UP, 1981.

————. "What Are We to Make of J. G. Ballard's Apocalypse?" In *Voices for the Future: Essays on Major Science Fiction Writers*. Vol. 2. Ed. Thomas D. Clareson. Bowling Green, Ohio: Bowling Green U Popular P, 1979. 82–105.

Fredericks, Casey. *The Future of Eternity: Mythologies of Science Fiction and Fantasy*. Bloomington: Indiana UP, 1982.

Fredericks, S. C. "Problems of Fantasy." *Science-Fiction Studies* 5 (1978): 33–44.

Frye, Northrop. *The Anatomy of Criticism: Four Essays*. 1957. Rpt., Princeton, N.J.: Princeton UP, 1971.

————. "Varieties of Literary Utopias." In *Utopias and Utopian Thought*. Ed. Frank E. Manuel. Boston: Houghton Mifflin, 1966. 25–49.

Guffey, George R. "Noise, Information, and Statistics in Stanislaw Lem's *The Investigation*." In *Hard Science Fiction*. Ed. George E. Slusser and Eric Rabkin. Carbondale: Southern Illinois UP, 1986. 164–76.

Gunn, James. "The Readers of Hard SF." In *Hard Science Fiction*. Ed. George E. Slusser and Eric Rabkin. Carbondale: Southern Illinois UP, 1986. 70–81.

————. "Science Fiction and the Mainstream." In *Science Fiction, Today and Tomorrow*. Ed. Reginald Bretnor. New York: Harper & Row, 1974. 183–214.

Hardesty, William H., III. "Semiotics, Space Opera, and *Babel-17*." *Mosaic* 13, 3–4 (1980): 63–69.

Harrison, Harry. "Inventing New Worlds I." In *Future Imperfect: Science Fact and Science Fiction*. Ed. Rex Malik. London: Frances Pinter, 1980. 73–80.

Heinlein, Robert A. "Science Fiction: Its Nature, Faults, and Virtues." In *The Science Fiction Novel: Imagination and Social Criticism*. Ed. Basil Davenport. 1959. Rpt., Chicago: Advent, 1969. 14–48.

Henkin, Leo J. *Darwinism in the English Novel, 1860–1910: The Impact of Evolution on Victorian Fiction*. New York: Russell & Russell, 1963.

Hienger, Jörg. "The Uncanny and Science Fiction." Trans. Elsa Schieder. *Science-Fiction Studies* 6 (1979): 144–52.

Hillegas, Mark R. *The Future as Nightmare: H. G. Wells and the Anti-Utopians*. New York: Oxford UP, 1967.

Holdstock, Robert, and Malcolm Edwards. *Alien Landscapes*. New York: Mayflower Books, 1979.

Hollow, John. *Against the Night, the Stars: The Science Fiction of Arthur C. Clarke*. San Diego: Harcourt Brace Jovanovich, 1983.

Horkheimer, Max, and Theodor W. Adorno. *Dialectic of Enlightenment*. Trans. John Cumming. New York: Seabury, 1972.

Houghton, Walter. *The Utopian Frame of Mind*. New Haven: Yale UP, 1957.

Huntington, John. *The Logic of Fantasy: H. G. Wells and Science Fiction*. New York: Columbia UP, 1982.

————. "Science Fiction and the Future." Rpt. in *Science Fiction: A Collection of Critical Essays*. Ed. Mark Rose. Englewood Cliffs, N.J.: Prentice-Hall, 1976. 156–66.

————. "Utopian and Anti-Utopian Logic: H. G. Wells and His Successsors." *Science-Fiction Studies* 9 (1982): 122–46.

Hynes, Samuel L., and Frank D. McConnell. "*The Time Machine* and *The War of the Worlds*: Parable and Possibility in H. G. Wells." Rpt. in The Time Machine *and* The War of the Worlds: *A Critical Edition*. Ed. Frank D. McConnell. New York: Oxford UP, 1977. 345–66.

Irwin, W. R. *The Game of the Impossible: A Rhetoric of Fantasy*. Urbana: U of Illinois, 1976.

Jackson, Rosemary. *Fantasy: The Literature of Subversion*. London: Methuen, 1981.

Jakobson, Roman. "The Dominant." In *Readings in Russian Poetics*. Ed. L. Matejka and K. Pomorsk. Cambridge: MIT P, 1971. 82–87.

Jameson, Fredric. "Of Islands and Trenches." *Diacritics* 7 (1977): 2–21.

———. *The Political Unconscious: Narrative as a Socially Symbolic Act.* Ithaca, N.Y.: Cornell UP, 1981.

———. "Progress versus Utopia; Or, Can We Imagine the Future?" *Science-Fiction Studies* 9 (1982): 147–58.

Keeling, Thomas H. "Science Fiction and the Gothic." In *Bridges to Science Fiction.* Ed. George E. Slusser et al. Carbondale: Southern Illinois UP, 1980. 107–19.

Ketterer, David. *New Worlds for Old: The Apocalyptic Imagination, Science Fiction, and American Literature.* Bloomington: Indiana UP, 1974.

———. "Power Fantasy in the 'Science Fiction' of Mark Twain." In *Bridges to Fantasy.* Ed. George E. Slusser et al. Carbondale: Southern Illinois UP, 1982. 130–41.

Khouri, Nadia. "The Dialectics of Power: Utopia in the Science Fiction of LeGuin, Jeury, Piercy." *Science-Fiction Studies* 7 (1980): 49–60.

Knight, Damon. *In Search of Wonder: Essays on Modern Science Fiction.* 2nd ed. Chicago: Advent, 1967.

Koyre, Alexandre. *From the Closed World to the Infinite Universe.* Baltimore: Johns Hopkins UP, 1957.

Lake, David J. "The White Sphinx and the Whitened Lemur: Images of Death in *The Time Machine.*" *Science-Fiction Studies* 6 (1979): 77–84.

Lawler, Donald L. "Certain Assistances: The Utilities of Speculative Fiction in Shaping the Future." *Mosaic* 13, 3–4 (1980): 1–14.

———, ed. *Approaches to Science Fiction.* Boston: Houghton Mifflin, 1978.

LeGuin, Ursula K. *The Language of the Night: Essays on Fantasy and Science Fiction.* Ed. Susan Wood. New York: G. P. Putnam's Sons, 1979.

Lem, Stanislaw. *Microworlds: Writings on Science Fiction and Fantasy.* Ed. Franz Rottensteiner. San Diego: Harcourt Brace Jovanovich, 1984.

Lemon, Lee T., and Marion J. Rice, eds. *Russian Formalist Criticism: Four Essays.* Lincoln: U of Nebraska P, 1965.

Levine, George, and William Madden, eds. *The Art of Victorian Prose.* New York: Oxford UP, 1968.

Lewis, C. S. "On Science Fiction." Rpt. in *Science Fiction: A Collection of Critical Essays.* Ed. Mark Rose. Englewood Cliffs, N.J.: Prentice-Hall, 1976. 103–15.

Lotman, Jurij. *The Structure of the Artistic Text.* Trans. Ronald Vroon. Michigan Slavic Contributions, no. 7. Ann Arbor: U of Michigan P, 1977.

McCarthy, Patrick A. "Zamyatin and the Nightmare of Technology." *Science-Fiction Studies* 11 (1984): 122–29.

McClenahan, Catherine L. "Textual Politics: The Uses of the Imagination in Joanna Russ's *The Female Man.*" *Transactions of the Wisconsin Academy of Science, Arts, and Letters* 70 (1982): 114–25.

McConnell, Frank. *The Science Fiction of H. G. Wells.* New York: Oxford UP, 1981.

McConnell, Frank D., ed. *H. G. Wells, The Time Machine and The War of the Worlds: A Critical Edition.* New York: Oxford UP, 1977.

McEvoy, Seth. *Samuel R. Delany.* New York: Frederick Ungar, 1984.

McHale, Brian. *Postmodernist Fiction.* New York: Methuen, 1987.

McNelly, Willis E., ed. *Science Fiction: The Academic Awakening.* Shreveport, La.: CEA Chap Book, 1974.

Malik, Rex, ed. *Future Imperfect: Science Fact and Science Fiction.* London: Frances Pinter, 1980.

Malmgren, Carl D. *Fictional Space in the Modernist and Postmodernist American Novel.* Lewisburg, Pa.: Bucknell UP, 1985.

Manlove, C. N. *The Impulse of Fantasy Literature.* Kent, Ohio: Kent State UP, 1983.

———. *Modern Fantasy.* Cambridge: Cambridge UP, 1975.

———. *Science Fiction: Ten Explorations.* Kent, Ohio: Kent State UP, 1986.

Merril, Judith. "What Do You Mean: Science? Fiction?" In *Science Fiction: The Other*

Side of Realism. Ed. Thomas D. Clareson. Bowling Green, Ohio: Bowling Green U Popular P, 1971. 53–95.

Meyerhof, Hans. *Time in Literature.* Berkeley: U of California P, 1955.

Meyers, Walter E. *Aliens and Linguists: Language Study and Science Fiction.* Athens: U of Georgia P, 1980.

Modern Fiction Studies 32 (Spring 1986): 1–151. Science fiction and fantasy special issue.

Mooij, J. J. A. "The Nature and Function of Literary Theories." *Poetics Today* 1, 1–2 (Autumn 1979): 111–35.

Morson, Gary. *The Boundaries of Genre: Dostoyevsky's "Diary of a Writer" and Traditions of Literary Utopias.* Austin: U of Texas P, 1981.

Mosaic 13, 3–4 (1980): 1–225. Special issue titled "Other Worlds: Fantasy and Science Fiction since 1939." Ed. John J. Teunisson.

Moylan, Tom. *Demand the Impossible: Science Fiction and the Utopian Imagination.* New York: Methuen, 1987.

Myers, Robert E., ed. *The Intersection of Science Fiction and Philosophy: Critical Studies.* Westport, Conn.: Greenwood P, 1983.

Nania, John S. "Exploding Genres: Stanislaw Lem's Science Fiction Detective Novels."*Extrapolation* 25, 3 (Fall 1984): 266–79.

Nicholls, Peter. "Science Fiction: The Monsters and the Critics." In *Science Fiction at Large.* Ed. Peter Nicholls. London: Victor Gollanz, 1976. 157–83.

———, ed. *Science Fiction at Large.* London: Victor Gollanz, 1976.

Nisbet, Robert. *History of the Idea of Progress.* New York: Basic Books, 1980.

Niven, Larry. "The Theory and Practice of Time Travel." In *Looking Ahead: The Vision of Science Fiction.* Ed. Dick Allen and Lori Allen. New York: Harcourt Brace Jovanovich, 1975. 363–72.

Nourse, Alan E. "Science Fiction and Man's Adaptation to Change." In *Science Fiction, Today and Tomorrow.* Ed. Reginald Bretnor. New York: Harper & Row, 1974. 116–32.

Parrinder, Patrick. "The Alien Encounter: Or, Ms Brown and Mrs LeGuin." Rpt. in *Science Fiction: A Critical Guide.* Ed. Patrick Parrinder. London: Longman, 1979. 46–58.

———. *"News from Nowhere, The Time Machine,* and the Break-up of Classic Realism." *Science-Fiction Studies* 3 (1976): 265–74.

———. "Science Fiction and the Scientific World-View." In *Science Fiction: A Critical Guide.* Ed. Patrick Parrinder. London: Longman, 1979. 67–88.

———. "Science Fiction as Truncated Epic." In *Bridges to Science Fiction.* Ed. George E. Slusser et al. Carbondale: Southern Illinois UP, 1980. 91–106.

———. *Science Fiction: Its Criticism and Teaching.* New York: Methuen, 1980.

———, ed. *Science Fiction: A Critical Guide.* London: Longman, 1979.

———, and Robert M. Philmus, eds. *H. G. Wells's Literary Criticism.* Sussex: Harvester P, 1980.

Pavel, Thomas G. *Fictional Worlds.* Cambridge, Mass.: Harvard UP, 1986.

Perry, Menakhem. "Literary Dynamics: How the Order of a Text Creates Its Meaning, with an Analysis of Faulkner's 'A Rose for Emily.' " *Poetics Today* 1, 1–2 (1979): 35–64, 311–61.

Petzold, Dieter. "Fantasy Fiction and Related Genres." *Modern Fiction Studies* 32, 1 (1986): 11–20.

Philmus, Robert M. "The Cybernetic Paradigms of Stanislaw Lem." In *Hard Science Fiction.* Ed. George E. Slusser and Eric S. Rabkin. Carbondale: Southern Illinois UP, 1986. 177–213.

———. *Into the Unknown: The Evolution of Science Fiction from Francis Godwin to H. G. Wells.* Berkeley: U of California P, 1970.

Pielke, Robert G. "Humans and Aliens: A Unique Relationship." *Mosaic* 13, 3–4 (1980): 29–40.

Platzner, Robert L. "The Metamorphic Vision of J. G. Ballard." *Essays in Literature* 10 (Fall 1983): 209–17.

Potts, Stephen. "Dialogues concerning Human Understanding: Empirical Views of God from Locke to Lem." In *Bridges to Science Fiction*. Ed. George E. Slusser et al. Carbondale: Southern Illinois UP, 1980. 41–52.

Prigogine, Ilya, and Isabelle Stengers. *Order Out of Chaos: Man's New Dialogue with Nature*. Toronto: Bantam, 1984.

Prince, Gerald. "How New Is New?" In *Coordinates: Placing Science Fiction and Fantasy*. Ed. George E. Slusser et al. Carbondale: Southern Illinois UP, 1983. 23–30.

Rabkin, Eric S. *Arthur C. Clarke*. Starmont Reader's Guide 1. Mercer Island, Wash.: Starmont House, 1979.

———. "Atavism and Utopia." In *No Place Else: Explorations in Utopian and Dystopian Fiction*. Ed. Eric S. Rabkin et al. Carbondale: Southern Illinois UP, 1983. 1–10.

———. "The Descent of Fantasy." In *Coordinates: Placing Science Fiction and Fantasy*. Ed. George E. Slusser et al. Carbondale: Southern Illinois UP, 1983. 14–22.

———. "Fairy Tales and Science Fiction." In *Bridges to Science Fiction*. Ed. George E. Slusser et al. Carbondale: Southern Illinois UP, 1980. 78–90.

———. *The Fantastic in Literature*. Princeton, N.J.: Princeton UP, 1977.

———. "The Rhetoric of Science in Fiction." In *Critical Encounters II: Writers and Themes in Science Fiction*. Ed. Tom Staicar. New York: Frederick Ungar, 1982. 23–43.

———, et al., eds. *No Place Else: Explorations in Utopian and Dystopian Fiction*. Carbondale: Southern Illinois UP, 1983.

Rawlins, Jack P. "Confronting the Alien: Fantasy and Anti-Fantasy in Science Fiction Film and Literature." In *Bridges To Fantasy*. Ed. George E. Slusser et al. Carbondale: Southern Illinois UP, 1982. 160–74.

Riley, Dick, ed. *Critical Encounters: Writers and Themes in Science Fiction*. New York: Frederick Ungar, 1979.

Rose, Mark. *Alien Encounters: Anatomy of Science Fiction*. Cambridge, Mass.: Harvard UP, 1981.

———, ed. *Science Fiction: A Collection of Critical Essays*. Englewood Cliffs, N.J.: Prentice-Hall, 1976.

Rosinsky, Natalie M. "A Female Man? The 'Medusan' Humor of Joanna Russ." *Extrapolation* 23, 1 (1982): 31–36.

Ruddick, Nicholas. "The World Turned Inside Out: Decoding Clarke's *Rendezvous with Rama*." *Science-Fiction Studies* 12 (1985): 42–50.

Ruppert, Peter. *Reader in a Strange Land: The Activity of Reading Literary Utopias*. Athens: U of Georgia P, 1986.

Russ, Joanna. "Amor Vincit Foeminam: The Battle of the Sexes in Science Fiction." *Science-Fiction Studies* 7 (1980): 2–15.

———. "On Setting." In *Those Who Can: A Science Fiction Reader*. Ed. Robin Scott Wilson. New York: New American Library, 1973. 149–54.

———. "The Subjunctivity of Science Fiction." *Extrapolation* 15 (1973): 51–59.

———. "Towards an Aesthetics of Science Fiction." *Science-Fiction Studies* 2, 2 (1975): 112–19.

Salvestroni, Simonetta. "The Ambiguous Miracle in Three Novels by The Strugatsky Brothers." *Science-Fiction Studies* 11 (1984): 291–303.

Sanders, Scott. "The Disappearance of Character." In *Science Fiction: A Critical Guide*. Ed. Patrick Parrinder. London: Longman, 1979. 131–47.

Schaefer, Martin. "The Rise And Fall of Antiutopia: Utopia, Gothic Romance, Dystopia." *Science-Fiction Studies* 6 (1979): 287–95.

Schlobin, Roger C., ed. *The Aesthetics of Fantasy Literature and Art*. Notre Dame, Ind.: U of Notre Dame P, 1982.

———. "From the Old on to the New: New Directions in Fantasy Criticism and Theory." *Extrapolation* 28, 1 (1987): 3–9.

———. "Introduction: Fantasy and Its Literature." In *The Literature of Fantasy: A Comprehensive Annotated Bibliography of Modern Fantasy Fiction*. New York: Garland, 1979. xvii–xxxv.

Schmidt, Stanley. "The Science in Science Fiction." In *Many Futures, Many Worlds: Theme and Form in Science Fiction*. Ed. Thomas D. Clareson. Kent, Ohio: Kent State UP, 1977. 27–49.

Scholes, Robert. "Boiling Roses: Thoughts on Science Fantasy." In *Intersections: Fantasy and Science Fiction*. Ed. George E. Slusser and Eric S. Rabkin. Carbondale: Southern Illinois UP, 1987. 3–18.

———. *Semiotics and Interpretation*. New Haven, Conn.: Yale UP, 1982.

———. *Structural Fabulation: An Essay on the Fiction of the Future*. Notre Dame, Ind.: U of Notre Dame P, 1975.

———, and Eric S. Rabkin. *Science Fiction: History, Science, Vision*. New York: Oxford UP, 1977.

Schuyler, William M. "Could Anyone Here Speak Babel-17?" In *Philosophers Look at Science Fiction*. Ed. Nicholas D. Smith. Chicago: Nelson-Hall, 1982. 87–95.

Science-Fiction Studies 13 (1986): 235–410. Special issue on Stanislaw Lem.

Scortia, Thomas N. "Science Fiction as the Imaginary Experiment." In *Science Fiction, Today and Tomorrow*. Ed. Reginald Bretnor. New York: Harper & Row, 1974. 135–47.

Sheckley, Robert. "The Search for the Marvellous." In *Science Fiction at Large*. Ed. Peter Nicholls. London: Victor Gollanz, 1976. 185–98.

Shklovsky, Victor. "Art as Technique." In *Russian Formalist Criticism: Four Essays*. Ed. and trans. Lee T. Lemon and Marion J. Reis. Lincoln: U of Nebraska P, 1965. 3–24.

Slusser, George E. *The Delany Intersection: Samuel E. Delany Considered as a Writer of Semi-Precious Words*. San Bernadino, Calif.: Borgo P, 1977.

———. "The Ideal Worlds of Science Fiction." In *Hard Science Fiction*. Ed. George E. Slusser and Eric S. Rabkin. Carbondale: Southern Illinois UP, 1986. 214–46.

———. *The Space Odysseys of Arthur C. Clarke*. Milford Series of Popular Writers of Today, no. 8. San Bernadino, Calif.: Borgo P, 1978.

———, et al., eds. *Bridges to Fantasy*. Carbondale: Southern Illinois UP, 1982.

———, et al., eds. *Bridges to Science Fiction*. Carbondale: Southern Illinois UP, 1980.

———, et al., eds. *Coordinates: Placing Science Fiction and Fantasy*. Carbondale: Southern Illinois UP, 1983.

———, and Eric S. Rabkin, eds. *Aliens: The Anthropology of Science Fiction*. Carbondale: Southern Illinois UP, 1987.

———, and Eric S. Rabkin, eds. *Hard Science Fiction*. Carbondale: Southern Illinois UP, 1986.

———, and Eric S. Rabkin, eds. *Intersections: Fantasy and Science Fiction*. Carbondale: Southern Illinois UP, 1987.

Smith, Nicholas D., ed. *Philosophers Look at Science Fiction*. Chicago: Nelson Hall, 1982.

Stableford, Brian. *Scientific Romance in Britain, 1890–1950*. New York: St. Martin's, 1985.

Staicar, Tom, ed. *Critical Encounters II: Writers and Themes in Science Fiction*. New York: Frederick Ungar, 1982.

———, ed. *The Feminine Eye: Science Fiction and the Women Who Write It.* New York: Frederick Ungar, 1982.

Sutherland, J. A. "American Science Fiction since 1960." In *Science Fiction: A Critical Guide.* Ed. Patrick Parrinder. London: Longman, 1979. 162–86.

Suvin, Darko. *Metamorphoses of Science Fiction: On the Poetics and History of a Literary Genre.* New Haven, Conn.: Yale UP, 1979.

———. "The Open-Ended Parables of Stanislaw Lem and *Solaris*." Afterword to Stanislaw Lem, *Solaris.* Trans. from the French by Joanna Kilmartin and Steve Cox. New York: Berkley, 1970. 212–23.

———. *Victorian Science Fiction in the United Kingdom: The Discourses of Knowledge and Power.* Boston: G. K. Hall, 1983.

Tolkien, J. R. R. "On Fairy-Stories." In *Essays Presented to Charles Williams.* London: Oxford UP, 1947. 38–89.

Toulmin, Stephen, and June Goldfield. *The Discovery of Time.* New York: Harper & Row, 1965.

Vernier, Jean-Pierre. "*The Time Machine* and Its Context." Trans. Frank D. McConnell. Rpt. in *H. G. Wells: The Time Machine and The War of the Worlds: A Critical Edition.* Ed. Frank D. McConnell. New York: Oxford UP, 1977. 314–23.

Waggoner, Diane. *The Hills of Faraway: A Guide to Fantasy.* New York: Atheneum, 1978.

Warrick, Patricia S. *The Cybernetic Imagination in Science Fiction.* Cambridge: MIT Press, 1980.

Weedman, Jane B. "Delany's *Babel 17*: The Powers of Language." *Extrapolation* 19 (1978): 132–37.

———. *Samuel R. Delany.* Starmont Reader's Guide 10. Mercer Island, Wash.: Starmont House, 1982.

———, ed. *Women Worldwalkers: New Dimensions of Science Fiction and Fantasy.* Lubbock: Texas Tech P, 1985.

Wells, H. G. *H. G. Wells's Literary Criticism.* Ed. Patrick Parrinder and Robert M. Philmus. Sussex: Harvester P, 1980.

Wendland, Albert. *Science, Myth, and the Fictional Creation of Alien Worlds.* Studies in Speculative Fiction, no. 12. Ann Arbor, Mich.: UMI Research P, 1985.

Williamson, Jack. "Wells and the Limits of Progress." Rpt. in *The Time Machine and The War of the Worlds: A Critical Edition.* Ed. Frank D. McConnell. New York: Oxford, 1977. 397–416.

Wolfe, Gary K. "Autoplastic and Alloplastic Adaptations in Science Fiction: 'Waldo' and 'Desertion.' " In *Coordinates: Placing Science Fiction and Fantasy.* Ed. George E. Slusser et al. Carbondale: Southern Illinois UP, 1983. 65–79.

———. *Critical Terms for Science Fiction and Fantasy: A Glossary and Guide to Scholarship.* New York: Greenwood, 1986.

———. "The Encounter with Fantasy." In *The Aesthetics of Fantasy Literature and Art.* Ed. Roger C. Schlobin. Notre Dame, Ind.: U of Notre Dame P, 1982. 1–15.

———. *The Known and the Unknown: The Iconography of Science Fiction.* Kent, Ohio: Kent State UP, 1979.

Wolfe, Gene. "What Do They Mean, SF?" *SFWA Bulletin* 75 (1981): 20–25.

Wymer, Thomas L. "Perception and Value in Science Fiction." In *Many Futures, Many Worlds: Theme and Form in Science Fiction.* Ed. Thomas D. Clareson. Kent, Ohio: Kent State UP, 1977. 1–13.

Wytenbroek, Jaqueline. "Science Fiction and Fantasy." *Extrapolation* 23, 4 (1982): 321–32.

Zavarzadeh, Mas'ud. *The Mythopoetic Reality: The Postwar American Nonfiction Novel.* Urbana: U of Illinois P, 1976.

INDEX

Actants, 7
Adams, Henry, 146
Adorno, Theodor, 3
Aldiss, Brian, 9, 102, 104, 169
Alien encounter SF, 17, 53–76
Allen, L. David, 140
Alterman, Peter, 67
Alternate society SF, 17–19, 76–101
Alternate world SF, 19–20, 119–38
Amis, Kingsley, 32–33, 56, 77, 170
Anderson, Poul, 12, 104, 148–49
Angenot, Marc, 24, 25, 42
Anthony, Piers: 151, 155; *Omnivore*, 57, 124; *Split Infinity*, 153
Asimov, Isaac: 77, 121, 170; *Foundation*, 14; "Nightfall," 123; *I, Robot*, 18, 19, 58, 103
Atheling, William Jr. (James Blish), 140
Attebury, Brian, 140
Atwood, Margaret, 175, 186n2
Austen, Jane, 24

Ballard, J. G.: 124, 172; *The Drowned World*, 20, 131–38
Bates, Harry, 56
Beauchamp, Gordon, 80
Benford, Gregory: 9, 60, 169, 175; *Heart of the Comet*, 125–31; *If the Stars Are Gods*, 57; *In the Ocean of Night*, 14, 57; *Timescape*, 148
Berryman, John, 58
Bloch, Ernst, 11
Bradbury, Ray: 172; *Fahrenheit 451*, 17, 186n2; *Martian Chronicles*, 18, 150
Bradley, Marion Zimmer, 151
Brin, David: *Heart of the Comet*, 125–31
Brunner, John, 12, 17, 186n2
Budrys, Algis, 104
Bulwer-Lytton, Edward, 177n2
Burgess, Anthony, 186n2
Burroughs, E. R., 151
Butler, Samuel, 177n2

Card, Orson Scott, 78
Chesney, George T., 177n2
Clareson, Thomas, 7, 121
Clarke, Arthur C.: *Childhood's End*, 17, 56, 57, 62, 69–71; *Rendezvous with Rama*, 104–11, 119–20
Clement, Hal, 20, 22, 58, 62, 124
Close Encounters of the Third Kind, 173
Concretization: 23–24; of SF worlds, 24–25

Crispin, Edmund, 56
Csicsery-Ronay, Istvan, 49, 57, 113, 114, 115, 116, 118
Cyberpunk, 175

Darwin, Charles, 3
Defamiliarization, 26–27
Delany, Samuel, 8, 18, 19, 78, 169, 175, 186n2
Dick, Philip K.: 18, 124; *The Man in the High Castle*, 18, 149–50, 151
Discourse of SF, 2–6, 24
Dolezel, Lubomir, 7
Dominant, the, 16–17
Doyle, Arthur Conan, 120, 133
Dystopia, 77–81

Effinger, George Alec, 62
Eiseley, Loren, 57, 58
Elgin, Suzette Haden, 153, 175
Eliot, T. S., 63
Ellison, Harlan: "A Boy and His Dog," 22; "I Have No Mouth, and I Must Scream," 17, 55–56, 62, 103
Ellison, Ralph, 7
Enlightenment, the, 2–3
ESP, 14
Estrangement, 26–27
E.T., 17, 62
Evolution, 4, 38–39
Extrapolation, 11–15, 31–41, 174–75

Fantasy, 139–41, 152, 154, 156–57, 191–192n1, 194n42
Farmer, Philip José, 104
Faulkner, William, 24
Frankfort, Henri, 13
Franklin, H. Bruce, 132, 134, 135
Fredericks, S. C., 139
Frye, Northrop, 80

Gadget SF, 19, 101–19
Garrett, Randall, 152
Gernsback, Hugo, 15, 101–102, 103
Gibson, William, 104
Godwin, Tom, 123
Grapholect, 8
Guffey, George, 144

Hard SF, 14, 180n55
Harrison, Harry, 149

206

CARL D. MALMGREN, Associate Professor of English at the University of New Orleans, is author of *Fictional Space in the Modernist and Postmodernist American Novel* and numerous articles on contemporary fiction.

www.ingramcontent.com/pod-product-compliance
Ingram Content Group UK Ltd.
Pitfield, Milton Keynes, MK11 3LW, UK
UKHW022245150325
456235UK00003B/14